Savannah Martin has always been a good girl, doing what was expected and fully expecting life to fall into place in its turn. But when her perfect husband turns out to be a lying, cheating slimeball - and bad in bed to boot - Savannah kicks the jerk to the curb and embarks on life on her own terms. With a new apartment, a new career, and a brand new outlook on life, she's all set to take the world by storm.

If only the world would stop throwing her curveballs...

When every member of a rural Sweetwater family is murdered in their beds, Maury County sheriff Bob Satterfield calls on the Tennessee Bureau of Investigation for help.

While Savannah's husband, TBI agent Rafe Collier, heads to their shared hometown to help the sheriff figure out who and what is behind the grisly massacre, Savannah goes along to assist her old friend Yvonne McCoy's quest to gain ownership of Beulah's Meat'n Three restaurant.

But when Beulah Odom's death turns out to have been murder, suddenly Yvonne's on the hot seat. And with the sheriff occupied elsewhere and Beulah's family gunning for Yvonne, it's up to Savannah to figure out the truth before her old friend lands in jail... or six feet under.

OTHER BOOKS IN THIS SERIES

BAD DEBT

Savannah Martin Mystery #14

Jenna Bennett

BAD DEBT
Savannah Martin Mystery #14

Interior design and formatting: B. Gallagher
Cover Design: Dar Albert, Wicked Smart Designs

Magpie Ink

ONE

The day started like any other. I woke up on my side—I was seven months pregnant, so I couldn't sleep on my stomach anymore, and the obstetrician had made it clear that lying on my back wasn't a good idea, either. Rafe was sleeping behind me, with a hand splayed on my stomach and his nose buried in my hair.

Or actually, he wasn't. By the time I woke up, the hand was moving north and his lips were doing things to the area behind and a little below my ear.

"Is that a banana in your underwear," I asked sleepily, "or are you happy to see me?"

He lifted his head long enough to tell me, "I'm always happy to be waking up next to you, darlin'," before going back to what he was doing.

Awww.

One thing led to another, and after we were done, I fell back asleep. It was still early, and it takes a lot of energy to create a baby. It takes a lot of energy to have sex with Rafe, too. I sleep a lot these days.

While I settled back in, Rafe got up and walked into the bathroom. I went in and out of hearing the shower and then the trickle of water in the sink as he shaved and brushed his teeth. Eventually he came out, wearing nothing but a towel, and I managed to open my eyes for long enough to enjoy the show. The towel disappeared, and I watched as he pulled on a pair of underwear and then a pair of jeans. Finally, he pulled a T-shirt down over all those muscles, and shrugged into a gray hoodie, before coming to bend over me. "I gotta go to work, darlin'."

I nodded. "Be careful."

"Always." He gave me a kiss and straightened. I happen to know that he's rarely careful, but he usually makes it home, and besides, I was too tired to argue. As his footsteps faded down the stairs, I snuggled back into the pillows and went back to sleep.

The second time I woke up was maybe an hour later. The footsteps were back, coming up the stairs this time. Almost running. Heavy soles thudding on the worn wood treads.

For a second, my heart shot up into my throat. What if it wasn't Rafe? What if it was someone else who had waited for him to leave, and who had broken in to hurt me?

But a second later he burst through the doorway—he, himself—and headed for the closet.

I pushed myself up on one elbow. "What's wrong?"

He glanced at me over his shoulder. "Got a call."

I sat up a little straighter, and watched as he pulled out a backpack and started shoving underwear and T-shirts into it. "From who?" Or whom?

"The sheriff." He chose another pair of jeans—other than the pair he was wearing—and shoved them into the bag on top of the T-shirts.

"The Davidson County sheriff?"

We live in Davidson County, which is the same as Metropolitan Nashville. There's a chief of police as well as a sheriff in charge of us. But I had no idea that Rafe was on speaking terms with the Davidson County sheriff. When he gets a call, it's usually from the Metro PD, and most often from our friend, homicide detective Tamara Grimaldi.

He shook his head. "Sheriff Satterfield."

Bob Satterfield is the sheriff of Maury County, which is

located an hour to an hour and a half south of Nashville, and encompasses the city of Columbia as well as the small town of Sweetwater, where we both grew up.

In addition to that, Bob Satterfield is my mother's gentleman friend. Once upon a time, in high school, I dated his son Todd, who is my brother Dix's best friend.

But I digress.

"Does this have anything to do with Mother?"

"I don't think so," Rafe said, looking around.

"Toothbrush?" I suggested, and watched him hurry toward the bathroom. "What does it have to do with?"

He came back, and dropped the backpack on the foot of the bed so he could close it. "Six dead."

"People?!"

You'll pardon the question. Maury County is a sleepy sort of place. Not even Columbia has much of a crime rate, and the rest of the county is even more laid back. The last time anything like that happened down there was six months ago, in May, when my ten year high school reunion was the occasion for a killing spree. Or maybe a case of serial murder. I'm not sure about the difference. Several people died, anyway. But that was the first time anything like that had happened in years, not to say decades.

And now there were six dead? "Who died? Anyone I know?"

"Prob'ly not. I don't imagine you had much to do with the Skinners growing up."

His voice was dry. Hard to tell whether it was a comment on my upbringing—as the youngest daughter of Robert and Margaret Anne Martin, I'd been limited in the sort of company I'd been allowed to keep; Rafe himself had not been on the list—or a comment on the Skinners themselves not being the sort of people I'd want anything to do with.

The name didn't ring a bell, anyway. "I don't remember the Skinners. Are they a family?"

Rafe nodded. "I went to school with Darrell Skinner. He was a couple years older than me, though. Woulda been gone by the time you came along."

We had spent a year of high school together, he and I. Or not together, but at the same school at the same time. Occasionally, he'd passed me in the hallway with a wink and a sly compliment. It wasn't until ten years later that I'd discovered he'd liked me back then.

Not that it would have made any difference if I'd known it at the time. My family would have pitched a fit, and at fourteen, I'd lacked the internal fortitude to stand up to my mother.

"And Darrell Skinner is... um...?"

"Dead," Rafe said. "Along with five of his relatives."

Yikes. "And the sheriff called in the TBI?"

My husband works for the TBI, the Tennessee Bureau of Investigation. When local law enforcement comes across something they can't handle, they can choose to call the TBI for help, since the TBI has more experience with things like serial murders and spree killers than a small town Southern sheriff would.

"He called me," Rafe said. "Because I'm from Sweetwater and he figured I knew the Skinners. It was up to me to square it with the brass."

"There's no reason why they wouldn't want you to go, is there?"

He shook his head. "They cleared it."

"Don't you want to go?" I'd gotten a very definite whiff of reluctance there.

"Unlike you," Rafe said, "I don't have a lot of good memories from growing up in Sweetwater. And a lotta those bad memories have to do with the sheriff."

Understood. For a lot of years, whenever something went wrong in Sweetwater, Rafe was the go-to guy who got blamed for it. "But he apologized for that. And he likes you now. And respects you."

Even if there was probably still a part of the sheriff who wished I had married his son instead of Rafe.

Rafe sighed. "I know. I just don't like going back there. And this looks like it's gonna be a bad one."

With six dead to start the day, I could well imagine that.

"Do you know any of the details?"

"Just that there were six people shot in their beds," Rafe said. "And one of'em was Darrell Skinner."

I winced. "That's enough, really."

He nodded. "I figure I'll have to stay there a couple days, at least. Something like this ain't likely to be solved in the first twenty-four."

No. Not with that many dead, and what would surely turn out to be six times however many motives.

But most likely just one killer.

"Give me five minutes," I said, throwing off the comforter. "I'll come with you."

"Darlin'..." He turned to watch me pad barefoot to the bathroom, and his mouth curved.

"I'm fat," I said crossly.

"You're pregnant. And gorgeous."

And he looked at me like he meant it, which helped even more than the words. He didn't, however, come into the bathroom to touch me. But since I was already slowing him down and he was waiting instead of leaving me behind, I guess I couldn't complain about that.

After brushing my teeth and hair and splashing some water on my face, I stepped into a pair of panties and got his help in fastening my bra. And then, since we were going to Sweetwater, where I might—probably would—come face to face with my mother at some point today, I regretfully gave up the idea of wearing something comfortable and instead dropped a dress over my head. It draped very becomingly over the stomach, if I do say so myself. Finally, after getting some help in pulling on a pair of socks—the stomach got in the way of bending over these days—I stuck my feet into a pair of ankle boots. Thus appropriately attired, at least according to my mother, I shoved a few pieces of clothing into an overnight bag and turned to Rafe. "I'm ready."

He was leaning on the door jamb, arms folded across his chest. "You sure you wanna do this, darlin'? Ain't like the sheriff's gonna let you interfere with his case, you know."

"It won't be his case," I pointed out. "It'll be yours."

He shook his head. "Still his. I'll just be there to give input and help. And ride herd on the forensic team and that kinda thing."

There had to be at least one crime scene, and if six people had been killed, it must be a bloody one. Far beyond what a small, rural, sheriff's department was accustomed to handling.

"Did you already arrange that?"

He nodded. "They're on their way."

"Then let's go, too." I headed for the door. He stepped aside to let me through and then fell in behind me.

"I've been thinking that I should make a trip to Sweetwater anyway," I told him, as we traversed the stairs with our respective bags. "It's been a couple of weeks since I was there. I don't think Mother is on speaking terms with Audrey yet. I'm not sure what's going on with Audrey and Darcy. And I think this is the week when they're starting the hearings into Beulah Odom's competency."

He glanced at me as we came off the stairs and crossed the foyer toward the front door. "Was there a question about that?"

"According to her family there is," I said, passing through the door he held open for me. "Thank you. She left her restaurant," Beulah's Meat'n Three, a Sweetwater staple for as long as I could remember, "to Yvonne," one of her waitresses, "and her sister-in-law and niece want it for themselves. So they've insisted on having a hearing into her competency, to see if they can't wrest the place away from Yvonne."

Rafe nodded, and locked the front door behind us. "Here." He took the bag out of my hand. "You shouldn't be carrying that."

It weighed no more than fifteen pounds, but I let him. "I guess we're taking the Volvo?"

It sat at the bottom of the stairs, in front of Rafe's big, black Harley-Davidson, the one he drives to work every morning.

He led the way to the car and popped the trunk so he could put his backpack and my bag inside. "We're gonna have to. I ain't letting you ride on the back of the bike the whole way there. Not in your condition."

And not only that, but it looked like rain. The sky was pewter gray, with low-hanging clouds.

"Maybe I should take you to the TBI," I suggested, "so you can pick up an official vehicle."

"Drive two cars?"

"It'll give us both something to drive while we're down there." Since I didn't want to be stuck sitting in the parlor at Mother's house while he took my car to work every morning and left me stranded.

He shrugged. "I'm sure the sheriff has a squad car he can spare."

"Yes, but are you sure the town of Sweetwater will be able to handle the sight of you driving a sheriff's vehicle?"

It wasn't just Bob Satterfield who had been wont to pin anything that went wrong in Sweetwater on Rafe. Everyone else in town had been only too happy to play along, too.

"They're gonna have to," Rafe said. "I prob'ly shoulda requisitioned a car when I was at work, but I didn't think about it. And now I don't wanna take the time to go back. I'm already running late."

"I'm sorry." I headed for the passenger seat. "You better

drive, then."

"Don't mind if I do." He walked around to the driver's side and got in. We took off down the driveway with spurt of gravel. "Fasten your seatbelt," Rafe said with glance at me.

"I'm trying." I fumbled with the buckle. "It isn't as easy as it used to be. One of these days, I'm afraid I'm going to get in the car and the belt just won't be long enough to fit around me anymore."

He grinned. "I don't think you have to worry about that. Not much more than a month to go."

An interminable month. Sometimes I felt like this was the longest pregnancy on record. Like I was an elephant waiting to give birth. And not just in girth, but in the time it took.

I didn't say so. He'd already talked me off the 'I'm fat, I'm ugly' bandwagon once today; it wasn't fair to make him do it again. "So tell me about the Skinners," I said instead. "I really don't remember them. Was Darrell the only one who was close to our age?"

"He wasn't close to yours." Rafe concentrated on maneuvering the car down Potsdam Street toward Dresden and the interstate. "He was a couple years ahead of me in school, making him maybe five years ahead of you. And they didn't live in Sweetwater."

"Where did they live?"

We had gone to Columbia High, which had drawn kids from all over Maury County. The two of us from opposite sides of Sweetwater, and Darrell Skinner from somewhere else, it seemed.

"Other side of the county," Rafe said. "Up in the foothills by the Devil's Backbone."

The Devil's Backbone is an outdoorsy area adjacent to the old Natchez Trail, now the Natchez Trace Scenic Parkway, which runs from the south end of Nashville all the way to Natchez, Mississippi. Originally, it was a dirt track that was used by the local Indian tribes to move between the Cumberland, Tennessee, and Mississippi Rivers. Later, it saw use by the early explorers and traders who settled in the area. Meriwether Lewis, of Lewis and Clark fame, died at Grinder's Stand on the Trace in October 1809. Apparently old Meriwether was addicted to opium, which may have contributed to his death. His mother claimed he'd been murdered, but William Clark along with then-president Thomas Jefferson, accepted a verdict of suicide.

Lewis was buried beside the trail, and since 2009, there's been a bronze bust marking his grave site.

At any rate, the Natchez Trace cuts through the upper northwest corner of Maury County, but by the time it reaches the area Rafe was talking about, it's well outside our county and into the adjacent one. The Devil's Backbone is not located in Maury County, but some of the foothills are, and apparently that's where Darrell Skinner had lived. And died.

"Sounds..." I hesitated, "rural."

Rafe's lips quirked as he maneuvered the car onto Dresden in the direction of Dickerson Pike and the interstate. "You can say that. The Skinners were what you mighta called hillbilly trailer trash."

"I would never call anyone that," I said, offended. "Especially now that they're dead."

Rafe chuckled. "Being dead don't mean Darrell wasn't all that and more, darlin'."

"Maybe not. But you're not supposed to speak ill of the dead." And I would assume that went double if they were murdered.

"The Skinners were trailer trash," Rafe said. "I oughta know."

Having grown up in a trailer himself, I assumed. In a trailer park called The Bog on the south side of Sweetwater, almost as far as it was possible to get from the Devil's Backbone while staying in the same county.

"You were not trailer trash," I said firmly. "Nor was your mother. Or even your grandfather, bless his—" *evil, rotten,* "heart."

Rafe grinned at me. "It is what it is, darlin'. Not much anyone can do about now."

I supposed not.

"Anyway, the Skinners lived in a couple trailers up in the hills. I never had much to do with'em. Darrell was older'n me, like I said, and he didn't like me much."

"Because... um...?"

He shot me a glance out of the corner of his eye. I'm getting better at articulating difficult thoughts, but sometimes it's very convenient that he can read my mind. "Cause my daddy was black?"

That's what I'd been getting at. Without saying it out loud, because that would be rude.

"So he was a racist?"

The corner of Rafe's mouth quirked. "No more'n a lot of other people."

Point taken. My family had taken a while to warm up to him, as well. It hadn't been just because he was half black—the fact that his mother had gotten herself in the family way at fourteen had had something to do with it, too, and so did the two years he'd spent at Riverbend Penitentiary—but the whole colored thing had played a part. Even if nobody was willing to say so. Out loud.

"I love you," I said.

He smiled. "I know, darlin'."

"Is this going to be hard for you?"

It was just a month since he'd stood over a dead body that had definitely hit close to home. I hated the idea that it would happen again. Especially so soon.

"Cause it's Darrell?" He shook his head. "I don't imagine so. I ain't seen him in close to fifteen years. And we weren't real friendly before that."

I didn't say anything, and he added, "It ain't supposed to be easy, Savannah. But I don't think this one's gonna be any harder than anything else I've had to deal with lately."

Point taken.

He gave me a searching look as he guided the car past the buffalo statues—Dickerson Pike used to be known as Buffalo Trail. Up ahead, we could see the entrance to I-24. "You gonna be all right?"

"It won't be up to me to figure out who killed six people," I said.

"I meant, with your mama and all."

"Oh." My mother had gotten some bad news last month, and she was still struggling with accepting it. "That. Sure. I'll be fine."

I'd probably have to listen to my mother moan, but there are worse fates. And if I kept busy with Yvonne and the Beulah problem, maybe I could cut down on the time I'd have to spend with her.

Maybe I could even get her to take an interest in Yvonne and the Beulah problem. It would give her something else to think about.

"You sure you wanna do this?" He gave me a sideways look, searching. "There's time for me to turn around and take you back home."

We hadn't reached the entrance ramp for the interstate yet, but it was right there on the other side of the intersection.

"I'm sure," I said. "Just drive."

Rafe nodded, and did.

TWO

Columbia is usually about an hour south of Nashville. Today, we made it in just over forty-five minutes. And we did it without lights or sirens, and without being pulled over by law enforcement. I'll admit to closing my eyes from time to time, though. Rafe's a safe driver, but he goes fast.

It was just before ten when we left the interstate at the Columbia exit and headed west. I caught Rafe glancing at the clock on the dashboard.

"Just go straight there," I told him. "If you take me all the way south to Sweetwater, and then drive north and across the county to the Devil's Backbone, it'll be another hour before you get there. The sheriff is probably already pacing, waiting for you to show up."

He gave me a look. "You sure?"

"I don't mind. If I drop you off, I'm sure the sheriff will give you a ride back. Or I can wait until you're done if you want."

"We can work something out." He headed west through Columbia instead of south toward Sweetwater.

Twenty minutes later, we were on our way up into the foothills of the Western Highland Rim. The hillsides were thickly forested, but the branches of the trees were mostly bare. Here and there, there was a fir tree, but mostly we were looking at oaks and maples and the occasional hickory. All trees that lost their foliage in the winter.

"How many Skinners are there?" I asked Rafe as he

maneuvered the car up the slick road. The drizzle had started just after we passed Columbia, but it hadn't developed into real rain yet. It was still enough to make the road wet and slippery, though. "More than six?"

"Not too many more. In fact—" He stepped on the brake, and the car fishtailed.

I uttered a faint scream and grabbed for the door handle. "What are you doing?!"

"Sorry. I just remembered that Robbie Skinner has a place up here." He backed up a few yards, going backwards down the hill at breakneck speed, before turning up an unpaved road that disappeared between the trees. A ghostly sign appeared out of the gloomy mist, and I leaned forward and squinted to bring it into focus. *'No Trespassing'* in red letters, with an outline of something underneath...

I sat back against the seat. "Is that an Uzi?"

"Looks more like an AK-47," Rafe said, running an experienced eye over it as we went by. "The Skinners ain't big on company."

"Seriously?"

He shrugged.

"I mean it. If he's threatening to shoot trespassers with an automatic weapon, what are we doing driving up to his house unannounced?"

"He ain't gonna shoot us," Rafe said calmly, his hands flexing on the wheel as he fought to keep the car on the road.

"Why? Do you think he's dead, too?"

He glanced at me, and I added, automatically, "Keep your eyes on the road." Or this sorry excuse for one that we were traversing.

"I wasn't thinking he was dead," Rafe answered my question. "More that he might know what's going on, and I oughta ask. I don't think the sheriff's gotten around to talking to any next of kin yet. But now that you mention it..."

"Or maybe he's the one who shot the rest of the family. With his AK-47 or whatnot."

"You just never know," Rafe said, and pulled the car out of the trees into a clearing.

I peered through the steady drizzle. A new, fancy pickup truck with big, beefy tires was parked next to an old Airstream trailer that had seen better days. It looked desolate and unhappy. While they were two different makes and models, I was reminded of the trailer where Rafe had grown up, on the other side of the county. Not a place I wanted to revisit, even in my mind.

A deep, reverberating bark echoed between the bare trees. It took a few seconds to spot the dog, as ghostly gray as the rain, at the end of a long chain extending from under the trailer.

"Don't turn off the engine," I said.

Rafe glanced at me. "Why not?"

"Remember that Stephen King story about the dog? What if the car won't start again? We'll be stuck here."

"He's on a chain," Rafe pointed out. "He can't reach us."

"If we get out of the car, he can." And if one of us got out of the car, the dog might even break the chain to attack us. "Let's just sit here and wait." With all this barking, surely the dog's owner would be out soon, to see what was going on.

Rafe shook his head when I said so. "I don't think so. Look over there." He pointed.

"Where?" I squinted through the rain. And then I saw what he had. A pale, longish lump on the ground a few feet from the dog. "Oh, no. Is that...?"

"Looks like," Rafe said. "The door's open."

It was. Hanging wide open in the rain. As if someone had stumbled out of the trailer, trying to make it to the truck, and had collapsed at the halfway mark.

Rafe opened his door. "I gotta see if he's still alive."

"But the dog..."

"He's protecting his owner," Rafe said, swinging his legs out. The dog went into a hysterical spate of barking. "I'm sure he's more afraid of me than I am of him."

"That's spiders! And he doesn't look afraid of you. At all."

Rafe shrugged. "Not much I can do about it. Somebody's gotta see if Robbie's still breathing."

"If you keep the dog away from me," I said, "I will."

He turned to look at me, brow arched.

"I mean it," I said. "We have a better chance if we work together. You have a gun. And you're better prepared to use it than I am. If you make sure the dog won't attack me, I'll go check if Robbie's alive."

Rafe thought about it. "I'd rather you stayed in the car," he told me.

I'd rather stay in the car, too. But I had a point, and he knew it. Rafe would have a harder time keeping an eye on the dog as well as checking on Robbie than if he just had to keep an eye on the dog while I checked on Robbie.

If it even was Robbie Skinner lying out there in the rain. We didn't even know that yet.

Rafe sighed. "All right. I'd rather you stayed here, but I ain't gonna waste time arguing about it. Not if there's a chance Robbie's still breathing."

I nodded, and opened my own door. "Just make sure the dog doesn't get to me. I don't really want you to shoot it—"

"I don't wanna shoot it, either," Rafe said. And added, "But if I have to, I will."

I swung my legs out of the car. Cold drizzle hit my knees. "On three."

"Two," Rafe said. "One. Go."

He got to his feet. The dog went into hysterics. As Rafe took a few steps closer, it threw itself at him. I gasped, even as the dog came to the end of its chain before it reached Rafe, and was yanked back with a strangled yip.

It was a scary-looking dog. Probably close to ninety pounds, with a big head, strong jaws, and ears that stood up. It was pale gray, with a blaze of white covering one eye and most of its square snout. It looked hostile.

However, when Rafe took a step toward it—and I could only guess at the expression on his face, since his back was to me—the dog shied back. It kept growling, but it didn't lunge again.

"Go," Rafe told me over his shoulder.

I went. Along the side of the car and then across the open expanse of mud and grass toward the lump—that I now could see clearly was a body—in the grass.

The dog backed off. Maybe because it recognized a stronger alpha, or maybe because it saw the gun and knew what it was. Or maybe it was because it realized, somehow, that we were trying to help.

The body was dressed in a pair of tighty whities and nothing else. He—definitely male—was lying on his stomach with one hand thrown over his head and the other trapped under his body. His hair was dark—or maybe that was just because it was wet from the rain. When it was dry, it might be more of a medium blond color.

He was a big guy. Shorter than Rafe, but hefty. Some muscle tone, but also some extra padding. And he was lying in a puddle, or maybe a pool, of what looked like blood.

I reached out and put a tentative hand on his back. He was freezing cold.

"Check for a pulse," Rafe instructed when I told him so.

I wasn't sure I knew how. I tried, but I couldn't feel anything, and I wasn't sure whether it was because the guy didn't have a pulse—likely—or because I just wasn't touching him in the right place.

"Hang on." I yanked open my purse and fumbled for my compact.

"Won't work," Rafe told me over his shoulder. "Too much

moisture in the air."

He was right. Holding the mirror in front of the dead guy's mouth and nose didn't do anything at all. But fog beaded the mirror nonetheless.

Rafe took a couple steps backward, with the gun still pointed at the dog, now huddled in the dryness underneath the trailer, and reached out with his other hand to grab the guy's wrist. After a few seconds, he shook his head. "Nothing."

I dropped the compact back in my purse and extended a hand. "A little help?" Squatting was hard. Getting to my feet without tipping over was harder. And I didn't want to have to brace myself on the body.

Rafe took my hand and hauled me upright. "Go back to the car. Call the sheriff."

"What are you going to do?"

"Find something to cover him with," Rafe said.

I glanced at the body. And then back at Rafe. "I don't think he cares."

"The sheriff will. His crime scene's washing away."

Good point. "I'll go call," I said. "Watch out for the dog."

"I think he's content to stay where he is now that he's figured out we're not a threat. But I ain't going near the dog."

He didn't. While I made my way back to the Volvo, he went over to the pickup truck—the one I suspected Robbie had been on his way to when he was felled—and peered into the bed. After a few seconds, he reached in and pulled out something blue. As he shook it open, I saw what it was: a plastic tarp. It was big enough to cover the body and a couple of feet of ground in each direction.

Meanwhile, I pulled out my phone and dialed Bob Satterfield. "Morning, Sheriff. Rafe said to call you. We're... um..."

"We?"

"I came down to Sweetwater with him."

"Of course you did." The sheriff sounded resigned.

"I'm not going to get involved in your case," I told him, even though I already was. "It's just that... um..."

"Spit it out, darlin'."

I spat it out. "We were on our way up to the crime scene. I was going to drop Rafe off rather than have him take me all the way to Sweetwater and then drive up to where you are. But on the way, he decided to check in on Robbie Skinner. I think we were driving right past his place, although I'm not sure." Rafe might have taken the roads he did on purpose, to get him here. "Anyway, it looks like Robbie's dead. Or at least someone is. Flat on his face outside his trailer."

"Shot?"

"I'm not sure," I admitted. "He's on his stomach. We didn't turn him over. But he's dead, and there's a lot of blood." Some of it had probably washed away in the rain, as well. "He's naked except for a pair of underwear, and the door to his trailer is hanging open. It looks like he was on his way from the trailer to his truck—" *in his underwear?* "—when someone shot him. Or maybe someone shot him, and he was trying to get to the truck to drive himself somewhere to get help." A likelier explanation.

"Huh," the sheriff said.

"What?"

"He wasn't shot in the head?"

Not that I'd noticed. And if he had been, chances were he wouldn't have made it out the door and halfway to the car before he collapsed.

"Rafe is putting a tarp over him," I said. "You should come over here and take a look. We're off Little Marrowbone Road, I think."

"I know where Robbie Skinner lives," the sheriff said, in a tone that indicated he'd been here before. After a second, he changed it to, "Lived."

"Good. Then I won't have to give you directions." Since I

technically didn't know exactly how we'd gotten here. "There's a dog. Chained under the trailer. Someone will have to take charge of it."

"There are dogs here, too," the sheriff informed me. "One more won't make a difference to Animal Control."

I hesitated. "What will happen to them?"

"The dogs?" The sheriff sounded surprised that I'd asked.

I nodded. And then, since he couldn't see me, I said, "Yes. If their owners are dead, what will happen to them?"

"I imagine they'll end up at the pound," the sheriff said. "Some of'em might get adopted. Most will probably have to be put down. The ones we've found here don't seem like they'd be pet material."

Probably not. "The one that's here doesn't seem too bad. It barked when we first got here, and tried to lunge at Rafe. But now it's just curled up under the trailer with its nose on its paws."

And part of me felt sorry for it. What kind of life could it have had, out here in the elements with no shelter other than the underside of the trailer? Robbie clearly hadn't been letting it in at night if it was outside now. He wouldn't have had time to chain it up after getting shot. And was it getting fed regularly? I couldn't see a food bowl anywhere.

"Then maybe it'll be one of the lucky ones," the sheriff said. "I gotta go, darlin'. Tell your husband to stay where he is until I get there."

I promised I would. "Hurry."

"I'll be there in ten minutes. The other Skinners don't live far." After a second he added, "Didn't."

"I'll let him know." I tapped the screen to disconnect, and called out to Rafe. "The sheriff is on his way."

He nodded. "I'm gonna take a quick look inside. Just in case he wasn't alone when it happened."

Oh, God. "Was he married? Involved?" Did he have children?

"No idea," Rafe said. "I ain't seen Robbie in fifteen years. He could have a whole harem, for all I know."

Not in this trailer, surely. And—not to speak ill of the dead—he didn't look like the kind of guy who could command a harem.

Rafe, on the other hand...

I watched as he made his way from the body toward the door of the trailer. And this time I was only peripherally enjoying the way he moved. I was more interested in what the dog was doing. If it suddenly lunged, Rafe would be in trouble. He had his gun in his hand again—he had nestled it at the small of his back to open the tarp and spread it over the body—but if the dog moved, I wasn't sure he'd be able to get it up and pointed in time.

Luckily, it didn't turn out to be necessary. The dog watched him, but made no attempt to come out from under the trailer. Not even when Rafe stepped up into the doorway and peered inside.

I rolled down my window and stuck my head out. "See if there's anything in there you can feed the dog."

He raised a hand to show me he'd heard me, and then he disappeared inside the trailer.

I waited, gnawing on my cuticles.

He wasn't gone long. Of course, there wasn't much space that had to be searched. It wasn't much more than a minute before he appeared in the doorway again, this time carrying a bowl. He jumped down, somehow managed to keep the dog food inside the bowl, and squatted to put it on the ground just within the dry section of the underside of the trailer. Then he backed up. The dog waited until he was ten feet away before creeping over to the bowl and starting to eat.

Rafe walked backward the whole way to the car, but the dog made no move to follow. Too busy wolfing down food.

"I feel bad for it," I told Rafe when he'd opened the door and slid behind the wheel. "It looks really hungry."

He nodded, his face grim. "I don't think he was starving it.

But if you keep it hungry, it'll be more likely to attack."

"That's terrible."

Rafe shrugged, but I could tell from his expression that he wasn't happy, either.

"Is anyone else inside? Or anything valuable, that the dog might have been guarding?"

He shook his head. "Nobody else. He either slept alone, or whoever he slept with, shot him."

"Is that likely?"

"At this point, anything's likely," Rafe said. "Or at least it's possible."

We sat in silence a moment, and then he added, "I didn't see nothing valuable. I didn't expect to. People who live in trailers don't usually have the Mona Lisa hanging on the wall."

I guess not. "Someone must have had a reason for killing all these people, though." Six—no, seven now. You don't do that kind of thing unless there's something valuable at the end of it.

Or unless you really, really hate those six or seven people.

"What do you think happened?"

Rafe rolled his head on the seat to look at me. "Here?"

"Here. There. Everywhere."

The corner of his mouth pulled up. "Doctor Seuss?"

"Not on purpose." Although in the next year or two, we'd probably get our fill of Doctor Seuss. I tried to imagine Rafe sitting on a small bedside in the nursery at home, reading *Green Eggs and Ham* to a small, faceless, genderless child whose curly, black hair spilled out over the blankets. (Yes, while I might not know yet whether we were having a boy or girl, I was pretty sure it would have dark, curly hair.)

The mind boggled. I shook it off. "The same person shot Robbie as shot everyone else, right?"

"Maybe," Rafe said. "Maybe not. Coulda been two shooters. Or more. Two strike teams going to two different places at the same time."

Strike teams? "Six people were shot at the other location, right?"

"Couple locations," Rafe said. "And yeah, that's what the sheriff said when he called."

"Who were they?"

"Mostly Skinners. Art and his wife Linda. Their daughter Cilla and her boyfriend. Their son A.J."

My stomach clenched. "Someone shot children?"

"Cilla was eighteen," Rafe said. "A.J. sixteen."

Someone had started the family early, then. Although sixteen was far too young to die. So was eighteen. So, for that matter, was thirty-five or forty.

"Art was the oldest brother?"

Rafe nodded. "Darrell was two years older then me, like I said. Robbie was a couple years older than Darrell, and Art was the oldest. He woulda been thirty-seven or thirty-eight, maybe."

After a moment, Rafe added, "Cilla had a baby."

"Someone shot a baby?"

He shook his head. "The baby was left alive. Still in bed with its mama and daddy."

God. I didn't know whether that made it worse or better. I mean, who kills an innocent baby?

But to kill the baby's mother and father, and leave the infant there, still in bed, maybe between them, maybe spattered with their blood... that was pretty bad too.

"God." I leaned my head against the seat and closed my eyes. If I hadn't, I'm afraid I would have fainted. Under my palm, I could feel my own baby moving around. "That's... I don't have the words to describe it. Who does something like that?"

Rafe didn't answer. When I slitted my eyes and peered at him, his face was grim.

I straightened. "You know who did this?"

He gave me a glance. And a head-shake. "No."

"Do you suspect something?"

He shrugged. "It's hard not to think."

Yes, it was. And while my thoughts were unpleasant, his were likely to be worse. He knew more about this—about all of it—than I did. Than I ever would.

"What are you thinking?"

He gave me another look. And a pause. But eventually he told me. "It's likely gonna be one of two things. Either it's personal, somebody with a beef against the Skinners, who drew the line at killing the baby."

"Or?"

"Or it's business. Somebody got hired to take out the Skinners, and there wasn't a price on the baby's head, so it was left alive."

And again, hard to wrap my brain around which was worse.

"If there had been a price on the baby's head, would a professional hitman have killed it?"

He glanced at me. "Maybe."

Yeah. Maybe. I had made the acquaintance of one of Hector Gonzales's minions a year ago. And I had no problem imagining him shooting a baby.

"Why would anyone send a hitman after a family of Middle Tennessee rednecks?"

"Can't imagine," Rafe said blandly, in a tone that indicated otherwise.

"Sure."

He slanted me a look. "It's too soon to tell."

I nodded, and waited for him to continue, since I doubted he was finished. After a second, he admitted, "Something about it feels off. One way or the other. But I don't know enough about anything yet, to even guess at a motive."

"It would have to be something big, to wipe out a whole family." Or most of one.

"You'd be surprised," Rafe told me, "what people'll do for not much profit. But right now, I can't tell you who did this and why. After I've seen the other crime scenes, maybe I'll have a better idea."

I nodded. "Let's just wait for Sheriff Satterfield to get here. Then you and he can talk, while I take the car and drive to Columbia. You can update me over dinner. If you get to take a break."

"I'm sure he won't let me starve," Rafe said and settled into his seat to wait for the sheriff.

THREE

The other crime scene mustn't be far away, because it couldn't have been much more than five minutes before we saw the headlights of the sheriff's SUV cut through the gloom.

Of course, at first we didn't know that it was the sheriff. For all we knew, it might be the shooter coming back to make sure the job was finished. Rafe tensed in his seat and got a better handle on his gun, which he had kept readily available in his lap. But then the vehicle exited the narrow path between the trees and pulled left to park beside us, and we saw the green stripe along the side that said Maury County Sheriff.

Rafe relaxed again, and when the sheriff opened his door, he did the same. So did I, since I didn't want to miss the conversation.

Sheriff Satterfield waved us both back into the car. "I'm already wet. No sense in y'all standing out here in the rain."

I was wet, too, but I obeyed the command to stay in the car. Rafe did not. He and the sheriff faced one another across the roof of the Volvo. "You made good time."

"The first crime scene isn't far," the sheriff said, looking around. His gaze snagged for a second on the blue tarp. "That Robbie under there?"

Rafe nodded. "I didn't turn him over, but I'm gonna guess he was gut shot. A slug to the chest and he never woulda made it out of the trailer."

The sheriff nodded back. "But with a bullet in the gut, he

mighta lived a couple minutes. Long enough to think he might have time to go for help."

"Long enough to know he was gonna die," Rafe said. "And long enough to feel it."

I fought back a shiver. It might have been that my clothes were still damp from earlier and the open window was giving me goosebumps. But I think it was more that that cold anger penetrated and made me feel chilled to the bone. There's a difference between shooting a man dead, and shooting a man in the gut so he'll stay alive a couple of minutes, feeling the pain and knowing he's going to die.

"Was it on purpose?"

I wasn't aware of having spoken out loud, but they both bent to peer in at me.

"Sorry," I added.

The sheriff shook his head. "It's a good question. Did someone want him to have a couple minutes to think about what he'd done—and he musta done something to someone to end up like this."

"Maybe it was an accident," I suggested. "Maybe whoever it was, meant to shoot him in the chest, but he moved."

I waited. They both shrugged. Maybe it was a stupid question.

"You didn't tell me much about the others," Rafe said, and the sheriff nodded.

"The M.E.'s gonna have to make the determination on who was shot first and last. But mostly I saw single shots to the head. No signs of struggle with most of'em. Looked like they were asleep when it happened."

"Someone just walked right in, shot them, and walked back out?"

The sheriff nodded. "Looks like."

We sat in silence a moment. I sat, they stood. "So maybe they didn't know it was happening?" I asked, optimistically.

"Maybe so," the sheriff agreed. I have no idea whether he actually thought so, or whether he just said so because he thought it was what I wanted to hear.

"Time for you to go," Rafe informed me.

"I don't mind waiting." I was curious now. It was horrible, of course, but fascinating, too, in a gruesome sort of way.

I mean, who would wipe out every member—or almost every member—of an entire family in one night?

"I don't suppose the Skinners were in any kind of family feud with anyone?"

Rafe's lips twitched. The sheriff's didn't, although he looked like he found the question amusing. "The Hatfields and McCoys?" he said, shaking his head. "I don't think so, darlin'. If there was that kind of thing going on in my county, I think I woulda heard about it."

I nodded. "It just seems like it would have to be a pretty big reason for someone to do this. Seven dead... that isn't just because someone beat someone else at cards. Or stole someone's girlfriend. Or even murdered someone else. I mean, even if one of the Skinners killed somebody—not that I'm saying they did, although I expect you'll look into it—but even if they killed someone, it wouldn't justify this."

"Nothing would justify this," Rafe muttered.

I glanced at him. "You know what I mean."

"It's overkill. Sure. Even if it was retaliation for someone's death, it's still too much. But that's assuming whoever did this was rational. And there ain't nothing rational about murder."

He had me there. "I'm just going to let you do your job," I said, and opened my car door. The sheriff moved out of the way, politely, and gave me a hand up. I made my way around the car to the driver's seat, where Rafe bundled me back inside. "Call if you need me. Or the car. I'm just going into Columbia, so I won't be far."

"What're you gonna do in Columbia?" the sheriff wanted to

know, and I turned to him.

"If I remember correctly, they started the competency hearing on Beulah Odom today. I want to see if I can find out how it's going. Beulah's sister-in-law and niece are trying to take the restaurant away from Yvonne."

The sheriff nodded. "I never saw no sign that Beulah wasn't all there. Getting older, like we all are. And she had some health problems. But diabetes don't make you lose your mind."

Not usually, no.

"I think they're probably saying that Yvonne exerted undue influence," I said. "You know, convinced Beulah to leave the restaurant to her."

The sheriff scoffed. "Never knew Beulah to do what anybody told her without a fight."

"Sounds like you knew her well."

"Wouldn't say that," the sheriff said. "She was a good ten years older than me. But she lived and died in Maury County. And I've worked for the sheriff's department most of my life. It's part of the job, knowing the people."

I guess it was. "So you don't think they'll be able to convince the judge that Yvonne shouldn't have the restaurant?"

"Depends on the judge," the sheriff said. "If he knew Beulah, I doubt it."

"I'm a little worried," I admitted. "Not that it's any of my business. Yvonne and I aren't that close. But she's had some bad luck in her life." Some of which I felt a little bit responsible for, since it involved Rafe. "And she's worked for Beulah since high school. She told me once that she didn't have much of a relationship with her mother, and that Beulah kind of became a substitute. If this doesn't work out, she'll be devastated."

The sheriff nodded. "I'll keep my fingers crossed."

I told him I appreciated it. And then they both stepped away from the car. "You know where you're going?" Rafe asked, as I put the Volvo into reverse. I guess he must have noticed that I hadn't paid a whole lot of attention on our way here.

"Down the hill." I waved a vague hand in the direction of the road. "And then straight down the road."

"Call if you get lost."

"I'm not going to get lost," I told him. "I grew up here. I can find my way to the courthouse in Columbia."

He nodded, but didn't look convinced. Or maybe there was something else that had put that expression on his face.

"Good luck," I added. "Let me know how it goes and when I can expect to see you, OK?"

He said he would, and then he went to join the sheriff by the blue tarp. I negotiated a careful sixteen-point turn in the wet grass, without hitting either the sheriff's SUV or the tarp, or— God forbid—what was under it, and then I headed back down the pockmarked dirt road with the No *Trespassing* signs.

I was just slowing down to negotiate the turn from the dirt onto the paved road when another car—big, with bright headlights that blinded me—zoomed across the road and onto the track. I stood on the brake, literally, and while the brakes didn't squeal, I did. To be honest, it was more like a high pitched scream. I thought for sure we were going to meet head to head— or front to front—but the Volvo came to a quivering stop less than a foot from the grille of a big, white truck.

For a second, nothing happened. My ears were ringing, probably because I'd been screaming so loudly.

Then the truck engine cranked, and it began to move slowly backwards, back toward the road. I crept along behind it—or in front of it, more accurately, as it backed away.

It took just a few seconds for it to reach the road and back out. As it made a forty-five degree turn, I saw the insignia on the side. *Maury County Animal Control.* The back of the truck was full of small doors with holes in them, and I could hear yipping and barking.

I rolled down my window. "Sorry."

"No problem." The driver was a woman my age, or a year or two older, with short, sandy hair and no makeup. "I didn't expect anyone to be here."

"My husband and I found the body," I said. "He's up there with the sheriff."

She nodded.

"Are you here to pick up the dog?"

Her face clouded. "Yeah. How bad is it?"

"The dog? It doesn't seem all that bad." I told her about how it had scared me at first. "It barked and came lunging out from underneath the trailer. But as soon as it figured out we weren't a threat, it went back where it was dry. My husband gave it some food, and it settled down to eat. I'm not sure it got fed enough."

"Bastards," the woman in the truck growled.

"The sheriff said there were other dogs at the other crime scenes. Were they hungry, too?"

"More than hungry," the woman told me, her voice tight. "The bastards used them for dog fighting."

The bastards being the Skinners, I assume. "That's illegal, isn't it?"

She nodded. "But there's a lot of money in it. And some people just don't give a damn about illegal. Or about the animals."

She revved the engine and glanced up the dirt road.

"I should let you get to it," I said. "I'm Savannah, by the way. Martin. Collier."

She arched a brow. "Can't make up your mind?"

"I haven't been married that long. But I'm getting used to it. You'll see my husband up there, with the sheriff."

She nodded. "I'll be sure not to poach."

"I wasn't warning you off," I told her. I've stopped worrying about women drooling over—and sometimes on—my husband. And anyway, no way was she Rafe's type. "Be nice to the dog, though. It didn't seem like a bad dog."

"I'm always nice to the animals," the woman told me, and put her truck in gear to climb the track to Robbie Skinner's place. I pointed the Volvo down the road in the other direction.

The Columbia city limits weren't far, and as I'd told Rafe, I had no problem finding my way. It helped, of course, that there was only one main road, and once I got on it, I just followed it. Between you and me, I will admit that I had never, to my knowledge, been up in the foothills by the Devil's Backbone before.

Columbia, however, was familiar. I found a parking spot just off the square, under the *Martin & Vaughan Hardware and Building Supplies* sign, and made my way across the square to the courthouse.

From there, a guard directed me to the small courtroom where the hearing was taking place. I opened the door as quietly as I could, thinking I'd just slip quietly into the back row without anyone being the wiser—only to have everyone in the room turn to stare at me when the door opened.

Oops.

"Sorry. I'm just going to... um..." I waved vaguely at the back row of benches, mostly empty, my cheeks hot. "Carry on."

Nobody said anything, but a few faces turned back to the front. Some watched me maneuver my bulk carefully onto the bench. I guess maybe I was more interesting than what was happening at the front of the room.

It wasn't a big room. The judge sat up front, on a low dais. There was no box to his left, the way you see on crime shows on TV, where the witnesses sit and give their stories. Instead, the box was up front, facing the judge, not the courtroom. The better for him to hear the testimony and judge their facial expressions, I guess.

Of course there was no jury, either, so the judge's opinion was the only one that counted.

At the moment, a man I didn't know was standing in front of the judge. Or at least I didn't know him based on the back of his head. He was tall and skinny, with a long neck, protruding ears, and a bald spot at the back of his head.

The judge nodded to him. "Carry on, Mr. Jackson."

"It's like I said," Mr. Jackson intoned. "She was always there early to open the place. She and I'd be the first ones there in the morning. And when she didn't show, I drove up to Columbia to make sure she was OK."

"And you found her dead."

Mr. Jackson nodded. "Saw her through the window. Half outta bed, she was, and looking just horrible. So I called 911, and a couple minutes later, the police came."

He pronounced it PO-lis, the way a lot of old Southerners do.

"How long had you been working for Ms. Beulah?"

Mr. Jackson had been employed by Beulah for thirty years, he said. Even the judge looked to be impressed by that. "Beulah's Meat'n Three was a good place to work?"

Mr. Jackson nodded. "Couldn't ask for better. I been working for Ms. Beulah since I got outta high school. Started out as a dishwasher, and then second cook. When old Norm retired, Ms. Beulah, she promoted me to head cook. I've been head cook ever since."

The judge nodded. "You knew her well."

"Known her all my life," Mr. Jackson said. "Wasn't a nicer woman alive. Hell, Judge, you should know that. You've known her your whole life, too."

The courtroom tittered. The judge rolled his eyes. "Yeah, yeah. Now work with me here, Grady. When did you find out she'd left the place to Yvonne McCoy?"

Grady Jackson glanced over his shoulder to where Yvonne was sitting, next to—I squinted—my sister Catherine. Catherine's dark curls were as familiar to me—more so—than Yvonne's bright red upsweep.

"Not until after Beulah died," Grady Johnson said. "The police went through her office behind the restaurant, and found her will in the safe."

"What did you think?"

Grady shrugged bony shoulders inside a blue shirt. "Wasn't my business to think nothing."

"So it didn't strike you as odd that Ms. Beulah left her property to one of her waitresses instead of her own family?"

"Didn't like her family," Grady Jackson said, "did she? Her brother, he left years ago, and moved up to Williamson County—"

Grady gave the words roughly the same inflection as Gomorrah, or maybe Hollywood. I guess maybe it was because Williamson County—just north of Maury—is the wealthiest county in the state, full of horse breeders and country music executives. Maury County is by way of being the poor country cousin, both to Williamson County, and to Davidson, Metropolitan Nashville, farther north.

"—and if he came back, it was only 'cause he had to. He's dead now, rest his soul..."

The whole courtroom took a collective breath, and a sort of respectful pause, before Grady Jackson continued, "but before that, it was years since I seen him."

"And the petitioners?" The judge indicated Beulah's sister-in-law and niece, sitting on the other side of the aisle from Yvonne and Catherine. The niece had shoulder-length, light brown hair, glossy and nice, while her mother's hair was a little shorter, a little lighter, not as healthy-looking, and cut in a severe wedge, thickly stacked at the nape of the neck.

Grady Jackson shook his head. "Never seen'em before."

"So it didn't surprise you that Miss Beulah left her restaurant to Yvonne, and not her relatives."

"Twas hers," Grady said, "wasn't it? She could do what she wanted with it. And it makes sense she'd leave it to Yvonne.

Yvonne worked there. She knew how to run the place. All the regulars knew her. She'd keep running it the way Beulah woulda wanted her to."

That made sense to me, too. It was a big legacy, sure. Financially, I mean. A thriving business with thirty years of regulars who kept coming back. A business Beulah had busted her butt for, for decades. Yvonne would be set for life, as long as she kept it running. Restaurants don't run themselves. But if Beulah hadn't liked her brother's wife and daughter, and she'd wanted someone to carry on her business the way she herself would, it made total sense that she'd leave it to Yvonne.

Up front, the judge thanked Mr. Jackson, who stood down. The judge glanced at his watch. "We have time for one more before lunch, I think." He nodded to Catherine.

I recognized the woman who got up as another of the employees from Beulah's Meat'n Three: a lifetime waitress with gray hair in tight curls and beefy arms that could rival Rafe's. Her name was Maureen Boyd, and like Mr. Jackson and Yvonne, she had spent most of her adult life working for Beulah.

"I knew her as well as anyone," she said, her voice quavering a little. "I'd seen her every day for forty years. That restaurant was her life. She never had a family of her own, and once Otis got married and settled down up there in Franklin, he hardly ever came back. I don't think I'd seen him more than half a dozen times in the last forty years."

"What about his wife? And daughter?"

Maureen Boyd shook her head. "Never saw neither of'em until last year. Otis died, and Miss Beulah, she went to the funeral. A couple months later, they showed up at the Meat'n Three."

"Maybe Miss Beulah had invited them?"

"She said she didn't," Maureen said. "She wasn't happy to see'em, neither. They ate and drank and didn't even offer to pay. And the whole time, they were looking around and trying to guess what everything was worth. I even caught'em checking the maker's mark on the bottom of the china."

"Is the china valuable?" The judge sounded surprised. So was I. I wouldn't expect a small country restaurant in the middle of Tennessee to be serving up chicken fried steak and stewed okra on Wedgwood or Spode.

Maureen shook her head. "Miss Beulah was valuable. The customers, they're valuable. Not the china."

Not much anyone could say to that.

"So it didn't surprise you when Miss Beulah left the restaurant to Yvonne?" the judge asked. "Instead of—say— you?"

Maureen cackled. There's no other word for it. "I don't want the place. I'm happy doing my job and going home at the end of my shift. And I'm sixty-three years old. You oughta know that, Judge. We grew up together, you and I."

The judge waved that away, the same way he'd waved away Grady Johnson's personal remarks earlier. "So you wouldn't mind working for Yvonne McCoy?"

"If Beulah thought Yvonne'd do right by the place," Maureen said firmly, "that was good enough for me."

"Did you have any indications that Yvonne pressured Miss Beulah into leaving her the place? Or tricked her?"

"Wasn't nobody could trick Beulah," Maureen said. "If she left the place to Yvonne, it was 'cause she wanted Yvonne to have it. And if Beulah wanted Yvonne to have it, then so do I."

The judge nodded and dismissed her. While she stepped back from the box, Beulah's niece leaned toward her mother and whispered something in her ear. The severe stacked bob nodded.

"Any more character witnesses?" the judge asked my sister. Catherine jumped halfway to her feet and shook her head.

"Not at the moment, Your Honor."

The judge nodded. "Time for lunch. We'll meet back here

at…" He pushed back his voluminous, black sleeve to glance at his watch and calculate, "one-thirty. Unless there's something new, I'll give my ruling then."

He got to his feet, and so did everyone else. As soon as the door closed behind him, everybody relaxed. People started seeping toward the back door, and up at the front, Catherine leaned toward Yvonne. I couldn't hear what she said, but I saw her lips move. "Look at me. Not them."

On the other side of the aisle, Mrs. and Ms. Odom got up and sailed toward the back.

I stayed where I was, the better to see them as they approached and walked by. And I have to say, my mother would probably have approved. (That undoubtedly says more about Mother than it does about either Odom.)

Both were elegantly dressed, in classic fashions, good fabrics, and expensive labels. Ms. Odom carried a Kate Spade bag, while her mother's shoes sported the double Cs of Coco Chanel. Otis Odom, may he rest in peace, must have done all right for himself after leaving Sweetwater.

Neither of them bothered to look my way. I waited until they'd gone through the door before I made my way into the narrow aisle—it was a very small room—and toward the front.

Catherine and Yvonne were still talking. When I stopped beside them, Catherine looked up at me with her brows furrowed, an expression that smoothed out when she saw who I was. "Savannah. What are you doing here?"

"It's a long story," I said, leaning in for a sideways hug, before turning to give Yvonne the same. We've never really been on hugging terms before, but she seemed to expect it, and I didn't want to be rude. "Rafe had to come down for something. I decided to tag along and see what was going on. I thought I remembered that this was when the hearing was scheduled."

Catherine nodded. "How long have you been here?"

"Just since Grady Johnson spoke. Whatever happened before

that, I missed."

"We'll fill you in over lunch." Catherine gathered me and Yvonne in front of her—the result of being an older sibling, or maybe a mother—and ushered us in front of her toward the back door.

FOUR

We ended up at a small restaurant just off the square, where I got updated on the hearing over salads and sweet tea.

Not that there was a whole lot to update, really. The judge had heard from several of the other employees at Beulah's Meat'n Three before I got there, and all the testimony had gone pretty much the same way as what I'd heard. All the employees liked Beulah, had no problem with her doing whatever she wanted with her property, and seemed to have no issues with the idea of working for Yvonne after things were settled. Beulah's doctor had started things off this morning, and had testified that while Beulah had high blood pressure and the accompanying diabetes, there had been nothing wrong with her mental faculties. She was free from dementia, Alzheimer's, and senility, and according to her doctor, was quite capable of making up her own mind about what to do with her property. There had been no indications, or at least none he'd noticed, that she had been pressured or coerced.

"Did you have to testify?" I asked Yvonne.

She shook her head, but since her mouth was full of lettuce, it was Catherine who answered. "She's the defendant, pretty much. She's not required to testify."

"But she can, right? Don't you think it would be good for the judge to hear from her?"

"I think it's better," Catherine told me, while Yvonne turned her head back and forth to follow the conversation, "for the judge to hear testimony from the people who knew both Beulah and Yvonne. I'd consider putting her on if I thought we needed it, but I don't think we do. Unless something happens in the next hour, I don't see how Judge Hopkins can do anything but rule that Beulah Odom was *compos mentis* and capable of making her own decisions, and the will stands."

Yvonne swallowed. "Really? Are you sure?"

"I can't be completely sure until the judge rules," Catherine told her, "but I haven't heard anything this morning that would give me any reason to think otherwise. I don't see why the judge would feel differently."

"So I'll get the restaurant?"

"The way it looks right now, I'd say so."

Yvonne broke into a wide smile, and Catherine added, "But let's not start celebrating yet. Let's wait until the judge has spoken. I'll be very surprised if he says anything different, though."

Yvonne nodded, and gathered another forkful of lettuce. Before putting it in her mouth, she told me, "Thanks for coming, Savannah."

"It's my pleasure," I said. "I didn't like how they tried to make it sound like Beulah wasn't competent. And I guess I wanted a look at them."

"What did you think?"

To be honest, they'd looked snotty. But since they looked like the sort of people of whom my mother would approve, and since my mother definitely didn't approve of Yvonne—and since I, myself, try my best to meet with Mother's approval and might look snotty too, to someone who doesn't know me—I chose my words carefully. "Well dressed. Well put together. There's some money there. Unless they're living on credit."

"Many people do," Catherine said.

I nodded. "They don't look like the sort of people who would want to run a meat'n three restaurant in a small country town."

"Maybe they think they can turn it into another kind of restaurant," Yvonne suggested, around the lettuce. "Something more fancy."

Maybe. But if so, they hadn't gotten a good look at the patrons the one time they'd been there. Beulah's catered to a small town clientele, and had done well because of it. Most of the people who frequented the small cinderblock building with the plastic table cloths and gravel parking lot wouldn't be caught dead forking up lettuce here in Columbia or in the Café on the Square in Sweetwater. If Mrs. and Ms. Odom thought they could turn Beulah's Meat'n Three into another fancy eating establishment, they hadn't thought things through well. The very reason for Beulah's success, was that the place wasn't fancy.

"Hopefully we'll never get the chance to find out," Catherine said, and turned to me. "Did you say Rafe came down here with you?"

I swallowed before I answered. "It was more that I came with him. He left for work this morning, and then showed up again an hour later because the sheriff had called and asked him to drive down. I thought I'd tag along, since he was going anyway, so I could check up on Mother as well as the competency hearing."

Catherine winced. "I don't like the way you put those two words together in the same sentence."

"Which two words?"

"Mother," Catherine said, "and competency hearing."

That was three words, technically. However… "Mother isn't incompetent. I realize that she can be a pretty tough pill, but there's nothing wrong with her mind."

Unless…

"Unless…" I added.

Catherine shook her head. "She's stayed off the booze since the incident last month. Or if she takes the occasional nip of something, it isn't mimosas for breakfast and whiskey in her tea every afternoon anymore."

Yvonne looked fascinated. "Your mother's drinking?"

"Not anymore. And don't you dare spread it around that she is. It just took a few days for her to process the news last month."

The news that my father had had a love child with someone else before he met Mother. And the news that the mother of that child had been my mother's best friend for thirty-three years, since before Catherine was born, and hadn't mentioned anything about it. The news that that love child happened to be the receptionist at the family law firm, and had been for a couple of years before any of us knew anything about the relationship.

Yes, it had taken Mother some time to process the news. I didn't think she was quite finished processing, to be honest. As far as I knew, she was polite and proper when she had to deal with Darcy, Dad's love child, Dix's receptionist, and our half-sister, but I didn't think she'd spoken to Audrey, Darcy's mother, since the morning we found out the truth.

But as long as she wasn't starting the day with a pitcher of mimosas, we were on the right track.

"She'll come around," I said. "Eventually."

"I'm sure you're right," Catherine added, without sounding sure at all.

Yvonne looked from one to the other of us, and with something approaching delicacy, asked, "So what's Rafe doing back in Sweetwater, Savannah?"

There was a time, about a year ago, when I'd been bothered by Yvonne's seeming fondness for my husband—who, at the time, hadn't been my husband, but had been someone I'd been in love with, even if I'd been unwilling to admit that fact, even to myself.

At any rate, Yvonne and Rafe had had a one-night-stand in high school. Yvonne had been willing to repeat the experience. Rafe, it seemed, had not, since they'd kept it to that one time. And since it was a long time ago, and since he was now mine, I didn't let it bother me. Much.

I hesitated. "The sheriff thought he might be able to help with a case that came up overnight, since he knew some of the people involved. Somewhat. A long time ago."

And also since it was a big case for a small sheriff's department to handle. The sheriff could—or might have—begged help from the Columbia PD, but having Rafe around certainly wouldn't hurt. Especially if my husband was right and there was a professional aspect to the crimes. That was something the sheriff as well as the Columbia PD would have had little experience with, while Rafe had spent the past eleven years working organized crime for the TBI.

Catherine wrinkled her brow. "Someone local?"

"Local to Maury County. Not to Sweetwater." Although like Rafe and me, and Yvonne, Catherine had attended Columbia High. She'd been a year ahead of Rafe, so if Rafe had known Darrell Skinner, Catherine might have known him—or at least known of him—too. "A family called the Skinners, up in the foothills near the Devil's Backbone."

Yvonne made a sound, as if a leaf of lettuce had gotten stuck in her throat. Catherine and I turned to her, concerned. She waved the attention away and reached for her glass.

"I remember Darrell Skinner," Catherine said. "I think he was a year or maybe two ahead of me in school. Has something happened to him?"

"He's dead."

Across the table Yvonne lifted her napkin from her lap to wipe her eyes, and I kept a surreptitious eye on her. "Along with his brothers Robbie and Art, his sister-in-law Linda, his nephew A.J., his niece Cilla, and Cilla's boyfriend."

Catherine stared at me, wide-eyed.

"A.J. was sixteen," I added, my voice tight. "Cilla was eighteen. Her boyfriend was probably around the same. They had a new baby."

Catherine looked sick.

"The baby survived. Both parents were killed, but whoever killed them, left the baby there. In bed with its dead parents."

"God." It isn't often I hear my sister blaspheme, but under the circumstances I couldn't really fault her. I'd done the same myself. "Who'd do something like that?"

I thought about sharing Rafe's thoughts on the matter, but decided I'd better not. It was one thing for him to share them with me. It was something totally different for me to share them with anyone else.

In fact, I probably shouldn't have mentioned anything about any of it. "You can't talk about this to anyone," I warned them both. "I don't think it's official yet. The only reason I know about it, is because I went up to Robbie's place with Rafe and we found the body."

Yvonne made another of those strangled sounds. Her eyes above the napkin were huge.

"I'm sorry," I added. I'd been pretty sure my sister hadn't been personally acquainted with the Skinners. Not on the approved list. But Yvonne might have been. She wasn't, as Mother might say, 'our kind.' "Did you know Robbie?"

She nodded.

"I'm sorry for your loss." By all accounts—those of the sheriff and Rafe, and the young woman from Animal Control—the Skinners hadn't been much of a loss, but Yvonne might well feel differently.

She pushed her chair back with a squeal on the concrete floor, and a muffled, "Excuse me." We watched her weave her way across the room, around the other tables, and disappear into the small hallway in the back, where the restrooms were located.

"I didn't realize she might know them," I told Catherine. "Rafe said Darrell was a couple of years older than him. Yvonne's Dix's age." A year younger than Rafe, if you want to get specific. "And Robbie was older than Darrell by a year or more."

"She might know them from somewhere other than high school," Catherine reminded me. "They're local. They might have frequented Beulah's Meat'n Three."

Come to think of it, they might. Although it would be a longish drive from the Devil's Backbone almost all the way to Sweetwater for a piece of chicken fried steak. Then again, it might not have been the food that was the attraction.

"I'll have to tell Rafe to have a talk with her. Or the sheriff."

"I'm sure your husband would get more out of her than Bob Satterfield would," Catherine told me. "She might be reluctant to talk to the police about anything she knows. But Rafe doesn't look or act like the police. And she seems to like him."

"What's not to like?" I asked flippantly. And added, "They slept together once."

"Rafe and Yvonne?"

I nodded.

"He married you," my sister told me. "And I imagine, if you're going to start worrying about all the women your husband has slept with, you wouldn't have time for anything else."

Too true. "I'll let him know the next time I talk to him. They've got their hands full up there, processing multiple crime scenes. I'm sure they won't get around to doing interviews for a while yet." Besides, Yvonne was on her way back to the table, more composed now, but with eyes that looked a little more naked than earlier. She must have wiped away some of the makeup along with the tears, and either hadn't bothered, or hadn't had what she needed, to fix the damage.

"We should head back," Catherine said with a glance at her watch. "By the time we've paid the check and walked back to the courthouse, it'll be time to see the judge again." She looked around for the waitress and the check.

"I'll meet you there," Yvonne said. "I'm sorry. I just…" She waved at the door. In my mind, I heard Greta Garbo's voice. '*I vant to be alone.'*

It didn't sound so good with a Southern accent.

"No problem." Catherine came across calm and unbothered. "Take the time you need. Just don't be late. It won't look good."

Yvonne promised she wouldn't, and ducked out. I let Catherine pay the check, since she makes more money than I do. I did make noises about paying my fair share, but I didn't insist when she told me I didn't have to.

We visited the ladies room, and headed out into the street. Yvonne was nowhere to be seen when we got there. Not surprising, perhaps, considering the minutes that had passed between her departure and ours. I just hoped she wasn't upset enough to blow off the rest of the hearing. It might not make a difference, since it had seemed to me that the judge shared Catherine's opinion that Beulah had been competent and Yvonne should get the restaurant, and whether Yvonne was present or not, it shouldn't affect that. But Catherine was right: it wouldn't look good if she didn't show up.

"I should probably call Rafe before we go in," I told Catherine as we approached the steps to the courthouse. "Let him know about Yvonne. Just in case she has some sort of insight into what happened."

Catherine nodded. "I'll see you inside."

She headed up the stairs without waiting for me. While she headed in, I found a quiet spot behind a pillar, where the misty rain didn't reach me, and dialed Rafe's number. I could have gone inside, I suppose, and tried to find a quiet corner somewhere, but since I assumed no one else knew about the Skinner murders yet, and since I didn't want anyone to accidentally learn about them from me, I did the best I couldn't not to be overheard.

The phone rang a couple of times, and then Rafe answered. "Darlin'."

"I know you're busy," I said. "But I wanted to tell you about

Yvonne."

"Now ain't really the time, Savannah."

"It's about the Skinners," I said. "Not the hearing. Although the hearing is going well. I think. Catherine thinks it's going well, anyway."

Rafe waited patiently. So patiently I could hear it, loud and clear.

"I think Yvonne knew the Skinners. She asked me what you were doing here, and when I told her it was about the Skinners, she started crying. She tried to hide it by pretending to get a piece of lettuce stuck in her throat, but I'm pretty sure she was crying. You should talk to her."

"I was planning to," Rafe said. "She and Darrell had a thing for a while. Long time ago now, but I thought she might have something to add to what we know."

"What do you know?"

"Not a lot more than when you left," Rafe said. "Seven dead. All of 'em shot."

"The woman from Animal Control said it looked like they'd been using the dogs for dog fighting. She says it's illegal."

"Very."

"I don't know how much money there is in dog fighting, but it might be a motive."

"It might could be."

"Did she take the dog with her? Robbie's dog?"

Rafe said she had.

"I hope it makes it," I said. "I hope they all make it, although she sounded like some of them wouldn't. So did the sheriff. But I hope that one does. I feel sorry for it."

"I'm sure it'll be all right, darlin'. She seemed like a nice woman. Who liked dogs."

"Let me guess," I said suspiciously, "she flirted with you?"

He chuckled. "She told me you'd warned her off."

"So if I hadn't mentioned that we were married, she would

have flirted with you?"

He shrugged. Sort of audibly. "A little flirtation never hurt nobody, darlin'."

"In that case," I told him, "maybe I'll just check and see if Todd's around." Being the assistant DA for the county, he's often to be found around the courthouse.

He sounded amused, and not at all threatened. "It's a little different, ain't it, darlin'? I never met the dog woman before in my life. Meanwhile, Satterfield proposed to you. Not just once, but several times."

"Ancient history," I said loftily.

"It don't sound like it when you tell me you're gonna go looking for him."

Maybe not. "Just stay away from the dog woman, and I'll stay away from Todd."

"The dog woman's gone, darlin'. Her name's June, and she took the dog and left. It didn't take more than five minutes. It's just the sheriff and me here." After a moment he added, "And the body."

So much for keeping it light. "What happened to the baby?" The dogs got picked up. Surely the baby had been, too.

"Children's services came," Rafe said.

"There's no other family?" Surely Cilla's boyfriend had a mother? Or a sister? Someone who could care for the baby instead of strangers?

"Not until we know what happened to the baby's parents."

"I'll let you get back to it. But plan to talk to Yvonne after we're done in court. She might not know anything about who would want the Skinners dead, but she might. They don't sound like the nicest bunch of people, but nobody deserves what happened to them."

Especially not A.J. and Cilla, who couldn't have had time in their short lives to do any mortal harm to anyone.

Rafe told me to let him know when court was over. I said I

would, and we hung up. I made my way into the courthouse and back to the room I'd been in earlier.

Most everyone else was back already. Catherine sat at the table in the front where she'd been earlier, but without Yvonne next to her. Ms. Odom was also back, but without her mother. Hopefully the two of them hadn't accidentally come face to face outside, and gotten into it. That wouldn't be good.

But no, the door opened, and Mrs. Odom arrived, looking just as stylish and pulled together as earlier. Obviously, if there had been an altercation, it hadn't descended from name calling to fisticuffs. Mrs. Odom made her way to the front, gave Catherine a haughty look, and settled next to her daughter. They got into a whispered conversation, and at the mother's request, the daughter turned and got the lawyer involved, too. The discussion looked intense, even though I couldn't hear a single word of what was said.

As the seconds ticked away toward one-thirty, I started to worry about Yvonne, and that she wouldn't make it. Maybe Mrs. Odom had caught her after all, had stabbed her with a sharpened nail file, and left her for dead in the alley beside the courthouse.

But no, with a few seconds to spare, Yvonne made it through the door and down the aisle. She had just managed to plant her posterior on the chair next to Catherine when the door opened and the judge appeared. We all stood again, until he had taken his seat.

For a long moment, nothing happened. The judge stapled his fingers together on the table in front of him and watched the courtroom. We all watched the judge.

"This is a bullshit case," he said eventually, and I don't think my jaw was the only one that dropped. Not only was he a distinguished old Southern gentleman, from whom one wouldn't expect that kind of language, but he was a judge sitting on the bench.

He waited for the whispers and titters to stop, before he

added, "You should be ashamed of yourself for wasting the court's time, Mr. Hamilton."

Mr. Hamilton, I assumed, was the plaintiffs' lawyer. The back of his neck didn't look particularly chastised, although his face might have told a different story.

"The court believes that there's no merit to the case," the judge continued. "According to her doctor and multiple witnesses, Beulah Odom was not under duress or undue pressure when she made her will, and she had the mental faculties to understand the ramifications of what she did. For that reason, the will stands."

The judge smacked his gavel on the desk. As he exited the courtroom in a swirl of black robes—like a giant bat, or Severus Snape—Yvonne turned to Catherine, eyes wide.

"Congratulations," Catherine told her.

"I get the restaurant?"

"The will has to go through probate. It can take a few months. But the will is valid. So I'd say you do."

Yvonne threw her arms around Catherine's neck with a squeal. My sister grimaced, but squeezed back. At the next table, Mrs. Odom and her daughter got to their feet and headed for the exit without looking left or right. Mrs. Odom's lips were so tightly compressed they were invisible.

FIVE

"That went well," I said to Catherine after Yvonne had bounced out with a lot more spring in her step than what she'd come in with.

Catherine gathered her paperwork together and shoved it into her bag. "It's like the judge said. Bullshit case. A last and desperate Hail Mary from two people who can't stand the idea of someone else getting the restaurant."

She swung the bag up over her shoulder and added, "I mean, really, Savannah. Could you imagine the two of them running a meat'n three in Sweetwater? The restaurant would go under in a month."

Quite possible. The Otis Odoms certainly didn't look like the type of women who'd worked a day in their lives. Not the hard manual labor of keeping a restaurant going. Although looks can be deceiving.

"Not that deceiving," Catherine said when I said so. "If that woman's ever lifted a finger for anyone but herself, I'll eat it."

The finger, I assumed. And Mrs. Odom, I assumed. As opposed to Ms. Odom, who might well have some sort of degree in restaurant management, or whatnot.

Catherine shook her head. "I don't doubt they want the restaurant. But I don't think it's because they want to run it. Maybe the land is valuable."

Maybe so. Land is increasing in value every day. They just don't make any more of it. And Nashville is expanding every day, as well. They say that within ten years, the city will be twice the size it is now. By then, Franklin will certainly have been swallowed up. Columbia would be next to go. Maybe the Odoms were planning for a future when the city of Nashville sprawled across most of Middle Tennessee, and when the land where Beulah's Meat'n Three sat, would be worth millions.

Or maybe they knew something we didn't.

It probably didn't matter. What mattered was that they'd wanted the place, but hadn't gotten it. Now they'd have to go back to Franklin empty-handed, their guns spiked. It was worthy of a celebration. But since it was only an hour since we'd eaten, I didn't say anything about it. At almost eight months pregnant, I can always eat. Catherine probably couldn't. And had children to get home to, anyway.

"Are you staying with Mother?" she asked when we were on our way across the street to her car. She'd been here earlier than I, and had snagged a spot closer to the courthouse.

"I'm not sure. She has the space. Or more of it than you or Dix. But I should probably ask first, before I assume anything."

"It's not like she has anyone else staying with her," Catherine said. "And she likes Rafe now."

"It would still be polite to ask, though. Instead of just showing up and expecting to be housed. What if she and the sheriff are dancing naked on the table in the parlor?"

My sister grimaced. "Thanks, Savannah."

"Sorry." It wasn't a mental image I particularly enjoyed, either. After a second, I added, "The sheriff's probably too busy tonight. Seven dead so far. Hopefully there won't be any more."

"I guess that would depend on how many other Skinners there are," Catherine said. Rather cold-bloodedly, I thought.

"I'm afraid I don't know. I don't even remember Darrell Skinner from high school. I think he might have left before I started."

Catherine nodded. "I'm almost four years older than you, so

I remember a few more. There was Darrell. Then there was Robbie. Then there was Art. I'm not sure there was anyone else."

"Then this might be it. Assuming someone went after the Skinners because they were Skinners, and not for another reason."

"It's disturbing," Catherine said, unlocking her car door.

I nodded. It certainly was. And she hadn't even seen Robbie's dead body. "Thank God it's on the other side of the county. If not, I'd worry about going to sleep tonight."

"You and me both," Catherine said. "But at least they left the baby alone. If anything happens to us, will you take care of my kids?"

"Of course." She and Jonathan have three: Robert, Cole, and Annie, ranging in age from eight down to three or so. "But nothing's going to happen to you. The Skinners were probably involved in something bad. If you're not, nobody would have a reason to want to get rid of you."

"Easy for you to say," Catherine said and opened her car door. "Take care, Savannah."

I told her I would, and stepped out of the way as she started the minivan. I waved until she was gone, and then I headed across the square and over to the *Martin and Vaughan* sign and the Volvo.

I had unlocked the door and was just about to get in when a voice called my name. When I turned in the direction of the sound, I saw Todd Satterfield coming across the square toward me. And I admit it, my heart sank a little. It had been awkward between Todd and me ever since I turned down his proposal and then married Rafe.

I did my best to smile naturally. "Hi, Todd."

"Savannah." He gave me a quick up and down. His gaze stopped on my stomach for just a second, but he didn't comment. "What are you doing here?"

"Your father called the TBI for help with a case," I said. "I came down with Rafe. If you're asking what I'm doing here, specifically, I just came out of the hearing into Beulah Odom's competency."

"How did Judge Hopkins find?"

"That there's no reason to think Beulah was *non compos mentis* or under undue pressure. The will stands."

Todd nodded. "So Yvonne McCoy gets the restaurant."

"If she doesn't," I said, "it won't be because of Beulah's mental state. I suppose the Odoms could come up with some other complaint, although I don't know what that would be."

"It would have to be something good." Todd changed the subject. "What kind of case does Dad need help with?"

I told him. "Do you know the Skinners? Are there any more of them?"

"Robbie has a daughter and an ex-wife," Todd said. "They don't live around here. Pulaski, I think. But..."

I nodded. "You should let your dad know, so he can check and make sure they're all right. Or I can tell Rafe."

"Go ahead. I don't want to get involved in my dad's job."

Fine by me. I had to call anyway, to let Rafe know that Yvonne was out of court and could be questioned.

But before I could do that, I'd have to get rid of Todd. "Was there something you needed?" I asked.

He shook his head. "I just saw you when I came through the door and thought I'd say hello. I'm on my way to a meeting."

"It was nice to see you," I told him. I suppose it had been. Or at least it had been less awkward than in the past. Marginally. Maybe he'd finally gotten over me and moved on.

Todd nodded. "I'll see you later, Savannah." He turned to go.

"Say hello to Marley," I told his back. He flinched, sort of like from a mosquito bite, but he didn't stop and he didn't speak. I waited until he was an appropriate distance away, and then I opened my door and slid behind the wheel. And pulled out the phone.

"Yes, darlin'," my husband's voice said a few seconds later.

"Sorry to bother you again. I just wanted to update you on a couple of things."

"Go ahead."

I told him what had happened in the courtroom, and that Beulah had been judged competent to dispose of her property the way she wanted. "So Yvonne gets the restaurant. Unless something else happens."

"What could happen?"

I had no idea, and said so. "The will has to go through probate. It'll take a few months. Anything could happen. The place could burn to the ground. Or Yvonne could keel over from a heart attack."

"Or something worse," Rafe said grimly. "Tell her to watch her back."

I told him I would, the next time I saw her. "I also saw Todd."

"Did you, now?"

"He came out of the DA's office and saw me. And decided to be polite."

"Bastard," Rafe said.

"He told me that Robbie had an ex-wife and a daughter. Todd thinks they might live in Pulaski. Someone should check and make sure they're all right." And, I suppose, tell them the news.

Notifying next of kin. One of my least favorite things to do.

"C'mon up here and get me," Rafe said. "We'll go do it now."

We? "I'm not sure the sheriff wants me to get involved in his case."

"It's one less thing he has to do himself. He's kinda busy. And I'm sure he'd rather have us do it, than ask the Giles County sheriff."

"I'm on my way," I said, as I put the car into gear and pulled away from the *Martin and Vaughan* sign, "but make sure the sheriff knows I'll be coming with you. I don't want him to be upset with me."

Rafe said he would. "But I don't think you gotta worry about that. It's not like we're gonna be investigating anything. We're just gonna do a notification."

And see what, if anything, Robbie's ex-wife knew. But since there was no sense in pointing that out, I didn't. "Twenty minutes," I said instead. "I'm on my way out of Columbia now. Tell me where to go once I'm past Robbie's place."

He gave me directions for how to get from Robbie's to Art's, where he was at the moment, and I hung up so I could concentrate on driving. The directions weren't complicated—it sounded like the Skinners had lived a couple of miles apart, if that—but it was still overcast and misty, visibility was poor, and I wanted to keep both hands on the wheel.

As a result, it took a little longer than the twenty minutes I had promised before I made it back up into the foothills and found Art's place, at the end of another long, winding dirt road liberally decorated with *No Trespassing* signs.

When I came out in the clearing at the end, I might as well have been back at Robbie's place. Same run-down trailer, same flashy, new truck with big beefy tires. Next to this one, a small Honda perched, and beyond that another truck, older and less flashy, a sort of poopy brown color. Off to the side, another Airstream—smaller than Robbie's—perched.

Several official cars rounded out the collection: the sheriff's SUV, of course, two other sheriff's department vehicles, a van with the TBI's logo on the side—the borrowed crime scene techs Rafe had sent down before we left, most likely—and a car from the Columbia PD, that said it belonged to the chief of police. He had no jurisdiction here, miles outside the Columbia city limits, but maybe the sheriff had called him in to consult.

Rafe was watching for me. No sooner had I pulled into the clearing, than he came out of the nearby trailer and made his way toward me, long legs eating up the distance between us. He yanked open the passenger door and fit himself inside. "Drive."

"Are you sure you don't want to drive?" I swooped around the wet grass and mud and headed back toward the road. Usually he wants to do the driving. I don't drive fast enough for him.

He shook his head. "Just get the hell outta here."

I glanced at him. A quick glance, since I was trying to make my way down the dirt track to the road, and since the track was narrow and wet and—if I got too close to the edge—a little loose. "What happened?"

He glowered. Not at me, out the windshield. "Politics."

"I was wondering what the Columbia chief of police was doing there."

"Big case," Rafe said. "I guess he don't want the sheriff to get all the glory."

"There's glory in solving a case like this?"

He shrugged. "He gotta taste of it back in the spring, I guess." During my high school reunion. "This is the biggest case to hit Maury County since."

The biggest case to hit Maury County ever, I would say. And did.

Rafe nodded. "This don't come along every day. He musta wanted in on it."

I flicked my turn signal on, peered left and right through the mist, and turned onto the paved road, back in the direction of Columbia. "The sheriff didn't call him in?"

"I dunno who called him," Rafe said, adjusting the passenger seat to get comfortable. His legs are a lot longer than mine. "He just showed up."

"Can't you ask him to leave? He's out of his jurisdiction, isn't he?" And on someone else's crime scene, spreading his own germs and DNA around.

He shook his head. "Cooperation goes a long way in a place

like this. If the sheriff tells the chief to get the hell off his crime scene, the chief won't be inclined to help the next time the sheriff needs a hand."

No, I could see that. It was annoying, and unquestionably a lot more annoying for the sheriff and for Rafe than it was for me, but there seemed to be no way around it. "Was he rude to you?"

Rafe shrugged. "Nothing I haven't seen before."

No doubt. He'd seen rather a lot. However— "What's the problem? Does he remember you from when you were a kid? Were you in trouble with the Columbia PD as well as Sheriff Satterfield?"

He shook his head. "I kept mostly to the county. And this guy's new, anyway. The old chief retired a few years back, the sheriff said."

"So what's the problem?" If they didn't know one another from before, and the chief had no preconceived notions about Rafe's questionable past, why didn't he like my husband?

"He just don't like the TBI," Rafe said. "Made it very clear that between the two of'em, they could handle this, and my services weren't required."

I arched my brows. "Isn't it a bit too late for that? I mean, you're here." And Sheriff Satterfield had invited him. "Is the sheriff telling you to leave?"

He shook his head. "Between the two of us, I think the sheriff'd rather have me."

I smiled. "That's a nice change, anyway."

Rafe grimaced, but didn't say anything. I added, "He's being nice to you, right?"

"Sheriff Satterfield? Sweet as pie. It's the Columbia chief who's the problem."

"Well," I said, "you don't have to work with him, right? Or does the sheriff seem inclined to let him play?"

"He seems inclined to tell him to go to hell. But he won't, since they're gonna be working in the same county long after this case is dead and gone."

Understandable.

"I guess you'll just have to put up with him. Maybe they'll find some kind of connection to Columbia, and he can focus on that."

Rafe muttered something unkind and folded his arms across his chest. "Take the road through Damascus."

"The one coming up?" There was an intersection up ahead.

He nodded. "No sense in going all the way through Columbia and Sweetwater when we can cut through the west side of the county. Unless you want I should drop you off at your mama's house and go to Pulaski by myself?"

"No," I said, my hands steady on the steering wheel as I made the turn onto the Pulaski Highway. "That won't be necessary. I want to come with you."

"This ain't gonna be a fun trip, you know."

"I'm sure it isn't." Best case scenario, we'd be telling Robbie's ex-wife that her ex-husband and the father of her child was dead. Worse case scenario, we'd have to tell Robbie's daughter that she was an orphan. She'd probably take it harder than her mother. If Mrs. Skinner had left Robbie, there might not be much love lost between them. And worst case scenario, we'd walk into another crime scene, and they both—or at least one of them—would be dead, too.

No, I had no illusions that this was going to be anything but difficult.

"You sure you don't wanna go home?"

"I'm positive," I said. If he was going, I was going. I might not be able to do much, no matter which scenario we found ourselves faced with, but at least he wouldn't be alone.

"Suit yourself." But he didn't seem upset as he leaned back in the seat and relaxed.

Neither one of us spoke for several minutes. I concentrated on driving, and Rafe on whatever thoughts were in his head. But as we neared Damascus, a small town southwest of Columbia on the way to Pulaski, he roused enough to ask, "D'you remember where Yvonne lives?"

"Of course. I was there just a couple of months ago." And not for the first time. Once, last year, I'd gone there—with Rafe—in time to save Yvonne from bleeding out on her living room floor. It wasn't a place I was likely to forget. Not in this lifetime.

"Remember how to get there?"

I did. Again, it wasn't that long ago that I'd been there. I had come from the other direction, from Sweetwater, granted. But it wasn't hard to find. A few minutes later, we pulled up in front of the tiny tract house Yvonne called home.

The living room light was on, a bright, happy beacon through the dreary gloom.

"Guess she's home," Rafe said.

I pulled into the driveway behind Yvonne's car. "Guess so. She had court this morning, so she's probably not working today." She wouldn't have known how long it would take Judge Hopkins to make up his mind about Beulah's competency, after all. I'm sure she wouldn't have scheduled a work shift after court.

"I thought the restaurant was closed," Rafe said, as I turned off the engine and withdrew the key from the ignition.

"It is. Didn't I tell you? She's working at the drugstore in Sweetwater while she's waiting to see how this whole thing pans out."

I had discovered that several months ago, and was pretty sure I'd told him. Then again, that was during the time he'd been involved in a gang war, and I'd been trying to figure out who Darcy's biological parents were, so we'd both had other things on our minds. I might have told him, and he'd forgotten, or I might not have told him at all.

Yvonne opened the door on the second knock. She'd changed out of the prim and proper court attire Catherine had had her dressed in, and into a pair of tights and a loose sweater. It was low cut enough that I could see the faint remains of some of the scars from the knife attack last fall. Not the worst of it—that was hidden below—but enough to remember walking into this living room and seeing Yvonne dead—or so I'd thought—on the floor.

She also looked like she'd been crying. Her eyes were red-rimmed and swollen.

For a second nobody moved. Then her bottom lip started to quiver and Rafe stepped through the doorway and pulled her into his arms. I closed the door behind us all as she started sobbing, and headed for the kitchen to make some tea.

SIX

"I dated Darrell in high school," Yvonne said five minutes later. To me, since Rafe had obviously known this already.

She and I were sipping tea. Rafe had declined. He's not a big tea drinker to begin with, and I think he might have been trying to maintain some semblance of official standing. Which wasn't easy when he'd just held the witness through a storm of sobbing. His shirt was still wet on the shoulder; a darker patch against the pale blue.

"I don't remember Darrell," I told her. "Rafe said he thought Darrell graduated before I started at Columbia High."

Yvonne nodded. "He was older than me. All the Skinners were."

And now all the Skinners were dead. "Did you have anything to do with them—with Darrell—after high school?"

This storm of tears seemed a little out of place, if not.

She sniffed. "On and off. We dated for a couple years a couple years ago."

"Why did you break up?"

"He was a bastard," Yvonne said. A tear leaked out of the corner of her eye, and she lifted the tissue in her hand to wipe it away.

OK, then. So the victim—one of them—had been a bastard, but she cried for him anyway.

"In what way?" I wanted to know.

Rafe rolled his eyes, but let me keep talking. Maybe he was

hoping he'd learn something from my curiosity. Or maybe he was waiting to come in for the kill, metaphorically speaking, after I had softened Yvonne up.

Not that she could get much softer than she was at the moment. She was slumped against the back of the sofa like her spine couldn't keep her upright, clutching a wet tissue.

"He cheated," Yvonne said. "Couldn't keep it in his pants."

Another tear appeared and she swatted at it.

"Who'd he cheat with?"

"Marcy Coble," Yvonne said.

I remembered Marcy Coble. She'd been several years older than me—Rafe's age; a high school senior when I was a freshman—and a cheerleader as well as, I thought, homecoming queen the first year I was in high school.

"Back then? Or now?"

"Then," Yvonne said, leaning her head back against the sofa. "Bitch."

I glanced at Rafe. He shrugged.

"How about more recently?" It wasn't likely that Marcy Coble—cheerleader and homecoming queen—would have shot Darrell Skinner and his entire family more than a dozen years later, after all. Even if he'd been a bastard. Or at least I wouldn't think so.

"Some high-class skank," Yvonne said, to the ceiling. "Someone he met at the Pour House."

"The poor house?"

"Bar in Thompson Station," Rafe said, naming a small community about halfway between Columbia and Franklin. "How long ago?"

"Last year." Yvonne was still talking to the ceiling. "It wasn't the first time. I took him back twice before that. All women he picked up in some bar or other when he was drunk." She lifted the tissue to dab at her eyes.

"Was he drunk a lot?"

Yvonne shrugged.

"I don't suppose you happen to have a picture of him?"

I was curious, to be honest, what this guy had looked like, to be able to attract women like flies to honey. From what I'd seen of Robbie—and admittedly, he hadn't been at his best, in his dirty tighty whities in the rain—he wasn't what I'd call a heart throb.

"Somewhere." Yvonne fought her way out of the sofa and padded across the floor in stocking feet. She disappeared into the back end of the house, where the bedroom was.

"Should I go with her?" I asked Rafe in a whisper.

He shook his head. "She's gonna come back. Not like she's hiding anything."

I guess not. "She seems distraught."

He nodded. "She was hung up on Darrell for a long time. And he on her. Remember that time you drove me back to the Bog from Columbia?"

Of course. It had been just after he graduated from high school. Maybe even the day of. He'd been eighteen, I'd been fifteen, and I'd been on my way home from the movies with Todd Satterfield, my brother Dix, and my best friend Charlotte, when we'd stumbled upon Rafe, drunk and bleeding, sitting on a curb in Columbia. I had insisted on taking him back to Sweetwater with us, and in the process, had ruined Dix and Charlotte's plans of necking in the backseat, while Todd had spent the entire ride worrying that Rafe was going to throw up all over the brand new leather interior.

"Don't tell me," I said. "That was Darrell Skinner?"

"And the other Skinners. He'd found out about Yvonne and me."

And had had his brothers help him beat Rafe to a pulp. Three of them, all older, for all intents and purposes grown men, beating up on someone who wasn't much more than a boy.

"I don't like the Skinners," I said. "I know they're dead, but I don't like them."

Rafe shrugged. "It was a long time ago."

And whatever broken ribs he had incurred had healed by now. He'd been hurt worse since. Nonetheless, it made me less kindly disposed to the Skinners, dead or not. "That says a lot about them, actually. That they were the kind of people who would gang up, three against one, on someone younger."

"I gave back about as good as I got," Rafe said.

Not bloody likely, if you'll excuse the word. Yes, he can fight, and probably could back then, too. But three against one is still three against one. However, before I could argue further, Yvonne came back into the living room and handed me a picture.

It was still in the frame, a nice tarnished silver, and taken somewhere that might be Lookout Mountain in Chattanooga. Somewhere high up, anyway, with a view over a city and a river in the distance. Yvonne was snuggled into the arm of a tall guy with middling-to-fair hair and a cocky grin, dressed in a T-shirt and faded jeans.

I could sort of see the appeal. He wasn't my type at all, but he looked like he could be charming, with a few beers on board, and to a woman who didn't have high expectations. I don't think I would have been tempted, but I could see why Yvonne might have been.

"When was the last time you saw him?" Rafe wanted to know.

Yvonne, back on the sofa now, shook her head. "Not for a while. He used to come into Beulah's once in a while, but it's been six months, at least."

"What about the other Skinners?"

"I've seen Linda at the Winn-Dixie out on the Lewisburg Highway a couple times. Saw Art at the Home Depot once, I think. Or maybe it was the Lowes. That was before last Christmas, though. I was buying lights."

"Robbie? Or the kids?"

Yvonne shook her head. "Not for a while." She hesitated, biting her lip and looking at Rafe from under her lashes. "Are they... all gone? Savannah said..."

"Darrell, Art, and Robbie," Rafe said, "Linda, A.J., Cilla, and Cilla's boyfriend."

Yvonne looked sick. "Cilla and A.J. are just kids. Who'd kill kids?"

"Who'd kill any of'em?"

Yvonne didn't answer, and Rafe added, "I could use some help here. It's been a long time since I lived down this way. I don't know much of what's going on in Maury County anymore, and I need to know what the Skinners were mixed up in."

Yvonne hesitated.

"The woman from Animal Control said something about dog fighting," I said. "Were they involved in that?"

Yvonne sighed. "Mighta been."

We waited, but she didn't say any more. "Anything else you can think of?"

"Darrell got around, you know. And he wasn't always particular about whether the women he bedded were single or not."

"So a jealous husband or boyfriend," I said, with a glance at Rafe. He nodded, but didn't look like he thought it a very likely motive. And I guess it wouldn't be. If Darrell had dipped his wick, so to speak, in the wrong woman, her husband or boyfriend might have beat up Darrell, but he wasn't likely to have wiped out the entire Skinner family. Certainly not the women. It had to be something bigger than that. Something that involved the entire family, or enough of it that they all had to die. Including sixteen-year-old A.J.

"Anything else?"

"I can't think of anything," Yvonne said.

"No idea who mighta had it in for them? Other than the dog fighting and maybe Darrell screwing around?"

Yvonne shook her head, teeth in her bottom lip.

"OK." Rafe got to his feet.

"We're on our way to Pulaski to talk to Robbie's ex-wife," I added, as I followed suit.

"Sandy?"

"I don't know her name. Todd told me Robbie had one. An ex."

Yvonne nodded. "Sandy. And a kid. A girl."

"Any idea why they aren't married anymore?" Rafe held out my coat, and I slipped my arms into it.

"You'd have to ask her," Yvonne said. "But I wouldn't wanna be married to Robbie, either."

"Was he a cheater, too?"

She shrugged. "He never hit on me. I just didn't like him much."

Rafe headed for the door. "Let me know if you think of anything else."

Yvonne said she would, as she got up to shut the door and lock it behind us.

"I'm glad the judge found in your favor," I told her as I passed over the threshold into the chill. "I'm sure the Skinner thing is probably taking precedence right now. But it's a good thing. Catherine was happy."

Yvonne nodded. "Just so long as the Odoms don't come up with something else." Like they'd come up with the suggestion that Beulah had been incompetent.

"I don't see how they can," I said, "when the judge has ruled."

Yvonne shrugged but didn't say anything. She also didn't look encouraged. Maybe she didn't believe me. Or maybe she understood the depths of depravity that lurked in the Odoms better than I did. Or perhaps the news about the Skinners was taking precedence, and that was all there was to it. "Thanks for coming by."

"It was a pleasure," I said, even though it hadn't been, really. Giving people bad news rarely is. Nor is digging in their memories after someone dies. "We'll be here a few more days. Rafe will be busy, but give me a call if you want to grab lunch or something."

Yvonne said she would, and then we headed back into the mist, which had turned into a driving rain by now, and turned the car south in the direction of Pulaski.

The town was founded in 1809, and named after Revolutionary War Hero Kazimierz Pulaski, who had absolutely nothing to do with the place. He was born in Poland, recruited by Benjamin Franklin in France in 1777, and came to America to serve under George Washington. He died during the Siege of Savannah in 1779, without ever—as far as I know—even visiting Tennessee.

Pulaski's—the town's—chief claim to fame otherwise, is as the birthplace of the Ku Klux Klan, which was founded by six veterans of the Confederate Army in 1865.

On a happier note, Frank Mars, founder of the Mars Candy Company, built a 25,000 square foot Tudor mansion with twenty bedrooms and fourteen baths just outside Pulaski in the 1930s. It's still there, just off the road, and serves as an event venue these days. People get married there. Rafe and I got married on the grounds of the Martin Mansion, my ancestral home in Sweetwater, but if I hadn't had a mansion of my own, I would have been all over the Manor House at Milky Way Farms.

Just the wedding dessert would have been worth it, I would think.

"That's gorgeous," I told Rafe as we zoomed past.

He glanced at it, the Tudor beams and stone half obscured by the rain, and grunted.

"So what did you think about what Yvonne told us?"

This time he glanced at me. "She didn't tell us nothing."

"She told us that Darrell slept around."

"I knew that," Rafe said. "He did it when he was twenty. I figured he was doing it now." After a second he added, "Guess I'm gonna have to dig up whoever he was sleeping with these days."

"Surely a woman wouldn't have wiped out every one of the Skinners just because Darrell was lousy in bed!"

His lips twitched. "I don't imagine so."

"Then why does it matter who he was sleeping with?"

"She might know something we don't," Rafe said. And since he was right, I didn't say anything more about it.

Sandy Skinner—or whatever her name might be these days; she might have taken her maiden name back after divorcing Robbie—lived in a small, white house on Chicken Creek Road. It was empty, which we should have foreseen, since it was still the middle of the workday and, unless Sandy was unemployed, she wasn't likely to be sitting at home watching soap operas or reruns of game shows. I couldn't imagine Robbie contributing much in alimony, so Sandy was probably mostly responsible for her daughter's expenses.

After this, she'd be solely responsible.

Rafe stuck his hands on his hips and looked around, a scowl on his face.

"I'm sure someone knows where she works," I said. "We could ask the neighbors."

"What's to say they're at home?" But he headed across the soggy grass to the next house, another small, white clapboard shack. I followed, ruing the beating my boots were taking today.

By the time I made it onto the tiny porch—more like an overhang over a stoop, really—Rafe had already applied his fist to the door. A moment later he did it again. I deduced he was annoyed, by the weather or the fact that Sandy wasn't where she was supposed to be or maybe just the situation in general.

"Yeah, yeah." We heard a growl and slow steps from inside.

"Hold your horses."

The door opened a crack. Rafe brandished his badge, and—when the door moved to close again—stuck his foot in the gap.

The ancient black man inside, his face as wrinkled as a raisin, scowled. "What you wanna do that for?"

"I'm looking for your neighbor," Rafe said, with a toss of the head in the direction of Sandy's house. "You know where I can find her?"

"No." The little old man pushed on his door. Rafe's foot stayed where it was. And he wears sturdy boots, so his voice wasn't even affected by the pressure.

"Listen, grandpa. I don't give a damn what you've got going on in there. I just gotta find Sandy Skinner, is all."

The little old man contemplated. After a second, I realized the sound I was hearing, sort of mixing with the dripping of the rain off the eaves, was him popping his dentures up and down inside his mouth. "Why?"

"Her ex-husband's dead," Rafe said.

The little man's jaw dropped, and the teeth with it, until he snapped his mouth closed and fitted them back in where they belonged. "How'd that happen?"

"Somebody shot him," Rafe said.

I waited for the old man to say something. '*How horrible,*' or '*That's too bad.*' Something along those lines. What I didn't expect to hear, was "Good riddance."

I don't think Rafe expected it, either. Or maybe he did, and that arched eyebrow was just an invitation to continue.

"Used to knock her around," the old man said. The door opened another few inches, the better to communicate. I peered past him into the gloom, but couldn't see anything he might have particularly wanted to hide. Unless he was embarrassed about the threadbare sofa and scarred table, and he might have been.

"Have you seen him around here?"

The old man sucked his dentures. "Not in a while. He used to come around more just after it happened. I ain't seen him in a couple months."

Rafe nodded. "What about Sandy? When was the last time you saw her?"

"When she went to work this morning. The school bus comes for the kid just after seven, and Sandy goes to work just after."

"Where does she work?" I asked.

He peered past Rafe to me, and I got the impression he might not have noticed me before.

"My wife," Rafe said briefly.

If the old man wondered what Rafe's wife was doing, accompanying him to do murder notifications, he didn't say anything about it, just nodded. "Down to the five'n dime. On Main Street."

"We'll see if we can find her there," Rafe said, and removed his boot from the door. "Thanks for your time."

The old man nodded. "I didn't know the bastard," he said, as the door closed, "but I'm glad somebody got him."

The door shut before either of us had time to formulate an answer. It might have been just as well. What, after all, could one say?

The five-and-dime store on Main Street was nestled between a cheap laundromat and an empty storefront that looked like it might have been a millinery store at some point, half a century ago, when people still wore hats. Now the window was streaked and dirty and the floor inside full of dust.

The five-and-dime wasn't a lot better. It also wasn't a five-and-dime, technically speaking. Five-and-dime has turned into dollar, it seems, as what we were looking at, was a Dollar Store. But I guess the principle was the same. A jumble of different things, from plastic flowers and discontinued DVDs to off-brand laundry detergent and candy bars.

There were two registers at the front. One was empty, while a young, black woman stood behind the other, picking at her nails. They were long and electric green, the better to match the tips of her hair. She glanced up when we walked in, and her jaw dropped when she saw Rafe.

It isn't unusual. He's a good-looking guy, the type who wouldn't look out of place gracing the front of one of those slightly irregular Hanes His Way boxer brief packages on the end-cap display right in front of her.

Not that she could see that at the moment. The six-pack was decently covered, by both a T-shirt and the hoodie. But he still looks and moves like a guy who has one.

He gave her a smile, designed to melt her down to a puddle on the floor. "Afternoon. We're looking for Sandy."

I'm not sure the plural registered at all. She never looked at me. And he'd obviously struck her dumb, because all she did was lift a finger and point, her mouth still hanging open. I could see a wad of pink chewing gum next to her teeth. And I wanted to say something about it, but I contained myself. She couldn't help it. God knows my own jaw drops plenty when he's around.

He flashed another smile. "Thanks, sugar."

We headed deeper into the store in the direction she'd pointed. Behind us, the girl—she couldn't have been much older than twenty—snatched up a circular and started fanning herself with it. I rolled my eyes and kept going.

We found Sandy down the food aisle, not quite in the direction the cashier had pointed us, but close enough. She was sitting on a low stool emptying cans of baked beans from cartons onto the shelves, and when Rafe said her name, she looked up and squinted. And promptly turned pale at the sight of his badge.

She jumped to her feet—not an easy task when she carried more than a few pounds too many, obesity being a common problem in poor areas where people have to make less money stretch farther—and for a second, I was afraid she was going to make a break for it. I think Rafe must have thought the same thing, because I saw his body tense.

But instead of running away, she stood there, sort of swaying, as what little color had been there leached out of her face. "Kayla! Something's happened to Kayla!"

She collapsed. Quite gracefully for such a large woman. Rafe was just in time to keep her head from cracking against the concrete floor.

"Ooof!" he grunted as his knees hit the floor. "Damn."

"Lay her down." I grabbed a couple of kitchen towels off a shelf and shoved them under Sandy's head. "Look, she's already coming around."

She was. It hadn't been much of a faint. I took a leaf out of the young cashier's book and used another kitchen towel to gently fan Sandy's face.

Her eyes blinked open and she looked around, vaguely. Then she sat up. "Kayla!"

"Nothing's wrong with Kayla," Rafe told her. And added, prudently, "At least not that we know."

She squinted at him. Her eyes were a faded sort of blue, like well-worn denim—much like the color of Rafe's jeans—and outlined in heavy black. Other than that, and the extra weight she carried, she'd probably been a pretty woman when she was young. At the moment, she looked like she was pushing forty, although I figured she was probably a few years younger than she looked. And I wondered whether it was Robbie or someone else who was to blame for her slightly crooked nose.

"I don't know you." Her voice had an accusatory edge.

"I'm with the TBI," Rafe said. He got to his feet and held out a hand to help her up. "Is there somewhere private we can talk?"

Not that the store was exactly teeming with customers at the moment. But the young cashier had realized that something was going on, and was gawping at us from the end of the aisle.

Sandy put her hand in Rafe's, and let him haul her upright.

"Why?"

"It's about Robbie," Rafe said. When Sandy didn't say anything, he added, "He's dead."

For a second, Sandy looked absolutely blank, like someone had taken one of those dish towels and wiped her face clean of every expression. I took a step closer, just in case she fainted again. Not that there was much I could do about it, in my condition, if she did. I probably shouldn't try to lift her. But I could at least make it so that my husband didn't have to crack his knees on the concrete again.

But Sandy didn't faint. "Really?" she asked, in the tone of one afraid of believing what she'd just been told.

Rafe nodded.

Sandy's eyes lit up and she began to giggle.

SEVEN

"I'm sorry," Sandy said, not for the first time. She had apologized at least once a minute since we'd sat down, and she still wasn't finished.

After the inappropriate—but perhaps understandable—attack of giggles in the canned food aisle, she had taken us into the tiny break room at the back of the store. It consisted of a single table with four chair, an old, golden refrigerator of 1970s vintage, that had probably been sitting in the same place since the days when the place really had been a proper five-and-dime, a small microwave, and a trash can. Oh, and a small and boxy TV on the kitchen counter. It was tuned to *Wheel of Fortune*.

"It's all right." Rafe had been repeating the same mantra every time Sandy apologized for the past several minutes, too.

"People deal with grief in different ways," I added, sympathetically.

She looked at me. "You ever been married?"

"Before now, you mean?" I glanced at Rafe. He looked back at me, his face impassive except for a quirk at the corner of his mouth. I turned back to Sandy. "Once. For two years."

A little less, actually. We hadn't quite made it to two years before the divorce.

"You still on good terms?" Sandy wanted to know.

Not at all. Bradley was in prison. And I couldn't be happier about that. I wouldn't have shed a tear if I'd been told he'd died, come to that. Although I hope my manners are good enough that

I wouldn't giggle when they told me.

"No," I said. Rafe, who knew the situation, suppressed a smile.

"Well, I ain't gonna lie about it. I'm glad he's dead. I didn't kill him, but I'm glad he's dead."

Sandy took a defiant sip of her diet soda.

"When's the last time you saw Robbie?" Rafe wanted to know. We watched as Sandy thought back.

"Musta been more than a month ago now. He stopped by with the check for Kayla."

"He's paying child support?"

Sandy tossed her head. The frizzy ponytail bounced. "He's supposed to. He don't usually. And when he does, it's late."

"Must be hard," I commented.

She glanced at me. "We do all right. I make money. And Kayla, she don't ask for much. She knows we don't have a lot, so she don't ask."

Good for Kayla. And for Sandy, I suppose.

"Were the two of you home together last night?"

Sandy looked at Rafe. "You thinking I killed him?"

"I gotta ask."

She nodded. "Yeah. We were home together. But Kayla, she's eleven. She goes to bed early and sleeps hard. I coulda left for a couple hours and she wouldn't know about it."

"Did you?"

"No," Sandy said, "but I can't prove it."

"You own a gun?"

"Don't everybody?"

I don't. Unless you count Rafe's. And Sandy must have realized that now wasn't the time to be flippant. She made a face. "Yeah. Robbie used to tune me up when he got drunk. After we left, I didn't want him coming down here to do the same thing. So I bought the gun. The first time he showed up drunk, I told him to stay the hell away from us until he was sober, or I'd shoot his pecker off. He stayed away after that."

I would have, too, if I'd had a pecker to lose. "I'm sorry."

Sandy shrugged. "It wasn't so bad in the beginning. Then it got worse, but by then we had Kayla, and Robbie said he'd kill me if I tried to leave. So I stayed."

A common story, from what I know about it, which isn't much. "What made you change your mind?"

"He hit Kayla," Sandy said. "He was drunk, she got in his way, and he knocked her across the room. I waited for him to pass out, and then I packed up our clothes and Kayla's book bag and put her in the car and left."

"Good for you."

There was a pause.

"How long ago?" Rafe asked. Sandy told him it had been more than a year, but not quite two.

"If I was gonna kill him, I woulda done it then."

"Can you think of anyone else who mighta wanted him dead?"

Sandy laughed. It wasn't a particularly nice laugh. "Most everyone who knew him woulda wanted him dead, I figure. He wasn't no prince."

No, he certainly didn't sound like he had been. "What about the others?" I asked. And closed my mouth with a snap when Rafe rolled his eyes. But of course it was too late.

"What others?" Sandy looked from me to him and back.

Rafe sighed. "They're all dead. Art and Linda, Cilla and A.J. Darrell. Cilla's boyfriend. And Robbie."

Sandy stared at him, her eyes widening. "All of'em? They're all dead?"

He nodded.

Sandy shook her head. "I wouldn't do that. I mighta killed Robbie, if he tried to hit me again. I woulda killed him if he laid a hand on Kayla. But not nobody else. I liked Linda. I liked Cilla."

And then her eyes widened. "Oh, God. Cilla. She was having

a baby. She was pregnant. She..."

"The baby's fine," Rafe told her. "It's with DCS until we figure out what happened. Any idea who mighta wanted everyone dead?"

But Sandy looked overwhelmed to the point of not being able to think anymore. "Kayla," she said. "I have to get Kayla. I have to tell her that her daddy's gone. And her aunt. And her uncles. And cousins..."

I glanced at Rafe. He got to his feet and dug a card out of his pocket. "Gimme a call if you think of anything we haven't talked about, OK? We'll let you go pick up your daughter."

Sandy nodded, but I'm not sure she even really heard what he said. She did grab the card, though. "I gotta leave. I gotta get Kayla. Before somebody else tells her. I gotta get Kayla."

She ran out, without even saying goodbye. Rafe pulled out my chair, and we followed, more slowly. By the time we got to the front of the store, Sandy was already gone. We could see her through the door, hoofing it across the street to a beat-up old Chevy parked at the curb. She was still wearing her Dollar Store apron over her jeans, and she must have forgotten to pick up her coat. Her shoulders were hunched against the drizzle as she put the key in the door and wrenched it open.

The young woman behind the register was staring, too, her mouth open. "What happened?"

"What did she say?" Rafe countered.

She looked at him, and this time, managed to string a couple words together. "Just that she had to go. To pick up her daughter at school. Is something wrong with Kayla?"

"As far as we know, not a thing," Rafe said, and brandished his badge. "It's about Robbie Skinner. Sandy's ex-husband."

The girl's eyes widened. Not at the mention of Robbie, but at the sight of the badge. And it wasn't an "*Uh-oh, I'm in trouble,*" sort of look. No, this was "*He's good-looking AND he has a badge.*"

I rolled my eyes. Rafe waited patiently, but eventually had to prompt her to answer the question. The answer was no. She'd never seen Robbie, or so she said. She must not have cared what happened to him, either, because she didn't ask. She did, however, suggest that she could give him a call if she remembered anything. A roundabout way of asking for his phone number, I guess.

"That won't be necessary," I said, with all the dignity I could muster. "Thank you for your time."

I took Rafe's arm and practically pushed him out the door. It was a good thing he wanted to go, or I wouldn't have stood a chance of moving him.

Outside in the spitting rain, he grinned at me. "I wasn't gonna call her back."

"I wasn't worried about that," I said, hustling across the blacktop to the Volvo. "I was worried about her calling you. And calling you. And calling you."

I glanced over my shoulder, to where the woman in question practically had her nose pushed up against the window, fogging the glass. "I'm not even sure she's old enough to drink!"

"Non-issue," Rafe told me, as he closed me into the car. I waited until he'd walked around the hood of the car and had gotten behind the wheel before I answered.

"She's too young to look at you like that."

He shrugged and glanced around. "Guess we're done here."

"I guess so. There's no point in following Sandy, I guess."

"If you wanna see where the youth of Pulaski goes to middle school. But otherwise, I don't think so. I'm sure she's just gonna pick up her kid, like she said."

He turned the key in the ignition and started the car.

"Did you believe her?" I asked.

He glanced at me as he pulled away from the curb. "About what part of it?"

"Any of it. The last time she saw Robbie. The reason she left him."

"Don't have no reason to doubt her. Robbie was always quick with his fists. Ain't no surprise to hear he used'em on his wife."

"A real peach." And yet another reason why someone might have killed him. His ex-wife just being one possibility. "She said they'd been divorced a while. Do you think Robbie had a new girlfriend?"

"I imagine he mighta had a few," Rafe said.

"Do you think he was hitting her, too? Or them?" Maybe one of his new girlfriends had killed him.

Hell—heck—maybe all his old girlfriends, including his ex-wife, had gotten together to kill him. And the rest of the family, too. Hard to imagine why anyone would take Robbie's transgressions out on the rest of them—especially Linda and Cilla—but I'm sure stranger things have happened.

"I imagine he mighta been," Rafe said. "Guess I'll have to find out."

He pointed the car northeast out of Pulaski, on the road to Sweetwater this time, instead of toward Damascus and Columbia.

"How are you going to do that?" I wanted to know. Sandy might have known, but if so, she hadn't said anything about it. Maybe Kayla knew, and maybe Rafe would have to talk to her. Although chances were neither of them had had anything to do with the murders.

He grimaced. "I might have to go out and do some drinking tonight."

"You mean, go to seedy bars and see who knew the Skinners?" Like that place Yvonne had mentioned, in Thompson Station. The Pour House?

He nodded. "Easier for me to do it than any of the sheriff's deputies. Most everyone's gonna know them."

And he'd been gone from Maury County, mostly, for thirteen years. Chances were he could slide right in and nobody would recognize him.

"Not alone," I said.

He arched a brow. "I ain't taking you, if that's what you're thinking."

It wasn't what I'd been thinking, actually. Under normal circumstances—say, a year ago—I would have been gung-ho to go with him, and would have accepted no reason why I couldn't. But things were different now. I was pregnant. I wasn't about to take any chances with the baby. And besides, I rarely stay awake past nine-thirty.

"How about Dix?"

His lips quirked. "Not sure your brother's the right man for this job, darlin'."

Well... maybe not. My brother is on the clean-cut side, not the type who spends a lot of time in dive bars. And he's a single father with two little girls at home. Dragging him out at night to go bar hopping might not be the best idea. "Who is?"

"I was thinking of Yvonne," Rafe said.

I stared at him. He drove on, placidly, as if he didn't notice my attention at all.

"Have you lost your mind?" I asked.

He shot me a look. "She knows the people I wanna talk to. And they know her."

"She's not going to be able to help you if something goes wrong!"

His lips curved. "She'd be more help than your brother, I figure."

Upon consideration, he might actually be right about that. She'd be more familiar with the ambience, at any rate. Although Dix could probably hit harder.

Then again, who knew? Yvonne had honed her muscles carrying trays at Beulah's. She could hold her own, no doubt.

"If you're taking Yvonne, maybe I should come, too."

"Maybe not," Rafe said. "You're pregnant. You need your

sleep. The baby needs his sleep. And I don't wanna have to worry about you."

"But it's OK to worry about Yvonne?"

"She ain't carrying my baby. And I prob'ly won't worry much. Yvonne can take care of herself."

I opened my mouth to tell him that I could take care of myself too, and he shook his head. "I ain't taking you. That's final."

"That's not fair." Between you and me, I'm not even sure why I was arguing. It wasn't like I wanted to come. I wanted to go home and sleep. I'd been OK with not coming when I thought he was bringing another man. But Yvonne...

He sighed. "I'd take you if I could, darlin'. But the sheriff would skin me alive if I let something happen to you. Can't you just stay home with your mama and let me do my job?"

I could. I wanted to. However— "I'd feel better if you'd take someone along who'd have your back in a fight."

His lips twitched. "It ain't like on TV, darlin'. Most nights out drinking don't turn into bar fights."

"Some of them do." One such had landed him in prison more than a dozen years ago. He had more reason than anyone to know that.

However, I wasn't about to remind him of that. I had something else I wanted to mention. "You remember what happened the day before we got married?"

His face darkened. "Not like I'd forget."

Not likely that I would, either. He'd gone out with the boys from the TBI for a last night of debauchery—drinks and pool—before donning the old ball and chain, and had gotten a lot more than he'd bargained for when he was hit over the head and loaded into a van, before being taken off by a serial killer and tortured for hours. He was damned lucky to have gotten out of it alive, and I wasn't about to let him forget it.

"I know I can't come with you. But I want you to be safe out there."

"I'll be safe," Rafe said. "Nobody in these part's got a reason to wanna hurt me. Nobody in these parts even remember who I am."

I hoped he was right about that.

"But if it makes you feel better," he added, "I can ask your brother to come along. Take both him and Yvonne."

"That's all right." Dix had a thing going with Tamara Grimaldi, my friend in Nashville. I wasn't sure exactly what kind of thing, but they'd gotten close since Sheila died. And Yvonne has always had a crush on Dix. I didn't want to be responsible for putting them together. "Just promise me you'll be careful."

"Always," Rafe said. I rolled my eyes, but didn't comment.

"So what happens now?" It was getting toward the end of the day. Or the end of the workday, at any rate. Rafe's day obviously wouldn't end for a long time yet. But it was after four o'clock, and the rest of the world was winding down.

"I take you to your mama's house and make nice for a while. And then I go back to work."

"And I stay with my mother." Great. "Just out of curiosity, what's the sheriff doing while you and I are driving all over Giles County talking to people?"

"Notifications," Rafe said.

"Who's left to notify? All the Skinners are dead." And we'd notified Robbie's ex-wife.

He glanced at me. "Cilla had a boyfriend, remember?"

How could I have forgotten? Cilla had had a boyfriend, and the boyfriend, presumably, had had parents. Maybe siblings. Like Cilla, he'd barely been more than a child.

No parent should have to be told that his or her child has been murdered.

"I'm glad he didn't leave that to us," I said.

Rafe nodded. "I think he was hoping they'd have some idea what mighta been going on with the Skinners."

"And he didn't think Sandy did, so he left her to us?"

Rafe shrugged, as if it didn't bother him. Maybe it didn't. When it came down to it, I guess getting out of doing the notification beat any feelings of being foisted off with second best.

"Ain't no second best in a murder investigation," Rafe said when I'd said so. "We all want the same thing. I don't get extra points for bringing in a juicy piece of evidence."

"You should."

He shook his head. "It ain't a competition, darlin'. We all just wanna figure out who did this and get'em behind bars before they can do it again."

I peered at him. "Do you think they would?"

I mean, it would seem to me that with all the Skinners dead, it was mission accomplished. Who was left to kill? "You don't think Sandy's in danger, do you?"

Rafe shook his head. "If somebody wanted to kill Sandy, she'd be dead. The locks on her door ain't worth spit."

He didn't say spit. I made a substitution.

"She has a neighbor, though."

"These ain't people who'd balk at killing innocent bystanders," Rafe said. "Seven dead. Two of'em teenagers. If they wanted Sandy and her daughter dead, they'd both be dead. And the neighbor too, if he got in the way."

I guess he had a point. "This is scary."

Rafe shrugged.

"Don't you think it's scary? Going after people who'd do something like this?" If they wouldn't balk at shooting Sandy's neighbor, they surely wouldn't balk at shooting law enforcement that came too close to them.

"I spent twelve years with people who'd do this," Rafe said. "Two years in prison and ten years undercover. Won't be the first time I've rubbed elbows with scum."

Maybe not. It didn't make me feel any better. And because it didn't, I changed the subject. "So what did you mean, 'before they can do it again?' If all the Skinners are dead, and you don't think Sandy and Kayla are in danger, who's left?"

"The rest of the county," Rafe said grimly. "We're investigating like the Skinners were specific targets. And maybe they were. God knows there were plenty of reasons somebody might wanna get rid of the Skinners."

"But?"

"But it might just be that somebody wanted to kill. Somebody wanted to kill a lot of people. And for some reason they chose to kill the Skinners. Maybe cause they were easy targets. They lived alone up there in the hills. No neighbors within a mile or two. Nobody to see or hear anything."

I nodded. I could certainly see why killing the Skinners, at least in the geographical sense, had been easy and safe for the murderer.

"If that's all it was," Rafe said, "somebody musta had a hell of good time last night. And that somebody's gonna wanna have a good time again. Before too long."

EIGHT

My ancestral home, the Martin Mansion, sits on a little knoll north of Sweetwater proper, on the road to Columbia. We got there just as the clock struck five, and pulled up to the grand entrance in what was still pouring rain.

"Go on up," Rafe told me. "I'll get the bags."

I thought about arguing, but I didn't. I didn't feel like getting any wetter than I had to be, and besides, the steps can be slippery when wet. So I left it to him to gather the two overnight bags from the trunk while I made my careful way up the steps to the double front doors.

"Key?" Rafe asked.

I have one, but I rang the doorbell anyway. "It's my mother's house. It seems more polite to ring the bell. At least the first time." Especially since I still hadn't called to warn her we were coming, and make sure it was all right that we were.

We waited. A moment later, Mother appeared in the far reaches of the hall and made her way toward us.

My mother is pushing sixty, but looks at least ten years younger. She's a bit shorter than me, with soft, champagne-colored hair and skin that's a testament to SPF 50. And even when she's just sitting around the house, like now, she's dressed to the nines. There were little gold studs in her ears, her makeup was perfectly applied with the lipstick refreshed, and her slippers had fur trim and heels.

"Savannah!" She seemed delighted to see me. "And Rafael!" She seemed no less delighted to see Rafe, which was nice. And quite a change from the early days, where she could barely bring herself to say his name. "Come in! What are you doing here?"

She stepped back so we could cross the threshold into the two-story foyer. I resisted the urge to shake myself like a wet dog, and instead let Rafe take my coat to hang up with his own.

"It was a spur of the moment thing," I said, while I leaned in and air kissed both her cheeks. "Rafe got a call from the sheriff. I decided to come along and see you."

A tiny wrinkle appeared between Mother's perfectly plucked brows. "Oh, dear. What's happened?"

"Shootings up by the Devil's Backbone," Rafe said, leaning in to kiss her cheek, as well. A real kiss, not the airy kind. Mother beamed. "Family named the Skinners."

"You probably don't know them," I added, since my mother, from everything I knew about her, would have nothing in common with the Skinners.

She shook her head. "I don't imagine I do. What happened?"

She started down the hallway toward the kitchen again, gesturing for us to follow.

"Someone came in overnight and shot'em," Rafe said, with a hand at the small of my back, pushing me along in my mother's wake.

Mother glanced at him over her shoulder. "How many?"

When he told her seven, her steps hitched. For a second, I was afraid she'd stumble, but then she righted herself again. "Dear me. Seven dead?"

"Yes, ma'am." We stepped into the kitchen, and Rafe steered me toward a stool at the island. "Everyone in the family over the age of sixteen."

"Except Robbie's ex-wife and daughter," I added, scooting my butt up on the stool. "They live in Pulaski. We were just down there to talk to her."

"Oh, dear." Mother turned on the tap and started filling a kettle. "Tea? It's a gloomy day out there."

It was a gloomy day out there, wet and cold and depressing. "Please," I said, making myself comfortable on the stool.

Rafe rubbed a circle on my back. "Not for me. I gotta head back out."

Mother put the kettle on to boil and turned back to him. "Not done for the day?"

"Not today." He dropped his hand and then stuffed both in his pockets. "When seven people are shot, it makes for long days."

Yes, it did. "You're taking the Volvo," I asked, "right?"

He nodded.

He'd driven here, so he already had my keys. "The key to the front door is on the chain," I told him. "I'll probably be asleep by the time you get back here. Just let yourself in and come upstairs. You know where to find me."

He nodded and bent to drop a kiss on my mouth. A quick one, since Mother was standing there watching.

But not so quick that my toes didn't curl inside my booties and my eyes didn't drift shut and stay that way.

It felt like reluctance when he lifted his head, although that could have just been on my part.

"Be careful," I said, uncurling my fingers from the fabric of his hoodie and smoothing it against his chest. I could feel his heartbeat through the layers of cotton. "Bring some backup. And maybe a weapon."

His lips curved. "I do that anyway. Don't worry."

Easy for him to say. However— "Take care."

"Always." He grinned, knowing full well how I feel about that not-quite-accurate response. I watched—Mother and I both did—as he headed out of the kitchen and down the hall. We heard the front door close and lock, and then the sound of the car engine starting.

I turned back to my mother. "How are you?"

"Fine," Mother said, taking a ladylike sip of her tea. "And you?"

"Very well, thank you. Tough situation."

"No doubt," Mother said.

We sipped in silence a few moments.

"I had lunch with Catherine," I said.

Mother put her cup down. "Did you?"

"When the sheriff called Rafe to come help with the Skinner murders, I decided to come along to provide moral support for Yvonne McCoy. The Beulah Odom hearing started today."

After a second, I added, "And ended today, too."

Mother's brows arched. "Catherine hasn't told me much about it. Client confidentiality, I assume."

Probably so. But at this point, the ruling was a *fait accompli*, as Mother would say—the Martins were French once upon a time, and so were the Calverts, Mother's family.

"She was representing Yvonne," I said. "Beulah Odom left Beulah's Meat'n Three to Yvonne in her will, and Beulah's brother's wife and daughter contested the will. I guess they want the place for themselves."

"And the hearing was today?"

I nodded. "Catherine brought a bunch of character witnesses. People who said Beulah was perfectly capable of making her own decisions and Yvonne wasn't pressuring her at all. So the judge ruled against the Odoms."

I took a sip of tea and added, "Of course, the will still has to go through probate. By then, Beulah's might have been closed so long that everyone has started eating elsewhere and Yvonne basically inherits a gravel lot and a cinderblock building with a kitchen inside."

Mother nodded. "Even so, it's good to have this first hurdle jumped. I'm sure Yvonne is celebrating."

"She's not, actually. She might have been, but I flapped my

gums over lunch, and told her and Catherine that the Skinners were dead. Turns out Yvonne used to date Darrell Skinner. Both in high school and a couple of years ago."

"Oh, dear." Mother put the tea cup down again. With a little click this time, as if her hands were unsteady. "How terrible."

"Apparently he cheated on her repeatedly. But she's still sad he's dead. And Robbie Skinner used to beat on Sandy. She's still upset he's dead, too." Although that was probably more for her daughter's sake than her own.

"They don't sound like a nice family," Mother said primly.

I shook my head. "Not at all. I wonder if that makes it harder or easier to investigate their murders." I'd have to ask Rafe. Who certainly had no reason to remember the Skinners fondly. But who'd have to do his best for them anyway.

"Maybe you should offer to meet Yvonne for dinner," Mother suggested. "To celebrate. And to take her mind off things."

"I would. But Rafe's taking her with him to case dive bars all night. She'll have plenty of opportunity to drown her sorrows. And I'm sure she'd rather be with him than with me."

Mother's brows crept up her forehead.

"They go back," I said. "Friends in high school." A little more than friends, too, but no reason to mention that to Mother. "He thinks having her there will make it more likely that people will talk to him."

Mother's brows wrinkled. "Are you sure you shouldn't go with them, darling?"

"I'm not worried," I said. "And if I go along, he'll spend half his time worrying about me. Besides, I usually conk out around nine these days. But you and I could have dinner. Since I'm sure you're not meeting the sheriff tonight."

Mother shook her head. "I'm not."

I smiled optimistically. "Maybe we could ask Catherine to join us." Mother looked positive to the suggestion. "And Darcy.

Make it a girls' night."

Mother's face clouded. "I'm not sure, Savannah..."

"You invited her to your birthday party," I reminded her. "And to Christmas Eve last year. And the Fourth of July picnic. And my wedding. You like Darcy."

"Yes," Mother said, "but that was before..."

"It isn't Darcy's fault that she's Dad's daughter. She couldn't help it."

"No," Mother said, "but..."

"She was just looking for her biological family. Since she lost her adopted family and was all alone in the world."

"Yes..." Mother said.

I smiled. "Great. I'll give her a call."

"No..." Mother said, but it was too late. I'd already pulled out my phone, and I guess she didn't feel comfortable actually saying that she didn't want to spend any time with her husband's love child and my half-sister, because she didn't stop me.

The law office was closed for the day, so I called Darcy at home. Or on her cell-phone, rather. "It's me," I told her.

"I know who you are. What can I do for you?"

"I'm in Sweetwater," I said, "and I wondered whether you'd like to grab some dinner. I was going to call Catherine, too." Although it was probably best not to mention Mother until later. Not that Darcy has anything against Mother, but she's sensitive enough to have realized that Mother has something against her. Or if not that, at least that Mother is uncomfortable around her.

Darcy hesitated.

"It's OK if you have other plans," I said. "Or if you don't want to, or whatever." Although I'll admit my feelings were a little hurt. I'd spent a lot of time with Darcy, trying to find her biological family—with absolutely no idea that Darcy's family would turn out to be my own—and we'd always gotten along well, both before and after we realized we were sisters. She didn't usually hesitate when it came to getting together.

"It isn't that," Darcy said. "Patrick has the night off, and I'm hoping maybe he'll call."

Ah. Patrick Nolan is a police officer with the Columbia PD, and he liked my sister a lot. She liked him too, as evidenced by her willingness to forego dinner with me to wait for a phone call from Nolan that might never come. "You could always invite him to join us. If he calls."

Darcy made a non-committal noise. I could understand that. I didn't always want to share Rafe, either.

"Or," I said, "it's possible he might not have the night off after all."

"What do you mean?" Darcy said.

I told her about the Skinners and the reason I was here in Sweetwater. "Apparently the Columbia chief of police wanted in on the action. He might have canceled time off for some of his officers to help with the case. Not that I have any idea what I'm talking about. But if you don't hear from Nolan, that might be why."

"That's terrible," Darcy said, presumably about the Skinners. I agreed that it was. "All right. I'll go to dinner with you. And if Patrick calls, maybe I'll ask him to join us. If you don't mind."

I assured her I didn't. I liked Patrick Nolan, or had the few times I'd met him. I especially liked the fact that he seemed so taken with Darcy. "How about we meet at the Wayside Inn at six-thirty?"

Darcy allowed as how that would work, and we hung up. I smiled at Mother. "She'll be there."

Mother looked less thrilled about it than I was, but she didn't say anything. I dialed Catherine, and told her what was going on. "Mother?" she said. "And Darcy? At the same table? Really?"

"Really."

"I definitely don't want to miss that." Her voice turned calculating. "Maybe I should call Audrey, too, while we're at it."

"One step at a time," I told her, conscious of the fact that Mother was three feet away and could hear everything I said. "I think this is enough for now, don't you?"

Catherine agreed, a little reluctantly, that maybe it was. "I'll see you at six-thirty. Just let me fix Jonathan and Dix up, so the kids can get together and play. That way, everyone's happy."

With the possible exception of Mother. I didn't say so. "See you there," I told her and hung up. "I guess you caught that?"

Mother nodded.

"I'm going to take my bag—and Rafe's bag—up to my room and put my feet up for a while before we have to go."

Mother nodded.

"I'll see you down here a little after six."

Mother nodded. I took my teacup to the sink, poured the last of the tea down the drain, and gently washed the porcelain with mild soap before putting it to dry in the dish drainer. That done, I wandered down the hall to grab the bags and take them upstairs. Throughout this, Mother stood like a statue by the island, staring into space while I moved around her. I deduced she was not looking forward to the evening's entertainment.

To be honest, half of me expected she'd be gone when I came downstairs again to go to the restaurant. I figured the house would be empty and Mother vanished.

She wasn't. She had even managed to move herself from the kitchen into the small parlor, and was perched on the edge of Great-Aunt Ida's uncomfortable turn-of-the-(last)-century sofa, looking like an aging Marie Antoinette waiting to be escorted out to the guillotine.

"Don't worry," I told her, since it was impossible not to feel bad for such obvious misery. "It's just dinner with your daughters. And Darcy's nice. You know that."

Mother nodded. "It's difficult," she told me. "I've known Darcy for several years. I never looked at her and thought she reminded me of either your father or Audrey. But now I find myself watching her face. To see if I can see him there. And when I do, it brings it all back again."

'It' being the feeling of betrayal, I guess. Or maybe the anger or whatever.

"He didn't know about Darcy," I reminded her. "Audrey never told him. He couldn't have told you, when he didn't know himself."

"I know that."

"And it was before he met you. He didn't cheat."

Mother nodded. "I'm not angry with him."

I wasn't too sure about that, but I wasn't about to argue. She continued, "And I'm not angry with Darcy. I know it isn't Darcy's fault." She shook her head. "But her presence is a reminder."

No question about that. However, it was what it was. Sooner or later, we'd all just have to learn to deal with that.

"We should go," I said, and reached out a hand. Mother contemplated it for a second before she took it and allowed me to haul her to her feet. We headed for the kitchen and the back door—closest to the carriage house—side by side.

The Wayside Inn is the nicest restaurant in Sweetwater. It's on the same road as Beulah's Meat'n Three, but in the opposite direction, and that isn't the only thing about it that's different. The Inn is an old building, late seventeen-hundreds, that actually was a wayside inn at one point, back when people traveled this way down to Birmingham and Montgomery and the Gulf. Not that either Birmingham or Montgomery existed at the time, but there were trails through the area. The Natchez Trail as well as others.

Anyway, it's a nice place. Old and full of atmosphere, with a German chef who really knows his stuff. We slid into a booth in the low-ceilinged dining room, and ordered a drink each. Chardonnay for Mother, and a sweet tea with lots of lemon for me, since I was off alcohol for the time being.

In the middle of the week like this, the restaurant wasn't all that busy. Less than half the tables were occupied, and the wait staff—small; just two people that I could see—huddled over by the hostess station, giggling together.

I turned back to Mother. "So how have you been? It's been a couple of weeks since I was down."

"I'm fine, darling." She took a sip of her wine. I watched, a bit enviously. Chardonnay had been my go-to drink when I'd go out to dinner, too, before the baby.

"You and the sheriff got things back on track again?"

She'd been pretty angry with Bob after the truth about Darcy came out. He'd figured it out before any of us—having been around back in the day when Dad knocked up Audrey—and he was the one who had convinced Audrey that it was time to come clean, before we figured it out on our own. Between the two of them, they had rounded up Mother and brought her to the law office for the denouement, and when the truth came out, she hadn't been particularly appreciative. I couldn't blame her. At first, I'd thought she was there because the sheriff was Darcy's dad. Then I thought they'd brought her to provide moral support to Audrey—her oldest and best friend—while Audrey told Darcy that she (Audrey) was Darcy's mother.

And then it had turned out that Mother was there because Dad was Darcy's father. No wonder she felt betrayed. Not only by her boyfriend, who knew the truth before her, but by her oldest and best girlfriend, who had known for thirty-four years.

At first, she had shut everyone out. I'd been staying with her at the time, and she'd all but kicked me out and back to Nashville. But Sheriff Satterfield had refused to give up. He'd given her time to process the news, but he simply hadn't allowed her to cut him off.

Mother nodded.

"What about Audrey?"

"She calls once in a while," Mother said. "I let the machine pick up."

"Don't you think you should give her a chance? It all happened before she knew you."

Mother sighed and put her glass down. "I'm not upset that she fell in love with your father, Savannah."

"You're not?"

She shook her head, and the diamonds in her ears sparkled when the candle light hit them. "I fell in love with your father. I'm not surprised that someone else would."

OK, then. "So...?"

"I'm upset," Mother said, "because she had his child, and for the thirty-three years she was my best friend, she never mentioned it."

"It's not like she could just blurt it out." Especially considering how Mother was handling the news now. In fact, Mother's response since the denouement was all the evidence needed that Audrey had made the right choice in keeping her mouth shut.

"Nonsense!" Mother snapped when I said as much. "She could have told me anytime at all. Perhaps not while your father was alive. I can understand that. But he's been gone a long time. She's had years to tell me."

"So she was just supposed to blurt it out? 'By the way, Margaret, I had an affair with your late husband and got pregnant'?"

"Of course not," Mother said. There were flags of color on her cheeks, and she took a sip of wine, perhaps to cool down. "But Darcy's parents were killed a few years ago. She could have told me then. 'Listen, Margaret, I gave up a child for adoption thirty-some years ago, before I knew you. And now her adoptive parents have died. What do you think I should do?'"

Well, yes. I suppose Audrey could have done that.

"I would have been sympathetic," Mother said. "I would

have understood why she hadn't told me before. And then we could have worked our way around to who the father was."

"So you're less upset about the fact that Audrey slept with Dad than that she didn't tell you about Darcy?"

Mother winced, but nodded. "It was before we were married. I'm sure he might have slept with someone else, too. And it wasn't like I was a virgin on my wedding night."

I resisted the temptation to plug my ears and hum. "I don't want to hear about it."

"It was the nineteen-eighties, darling. The sexual revolution had come and gone."

After a moment, she added, pensively, "Not that people didn't sleep around before the sexual revolution, too."

Of course they had. But none of them were my mother. "Just don't talk about it."

"Don't be hypocritical, Savannah," Mother said. "You certainly enjoyed your husband before you married him."

No argument there. I'd been visibly pregnant walking down the aisle. I just never thought I'd hear my mother—my *mother*, for God's sake!—chastising me for being too prudish.

But hey, I could live with it. I grinned. "I did, as a matter of fact. And still do. As often as I can."

"There's no need to be crude," Mother said repressively, and lifted her hand. "There's Catherine."

So she was. And since she was—and since my mother was back to herself again—I shelved the discussion.

Catherine slipped into the booth on the other side, next to Mother. "This was a good idea." She stuffed her purse behind her legs on the floor and grinned at me across the table.

"Rafe's working," I answered, "and I needed food."

"Sure. But it's nice." She leaned over to give Mother an air-hug, and then looked around. "Sheila and I used to do this once in a while."

"Really?" I hadn't known that. Sheila and I hadn't been

particularly close, and for some reason I had assumed that she and Catherine hadn't been, either.

Catherine nodded. "Sometimes Mom would come with us, but sometimes it was just her and me."

"I didn't realize you and Sheila were close."

"I don't know that I'd say close," Catherine said, "but she was Dix's wife. We spent time together."

"That's nice."

"Jonathan and Dix would get together to have beer and pizza with the kids—the kids didn't get beer—and Sheila and I would go out and eat somewhere like adults. I miss that."

I probably would, too. "I'm sorry I don't live closer."

Or actually, I wasn't. I'd hate to have to live in Sweetwater again. But it seemed like a nice thing to say.

Catherine shrugged. "It's been a year. I don't think about it a lot. This just reminded me."

"Now you have Darcy," I reminded her, and tried not to notice Mother's wince. "Do you and she get together?"

"We have lunch once in a while. Mostly when I'm in the office at lunch time. We go down to the Café on the Square and grab something." She was quiet for a second before adding, "At least we used to do that before I knew she was my sister. We haven't lately."

"You don't mind, do you? About Darcy?"

"I wouldn't say I mind," Catherine said. "I mean, I like Darcy. I liked her before I found out who she was. But it's a little weird."

It was a little weird. And being here, in Sweetwater, with the constant reminder sitting at the front desk at the law office every day, was probably weirder than being an hour away in Nashville where a lot of the time I didn't even think about the fact that I had a new half-sister.

"You're OK with having dinner with her, aren't you?"

"Of course," Catherine said, glancing around. "Although

she's late."

"Not that late. And she lives in Columbia. She has a longer way to drive than the rest of us."

Catherine nodded. "I'll have a glass of Pinot Grigio," she told the waitress who appeared next to the table. "And an order of the crab dip while we wait, please."

She turned back to me as the waitress hurried away. "So what's Rafe doing tonight?"

"Taking Yvonne to every dive bar in Maury County." I refrained from rolling my eyes and took a sip of tea instead.

Catherine wrinkled her brows. "Why?"

"He's hoping that the fact that Yvonne knew the Skinners will loosen people's tongues. He's looking for an angle for why someone would have killed them all."

"I wish he'd asked me first," Catherine said.

"Why? You didn't know the Skinners, did you?"

"Don't be ridiculous, Savannah," Mother said, and took a sip of wine.

Catherine shook her head. "I remember Darrell. Barely. But I don't want her getting mixed up in this."

"Why not? The hearing's over. The judge ruled that Beulah was competent. Whatever Yvonne does now, doesn't matter." And oughtn't to have mattered before, either, since it wasn't her competency in question.

"Tell that to the Odoms," Catherine said. She dug for her purse. "I have to make a phone call. Don't eat all my crab dip."

She walked away before I could tell her that she'd better make it back to the table quickly, in that case.

NINE

When Catherine came back, she had Darcy with her. As they made their way between the tables, I found myself looking at them for similarities.

Dix and I take after Mother's family, the Georgia Calverts. We're on the taller side, and medium to fair. Catherine takes after Dad's family, the Martins, who are shorter and dark.

Darcy... Well, Darcy is tall. Taller than me, and slender. Not much in the way of curves. She gets that from Audrey, who's also tall and thin. Both of them have the build of runway models. Long and leggy. But where Audrey's eyes are blue and her skin pale, Darcy almost has Rafe's coloring. A little darker than Catherine, whose skin is a degree or two darker than mine, with short, black hair and brown eyes.

I'd be more inclined to say she looked like Rafe's sister, to be honest, than either of ours. I could definitely see Audrey in her, especially now that I knew the truth. Seeing Dad was more difficult. A little in the mouth and chin, maybe...

She gave me a smile, although I could see trepidation in her eyes.

"You're next to Savannah," Catherine said, giving her a nudge. "Where's my crab dip?" She looked at the table.

"I scarfed it down while you were gone, and sent the bowl back," I told her while I scooted deeper into the booth to make room for Darcy. "You snooze, you lose."

Catherine stared at me.

"They didn't bring it yet," Mother told her. "Hello, Darcy."

She met Darcy's eyes for a nanosecond across the table.

"Hi, Mrs. Martin." Darcy didn't sound any more comfortable about the situation.

"Margaret," Mom said. "Please."

Now, there was a nice, semi-friendly overture. Not too friendly—"*Call me Mom; after all, your father was my husband,*"— but just friendly enough. And anyway, Darcy had a mother, so that wouldn't work out well in either case.

Darcy smiled. It was a little strained, but pretty convincing. "Thank you."

"It took you a while to get here," I told her. "Did Nolan call?"

She shook her head. "Car accident on the Columbia Highway. Traffic was stopped for ten minutes while they towed the cars."

"Oh, dear," Mother said. "The weather, I suppose."

Darcy nodded. "It's slick out there. It didn't look too bad, though. I didn't see an ambulance. Just a tow truck. One car was nose first in the ditch. The other looked OK."

We all agreed that was good. "It wasn't anyone we know, I suppose?"

"I don't think so," Darcy said. "I didn't recognize either of the cars." She turned to the waitress as the crab dip descended to the table, surrounded by a ring of toasted baguette slices. My mouth watered. "I'll have sweet tea, please."

"Are you sure you wouldn't like some wine?" Catherine asked as the waitress walked away. "Mother and I are indulging. Savannah can't, of course."

"Tea is fine." Darcy smiled, but it was the kind of smile that didn't invite to further conversation. I thought I knew why. Her parents had died in a traffic accident a few years ago. I have no idea whether alcohol had played any part, but it was possible. And she had just driven past another car accident on the way here. It probably brought back memories. And she'd be driving herself home after we ate. It made sense that she'd be a little extra careful.

"We better decide what we're going to eat," I said, and reached for my menu. "The waitress will ask when she comes back with Darcy's tea. We might as well be ready. I'm starving."

"Have some crab," Catherine said. "You too, Darcy." She nudged the bowl an inch in Darcy's direction, without taking it out of Mother's or my reach.

"Thank you." Darcy took an obligatory baguette piece and an obligatory scoop of crab dip. Hopefully she actually liked crab, and wasn't just doing it to be polite.

If the whole situation sounds awkward, it's because it was. Clearly Mother was uncomfortable with Darcy, and equally clearly Darcy knew it, and it made her uncomfortable, too.

"I'm thinking about the salmon," Catherine said, with her eyes on the menu.

I nodded. "I've had it before, and it's good. What do you think, Mother? You've probably eaten here more than the rest of us."

"The salmon is usually excellent," Mother said. "So is the veal."

Of course.

Catherine and Darcy choose the salmon, Mother the veal. I bucked the system and had the mushroom pasta I'd had on a previous occasion. It had been good then. It would probably be good now.

Once the food arrived, things got a little easier. We were all eating, and too well brought-up to speak with our mouths full. Darcy hadn't had Mother drilling manners into her as a child, of course, but I was happy to see that her own mother must have done the same thing, since she was thoroughly unobjectionable. Not that I'd expected anything different, but Mother might have, and it was nice that Darcy didn't give her an excuse.

We talked about Yvonne and the hearing into Beulah's

competency, and then we talked about the Skinners and possible motives for the murders. Since neither of us had any recent experience with the Skinners, all we could come up with were wild theories with no basis in fact, but it was interesting. Catherine remembered Darrell as being a ladies man, even in high school, which coincided with Rafe's memories and Yvonne's story. The entire family was shocked and appalled when I told them that all three Skinners had beat the crap out of Rafe once in high school.

"We drove him home," I said, "although nobody was happy about it. He ended up in the backseat with Dix and Charlotte, and ruined their plans for necking the whole way home. And Todd was upset because Rafe was bleeding on his new leather interior."

Mother straightened on the chair. "You never told me this."

"Because I knew you'd have a fit. Rafe wasn't exactly on the approved list back then. Just the fact that I'd breathed the same air he did would have set you off."

There was nothing Mother could say to that, so she didn't try. "Dessert?" she asked instead, brightly.

I'm never one to turn down dessert. And although Mother often tells me to be careful what I put in my mouth, since I'll have to get rid of it again once the baby is born, this time she didn't.

So I had cheesecake. Catherine, perhaps in an effort to at least sound like she was watching her weight, had the carrot cake. Mother picked at the Crème Brûlée, and Darcy devoured a piece of pie. Of all of us, she had the least to worry about when it came to gaining weight.

And after that we went home. Catherine to her husband and kids, Darcy to her empty house in Columbia, and Mother and I to the mansion.

It's a quick drive from downtown Sweetwater to the Martin Mansion, and neither of us spoke. It wasn't until Mother had parked the Cadillac in the old carriage house and we were on our way to the back door that she opened her mouth. "I wonder if one of us should say something to Darcy about the dangers of tanning beds."

I turned to arch my brows at her. "Why?"

"Because it can't be good for her skin. If she's not careful, she'll start to look old before her time."

"That's not what I meant," I said, while Mother unlocked the back door and ushered me in. "I know all about how the sun gives you wrinkles and makes you look old." Mother is a living, breathing testament to the opposite. She hardly ever goes out in the sun, and her skin is lovely. "What does it have to do with Darcy?"

"Well," Mother said reasonably, "she must go to a tanning salon to keep herself looking so..." She hesitated before landing on, "...healthy."

I shrugged out of my coat and hung it over the back of one of the kitchen island stools. "I think that's her natural complexion."

"Oh, no," Mother said, shaking her head, "that's not possible, darling."

"Why not?"

She stared at me. "Well, her mother is Audrey, isn't she? And your father was her father?"

I nodded.

"Well, no offense, darling, but then she shouldn't look like your husband, should she?"

"No offense taken," I said, although I'll have to admit to a little. "I like the way my husband looks. I like the way Darcy looks, too, for that matter. She's pretty."

Mother agreed that Darcy was attractive. "But her coloring, darling..."

"She's only a little darker than Catherine," I said. "And this stuff can lay dormant for generations before it pops up again. Maybe there's some mixed blood in Audrey's family, too, a few generations back. That would explain it."

Mother stared at me. Apparently it explained nothing for her. And a little too late, I remembered that my mother didn't know what I had gotten used to taking for granted: the fact that during the War Against Northern Aggression, while her husband was away defending the gallant South against the damn Yankees, my great-great-great-grandmother Caroline had had an affair with one of the grooms and gotten pregnant.

"Oops," I said. "You know, forgot I said anything. I'm going to bed." I headed for the door.

"Not so fast," Mother said, and stepped in front of me. "What did you mean, 'too'?"

I avoided her eyes. "Nothing. It's not important. Forget I mentioned it."

"It's a little late for that," Mother said, putting her hands on her hips.

It was. But that didn't stop me from trying to squirm out of telling her. "You know, it isn't really my place to talk to you about this. You should call Aunt Regina. She was the one who told me."

"Told you what?" Mother wanted to know.

"About great-great-great-grandmother Caroline."

"What about great-great-great-grandmother Caroline?"

I sighed. I'd gone this far; I might as well go the rest of the way. "On Christmas Eve last year, Aunt Regina and I were talking about Rafe. I was here, remember, for the party?"

Mother nodded. "And then Rafael showed up."

He had. A bit later. "Before he came, Aunt Regina and I were talking. And she told me about great-great-great-grandma Caroline."

"What about Caroline?"

"She was the Mrs. Martin during the Civil War. I'm not sure who she was married to, but whoever he was, he went off to fight the Damn Yankees, and left her in charge of the plantation."

In case I haven't mentioned it, the Martin Mansion was a working Southern plantation at the time, with fields and slaves and all the usual things. The fields are gone now, and so of course are the slaves. All that's left is the mansion itself, a couple of outbuildings, and an acre or two of grass for them to sit on. Plus a few trees and an old family cemetery.

"Caroline was here, and what's-his-name was gone. And I guess she got lonely. Or maybe he died, and she got lonely after that. Either way, she took up with one of the grooms."

Mother stared at me, her mouth half open. If it had been anyone else, I'd have said she was gaping. Since she's my mother, and extremely elegant, I'll just say she stared. With her mouth open.

"Apparently she got pregnant, and the result was great-great-grandpa William."

Mother closed her mouth. And opened it again. "There's a picture of him in the hallway upstairs."

I nodded. That had been my first reaction, too. I'd seen great-great-grandpa William's face my whole life—so long, probably, that I didn't even notice it anymore. But it had never crossed my mind that he looked black. Not until I spoke to Aunt Regina. "If you look closely, you can see it."

For a second, neither of us moved. Then Mother swung on her heel and hurried down the hallway. I grabbed my purse and coat and followed. If we were going upstairs, where my room was, I might as well bring my things. That way I wouldn't have to come back down for them.

Mother's heels clicked on the floors and the treads of the stairs. She was already halfway to the second floor by the time I got out into the foyer.

By the time I gained the second floor, Mother was halfway down the hallway, standing in front of the photograph of William. I bypassed my own door to come and stand next to her.

Like most of the early family portraits in the house, this one was black and white. An early photograph rather than a painting. (We do have some of those, too.) It showed William's head pretty much from the shoulders up, a bit smaller than life size, and it had become somewhat faded with time. Not surprising, maybe, considering how many years had passed.

William might have been around thirty, or maybe he was younger and people just looked older earlier back then. He was wearing a dark jacket, buttoned higher than we're used to seeing these days, with a high-necked white shirt underneath. The tie was also dark, and while it wasn't quite a modern-day bowtie, it was closer to that than the ties men wear now. Above, his face was almost as familiar to me as my own, and certainly as familiar as those of my brother and sister.

He'd been a good-looking guy, with a strong jaw and a firm, full mouth. He had thick, black eyebrows over dark eyes, and his hair was slicked back wetly, as must have been the fashion at the time. The photograph must have been taken—I counted on my fingers—sometime between 1890 and 1895, perhaps, if William had been born during, or just after, the War Between the States.

Mother didn't say anything. I slanted a glance her way. "He looks a little like Catherine, don't you think? Or Dad?"

Mother didn't answer. Not the question. "Are you sure...?" she began instead, and then trailed off.

I shook my head. "All I know is what Aunt Regina told me. I haven't looked into it. And I don't know that there's any way to find out for certain, either, after all these years. Aunt Regina said he was raised with Caroline's other children. She had a bunch, I guess. But given the times, I'm sure the name on his birth certificate was Caroline's husband's."

Mother didn't respond.

"I think it was one of those family secrets that was passed down from generation to generation, orally. Aunt Regina said her father told her and Dad. I'm not sure there's any written proof anywhere."

"So it might not be true," Mother said.

I shook my head, even though I recognized the grasping at straws. "It might not. But if you look at him, you can kind of see it. And let's be reasonable here. The Martins got that black, curly hair and sallow skin somehow."

Mother had no response for that.

"It doesn't matter," I said.

"Of course it matters." Mother's voice was sort of faint.

"Not to me. It was a hundred and fifty years ago. I'm still the same person I was before I found out. So was Dad."

"He never told me," Mother said.

I figured he hadn't. Aunt Regina had told me she didn't think he had, that she didn't think Mother knew.

I had my mouth open to tell her I knew that when I realized what Mother meant: that this was yet one more thing someone had kept from her. Dad might not have known about Darcy, and he obviously hadn't seen the need to tell Mother that he'd slept with Audrey before the two of them got together. But this, this was something he could have told her. And maybe should have told her. And hadn't.

She looked at me. I opened my mouth again, but there wasn't much I could say. To explain why he might not have—she wouldn't have been happy with the news—would only make her feel worse.

After a moment, she turned away. "I'm going to go to bed."

"It isn't even nine yet," I said. And unlike me, Mother wasn't pregnant.

She didn't answer. Just continued up the hall to her door, her feet managing to drag even in the high heels. I watched as she crossed the threshold, head bowed. The door closed with a soft but final click.

TEN

I don't know if she lay awake tossing and turning all night. I don't know if she cried herself to sleep. I put my own head on the pillow and dropped off, even though it wasn't nine yet. I didn't stir when Rafe slipped into bed in the middle of the night, or if I did, I don't remember. The first I knew he was there, was the next morning, when I woke with sunlight slanting through the windows, with his breath in my hair, his body spooned around me, protectively, and his hand on my stomach.

I figured I'd let him sleep—he hadn't gotten to bed as early as I had—but it soon became apparent that he was awake.

"Morning, darlin'." The hand started moving.

"Good morning," I said, stretching.

And that was all that was said for the next little bit. It wasn't until thirty minutes later that I got a good look at him. My eyes widened. "What happened to you?"

"Nothing," Rafe said, putting a hand to the side of his jaw and the bruise there. There was a small cut on his bottom lip, too, and the lip itself was a little swollen. The cut didn't look deep and had already scabbed over, so I didn't mention it.

"Did someone hit you?"

He shook his head. "I walked into the door on my way home."

Sure. "Who did it?"

"Just some guy in a bar," Rafe said. I stared at him until he added, "It's no big deal."

It didn't look like a big deal. I'd certainly seen him look worse. And he's perfectly capable of assessing his own damage. However— "Is this all of it?"

"Pretty much," Rafe said.

"What else is there?"

He showed me his knuckles. They were bruised, too. I tilted my head. "Who did you hit?"

"The guy who hit me first," Rafe said.

"Why did he do that?"

He sighed. "I shoulda known better, OK? It was my own fault."

"What did you do?"

He flopped back down on the bed so I was forced to sit up to see his face. The blanket slipped off and down to my waist, and his lips curved.

I hiked it up. "Don't get any ideas about distracting me. I want to know what happened."

Trust him to take it all the way back to the top instead of just telling me what I wanted to hear. "I took your car to Yvonne's and talked her into going with me. We started at a place in Columbia that she said she and Darrell used to frequent. I walked up to the bar to order two beers, and the bartender objected."

"Why would he do that? Isn't that his job?"

He made a face. "It was the same bar where I found Billy Scruggs thirteen years ago. And the same bartender."

Ah. "I guess he liked Billy?"

"Not so much," Rafe said. "But while I was doing my best to kill Billy, and he was doing his best to kill me, we broke a lot of chairs and tables. And glasses and bottles and everything else."

"So the bartender was holding a grudge."

"Seems he musta been. I shoulda thought of it. It's just..." He glanced over at me for a second, and away again, "—it feels like a different life, you know?"

I nodded. The altercation with Billy Scruggs—the one that had sent Rafe to prison for two years—had taken place when he was eighteen. Before he was recruited by the TBI. Before he and I hooked up. Before he'd turned his life completely around. "So what happened? Did you arrest him?"

"I guess I coulda done that."

I happened to know he could. He has a badge, and a pair of handcuffs, and the authority to make arrests anywhere in Tennessee. And someone had attacked him, unprovoked. He'd had every right to do just that. "But you didn't."

"I figure I knew where he was coming from. He just wanted some of his own back."

"By hitting you?"

He shrugged. "I hit him back."

"Only as hard as you had to, I hope?"

He grinned. "Naturally." And then he muttered a curse and swiped at his lip.

I leaned over to grab a box of tissues from the bedside table. The blanket slipped again, and Rafe's grin widened.

"Knock it off," I told him, as I dropped the box on the bed between us.

"I'm already bleeding." His voice turned muffled as he picked up a tissue to dab at his lip. "I might as well enjoy my wife."

"You've already enjoyed your wife this morning." Although I didn't bother hiking up the blanket this time. If the sight of my breasts made him forget the way his face no doubt hurt, I was happy to sacrifice for the cause. "I don't suppose, after that fiasco, the bartender told you anything about the Skinners."

Rafe shook his head. "We left, after I waved my badge in front of his face and told him he was lucky I didn't haul him in for assault. Wasn't nobody in that place gonna talk about the Skinners after that."

No. They'd spend the rest of the evening discussing Rafe and his many failings, and probably drinking to Billy Scruggs's memory. And the Skinners' too.

"I don't suppose you packed up and came home after that fiasco?"

He shook his head. "No, darlin'." He took the tissue from his mouth and inspected it. The result must be satisfactory, because he dropped it, and his hand, to his lap. "We went to the next place on the list. Nobody hit me there."

Good to know. "How did Yvonne handle the whole thing?"

"Offered to kiss it and make it better," Rafe said.

My eyes narrowed. "Really?"

"I told her no thanks. But *you* can kiss it and make it better if you want."

"I already kissed it." And a lot of other things. Although I could kiss it again. I had nowhere else to be. So I leaned forward and put my lips, very gently, on his. His arm went around my back, and one thing, as they say, lead to another.

"So how did you spend the evening?" he asked me when another thirty minutes had passed, and we'd come up for air again.

I told him I'd gone to dinner with Mother, Catherine, and Darcy, and watched his eyebrows rise. "All of them?"

I nodded. "Mother was worried about getting together with Darcy, but I talked her into it." Or guilted her into it. Whichever. "It was all right. A little awkward at times, but we got through it. It'll be easier next time."

"Will there be a next time?"

"Well..." I thought about it. "Maybe not, now that you mention it. The dinner was all right. If that was all it was, I'd say yes. Nothing happened that would have made Mother refuse to have a meal with Darcy again. It was what happened later."

He scratched his chest. It's a lovely chest, and for the next few seconds I was distracted. Then I pulled it together. "She wondered whether she should tell Darcy about the dangers of tanning beds. Since Darcy must be going to a tanning salon to look so tan all the time."

"Oh," Rafe said.

I nodded. "I ended up telling her about Caroline and William. It wasn't really a conscious decision. One thing just sort of led to another, and it fell out of my mouth when I wasn't looking."

He arched a brow. Just one this time. "You sure about that?"

"Positive." I nodded. "If it had been deliberate, I would have planned it better. I was keeping that in reserve for some time when she insulted you and I had to get her back. I didn't mean to throw it away on something like this."

A corner of his mouth quirked, but he didn't say anything else. "How'd she take it?" he asked instead.

I grimaced. "About as well as you'd expect. Disbelief. Denial. Anger."

Something flashed in his eyes. "She angry with you?"

"I don't think so. Mostly she was angry with my dad. He didn't know about Darcy, and I can see why he wouldn't want to tell her he'd slept with Audrey, when she and Audrey were living in the same town and ended up being friends. But this was something he could have told her, and didn't. She's feeling betrayed all over again."

Rafe nodded. "Hard to blame her for that."

It was. Even though I could understand why Dad hadn't. He must have known she wasn't likely to take it well, and had thought it safer to keep the information to himself. Although I have to say it was something of a miracle that after thirty-three years, someone else hadn't told her. Sweetwater is a small town, and in small towns, people always know all your secrets. Someone around here—someone other than Aunt Regina—had to know the truth, as well.

"I'm sure she'll get over it," I said. "There isn't much else she can do, after all. I mean, it is what it is. A fact. And it's not like she can divorce him, posthumously."

Rafe shook his head. "Not like she'd want to, either, I guess, once she thinks about it. Just as long as she doesn't take it out on you."

"I don't think she will. She didn't last night. Just gave me this sort of sad, betrayed look before she locked herself in her room for the night. It wasn't even nine o'clock!"

"At least she didn't start drinking again."

Oh, God. For a while after learning about Darcy and my dad, Mother had drowned her sorrows in a bit too much alcohol. Not that she became a raging drunk or anything. But there were mimosas for breakfast and a dollop of brandy in the afternoon tea when there usually isn't. Hopefully she wouldn't start that again.

I threw off the blankets. "Maybe we should go downstairs and make sure she hasn't fired up the blender."

"We'd hear it," Rafe said, although he rolled out of bed, too, his movements lazy. When he stopped beside the bed to stretch, my tongue got stuck to the roof of my mouth. He grinned. "You wanna share the shower with me?"

"I don't think there'd be room for both of us." Not with the way I was bulging these days. And frankly, if we were both wet and naked and in the shower together, I'd probably be tempted to jump him again, and this much sexual activity might not be good for the baby. The doctor had said we could continue normal activities as long as I was comfortable. Even though I'd had a couple of miscarriages prior to this pregnancy, I'd had a perfectly normal pregnancy this time, and sex was allowed. But I wasn't sure three times within a couple of hours constituted 'normal,' and the last thing I wanted, was to put the baby at risk. Losing the previous one at just a couple of months had been devastating. I was into my third trimester now, but it was still too early for the baby to be OK outside my body, and I didn't think I could handle it if anything happened to him or her.

Rafe studied me. "You sure?"

I nodded. "I'll wait. You go ahead."

He went ahead, but before he did, he came around the bed and bent to kiss me. I resisted the temptation to pull him back down, and instead let him straighten. "Everything all right?"

I nodded.

"No stomach cramps? Nothing like that?"

I assured him I had nothing like that. "As far as I can tell, everything's fine. And I want to keep it that way."

"You and me both." He gave my stomach a stroke before he padded across the floor toward the door.

"Check the hallway," I told his back, "before you walk out. My mother might be out there."

"God forbid." He opened the door a crack and peered out. The coast must have been clear because he slipped through. A few seconds later, I heard the bathroom door close and the shower come on.

He came back a couple minutes later, with a towel hanging low on his hips and water droplets still clinging to his skin. "All yours."

I rolled to my feet as he headed for the chair where his overnight bag sat. "Why don't you give me the towel. I'll take it back to the bathroom and hang it up."

He grinned at me over his shoulder. "You just want to see me naked."

Damn—darn—straight. "Who wouldn't?"

He chuckled, but whipped off the towel and tossed it to me. He even added a playful little swivel of his hips, stripper style, and then winked. "You better go. Or we'll never get outta here."

He was right about that. I took the towel and left.

By the time I had finished my own ablutions and got back to the bedroom, it was empty. He hadn't stuck his head into the bathroom to tell me he was leaving, so I had to assume he was somewhere in the house still. It was a slightly disconcerting idea. While my mother and my husband get along these days, I couldn't remember them ever spending any time together, just the two of them. I'd always been there as a buffer.

Although Mother might still be wallowing in bed, and in her suffering. Rafe might just be in the kitchen by himself, feeding himself breakfast. All by himself.

That possibility was more reassuring. Nonetheless, I hurried through dressing and drying my hair. It was still slightly damp when I made my way down the stairs.

Mother's bedroom door had been closed. Just in case she was sleeping, I hadn't knocked. When I got down to the foyer, I heard voices, however. My husband's baritone—he usually sounds like he's just rolled out of bed, all husky and a little rough—and my mother's well-modulated tones.

They weren't yelling. That had to be a good thing.

They heard me coming, of course, and stopped talking before I reached the door to the kitchen. I don't know whether that was because they were talking about me, or just talking about something they didn't want me to hear. Or maybe they were just being polite. Both of them were looking at the door when I appeared.

"Good morning, Savannah," Mother said graciously. "Coffee?"

Rafe didn't say anything, just saluted me with his cup. The corner of his mouth was turned up.

"No," I said. "Thank you. It isn't good for the baby."

Mother nodded. "There's milk and orange juice in the refrigerator."

Looked like I was on my own. I headed that way and fixed myself a glass of milk. "What's going on?"

Mother didn't answer.

"Just talking," Rafe said.

Right. Message received. None of my business.

I put the glass down and leaned on the counter, tucking the stomach under the edge. "I forgot to ask. Did you learn anything interesting last night? Other than the fact that the bartender at Dusty's knows how to hold a grudge?"

He made a face. "Not much. Got it confirmed that Robbie Skinner liked to throw his fists around. More so with people who couldn't fight back—"

"Like his wife."

"—than with other guys, but he'd get drunk once in a while and pick a fight with somebody. Nobody could think of a reason why anybody'd wanna kill him over that, though, since that kinda thing's pretty common when a bunch of guys get drunk."

I nodded. "What about the dog fighting? Did that come up at all?"

"We got confirmation on that, too, pretty much. The Skinners were running dog fights."

Mother wrinkled her nose. We never had a dog growing up—or any other kind of pet—but she obviously doesn't hold with hurting them. Nobody decent would. And while my mother might be concerned with appearances, and with keeping the furniture looking nice, she's a decent person.

"You said there's a lot of money in dog fighting," I said, "didn't you? Maybe somebody else is running dog fights, too, and the Skinners were honing in on the action and siphoning off their income?"

"It's possible. And something we'll have to look into."

"So you'll have to go to dog fights?"

He made a face. "If we can find one to go to. If somebody killed all the Skinners over dog fighting, I'd think they'd have enough sense not to put on any dog fights while the investigation's going on."

He had a point. "I don't want to come with you," I said.

"I wouldn't want you to, darlin'. I don't wanna go, either, but it's part of the job. But there might not be anybody else doing dog fights."

"Then who killed them?"

"We don't know that they were killed over dogs," Rafe reminded me. "But if they were, there's the other side. The folks who are against dog fighting and want the people who abuse animals dead."

It's hard to drum up any sympathy for people who abuse animals. But that doesn't mean I think it's OK to kill them. Even if maybe it would feel good. At least in theory.

"The woman from Animal Control might be able to help you there. She knew about the dog fighting. And she'd probably know other people who like animals."

"Believe me," Rafe said, "I'm gonna be talking to her."

Something in his voice was a little off, and I looked at him, just as the telephone rang. Mother murmured an excuse and took herself off to answer it. I turned back to Rafe. "Surely you don't suspect that she had anything to do with it?"

He shrugged. "No more'n anybody else. But I can't write her off, either."

"She didn't seem crazy. And somebody would have to be crazy to kill seven people over dogs, wouldn't they?"

"Yes," Mother told the phone, with a glance over her shoulder in our direction. "He's right here. Do you...?"

The person on the other end of the line must have declined to talk to Rafe, because Mother didn't wave for him. He was already on his way across the floor to her, anyway. And she must not have realized it, because she jumped when he took the phone out of her hand and lifted it. He put a hand on her back to steady her, and for a second she stiffened before she relaxed again.

"Who's this?" Rafe asked the phone.

I have no idea what the phone said. Probably nothing, because it was only a second later that he hung it back on the wall. (Yes, it's the kind of old-fashioned kitchen phone that hangs on the wall next to the door. We've had it since I was a little girl. The kitchen's been updated since then, but around the phone. The phone stayed.)

"Who was it?" I asked.

He shook his head. "He hung up when he heard my voice. Or she."

"He," Mother said, and stepped away from him. She headed back toward her cup of coffee. After a beat, Rafe did the same. "I don't know who it was," Mother continued. "He didn't introduce himself, and I didn't recognize the voice."

No reason why she would. She and my husband don't exactly travel in the same circles.

"What did he want?" Rafe picked up his coffee mug and took a sip. I had another of my milk.

"To give you a message," Mother said. "'Look behind Robbie's trailer.'"

"That's the message?"

Mother nodded.

"Look for what?" I wanted to know.

Mother shook her head. "He didn't say. Just to look behind Robbie's trailer. Robbie Skinner, I assume."

It was a safe assumption.

"Wasn't there crime scene crews crawling all over the crime scenes yesterday?" I asked Rafe.

He nodded. "I don't think they found much. Wasn't much to find, what with the weather. Anything that was there woulda washed away."

"But if something was there, they would have found it."

"You'd think."

"But you're going over there anyway."

"I figure I better, don't you?" He drained the coffee cup. "Maybe there ain't nothing there. Maybe they missed something yesterday. Or maybe somebody wants to talk to me, and this is a way to get me out there."

"If he wanted to talk to you," I wanted to know, "why didn't he talk to you on the phone?"

"Maybe he was afraid I'd recognize his voice."

"In that case, I doubt he'll be there waiting for you, since you'd certainly recognize his face." Unless he never got the chance to tell anyone who he was meeting. Because someone was trying to lure him there to kill him.

"I'm coming with you," I said.

"Like hell you are. I'm gonna call the sheriff for some backup. Just in case."

At least he seemed to be aware of the possibilities, too. Although it didn't actually make me feel a lot better. "It might take them a while to get there. It's better if I come along."

He shook his head. "You can't come along, darlin'. This is a criminal investigation. And you've heard that saying about the murderer returning to the scene of the crime?"

"All the more reason for me to go with you," I said. "Just let me get my coat."

He looked mutinous. I added, "And if you try to leave without me, I'll borrow Mother's car and follow you. I remember where Robbie lives." Or lived.

He sighed. "Make it quick."

I scurried out of the kitchen to visit the bathroom and find my coat. Behind me, I heard Rafe begin to ask my mother questions about the man who had called.

ELEVEN

When I came back downstairs, he was waiting in the foyer, obviously more than ready to go.

"I brought your coat." I handed him the gray hoodie he'd worn yesterday, and watched him shrug into it. "Are you ready?"

He nodded. "You sure you wanna do this? It might not be a lot of fun."

If someone tried to kill him, it certainly wouldn't be. But I wasn't looking for fun. I nodded and reached for my coat.

He took it and held it for me even as he kept arguing. "It could be nothing. We could drive all the way out there, and there's nothing to see. Nobody and nothing."

"I'd rather do nothing with you than sit here and wait," I told him.

He sighed. "Fine. C'mon."

He turned to the door, only to stop again when Mother came hurrying down the hallway from the kitchen, her heels clicking on the wood. "Wait!"

She handed us each an English muffin with jam. They must have been hiding in a drawer, and she had taken the time to make sure we wouldn't leave the house without something to eat. My stomach thanked her. So did I. "I'm starving."

"Be careful," Mother said and took a step back. She watched while Rafe ushered me out the door—without touching me, since his hands were full of muffin—and down the stairs. I heard the front door lock click when we reached the gravel.

"That was nice of her," I said when we were properly buckled into the car and on our way down the driveway a minute later. "My mother made us breakfast. With her own hands."

Rafe glanced at me. He was driving with one hand, with half an English muffin in the other, and the second half balanced on his thigh. It was liberally spread with strawberry jam, as was mine, so I hoped it wouldn't slide if he had to stop quickly, and wouldn't accidentally smear red all over his zipper. "Didn't your mama make breakfast for you when you were growing up?"

"Did yours?" Somehow I wouldn't have expected that.

His lips curved. "She liked Lucky Charms. I did, too. We had cereal together."

That was actually kind of sweet. And maybe I should have guessed it. LaDonna had only been fifteen when he was born. Just a kid herself, really, if one who had to grow up fast. But it wasn't surprising that she'd liked sugary cereal. I had, too, at that age. Not that Mother would allow it in the house.

"I rarely ate a lot for breakfast."

"Dieting?" Rafe guessed and bit into the muffin.

"Something like that." Mother's idea of breakfast had been a cup of tea—no milk—and a piece of dry toast. Is it any wonder I grew up with body issues? "So what did the two of you talk about before I got downstairs?"

"None of your business," Rafe told me, and stuffed the rest of the first half of English muffin into his mouth.

I nibbled on the edge of mine while I waited for him to chew and swallow. When he had, he didn't say anything else, though, just rescued the second half of muffin from his thigh and bit into that, as well. "You looked comfortable."

"Your mama's all right," Rafe said. "It took her a while to get used to me, but we're all right now."

Good to know. "Did she mention Caroline and William and

that whole mess?"

He licked a smear of strawberry off his thumb. "Some part of 'none of your business' you didn't understand?"

No. But— "She's my mother. And she was very upset last night. I just want to make sure she's all right."

"She's working her way through it," Rafe said, with both hands on the wheel now. We were just passing Beulah's Meat'n Three, zooming toward Columbia. "If it helps, she's more upset that nobody told her than because her kids are some unknown percent black."

"That's good." I'd been concerned. My mother is old-time Southern, and there's some lingering racial prejudice there. It was nice to hear that her priorities were in order, even if she'd come to them late. "Was she able to tell you anything else about the person who called?"

He shook his head, his expression—or at least his profile— frustrated. "She's pretty sure it was a male. She didn't recognize the voice. She couldn't tell whether he was young or old. She thought he might have been talking through a handkerchief to disguise his voice."

"In my mother's world, men still carry handkerchiefs." While the rest of us had moved on to disposable Kleenex.

Rafe smiled. "More likely he used his T-shirt or a towel, but it does work."

"Does that mean it was someone whose voice she'd recognize if he hadn't disguised it?"

"Mighta been. Or could just be someone who thought he'd have some fun."

Sure. "Did you try to call back?"

He nodded. "No answer."

Big surprise. "You can ask the sheriff to check the phone records, can't you? And find out where the call came from?"

He nodded. "Or do it myself. And if this little trip don't pan out, I might do that. We'll see what happens."

We would. "You have a gun, right? Just in case?"

He smiled. "Yes, darlin'. I have a gun."

"Good," I said, and sat back in the seat to nibble on my muffin.

The weather was a lot nicer today than yesterday. Sometime during the night, the rain had stopped and the clouds had blown through. By the time we got to Robbie's place, the sun was slanting rays of yellow between the trees lining the road.

"Can you see any tire tracks?" I asked Rafe, as he maneuvered the Volvo along the ruts in the dirt road.

He didn't look away from the windshield. "Plenty. Dunno if any of'em are from today."

I nodded. No way to know whether anyone had gotten here before us, then, or whether the tire tracks were all from yesterday.

There was no car parked outside Robbie's trailer, anyway. Not except for Robbie's truck, that had been there yesterday, as well. "Would Sandy inherit that?"

"His next of kin's prob'ly the kid," Rafe said. "Kayla. She ain't old enough to drive, so yeah, I guess Sandy'll keep it safe for her."

It seemed like justice, as long as she didn't mind driving a big truck. It was a much nicer vehicle than the one Sandy had gotten into yesterday, at any rate.

"You don't think... no, that's stupid."

He glanced at me as he turned the car off. "People have killed other people for a lot less than a truck. Specially if there are other considerations."

Like in this case, when Robbie had beaten Sandy and started hitting the girl. That alone might have been reason enough for Sandy to kill him. A new truck was just a bonus.

The trailer door was closed today, with bright yellow crime scene tape across it, running from the door handle to the truck mirror to a stake in the ground beyond the point where Robbie's body had lain.

"Stay here," Rafe said. He opened the car door and slipped out onto the grass, his hand reaching for the gun at his back.

I opened my own door. "If you're going, I'm going."

He put his finger across his lips to tell me to keep my voice down. "You'd be safer in the car."

"Not necessarily," I told him. "If someone's coming after you, they might be here already. Somewhere behind the trailer. But they might not. And if you go behind the trailer and leave me here, they could show up and shoot me."

He didn't disagree with me on that. "Can you at least stay in the car while I make sure nobody's inside the trailer?"

I told him I could do that.

"Lock the door." He waited for me to get back inside the car and close—and lock—the door before he headed for the truck, gun in his hand but down at his side.

The truck cab must have been empty, because he moved on to the door of the trailer. The crime scene tape drooped when he pulled the screen door out. It flapped in the breeze. While the weather was prettier today, the temperature had dropped at least ten degrees, and it was windy.

He disappeared inside, gun up and ready. I looked around, but nobody jumped out from concealment to take him on now that he was cornered.

He came back out a few seconds later. I held my breath for the moment he stood framed in the doorway—it would be such a perfect moment to shoot him—but nothing happened. He hopped down and came over to the car. "It's empty. Looks just like yesterday."

I nodded. "I guess we go behind the trailer, then, and see what—or who—is back there."

He sighed. "Stay behind me. And if I tell you to run, you run."

I told him I would, although between you and me, I wasn't sure how fast I'd be able to move, carrying all this extra weight on my stomach.

But I fell in behind him, and stayed a step behind—and slightly off to the side—as we made our way past the truck and around the corner of the trailer.

It looked about as you'd expect. Patchy grass and mud, and about twenty feet away, the tree line. The trailer itself sat up on a few courses of bricks. One at each corner, a few in the middle. There was an old, rusty HVAC condenser halfway down, sitting on a little platform of bricks. The various tubes and pipes went through the wall of the trailer and inside. Other than that, there was nothing to see back here. I might have expected some trash, maybe, but it was possible the crime scene techs had picked anything like that up.

"Nobody," I said.

Rafe shook his head, looking around.

"There's a path." I pointed.

There was an opening behind the trailer into the brush and trees. Not a wide path, just enough for a single person to walk. But it was worn, with no grass growing there, so it looked like it might have been used a lot.

"Mighta been where Robbie walked his dog."

Might have. If he'd bothered to walk the dog. "We should take a look," I said. "I mean, it's behind the trailer. We were supposed to look behind the trailer, right?"

"*We* weren't supposed to do anything," Rafe told me. "*I* was supposed to look behind the trailer."

I gestured to the beginning of the path. "Be my guest. I'll be right behind you."

He made a face, but went. I followed.

The path widened a little once we were through the tree line. Not enough for us to walk side by side, but enough that it was obvious that someone—probably Robbie—had kept the path clear. It was easy to see where he had trimmed bushes and small trees to make the path more comfortable to walk. In fact, it was so easy to walk, I wondered why Rafe moved so slowly.

After about three minutes, I got my answer. He stopped, and put out an arm to keep me from passing him. "See that?"

"What?" I peered past him.

"Fishing line."

Fishing line?

I looked closer—maybe it was time for new contacts?—and saw it, too. A thin, clear, practically invisible thread strung across the path roughly at ankle height.

"Don't touch it," Rafe said.

I'd had no intention of touching it. "Why would somebody string fishing line across the path?"

"Could be a couple reasons." He looked around. "Could be hooked up to a bell. To let Robbie know people are coming. Or it could be a booby trap."

"Booby trap?" My mind conjured up visions of a net falling down and then yanking us back up into the trees, followed by the sound of cannibals beating drums.

I looked up. There was no net waiting to fall.

"Gimme a second, and we'll see." He looked around.

"Branch." I pointed.

He picked it up. "You stay here. At least six feet away from the string."

"Where are you going?"

"To the other side." He stepped carefully over the fishing line, giving it as much room as he could. "I have to get to where I can pull the string that way. The way somebody would pull it if they walked into it."

That made sense. Whoever came from the other direction would know about it. Or so it seemed safe to assume.

So I stayed six feet back, up on the path, and watched as Rafe moved as far away from the string as he could, while still being able to reach it with the tippy-top of the branch. He snagged it, and pulled.

For a second, nothing happened. Then there was a whistling sound, and a long branch came whipping through the air. It hit the path a few feet beyond the wire, and a little too close to where Rafe was standing. He must have thought so too, because he jumped back. "Shit!"

No kidding.

"What is it?" I asked from where I was standing.

He waved to me. "You can come this way now. I don't think anything else is gonna happen."

After a second he added, "Not here. But we're gonna have to be careful as we go on."

I moved forward. Meanwhile, he lifted the branch. When I came close enough, I saw the line of nails that had been pounded through it. Five of them, in a straight line, all about three inches long.

"That would have hurt if it had hit you." The nails had dug deep into the ground, soft from yesterday's rain.

Rafe nodded and let it go. "Robbie's got something back here he didn't want anybody to see."

"Dog fighting arena?"

"Could be. There's gotta be a different way to get to it, if so. The people coming to watch wouldn't walk in this way. They'd drive in."

"There were other driveways we passed on the way here," I said. "It might be one of them."

He nodded. "If that's what's back here, I guess we'll find the way out and follow it. C'mon."

He started moving again, even more slowly. This time, I didn't wonder why.

Two minutes later, we came across one more booby trap. Not a whippy branch with nails hammered through it this time. A shallow pit dug in the path, a foot or so deep and maybe two feet across, filled with sharpened sticks standing on end. Six or eight of them, close enough together that if you stepped in, you had no chance of avoiding at least one of them. It wasn't fatal—the branch with the nails wouldn't have been, either—but at the very least you would have impaled your foot, and at worst broken it. I wouldn't want to be out here with a broken foot. Not with Robbie's dog—and Robbie himself—around.

To add insult to injury, it was sheer luck that we even saw it. All the rain yesterday must have washed the grid of thin branches clean of mud so the pit was visible. On a rainy day with bad visibility, or even a sunny one with the grid of branches properly covered with dirt and mud, I'm not sure we would have noticed. Or at least I'm pretty sure I wouldn't have.

"Robbie meant business," I said.

Rafe nodded. "Let's move past."

We went past.

There were no other traps after that. Not on this path. But after another few steps, I could hear a sort of humming sound. There was also a not-so-nice smell wafting our way on the wind. My nose wrinkled, but before I could comment on it, we came out of the trees into a clearing with a building in the middle.

Rafe stopped. I did the same.

The building was twice the size of Robbie's trailer. And it looked home-built, but it wasn't one of the old log structures you see up in the hills, sagging and awful from sitting in the same place for a hundred years with no maintenance. No, these materials looked new. The planks hadn't faded too much yet, but still looked yellow and sort of fresh. The reek was stronger here, and I covered my nose and mouth with my hand. "What is it?"

Rafe shot me a glance. "Can't you smell it?"

"Of course I can. It smells terrible. Was Robbie having skunk fights, too?"

Rafe's lips twitched. "This ain't a dog fighting arena, darlin'."

"What is it, then?"

There was a door in the side wall. He walked toward it. After a second, I scurried after. It was locked by a hefty padlock, and it took him a minute or so to open it, with the tools he keeps in his pocket. I was peering over his shoulder when he pulled the door open. Into a green world of bright lights and plants. Hundreds of plants. Some as small as houseplants, in little pots, and some as big as Christmas trees. All of them with spiky, jagged leaves.

They looked familiar, but it took me a second to place them. "Is that...?"

He nodded.

Pot plants. A lot of them. And I mean *a lot*. "How much would this be worth on the open market?"

"Plenty," Rafe said. "More than enough to kill someone over."

He reached for his phone. I watched the fortune of pot plants growing under the bright lights and breathed through my mouth while he dialed the sheriff.

TWELVE

There was indeed another way out of there. A rutted track led through the trees in the other direction of the one we'd come in, and while we waited for the sheriff to arrive, we headed down that way. It was going to take him thirty or forty-five minutes to get here, after all, and there wasn't anything else to see.

"Do we need to look for booby traps?" I asked Rafe as we trudged along, side by side now, separated by a broad strip of grass that separated the two tire tracks.

He shook his head. "This looks like a private road. They prob'ly drove along it, and they wouldn't want nothing to happen to their trucks. We'll keep an eye out, but I don't think we'll find anything."

We didn't. After about fifteen minutes, though, we ran into another structure, much like the first one. New wood, some modular pieces—to make it easier to put up quickly, I guess— and motion detector lights on the corners.

"Another marijuana grow," Rafe said.

It was a safe bet. But to make sure of it, he went to work on the padlock again, and opened the door into another brightly lit room full of spiky, green plants. The reek flooded out and hit me in the face with the force of a dead fish.

"Gah!" I stumbled back a couple of feet as my stomach turned.

"Sorry." Rafe slammed the door shut again.

"It's all right. It's a strong smell." The morning sickness had followed me into the second trimester, but had left soon after. I'd thought I was finished with it. Now I felt my stomach heave in a way I hadn't felt in a few months.

Rafe's arm came around me. "Deep breaths."

He supported me while my stomach lurched. After a minute the nausea passed, and I was able to breathe without smelling that awful stink again. But it was nice to lean on Rafe, to hear the steady beat of his heart against my ear, so I took my time before I straightened and pushed away. "I'm all right."

He kept his hand on my back for a moment, rubbing circles, before he dropped it. "Ready to walk? Or do you wanna stay here and wait for me?"

"The farther I get from the smell, the better I think it is. Back the way we came, or forward?"

The track continued past the building.

"How long since we called the sheriff?" Rafe asked.

I thought it might have been twenty minutes, at most. "I don't think he'll be here quite yet. It's a bit of a trek from Sweetwater."

"We can probably spare a couple more minutes. This way."

He headed off, not down the track, nor back the way we'd come, but around the building.

"What are we looking for?" I asked, trudging after him.

"That." He pointed.

"Another path."

He nodded. "I'm pretty sure where we are, but we can take five minutes to make sure. C'mon." He headed for the entrance to the path. Just before he got there, he added, with a glance over his shoulder at me, "And this time, we do need to keep an eye out for traps."

Of course we did. But since we'd already found a few, it was easier to spot them this time. We knew what we were looking for. We circumvented another pit full of stakes, another tripwire resulting in a branch with nails whipping through the air and smacking into the ground between us, and—just as we reached the tree line, where the growth was more dense—a good, old-fashioned bear trap. Luckily, Rafe was looking for it. If one of us had stepped on it, the sharp metal teeth would have bit deeply into our ankle.

Rafe pushed the brush aside and peered out. "Thought so."

I peered out past him, at the back of another mobile home, and—some yards away—an old, dented Airstream trailer. Beyond both of them, yellow crime scene tape flapped in the air.

"Art Skinner's place?" It looked familiar, if backwards from what I'd seen yesterday.

Rafe nodded and let the brush go. It closed back up to screen the path from prying eyes. "Cilla and her boyfriend were killed in the Airstream. Art, Linda, and A.J. in the trailer." He turned away from the crime scene. "C'mon. It's time we get back."

It was. I followed him back down the path, hopping over the various booby traps, until we got to Art's part of the marijuana operation. From there, we headed down the track toward Robbie's place.

"If we went that way," Rafe told me, with a thumb over his shoulder in the other direction, "we'd prob'ly end up at Darrell's place. The Skinners must own all the land up here on the hill. I wonder what else is tucked away in the woods up here."

"Maybe nothing. I mean, this is enough, isn't it?"

"It's plenty. Hundreds of pot plants. Some of those plants in there—the big ones—are probably worth a couple grand each, if not more."

"How much pot can a plant produce?"

He shrugged. "I don't know a lot about the drug business. Hector had his fingers in it, but I didn't. But I know it's big money. There could be half a million dollars worth of weed between those two buildings. More if Darrell's got a greenhouse up behind his place."

"You'll have to find out."

He nodded. "Easier to come at it from the front. Drive in and walk the path. And take out any booby traps while we're at it."

"There has to be a way to drive in," I said. "These tracks," the ones we were walking along, "were made by some kind of vehicle."

"It might be up at Darrell's place. We'll check and see. But first we better get back and meet the sheriff."

He held out a hand. I took it and focused on keeping up as we made our way back to Robbie's place.

The sheriff had arrived by the time we had skirted Robbie's marijuana barn and made our way up to the trailer.

"I wanna take the cars up to Darrell's place," Rafe told him. "There's no way to drive in from here or from Art's, but there could be from Darrell's. I think they're all three connected through this road in the back. And the boys had to get all those materials in there somehow, and I don't think they carried'em in by hand."

I shook my head. The sheriff nodded. "Let's go."

Rafe turned to me. "You go on back, darlin'. I'll get a ride with the sheriff."

Fine by me. I'd already seen what the mysterious caller had wanted us to see. And now that I knew that Rafe was safe, that nobody was out here to get him and that he had backup if something happened, I had no more desire to tramp around the woods, on soggy ground with still-wet branches slapping me in the face. Darrell's place would just be more of the same. "Look out for booby traps," I warned them.

Rafe said he would. "See you later, darlin'."

He leaned down to kiss me. The sheriff looked away, politely, but Rafe kept the kiss brief. "Be careful."

"You, too. I'm not going to be the one stumbling around the woods where seven murders took place just a day or two ago."

"Good point." He gave me a nudge. "Get going. And stay outta trouble."

"You, too." I twiddled my fingers at Bob Satterfield. "Bye, Sheriff."

He twiddled back. "Give my love to your mother."

I promised I would. "She could use a shoulder to cry on. I know you're busy with the investigation, but if you could spare thirty minutes sometime today, I think she'd appreciate it."

The sheriff's grizzled brows rose. "What happened?"

"I'll let Rafe tell you about it," I said, with a glance at him. It would give them something to talk about on their walk through the woods. "He and my mother talked this morning. He might be more up to date than I am on how she's feeling."

Rafe nodded. The sheriff looked at him, and looked curious, but didn't ask any questions. "Let's get going," he said instead, and slid back into the sheriff's department SUV. I headed toward the Volvo while Rafe got in on the other side. The two of them waited until I'd made my sixteen point turn and was going in the right direction, and then they followed me down the driveway to the road. Once there, I headed down the hill and they headed up.

It was a much nicer day than yesterday to go driving in the country. The sun was shining, and I didn't have to worry about hydroplaning and slipping off the road.

Like yesterday, I took the turnoff to Damascus instead of going through Columbia. And since I was going that way, I decided I might as well stop by Yvonne's house and ask her about the pot, as well as about the mysterious caller who had drawn our attention to it.

At this point, I had to assume the grow operation was what the mysterious caller had wanted us to find. There sure hadn't been anything else of interest behind Robbie's trailer. Not unless something had been there, and it had blown away in the rain and wind yesterday. Or the crime scene crew had picked it up, but if so, we would have already known about it. Or at least Rafe would.

So it appeared somebody knew the Skinners had been

growing pot. Large quantities of pot. I didn't know much about it, either—less than Rafe—but I do know it's big business. I tended to agree with him that a half million dollars worth of weed made for a dandy reason for murder.

Except... nobody would benefit from this. As Rafe had said earlier, Kayla would probably inherit anything of Robbie's, as his next of kin. Cilla's baby would eventually inherit anything she or her parents had own, I guessed. And who knew who benefitted from Darrell's demise?

But the pot was illegal, so it wasn't like Kayla would get any of that. As soon as the police got involved, the value of the pot dwindled from half a million to nothing. The sheriff or the TBI would confiscate the plants and destroy them.

Maybe the caller had been someone who didn't care about padding their own pockets, but who just didn't want the Skinners to benefit, then.

Although in that case, they could have just called the police about the marijuana earlier. No need to kill the Skinners to stop the drug dealing. All they'd have to do was turn the Skinners in. The evidence was right there. The result would have been the same: the pot would be confiscated and destroyed, and the Skinners wouldn't benefit from it.

So maybe this wasn't as cut and dried—no pun intended—as I'd assumed. I turned down Yvonne's street still mulling it over. The pot had to be connected somehow, or so it seemed, but damned—darned—if I could see how.

Yvonne's decrepit little car was parked in the driveway, so I parked the Volvo behind it and got out. She must have heard the engine, because she opened the door before I made my way up to it, and certainly before I'd had the chance to knock. "Savannah. What are you doing here?"

"I'm on my way back to Sweetwater from the Devil's Backbone," I said, "and thought I'd stop by and see how you are."

She turned a shade paler. "Did something happen? Who else is dead?"

"Nobody that I know of. May I come in?"

While the weather was nicer, it was still chilly to stand out here.

She stepped back. I climbed the couple of steps to the stoop and crossed the threshold.

She shut and locked the door behind me. "You want something to drink? Sweet tea? Coffee?"

I told her that tea would be all right, and watched her walk past me to the little kitchen. "How's Rafe today?" she asked on her way past.

"A few bruises and a split lip. Nothing too bad." I leaned in the kitchen doorway and watched her pull a pitcher out of the fridge and pour tea over ice in two glasses. "He said the bartender at Dusty's hit him."

Yvonne nodded. "We walked in, and the next thing I know they're going at each other." She shook her head. "It was crazy."

"At least it didn't last long."

She shook her head. "He had the guy on the ground in under twenty seconds. One swing, and that was it."

I'm not sure whether the one swing had come from my husband or the guy he'd put on the ground, and I preferred not to know. Changing the subject, I told her, "We got a phone call this morning from someone—a man—who told us—or Rafe—to go look behind Robbie Skinner's trailer. Can you think of anyone you met or talked to yesterday who might have called my mother's house to leave a message for Rafe?"

"Princess," Yvonne said as she handed me my glass and walked past me to curl herself up on the sofa, "everyone knows Rafe married you."

"Surely not everyone." How could that be interesting to the kind of person who spent their time in Dusty's Bar or the Pour

House in Thompson Station?

"Your aunt put it in the newspaper," Yvonne said, "remember?"

Oh. Right. She had.

My Aunt Regina, in addition to being the keeper of family secrets, is also the society reporter for the local newspaper.

I took a seat in the chair on the other side of the coffee table. "Who do you know who reads the society column in the *Sweetwater Reporter*?"

"Word gets around," Yvonne said.

"Well, can you think of anyone who might have been at either of the bars yesterday, who might have known that Rafe would be staying at my mother's house, and who would have known that Robbie had a pot growing industry in his backyard?"

Yvonne didn't say anything for a moment. "Is that what he was doing?"

"I assume that's what we were supposed to find. It was there, and nothing else was."

She didn't answer, and I added, "Did you know they were growing pot?"

"They?"

"After we found Robbie's greenhouse, we followed the track up to Art's place. He had one, too. By then it was time to go back and meet the sheriff, but the track went on up toward Darrell's place, or so Rafe said. I didn't go up that way, so I don't know if he was doing the same thing, but I assume he was." Rafe and the sheriff had certainly assumed so.

Yvonne sighed. "No, I didn't know they were growing pot. But it doesn't surprise me."

"Why is that?"

"Money," Yvonne said. "They were always looking for ways to make money. Didn't really matter whether it was legal. And drugs are big business."

Yes, they are. Big business worth lots of money.

"Do you know anyone else around here who deals in pot?" And who might have reason to want the Skinners out of the game?

"No," Yvonne said. "Why would I know something like that?"

"Sorry. I thought maybe it was common knowledge."

She shook her head. "Billy Scruggs used to deal in some stuff. A lot of it prescription. But he's dead now."

Yes, he was. As of about six months ago. "Any idea who took over his business?"

But Yvonne said she didn't.

"Any idea who would know?"

"Some of the same guys we talked to last night," Yvonne said. "If Rafe wants to go out with me again, just let me know." She grinned.

"I'll be sure to do that." I got to my feet. "Thanks for the tea." I hadn't had much of it, but it was the thought that counted.

She stayed where she was. "Any news on the investigation?"

"Not aside from the pot." I headed for the door, just as somebody knocked on it. "Perfect timing."

I didn't even think to ask whether she wanted me to answer the door, or whether she was expecting someone she maybe didn't want to see. In my defense, she didn't say or do anything to stop me when I took the last couple of steps and pulled the door open. "Good... oh."

Two uniformed police officers stood on the stoop. It took me a second to go from the general impression of 'this can't be good,' to realizing I knew them. "Good morning."

They nodded to me, and Patrick Nolan, at least, looked a bit disconcerted. His partner, a short, Hispanic woman by the name of Lupe Vasquez, a few years younger than me, made a face. "Miss... Mrs..."

"Savannah," I said.

"What are you doing here?"

"I could ask the same of you." She didn't answer—Nolan didn't, either—and I added, "I'm talking to Yvonne. We're friends. And she used to date Darrell Skinner a couple years ago. You've heard of the murders?"

They both nodded. "That's why we're here," Nolan said, and Lupe Vasquez glanced at him, a little wrinkle between her brows.

"The sheriff says your chief of police has been trying to horn in on the investigation."

It might not have been the most polite way to put it. They might feel some loyalty to their boss, after all, and resent my implication.

I added, "What I meant to say, is that he offered his assistance, and that of the Columbia PD."

Lupe Vasquez's lips twitched. "Is that what you meant to say?" She didn't wait for me to confirm or deny, just continued. "It's the biggest case to hit Maury County since the serial murders in May. And the case is outside his jurisdiction. He wants a part of it."

"Like we don't have enough work of our own to do," Nolan added.

I took a step back. "Why don't you come in? I still don't understand what you're doing here. Rafe and the sheriff both know that Yvonne used to date Darrell. They've talked to her about it. Why do you need to?"

"We don't," Nolan said, crossing the threshold and nodding to Yvonne. He didn't seem the least bit threatening, not like he was about to whip out his handcuffs and start reading her her rights, but she looked apprehensive anyway. "Not about that."

"About what, then?" I waited for Lupe Vasquez to pass through the doorway before I closed the door behind them. "What's going on?"

"You'll have to come with us to the station," Nolan told Yvonne.

Her voice was faint, and she kept pleating a fold of her sweater between her fingers, over and over again. "What for? I didn't have anything to do with what happened to Darrell and the others."

"Is this about the pot?"

They both turned to look at me. "Pot?"

"Never mind." If they hadn't heard that the Skinners had been running a large scale pot growing operation up there in the hills, chances were their boss didn't know yet, either. And I didn't want to be responsible for passing the word to him.

Lupe Vasquez gave me a considering look, but her partner turned back to Yvonne. "We'd like you to come into Columbia to the police station and talk to the detective in charge of the Beulah Odom investigation."

"What Beulah Odom investigation?"

This was me again, not Yvonne. She was scared, and perhaps rightfully so. I had no reason to be, so I barreled ahead. "There's no Beulah Odom investigation. The M.E. ruled natural causes. You were there, at the crime scene." I looked at Lupe Vasquez, who had told me as much a couple of months ago. She nodded. "You said it was all tied up, and that there were no signs of foul play. Why does he want to talk to Yvonne about it now? Beulah's dead and buried."

"New evidence has come to light," Nolan said ponderously.

"What new evidence?"

He shook his head. "I can't tell you that."

"You know," I told him, "if you're going to be like that, I'm not sure I'm OK with you dating my sister."

Nolan opened his mouth and closed it again, and flushed, all the way out to his prominent ears. Lupe Vasquez chuckled, and tried to hide it behind a cough, not too successfully.

"I'm just doing my job," Nolan told me. He turned to Yvonne. "You're not under arrest. The detective just wants to ask you a couple of questions."

"If she's not under arrest, why couldn't the detective just get in his car and drive out here?"

But I knew the answer even before I'd finished asking the question. If he'd come here to ask his questions, on Yvonne's home turf, she'd have felt more comfortable. By bringing her to the police station, she'd already be nervous and maybe more prone to let something slip.

"I'm going to call Catherine," I told Yvonne. "My other sister," I added, for Nolan's and Lupe Vasquez's benefit. "She's a lawyer in Sweetwater. She represented Yvonne for the competency hearing. Beulah Odom's competency hearing."

I turned back to Yvonne. "You can go with them." If she didn't, it would look like she had something to hide, when I knew she didn't. "But don't say anything to anyone until Catherine gets there."

Yvonne nodded, and looked a little less scared as she went to get her coat.

THIRTEEN

I got Catherine on her way, and by then, Nolan and Lupe Vasquez had loaded Yvonne into the back of their squad car.

"I'm going to follow you in my car and meet her there," I told them, while Yvonne had a sort of deer-in-the-headlights look in the backseat.

"You won't be allowed in the interro... interview room," Nolan told me. I could tell he was becoming a little irritated by my persistence.

"I'm aware of that. But this way I'll be able to drive Yvonne home after the interro... interview."

Yes, it was deliberate. Nolan scowled. Lupe Vasquez hid a smile, although I could hear it in her voice.

"You're welcome to follow us. We're just going to the police station in Columbia. Do you know where it is?"

I did know where it was. "I'll see you there. Drive carefully."

Nolan grumbled something and opened his door. Lupe Vasquez slid into the passenger side without comment. I fired up the Volvo, and we all rolled backwards down the driveway and onto the street.

It wasn't a long drive. Just over ten minutes, and we were there. Right down the hill from the courthouse, in a big, brick building with arched windows, that housed the Columbia PD.

"You can wait here." Lupe Vasquez pointed to a bench in the lobby, just inside the doors. "When your sister gets here, have her tell the sergeant on duty who she is. I'll tell him what to do with her."

"That sounds a bit ominous."

She smiled, although it didn't reach her eyes. We usually get along pretty well, she and I—we'd first met in the spring, during my high school reunion, and all the murders that went along with it—but I surmised that in this case, her liking for me was warring with her need to do her job.

"I'll just wait here," I said, and took a seat on the bench. Lupe Vasquez nodded, looking relieved. I added, "If you have a minute later, would you come back here? I need to ask you something. Not about this. About something else."

She nodded. "Sure. I'll come back out if I get a chance."

I told her I appreciated it. She followed Yvonne and her partner into the bowels of the building, and I leaned back and waited for my sister to get here.

She had twice as far to drive from Sweetwater, pretty much, as we'd had to go to get here, so I figured there'd be a few minutes yet, before I saw her. I decided I'd better give Rafe a call and let him, and thus the sheriff, know what was going on. It probably didn't have anything to do with anything, but Nolan had mentioned the Skinner murders when I first opened the door, even though the rest of the conversation had been about Beulah.

"Darlin'." I could hear from the cadence of his voice that he was walking.

"Still tramping around in the woods?"

"We found Darrell's greenhouse. It was out back of his trailer, like the other two. Looked the same, with the same number of plants in it. But there was just a path leading there from his place, too. So I'm walking the track to see where it comes out. It's gotta lead somewhere. The sheriff went back to his car and he's gonna meet me wherever I end up."

"Will you know where you end up?"

"I hope so," Rafe said, "or I could be in some trouble. But this track goes somewhere. They drove in on it. I'm gonna get to some kind of road eventually."

So it would seem. I mean, not only didn't I think they had hauled all the lumber and the generators and the estimated three hundred marijuana plants into the woods by hand, but they needed a way to get the pot back out again, too, once it was ready for sale.

"What's going on?" Rafe added.

"Oh." Right. I'd had a reason to call. "I'm sitting at the police station in Columbia."

"What the hell?"

There was anger in his voice, and I was reminded of one of those differences between us that cropped up every so often. If I had told my mother I was sitting at the police station, she would have assumed I was reporting a crime. That someone had hit my car in a parking lot or something, and driven off without leaving a business card. Rafe assumed I'd been arrested.

"It's fine," I assured him. "I'm just sitting in the lobby, waiting for Catherine."

Somehow, that didn't seem to make it any better. "Why?"

I told him why. "So it isn't about me at all," I finished. "It's about Yvonne. I thought you ought to know. It sounds like it's about Beulah's death and not the Skinners, but I don't really understand why. Beulah's case is closed. It was natural causes."

"Maybe they've learned different," Rafe said.

"Sure. But how? She's dead and buried. I don't think they've dug her up. We would have heard, don't you think? It's not the kind of thing that happens every day. And anyway, why would they bother? Nothing's changed."

Other than that the competency hearing yesterday came down in favor of Yvonne, I guess.

"Do you think the Odoms are doing this?" I asked.

"Could be," Rafe told me. "They couldn't get the will overturned, so now they're trying to say that Yvonne killed

Beulah."

"But she wasn't killed!"

"She mighta been," Rafe said. "There are plenty of ways to kill somebody that looks like natural causes. And the lab can't test for all of'em. Usually, they only test for the usual stuff."

I pondered. "That's not encouraging."

"I don't think Yvonne killed nobody," Rafe said.

I didn't, either. But proving it would be more difficult. It usually is.

Through the door, I could see my sister's minivan pull up and the door open. "Catherine's here," I told him. "I have to go. Enjoy your walk in the woods."

"I'd enjoy it more if you were here, keeping me company," Rafe said.

Awww. "I love you."

"Love you, too. Be careful."

He hung up before I could tell him the same. I dropped the phone into my purse and got to my feet to greet Catherine.

It didn't take long to get her up to date—I didn't know much, just that Yvonne was answering questions about Beulah and my speculation as to why—and then she approached the sergeant at the desk and was taken into the back. I returned to the bench and took a seat. After a couple of minutes, I got up again, and wandered over to the desk sergeant. "Excuse me."

The look he gave me, told me that he'd already pegged me as a troublemaker.

"I don't suppose you have anything I can read? A magazine or something?"

He looked at me for a second. Then he stretched sideways to fetch something. He held it up. *Guns and Ammo,* it said, over a picture of a guy in camouflage holding a rifle.

"That's it?"

He nodded.

I sighed. "Thank you." It was better than nothing, I guess.

He kept his face impassive when he handed it across the desk to me, but I'm pretty sure that inside he was smirking.

As it happened, I didn't have much time to read. No sooner had I sat down and started desultorily flipping through the magazine, than the door into the building opened again, and Lupe Vasquez came out.

I closed the magazine. Lupe Vasquez looked at it, and her brows rose.

"It was all he had," I said.

She shook her head and sat down beside me. "Your sister got here."

I nodded. "I saw her. For a second. I don't suppose you'd be willing to tell me what's going on?"

"They don't tell me what's going on," Lupe Vasquez said.

Figures. "The case was closed, though. Why is it suddenly open again?"

Vasquez shrugged. "Someone must have suggested to Jarvis it'd be a good idea to take another look."

Jarvis was the detective in charge, I assumed. "Who would do that? And why?"

"He might have gotten a tip," Lupe Vasquez said. "That happens sometimes. People will call in with a new piece of information, and a case will get reopened."

"But this wasn't even a murder! It was an old lady with a weak heart who died from natural causes. You said so. The sheriff said so. The M.E. said so."

"I don't know," Lupe Vasquez said. "It looked cut and dried to me. I don't know why Jarvis is looking into it again. But he is. Some kind of connection with the Skinner murders?"

If there was a connection, I hadn't noticed. And Rafe hadn't mentioned it, either.

"I'm sorry I can't help you." She made to stand up, and I yanked her back down.

"Wait a minute. That wasn't what I was going to ask. If I

wanted to buy some pot around here, where would I go?"

She looked at me, brows slowly creeping up her forehead. "You're asking a cop where to go buy weed? And when you're pregnant? I could arrest you for child endangerment."

Sheesh. "I don't actually want to buy any. I just want to know who runs the pot industry around here."

Lupe Vasquez hesitated. She glanced around, made sure the sergeant at the desk wasn't paying any attention to us, and lowered her voice. "Does this have something to do with the other case?"

I probably wasn't speaking out of turn by admitting that. Chances were Sheriff Satterfield would notify the Columbia chief of police soon, if he hadn't already, about the greenhouses. It wasn't the kind of thing he'd keep to himself, especially since the city of Columbia probably served as the Skinners' biggest sales market. At least locally.

I lowered my own voice. "Your chief of police may not know yet. But this morning, we discovered that the Skinners were growing marijuana. A lot of it."

Lupe Vasquez's eyebrows rose, but she didn't speak.

"Someone called my mother's house this morning, and told Rafe to look behind Robbie Skinner's house. We went into the woods and found a big building full of marijuana plants. And then we found another building behind Art's place, and another behind Darrell's."

Lupe Vasquez nodded.

"There's enough pot there to make a very fine motive for murder. Especially if the Skinners were honing in on someone else's business. And that someone else didn't like seeing their own profits dwindle."

"I can see that."

"So I'd like to know who the big players are, in pot distribution in this area. And I'd also like to know who might have wanted to make sure that the police found the pot.

Someone who knew that Rafe was here, and that we're married and that he's likely to be staying with my mother."

"I can't help you with that," Lupe Vasquez said. "For what it's worth, I had no idea who either of you were until six months ago."

I nodded. "You're a few years younger than we are. And not from Sweetwater. But Rafe and I both went to high school in Columbia, so we know people here. And they know us."

She didn't respond, so I went on, talking to myself as much as to her, working it out in my head. "It had to be someone he met last night—he went bar hopping, trying to find out what people were saying as far as the Skinners were concerned. Someone must have recognized him and realized he was investigating. That means it's someone who knew he works for the TBI, because I'm sure he didn't flash his badge around. A lot of people are leery around badges."

Lupe Vasquez nodded. She'd know that, too.

"Although he did once. At Dusty's. So it might have been someone there. In any case, whoever called knew enough about Rafe to figure he'd be able to get in touch with him through my mother, and enough about the Skinners to know that they were growing pot on a large scale. And he had some sort of incentive for wanting that fact known."

"I can't help you there," Lupe Vasquez said. "I have no idea who'd fit that criteria. It wasn't about getting the Skinners put in jail, obviously, since they're already dead."

I shook my head. "It can't have been. And it couldn't be about making sure the pot got off the streets either, since—with the Skinners dead—who's left to deal with it?"

We sat in silence a moment.

"They might have had a partner," Lupe Vasquez suggested. "And whoever called your husband wanted to make sure the police found the plants before the partner could move them."

Possible. Although moving three hundred marijuana plants,

some of them close to ten feet tall, would be a big undertaking.

Doing it in close proximity to three crime scenes would be crazy.

On the other hand, the prospect of losing close to a million dollars would make a lot of people do crazy things. And if the partner just lay low, there was always the chance that the police wouldn't notice the grow sites. They hadn't until the mysterious caller had drawn Rafe's attention to them.

"Another possibility," Lupe Vasquez said, "is that the pot was the reason for the murder. They were killed because they were messing in someone's business. Your caller knew that, and wanted to make sure the police knew, as well."

I nodded. Then the pot wasn't the reason for the call, or only peripherally. The real point had been to give the police a clue as to the motive for the murders. The Skinners had been involved in the pot industry, and that's why they'd been killed. "So we're back to the same question. Who runs the drug business in Columbia? I'm sure the sheriff has some idea as far as the rest of the county goes, but in this area, you'd know better. You're a patrol officer. You see things. Who would I talk to if I wanted to buy pot?"

"If you think I'm going to tell you that," Lupe Vasquez told me, "you're nuts. I'm not going to be responsible for a civilian going head to head with someone who deals drugs for a living, trying to get him to tell you who killed the Skinners. No way."

"But I need to know!"

"No," Lupe Vasquez said. "You don't. Your husband does."

"If this is an excuse to talk to my husband..."

She rolled her eyes. Big, expressive, brown eyes. "I'm not interested in your husband. He looks good, sure, but he's married. And anyway, he isn't my type."

Fine. "How about you tell me, and I tell Rafe? And I promise not to go near the guy myself. Whoever he is."

She snorted. "Like I'd take your word for that. I know you

have a habit of sticking your nose into everything. It's just a couple of months ago that I came this close—" She held up a hand, thumb and forefinger an eighth of an inch apart, "—to arresting you and your brother and sister for burglary."

"They were medical files!" Thirty-five year old medical files. "Darcy had to find her birthmother!"

"Still burglary," Lupe Vasquez said. "Here's what you need to do. Call your husband. Have him call Chief Carter and ask for two uniforms to help out with the case. Tell him to mention, sort of off-hand, that he was involved in the serial murder case back in May, and that he'd like the same two officers he met then, since he's already familiar with them. See if the chief will agree to assign me and Nolan to the Skinner case. There's a good chance he will. The sheriff sort of brushed him off, since it's out of our jurisdiction, and if the chief can get someone assigned, so he can keep his hand in, I think he'll grab it."

That sounded like a plan. A good one.

"I'll call right now." I reached for my phone.

"At least wait until I'm back inside," Lupe Vasquez said, getting to her feet. "And maybe step outside while you talk. Just in case."

In case the walls had ears. Or in case the sergeant on duty at the desk decided to share the conversation with his boss.

"How long do you think they'll be in there?" Yvonne and Catherine and Detective Jarvis.

"Probably a bit longer," Lupe Vasquez said.

"He won't arrest her, will he?"

"What for?" Lupe Vasquez headed for the door to the interior of the building. "If it wasn't murder," she added over her shoulder, "there's nothing to arrest anyone for."

She ducked through the door. I put *Guns and Ammo* on the bench and headed for the door to the outside to make my call.

Rafe was still walking. I guess it hadn't been that long since I spoke to him, really. It felt like a lot had happened, but it had really only been twenty minutes or so.

"You're walking a long way," I said.

"It's been a couple miles, I guess. Good thing I'm wearing comfortable shoes."

"Any idea how much farther you have to go?"

But no. Of course not. "This is all Skinner land, I'm betting. Private. I tried to look on the phone, but I'm just a blue dot moving through a big area of white. The track I'm walking on isn't on there. There's a road looks like about three miles away, but I'm hoping I'll get to something before I have to walk all the way there."

I hoped so, too.

"So what can I do for you?"

I told him about Lupe Vasquez. "She wouldn't tell me anything. But she said if you can get the Columbia chief of police to agree to assign her to you, she'll help you out."

"You think she knows anything?"

"I got the impression that she might. Or at least that she thinks she does. You remember her, don't you? From back in May?"

Rafe said he did. "Fine. I'll tell the sheriff later."

"Did you let him know that the Columbia PD has pulled Yvonne in for questioning?"

"Not yet."

"Why not?" I had wanted him to tell the sheriff right away. Just as I wanted him to share this news right away.

"I'm out here in the middle of nowhere," Rafe said. "I don't know how long before my phone runs outta power. There ain't nowhere I can charge it until I get back to the house. The sheriff might not be carrying a charger in his car."

True.

"I wanna make sure I don't run outta juice. I'll tell him when I call to let him know I'm outta the woods. If I still can."

And every second I kept talking to him was leaching more power from his phone.

"I love you," I said. "I won't call again. Be careful out there. And call me when you get back to civilization."

I didn't even give him time to respond, just shut the phone down with a snap. And headed back inside the police station to wait for Yvonne and Catherine to come out.

FOURTEEN

By the time that happened, my stomach was howling and I was feeling faint. Catherine took pity on me and suggested lunch. We ended up in the same little restaurant as yesterday, eating the same salad. Yvonne looked a little the worse for wear, and my sister was snapping her teeth on bites of lettuce, leading me to deduce she was upset.

"So tell me what happened."

Yvonne glanced at Catherine. Catherine masticated furiously, her eyes angry. Yvonne turned back to me. "They're trying to say that I killed Beulah."

"But that's crazy. Beulah wasn't killed. It was determined to be a natural death. And who are 'they?'"

"Detective Jarvis," Catherine said, in the same tone she might have used to say Detective Fathead or Detective Dipstick. "But I'm pretty sure I sensed the presence of the Odoms in the background."

"The Odoms told Detective Jarvis they thought Yvonne killed Beulah? Why didn't he tell them to go pound sand? She wasn't murdered."

"They have to investigate," Catherine said, sounding a little bit calmer now. Maybe talking about it helped. "It's new information. Or could be. There's always a chance the natural death determination was wrong. It happens."

"Sure. People miss things, whatever. But there's usually some reason to suspect foul play, even if there's no evidence of it.

Like when LaDonna Collier died."

Rafe's mother. She'd died of an overdose a year and a half ago.

I added, "The sheriff was absolutely convinced Rafe had something to do with it, remember? Even though there was no evidence whatsoever that she didn't just give herself the drugs."

Catherine nodded. "But that time he was actually right. Someone did kill her."

"But there was no evidence. Not against Rafe, and not against anyone else."

"So maybe he just had a gut feeling," Catherine said.

Maybe so. "In any case, he didn't have one this time. I asked him about it at least a month ago, probably more, and he said he'd been there at the crime scene and it looked normal. He discouraged me from wondering whether it was murder, because there was no evidence that it was."

"Why did you wonder whether it was murder?" Yvonne wanted to know, finally getting a word in edgewise.

I turned to her. "No real reason. I'm just suspicious. I asked both him and Lupe Vasquez, the girl cop who drove you here, and they both said it looked normal. No signs that anyone else had been there, no evidence of foul play."

"Well, they must have found some," Catherine said. "Either that, or they're grasping at straws. That would be the Odoms, I guess. They thought they could get the will overturned, and when that didn't work, they came up with this."

Yvonne and I both nodded. That was the most logical explanation.

"Hopefully it'll just die a natural death. If there's nothing to it, I'm sure it will."

I wasn't, but I didn't contradict her. It would only serve to make Yvonne more nervous and upset. But between you and me, I wasn't sure the Odoms were finished. Even if this turned out to be nothing, I had the feeling they'd come up with something else. They seemed bound and determined to get their hands on that restaurant.

"Did the detective say anything else?"

"He was asking me about Darrell," Yvonne said. "About our 'relationship.'"

Her tone made air quotes around the word.

"Why would he care about that? It doesn't have anything to do with Beulah."

Was it possible that this whole thing was just an excuse for Detective Jarvis—and I guess in turn his boss—to fish for information about the murders that they thought Sheriff Satterfield hadn't shared with them?

It seemed like a roundabout way of gathering intel. It also made it seem like they—or the chief, at least—was inordinately interested in the Skinner murders. And maybe a bit paranoid in his fear that people were keeping things from him.

Or maybe I was just imagining the whole thing. I forked up a bit of lettuce and ferried it to my mouth.

"I think," Yvonne said, in response to my question, "he thought I might have talked Darrell into killing Beulah, and then, the day before the hearing, I got worried that he might rat me out, so I killed him."

"That's crazy. And anyway, what about the other Skinners?"

"He probably thinks I killed them, too," Yvonne said. She was picking at her salad, just pushing lettuce around on her plate. If I'd been in her position, I might have lost my appetite, too.

Or maybe not. I couldn't seem to not eat these days.

"But that doesn't make any sense," Catherine objected. "If you wanted Beulah dead, it would have been much easier for you just to kill Beulah. This way, you had to shoot all seven of the Skinners."

Yvonne shrugged, a bit jerkily. "I didn't want Beulah dead. I loved Beulah. By now, I'm not even sure I want the restaurant anymore."

"Oh, no." Catherine shook her head. "After all this, you're not giving up until you do. You'll get it, and you'll run it, and you'll thumb your nose at the Odoms for the rest of their natural lives. They're not getting away with this."

I nodded. "If you give up now, they'll win. And anyway, if anyone killed Beulah, it was probably them. They seem crazy determined to get their hands on the place. Just won't accept the fact that they won't."

"Nobody killed Beulah," Yvonne said, but she seemed a bit cheered by the thought that the Odoms might have.

I rather liked the idea myself. It made sense. There she was, an older woman with a successful business, health problems, and no other family. It must have seemed a no-brainer. Put something in her medicine to make it look like a natural death, and presto, you owned her restaurant. There was no other family to consider, and who would have guessed that she had made a will giving it away to strangers? They might even have checked her house before they killed her, sometime when she was at the restaurant working her usual ten-hour shift. There was no will in the house, so they'd assumed one didn't exist. Bump her off and get it all.

Except there'd been a will at the restaurant, where they hadn't looked for it, and suddenly they'd committed murder for nothing.

No wonder they were behaving like crazy people.

"That's horrible," Yvonne said when I laid it out. She shuddered. Since she's generously endowed, the shudder resulted in a corresponding jiggle of the assets under her sweater, and a man on the other side of the room stopped chewing for a second and just stared, mouth open and eyes bulging out of his head.

"Maybe, but it makes sense."

"Hypothetically," Catherine warned me. "You have no proof,

and you can't go around accusing people of things like this, no matter how much sense it makes."

"Isn't that what you said the Odoms did to Yvonne?"

It was, but Catherine still stuck to her guns. "You said it yourself. There's no proof that Beulah was murdered. Sure, you can spin any kind of story you want about her death might have happened, but that's all it is. Stories. Until you can prove that Beulah was murdered, you can't accuse people of killing her."

I most certainly could, at least here among friends. "We might just mention it to Detective Jarvis. It makes as much sense as his theory—or the Odoms' theory—that Yvonne did it. More. The whole Darrell angle is insane."

They both agreed with me. However— "I don't think Detective Jarvis will be open to an alternate explanation," Catherine said, "whether it makes sense or not."

"You're saying he's going to pursue this, even though there's no evidence that Beulah was even murdered? He's going to come after Yvonne for a murder nobody committed?"

"I hope not," Catherine said, while Yvonne paled, "but I didn't get the impression he had a very flexible mind, if you understand what I'm getting at."

I understood exactly what she was getting at. One of those people with mental constipation, who got an idea into their heads and weren't willing to relinquish it, even in the face of evidence to the contrary.

"Well, he's going to have to prove it was murder before he can prove anything else. You can't charge and convict people of murder when the M.E. determined natural causes."

"Tell that to O.J. Simpson," Catherine told me.

"What are you talking about? The O.J. Simpson murder wasn't natural causes."

"But he was acquitted. And they threw a civil suit at him anyway, and won. He had to pay twenty-five million in damages."

Yvonne gasped.

I glanced at her, and back at Catherine. "So you're thinking the Odoms will try to file a civil suit? Even though it wasn't determined to be murder?"

"I think we should be prepared for it," Catherine said. "They've already shown they're willing to accuse Beulah of being *non compos mentis* and Yvonne of murder. I wouldn't be surprised if that's their next step. At this point, it looks like they'll do anything they can to get their hands on that business."

"It's mind boggling." A second after the words were out of my mouth, I realized what I'd said, and shot a guilty glance at Yvonne. "I mean, I know it was a popular place. People around here liked it. But it surely wasn't that big a money maker. The prices weren't very high." You could get breakfast for well under ten dollars, and the blue plate special was something like $6.99. "And the Odoms don't look like they're hurting for money. Not the way they're dressed."

"Otis Odom died a couple years ago," Yvonne said. "He was the one making the money."

Catherine nodded. "Maybe they were living above their means. Maybe things were all right for as long as Otis was bringing home the bacon, but they may not have been able to save anything. And now that he's dead, they don't have the income they're used to. Maybe that's why they want the restaurant."

That all made sense. "I really can't see either one of them wanting to run a meat'n three, though. Can you?"

The mental picture of Mrs. Odom sitting behind the cash register inside the door at Beulah's, her hair perfectly done and her nails manicured, was incongruous, to say the least. And her daughter... I tried to imagine the elegantly turned out Ms. Odom in an apron and support hose, with her hair in a ponytail, waiting tables. The brain rebelled.

"Maybe they're planning to hire someone to run it for them,"

Catherine said.

Maybe. "But that would cut down on the profits. And defeat the purpose."

Catherine shook her head. "I doubt we'll ever find out. And I, for one, intend to do anything I can to ensure that they won't get their hands on the place. Now more than ever. It was one thing to question Beulah's competency. She was old, and they didn't know her well. But to accuse Yvonne of murder, when there isn't even any evidence that a murder was committed... I'm not going to stand for that."

"Good for you!" I applauded. "I'll stand with you."

"I might hold you to that." She turned to Yvonne. "How about you?"

"I don't think I can afford you," Yvonne said. "I'm working at the drugstore for minimum wage."

Catherine reached over and patted her hand. "Don't worry about it. When you own Beulah's and I come in to eat, you can give me free pie for life."

Yvonne looked relieved. And since I'd never in my life seen or heard about my sister eating anything at Beulah's, let alone pie, I figured Yvonne was probably safe.

"So is there anything I can do to help you?" I wanted to know. "Any snooping you need done, or anything like that?"

Catherine snorted. "You think I'd risk making your husband angry by sending you out to snoop? No way. And anyway, I don't think there's much of anything that anyone can do right now. We'll just have to see what happens. I'm going to go read some case law about civil cases in situations like this. See if I can do anything to prepare, if indeed they plan to bring a civil suit."

"I could talk to the sheriff," I suggested. "See if he'll check with the M.E. to see if there's any chance at all that Beulah might have been murdered."

"We don't want Beulah to have been murdered," Catherine reminded me. "We want there to be no question at all about whether Yvonne could have killed her."

"Sure. But isn't it better to know for sure?"

Catherine allowed, a little reluctantly, that maybe it was. "Don't spend a lot of time on it, though. If everyone said it was natural causes, it probably was."

I promised I wouldn't do more than make a quick inquiry.

"What about me?" Yvonne wanted to know.

Catherine shook her head. "Don't worry about it. I realize that's probably easier said than done, but we made it through the hearing. And we won. We're going to make it through this, too. And win again."

Whatever 'this' turns out to be.

I thought the words, but I didn't say them. There was no point in fouling up my sister's pretty little speech with dire predictions. Yvonne was already worried enough.

Catherine said she'd drive Yvonne back to Damascus, so I headed back up into the foothills to find my husband and the sheriff, to update them on what had happened. And since Rafe had been concerned about his phone, I didn't call him first. Instead, I called Sheriff Satterfield.

"Good afternoon, Sheriff. It's Savannah."

"Afternoon, darling." From the background sound—a sort of humming—I thought he was either driving, or standing next to one of the generators.

"What's going on? Has my husband made it out of the woods yet?"

"Not quite," the sheriff said, "but he's found a road and gotten his bearings. I'm on my way to pick him up."

"I'm on my way to talk to the two of you." He didn't answer, and I added, "I brought lunch."

Before I left the café in Columbia, I'd had them pack up a couple of chicken wraps for me. I'd thought the offer of food might come in handy—aside from the fact that I had assumed my husband hadn't had a chance to eat—and I turned out to be right.

"Why don't you go on up to Robbie's place," the sheriff said, "since you know the way. Meanwhile, I'll go pick up your husband and meet you there."

That worked for me, and I told him so. We both hung up, and I continued driving. I assume he did, too.

I thought they might beat me there, but Rafe must have ended up farther from the Skinners' properties than I'd thought. When I came up the rutted driveway and into the open area in front of the trailer, there was no police car there. Just Robbie's blue truck and the trailer, just like earlier.

I turned off the engine and looked around. Everything seemed quiet. Nothing moved, other than the bare branches of the trees.

I opened the car door, the bag with the sandwiches in my hand, and got out. The dry branches creaked and sort of snapped when they rubbed together.

But there was another sound, too. Sort of squeaky. A little bit like crying.

I should have gotten into the car and waited. But it sounded pitiful. And I thought someone might be in trouble and I could help. So I made my way carefully around Robbie's truck, toward the back of the trailer. We'd been here earlier, after all. There hadn't been anything scary here then. And Rafe and she sheriff were coming.

I guess I thought it was someone mourning Robbie. That girlfriend we'd surmised he might have. Or maybe Kayla, Robbie's daughter. Rafe's son David had once bicycled all the way from his summer camp on the Cumberland Plateau to Sweetwater to look for his father. He was only a year or so older than Kayla, and it was a very long distance. I wouldn't put it past her to have bicycled from Pulaski to the Devil's Backbone to see her dad's place.

And I didn't want to scare her, so while I picked my way across the still-muddy ground, I called out. "Hello? Is someone there? Do you need help?"

The whining ceased. I turned the corner of the trailer... and stopped when I found myself face to face—or nose to kneecaps—with the gray dog that had been chained under the trailer yesterday.

It wasn't chained now. It was unchained, off the leash, and standing six feet in front of me, with its feet planted and its head lowered.

I think I might have squeaked. I don't think it was a scream, but that was only because my voice got caught in my throat. It wasn't because I didn't want to scream.

Up close, it looked even bigger and scarier than yesterday. And it was big, and plenty scary.

I thought about running, but only for a second. In addition to being big and scary, it was muscular. A bit on the thin side—I could see ribs—but if I ran, I had a feeling it would chase me. And probably catch me. And then eat me.

The dogs nose twitched. I remembered the bag in my hand.

I reached in and closed my fingers around a chicken wrap. "Here, doggie." My voice shook as I pulled the wrapped sandwich out of the bag. "Are you hungry?"

I thought about just throwing it the package, and then taking off while it ripped at the paper. But it's tail twitched, in a sort of tentative, aborted wag, and I found myself feeling sorry for it. Still scared practically out of my mind, but sorry enough that I took off the outer paper. My hands shook so much I almost dropped the sandwich on the ground.

The dog kept its eyes on it, but it didn't—as I'd been afraid of—attack me and try to tear the sandwich out of my hands. Maybe someone had taught it to wait—and I didn't really want to think too hard about that, since it might have involved hurting the dog.

"Sit," I tried.

It sat. I tossed the first sandwich at its feet. It leapt on it, and devoured it practically whole, in a single gulp. Inner wrapping and all.

"Wow." It looked up at me, expectantly. "Um..."

The second sandwich was still in the bag. And I might as well sacrifice that one, as well, since I didn't have food for both Rafe and the sheriff now. They'd understand that I'd had to use what I had to defend myself.

I pulled the second sandwich out of the bag. My hands were still a little unsteady, but better than earlier. If nothing else, I knew that the dog would sit and wait, and wouldn't attack me.

Unless it would leap on me once it figured out that I was out of food...?

I determined that as soon as I'd given it the second sandwich, I'd make a break for it. I could probably make it over to Robbie's truck, at least, before the dog caught up.

Assuming it would stop and eat the sandwich first. If it left the sandwich behind in pursuit of me, I'd be out of luck.

I took the paper off the second sandwich. Each half was still wrapped in a thinner wrapping paper, and I removed that, too, from one half. "OK. Here's the deal. I'm going to give you this."

The dogs stub of a tail made that twitch again.

"And then I'm going to leave the second half over here and back away. And it would be really nice if you'd just eat the food and let me leave. I'm giving you my husband's sandwich. He's probably not going to be happy about that. And I'm pregnant. I really don't want to be mauled by a dog. You know?"

The dog twitched its tail, eyes on the sandwich in my hand.

"OK, then." I took a deep breath before I tossed half the sandwich in its direction. It snapped it out of the air, before it even landed on the ground.

"Shit. I mean—" Shoot.

"OK." I took another breath. "Stay. OK? Stay where you are.

Wait."

I bent, to the best of my ability, and placed the second half of the sandwich on the ground in front of my feet. And then I took a step back. "Stay."

The dog stayed.

I stepped back again. "Wait."

The dog waited. It was looking at the sandwich, not me. I made it to the corner of the house.

"OK," I told it. "Go ahead."

I ducked around the corner, but not before I'd head the rush of displaced air as the dog moved, and then the snapping of its jaws. Catherine's table manners were absolutely perfect in comparison.

I knew it wouldn't take the dog long to swallow the second half of the second chicken wrap, so I threw the plastic bag on the ground—maybe it would serve as a momentary distraction; maybe it still smelled like food—and then I booked it as fast as I could in the direction of the Volvo.

FIFTEEN

I was halfway there when a car crested the driveway and bumped its way into the parking area.

It slowed me down for a second. I knew the sheriff and Rafe were on their way, but I also hadn't forgotten my earlier fear that someone would be at Robbie's place to harm Rafe. So I slowed down. Just long enough for the dog to round the corner of the trailer and bound past me.

The car did belong to the sheriff, as evidenced by the light bar on the roof. But by then, the dog was between me and the car, it's feet planted and the hairs at the back of its neck standing up. It was barking, those same threatening barks we'd heard yesterday morning.

The car stopped. At an angle. The passenger side door opened and Rafe got out, his movements smooth and, even from this distance, sort of deadly. It didn't surprise me to see him brace his forearms on the hood of the car, his pistol aimed at the dog.

"Wait," I yelled, over the dog's barks. "Don't."

My phone rang. I fished it out of my pocket and looked at it. It was the sheriff. "You need to get out of the way," he told me tersely. "Your husband can't shoot with you that close to the dog."

"Tell him not to. The dog's protecting me."

The sheriff didn't say anything, but I could hear him relay the message to Rafe. He didn't move.

"I swear," I said. "He's standing between me and you. And he just ate both your sandwiches. I think he's trying to make sure I'm safe."

"Not sure I want to take that chance," the sheriff told me. "If something happens to you, your mama'll have my hide."

I could hear Rafe's voice in the background. I didn't bother to ask what he said. I could guess.

"Just let me try to talk to it," I said. "It listened to me earlier."

I waited while the sheriff relayed the message to Rafe. "He says to hurry up," the sheriff told me. "And if you can't, get out of the way so he can have a clear shot."

"I'm not letting him shoot the dog. Not unless he has tranquilizer darts in that gun." I dropped the phone back in my pocket, but without turning it off. I wanted them to be able to hear what was going on.

And I admit it, it took everything I had of courage to step up to the dog. It was about six feet in front of me, feet planted and compact body tensed and ready to go on the attack if it felt the need.

"It's OK," I told it, doing my best to keep my voice calm and even. It wasn't easy. Although I hoped and prayed that it wouldn't, I knew there was a chance the dog might turn and attack me. If it did, I hoped Rafe could shoot it before it mauled me and the baby. And if he had to, I hoped his aim was true enough that he didn't accidentally shoot us instead of the dog. "It's all right. You can stop barking. They're friends. They won't hurt me. Or you."

Hopefully I was right about that.

The dog glanced over its shoulder at me between barks.

I nodded. "I promise. It's all right. Nothing's going to happen. If you'll stop doing this, I'll make sure you get another chicken sandwich." Even if I had to go buy one. "Or a hamburger. Something good."

The dog hesitated before the next bark.

"I swear. All you have to do is stop barking, and then show them that you're not going to hurt me. And they'll put the guns away, and we'll all walk away from this."

The dog wouldn't, of course. I had no idea how it had even made it here, now that I thought about it. The woman from Animal Control had picked it up yesterday. Maybe it had gotten away from her and run back home.

"It'll be all right," I told it, between barks that were becoming less and less frequent now. I don't know whether it was my voice, or the fact that nobody moved, but either way, the dog was calming down. The scruff at the back of its neck was no longer standing at attention. "Why don't you come with me? We'll go get in the car. That way we'll both be safe. And nobody'll shoot at you."

I took a step to the side. The dog glanced at me and followed, making sure to keep itself between me and the police car.

We kept walking. I could feel the muzzle of the pistol following along as we did, until we—or at least the dog—disappeared behind the front of the Volvo. It was a big dog, but not big enough that it showed over the hood of the car.

Out of the corner of my eye, I could see Rafe holstering the pistol and stepping out from behind the sheriff's vehicle. I hoped he had enough sense to stay out of the way until I had—hopefully—managed to tuck the dog away in the backseat of the Volvo.

We stopped at the back door, and I opened it. "Here you go. You'll be safe in here."

The dog looked from me to the open door.

"It's OK. I won't let anything happen to you. I'm not sure why you ran away from Animal Services. Maybe you just wanted to go home. But there's nobody here anymore. So we'll find another home for you."

I waited. Eventually the dog crouched, and then jumped into the backseat. I waited until it was clear of the door. "Go ahead.

Lie down and take a rest. You must have walked a long way to get here. Just take it easy. I'll be right here."

I had no idea how much it understood. Probably very little. But it understood the tone of my voice, I think. When I shut the car door, it didn't object.

I got to the front of the car just as Rafe did. The sheriff had exited the vehicle, but seemed to think it would be best to let the two of us handle this without interference. Maybe he thought we were about to have a married spat.

Rafe arched a brow at me.

"Sorry," I said. "But it seems like a nice dog. I couldn't let you shoot it."

He glanced at the car. The dog was standing up on the backseat, staring a hole through the windshield.

"I think it's just very protective," I added. "It was probably trained to protect Robbie. And maybe Sandy and Kayla when they were here. Do you think they might want it?"

He shook his head. "I wouldn't wanna trust that dog with a little girl. And anyway, that was a small house they lived in. And no fence. They'd have to chain it under a tree in the yard."

I definitely didn't want that. I was still bothered by the way Robbie had kept the dog chained.

"Maybe we'll just have to take it home with us."

His brows rose. Both of them this time. "Have you lost your mind?"

"We have the room. The backyard is fenced. And the house is huge." Three stories. Not quite as big as the Martin Mansion, but plenty for two people and a dog. And soon, a baby. "And we could use a dog. You've said yourself it isn't the greatest neighborhood. How many times have people broken into our house now? Three? Four? All in the last year?"

He had no answer for that.

"In a couple of months, I'll be home with the baby," I said. "Alone. And you'll be at work. Having a protective dog around isn't a bad idea."

He glanced into the car again. The dog was still standing at attention.

He turned back to me. "Does it have to be that one? Couldn't we get a nice, normal dog from a store, or somewhere? The pound, even. Just not that one?"

"I like that one," I said. "And I think it likes me. I may have bought its affection with chicken wraps, but after I fed it, it tried to protect me."

Rafe sighed. "How's your mama gonna react when you bring that monster back to her house?"

I hadn't thought about that. Chances were she wouldn't react well. Then again, she had surprised me before. "Worst case scenario, it can sleep in the carriage house for a couple of nights. Until we go home."

He sighed again. "I'm not opposed to a dog. You're right, a dog might be a good idea. But I want it to be a dog that likes me. I don't wanna have to worry about getting my throat ripped out when I walk through my own door."

"It'll learn to like you." Just like I had. "It'll just have to get to know you first. Next time, you can feed it." And it probably had to realize that Rafe was no threat to me. If the dog had attached itself to me, once it realized that Rafe's whole purpose was to protect me, too, the two of them would be best of friends.

"Give me a hug," I told him.

He arched a brow. "Scuse me?"

"Show the dog that you don't mean to hurt me. Once it sees that, it'll be fine." I hoped.

Rafe didn't look convinced, but he doesn't usually refuse to touch me, either. He reached out and put an arm around me. I leaned in, making sure the dog could see that I was safe and happy. It was watching through the window, but it wasn't barking, or throwing itself at the windshield trying to get out, and I couldn't see where it was showing teeth.

"I love you," I told Rafe.

He sighed into my hair. "I know, darlin'."

"I'm sorry I scared you. I came around the corner, and there it was. I was afraid it was going to attack me, so I threw the sandwich at it. But I think it's sad. When I first heard it, I thought it was crying."

A second later, I added, "I thought someone was crying. I thought it might be Kayla. If I had realized it was the dog, I wouldn't have gone back there."

Rafe nodded. His cheek rubbed against the side of my head.

"I'm glad you didn't shoot it. I'm not sure why, but I kind of like it."

"I'm glad I didn't shoot it, too." He lifted his head to drop a kiss on top of mine, and then he stepped away. I straightened, and we both looked toward the car. The dog was nowhere to be seen.

"I guess it lay down," I said.

Rafe nodded.

"That probably means it won't attack you when you get in the car."

"Let's hope so." He turned toward the sheriff as the latter reached us.

"Everything all right?"

"Everything's fine," Rafe said. "Savannah wants to take the dog home."

The sheriff's eyebrows rose. "Not sure how Margaret's gonna like that, darling."

"If she doesn't like it, it can spend a couple of nights in the carriage house," I told him, just as I'd told Rafe. "But I'm not giving it back to the Animal Control people. It ran away from them. If for some reason we can't keep it ourselves, I'll find another home for it."

Surely I knew someone who could use a guard dog.

Not that I was worried. The dog was already more accepting

of Rafe—if not, it would have continued to stand and stare at him—and by the time we got back to Nashville, it would love him as I did. And, I hoped, vice versa.

"We're gonna have to let'em know we got the dog," Rafe said. "Just in case they're out looking for it."

I thought they probably had better things to do than look for one runaway dog, but— "That's fine. You can ask what's-her-name about the dog fighting. I know the pot would make a good motive for murder, but so would animal abuse. When she was out here to pick up the dog, she certainly looked angry and disgusted enough to murder somebody."

The sheriff stared at me. "You think the woman from Animal Control shot all the Skinners because they used their dogs for fighting?"

"Rafe said there's a lot of money in it. So did the woman from Animal Control. And there are a lot of people who are against it. And it's illegal, right?"

They both agreed it was illegal.

"Then shouldn't you at least investigate it?"

The sheriff sighed. "You go on, son. Take your wife down to Animal Control, tell'em you've rescued Robbie's dog, and ask about the dog fighting. If you get a feeling the folks there are involved in the killings, you know what to do."

Rafe nodded.

"Before we go..."

The both turned back to me. Rafe's brows were lowered.

"I just want to tell the sheriff about Officer Vasquez," I said defensively.

The sheriff threaded his thumbs through his belt loops, Old West style. "What about Officer Vasquez?"

"She works for the Columbia PD. I met her back in May."

The sheriff nodded. "I know Lupe Vasquez. I sent her looking for you and your brother and sister when you decided to burglarize Doc Seaver's house, remember?"

Now that he mentioned it, I did remember. "Well, she and her partner picked up Yvonne McCoy earlier. When we got to the police station, I asked her who might be in control of the drug trade in Columbia. She wouldn't tell me who it was—"

"Prob'ly knew I'd have her hide if she did," Sheriff Satterfield growled.

"—but she did say that if you could finagle getting her attached to the Skinner investigation, she might be able to help you. She thought her boss would probably go for it, since he'd get one of his own people on the inside of things."

The sheriff muttered something. Since he didn't say it out loud, I figured it wasn't intended for my ears. I took it to be a pejorative remark on the chief of police, although I suppose it could have been one on me. An even better reason not to ask him to repeat it.

"She said you should call him and ask if he could spare an officer. Perhaps the nice female one you worked with on the serial case this spring."

The sheriff said he would. "Now get on outta here. I don't need anybody doing my job for me."

"I was just trying to help," I said. "Somebody has to run the drug trade in Columbia. Unless the Skinners did. And if the Skinners didn't, whoever does might be the one who killed them."

"Yes, darling." His voice was very patient. "I can connect the dots, too. I've been holding down this job for a while now. Take your husband and your dog and go. I've got this."

He sounded irritated enough that I figured I'd probably best just do what he wanted. While I trudged toward the passenger seat, Rafe told the sheriff that he'd be in touch after talking to Animal Control. The sheriff nodded, and we got in the car and drove off.

That might make it sound a little too facile, actually. As soon as I opened the passenger door, the dog came alive in the backseat. When it saw that it was me, it settled back down. Until Rafe opened the driver's side door and slid across the seat. The dog growled, a deep-in-its-throat, menacing rumble.

Rafe froze with his excellent posterior two inches above the seat.

"It's OK," I said, as much to him as to the dog. "He won't hurt you. Or me. You can settle back down."

The dog kept growling. Rafe slowly lowered his butt onto the seat. He turned his head to look at the dog. "You know," he told it, "that was my lunch you gobbled up earlier. You could show a little gratitude."

The dog tilted its head and looked at him.

"That's right. You're full of food, and I'm hungry. I'm gonna have to stop somewhere and get something to eat. If you behave, maybe I'll get you something, too. But not if you show teeth at me."

The dog seemed to be considering.

"Why don't you lie down and rest?" I told it. "We'll be driving for a while. You'll probably be safer if you're not standing up."

It looked from me to Rafe and back for a second. Then, when Rafe put the car in gear and we started bumping across the uneven ground, the dog must have realized the sense of my suggestion. It walked in a sort of truncated circle before it settled on the backseat with sound halfway between a groan and a grunt.

"That went well," I told Rafe.

He grunted, too.

"I think this will work out well."

"From your lips to God's ears," Rafe said, but he didn't sound too upset about it.

We drove for a moment in silence. When we'd navigated Robbie's rutted track and wound up on the paved road in the direction of Columbia, I opened my mouth again. "I've been thinking."

He slid me a look. "Uh-oh."

I lifted my hand to smack his arm, but thought better of it. Not just because he was driving, but because the dog might see it as a sign that I was fighting and come to my rescue. "There's no need to be smart," I said instead, primly.

Rafe grinned. "What were you thinking about?"

"The dog. It's OK now. But when we first got to Robbie's place yesterday, it was going crazy."

"Protecting its owner."

Right. "But somehow, someone had gotten past it and into the trailer to shoot Robbie. You said he was shot inside, right?"

Rafe nodded. "Blood spatter. Trail from the bed to the door."

"And then that someone got out again. Without being mauled by the dog. How?"

"Fed it?" Rafe suggested.

It had worked for me. "Someone had to know there was a dog there, then. Because I'm not going to buy that some guy—or woman—with a rifle, intent on killing every Skinner he or she could reach, just happened to be carrying a sandwich or steak along in case they got hungry in the middle of the night."

Rafe nodded. "If the dog was kept busy with food, or was given food that made it sleep, somebody knew the dog was there. It seemed pretty hungry yesterday morning, though. I didn't get the impression it'd had a lot to eat lately."

I hadn't either, now that he mentioned it. He'd had to fill a bowl for it inside the trailer, and it had wolfed the food down. Not as if it were full of steak or chicken wraps.

"So if nobody gave the dog food to keep it busy..."

"Whoever it was prob'ly knew the dog. It was somebody the dog was used to seeing. Somebody the dog wouldn't see as a threat."

"Sandy," I said. "Or Kayla."

"I don't see Kayla killing all the Skinners, do you? And

anyway, how'd she get here in the middle of the night? She'd need her mama's help."

"Maybe she had it. Maybe it was both of them."

He didn't answer, and I added, "Who else?"

"What makes you think I'd know?" Rafe wanted to know, as he maneuvered the car down from the foothills. The dog gave a slight rumble at the impatience in his voice, and he made a concerted effort to sound calm. "The other Skinners. But they're all dead. He mighta had some friends. Or a partner for the pot operation. Some kinda middle man between the growers— Robbie and his brothers—and the distributers."

Maybe so. But— "Why would the partner kill him? Kill all of them? Wouldn't he be out of a job?"

"Unless he was offered a better job," Rafe said. The car picked up speed along the flat road leading to Columbia. "The Skinners and their little operation mighta run afoul a much bigger operation who decided they didn't like the interference. So they turned the middle man and made him take care of the problem."

"In that case, it probably wouldn't have been him who called you this morning."

Rafe shook his head.

"It's confusing," I said. "Too many options. Too many motives."

Rafe disagreed. "Not that many. It don't seem personal. Anybody with hard-on for Robbie, say, ain't gonna take the time and trouble to drive to Darrell's and Art's to kill everybody there, too. If it was Robbie or Darrell who was the target, whoever wanted to kill them woulda killed just Robbie or Darrell. They both lived alone. The killer didn't have to shoot nobody else."

That made sense.

"If the target was Art, they mighta killed Linda, too. And A.J. He was in the same trailer as his parents. But there was no need to go after Cilla and her boyfriend. If they heard the shots and woke up, that'd be a different story, but they didn't. They were still in bed when they were killed. They didn't hear nothing. And Robbie and Darrell were at least a mile away, in opposite directions. If all the killer wanted, was Art dead—or even A.J. or Linda dead—he didn't have to go after Darrell or Robbie."

That made sense, too.

"This was somebody who wanted all the Skinners gone. Either because they thought all the Skinners were guilty, or because Cilla and A.J. were old enough to be able to tell people who the killer was. If all the Skinners were involved, Cilla and A.J. woulda known what it was about."

"So someone who blamed the Skinners for the pot trade. Someone whose kid became a drug addict, maybe."

Rafe nodded.

"Or someone who knew the Skinners were involved in dog fighting, and wanted to stop them."

"Something like that. Or something else we don't know about yet."

"If there was something else, don't you think you would have discovered it by now?"

"We only found the pot this morning," Rafe said. "It's been less than forty-eight hours since the murders. Not much more'n twenty-four since you and I got here. I'd say we're doing all right."

Maybe we were. Or they were. Whatever.

So we—they—were looking for someone who knew the Skinners and blamed them—all of them—for something. Someone who knew where they all lived, and knew about the dogs. Someone the dogs knew. Someone the dogs didn't attack.

Sandy fit the bill on all counts. It was hard to imagine her cold-bloodedly killing Cilla and A.J., though. They weren't much older than Kayla. And she had seemed genuinely distraught when we told her the news that they were dead.

I opened my mouth to say something, but before I could, Rafe's phone rang. In the backseat, the dog's ears pricked up, but it didn't move. Rafe dug in his pocket for his phone. "Yeah, Sheriff?"

I could hear Sheriff Satterfield quacking on the other end of the line.

"Sure thing," Rafe said. "We'll take care of this dog situation, and then she and I'll look into the other thing."

Somehow, I didn't think 'she' in this situation was me.

"I'll let you know how it goes." He dropped the phone back in his pocket.

"Lupe Vasquez?" I guessed.

"She's gonna meet us at Animal Control. Just in case there's something to this crazy theory of yours that the nice Animal Control lady killed all the Skinners so she could rescue their dogs."

"Hey," I told him, "I'm sure people have been killed for less."

He arched a brow, but didn't argue, so I was probably right. In the backseat, the dog made a rumbling sort of sigh and put its massive head down on its huge paws.

"After that," Rafe continued, "you can take Cujo here back to your mama's, and explain to her why the dog's there. Officer Vasquez and I are gonna go looking for drug dealers."

"I'd like to come," I told him.

He grinned. "Tonight, darlin'."

I rolled my eyes. I'd walked right into that one. "Thank you, but that wasn't what I meant, and you know it. I'd like to come with you and Lupe Vasquez to see the drug dealers."

"I'm sure you would. Over my dead body."

"It's not like anything would happen." Not in broad daylight, with a cop and a special agent guarding me.

"You don't know that," Rafe said. "Drug dealers don't always like it when cops show up to ask questions. Sometimes they do stupid stuff. And you don't have bulletproof windows."

I didn't. When I bought this car—when my ex-husband bought it for me just after we got married—I'd had no idea my life would take a turn where bulletproof glass would become a concern. And I wouldn't have believed it if someone had told me.

"Fine," I said. "I'll take the dog home and tackle my mother. You go have fun."

If I'd tried to make him feel guilty, it backfired. "Sure. Talking to violent criminals about whether they mighta killed seven people is always a joy."

"You'll be careful, right?"

He reached out and took my hand. "Always."

Never. But— "Does Lupe Vasquez have bulletproof windows?"

He smiled. "I dunno. But she's got a gun."

"Good." I held on to his hand as we entered the Columbia city limits and wound our way in the direction of Animal Control.

SIXTEEN

The Columbia PD squad car was already waiting beside the entrance to Animal Control when we came into the parking lot. Rafe pulled the Volvo to a stop beside it and cut the engine. Lupe Vasquez opened her door and got out. We did the same. In the backseat, the dog got to its feet, stretched, and sat down to watch the window.

Lupe Vasquez nodded to me. We'd spoken just over an hour ago, after all, so no need for much of a greeting. Instead, she turned to Rafe and held out her hand. "Agent Collier."

He took it. His hand swallowed hers completely, of course. She's a small woman, and he's a big guy. "Officer Vasquez. Thanks for offering to help out."

The corners of his mouth twitched as he said it, and Lupe Vasquez grinned. "Chief Carter would have given his left nut to get into this investigation. Getting me into it was second choice, but better than nothing."

They both stepped back from the handshake. Rafe put his posterior against the side of the Volvo and folded his arms across his chest, and Lupe Vasquez mirrored the movement against her own car. Inside the Volvo, the dog eyed Rafe's butt like it wanted to take a bite. I knew the feeling.

"Savannah says you might have some information about the drug trade in Columbia."

Lupe Vasquez nodded. "She told me about the greenhouses. I have to say, I never heard anything about the Skinners being involved in any drug distribution. Could be they were just growing for someone else."

Rafe nodded. Even in jeans and a gray hoodie, leaning against a Volvo, he didn't manage to look relaxed. His eyes kept scanning the parking lot over Lupe Vasquez's head. "Who'd that be, around here?"

She sighed. "It's the same thing here as most everywhere else. The South Americans have taken over most of the drug trade. You get the occasional good old boy—like Billy Scruggs before he was killed last year—but it's mostly the South Americans."

I don't know whether she noticed the way Rafe tensed. I know I did. "South Americans?"

"And Mexicans. Hispanics."

There was a pause.

"You're Hispanic yourself," I said, "aren't you?"

She turned to me. "Yes, ma'am." And while she didn't say it out loud, her tone very clearly asked me whether I was going to make something of it.

"I worked undercover for ten years," Rafe told her, "trying to take down a South American theft gang. It damn near killed me."

More than once.

Lupe Vasquez nodded. "We heard about it. This isn't Hector Gonzales's organization. It's someone who moved into the vacancy after Hector's organization blew up."

"Any connection?"

She shrugged. "Could be. I doubt they swept up everyone who was involved. Especially on the lower levels."

Wonderful. A blast from the past. Just what we needed. Someone who knew Rafe and knew he'd been responsible for putting Hector in prison.

I opened my mouth. He got in before me. Probably because he knew what I was thinking. "If it's someone who used to work for Hector, chances are he's gonna be pleased as punch he moved up in the world."

I closed my mouth again. Maybe so. "Can I at least come inside with you while we talk about the dog?"

"Sure," Rafe said magnanimously. He gestured me to go in front of him. I nudged Lupe Vasquez in front of me, and we headed up the steps in our little parade.

We headed back out two minutes later. The woman we wanted to talk to, the one who had picked up the dogs from the crime scenes and who had told me about the dog fighting, wasn't in the office. She was out in the car somewhere picking up someone else's dog. A throwaway mention of dog fighting got us a blank stare from the guy behind the front desk. And nobody cared that I'd found Robbie Skinner's dog. I'm not sure anyone knew it was missing. They certainly didn't care that I wanted to keep it. I had expected to have to fill out paperwork, at least, but since the dog wasn't in their possession to begin with—even if it had been, up until a few hours ago—there was nothing at all needed. All I had done, I was informed, was pick up a stray dog I had found in the woods, and I was welcome to keep it.

So that was that. We went back outside, and congregated in the same spot between the two cars.

"Sorry, darlin'," Rafe told me.

I shook my head. "No need to be sorry. I'm getting to keep the dog. And it didn't even cost me anything. I just think the dog fighting angle needs to be looked into. That's all."

"We'll look into it." He put a hand on my shoulder. "And the drug angle. Anything else you want me to look into while I'm at it?"

"That's probably enough. If I think of anything else, I'll look into it myself."

That statement earned me a raised eyebrow, as I should have expected it would. Before he could respond, however, Lupe Vasquez opened her mouth. "That reminds me. After you left the police station, I found out from Detective Jarvis that the Odoms did talk to Chief Carter and suggest that Beulah Odom had been murdered by Yvonne McCoy."

I nodded. No surprise there. I'd been sure of it, especially after talking to Catherine and Yvonne over lunch. "It's going to be hard to prove murder when the M.E. ruled natural causes, isn't it?"

"That's why they're digging her up to try again," Lupe Vasquez said.

My jaw dropped. "What?"

"They're..."

I waved my hand. "Never mind. I heard you. They're exhuming the body?"

She nodded. "Chief Carter talked to a judge—not the same one who ruled on the competency question—and got a court order. Jarvis is headed to the cemetery at four this afternoon."

I glanced at my watch. It was almost that now. "Which cemetery?"

She told me.

"I have to go," I said, making my way around the Volvo as I talked, my voice getting progressively louder the farther away from them I got. "Be careful when you're talking to the drug dealers. Try not to get shot. I hope you discover something helpful."

I opened my car door.

"Darlin'..." Rafe began.

I waved at him. "Later. I have to call Catherine."

I started the car. He removed his posterior from the window. The last thing I saw as I zoomed out of the lot, was him wedging himself into the passenger side of the squad car. Apparently he was letting Lupe Vasquez do the driving. Good for her.

And then I was on my way down the road toward Sweetwater while I fished for my phone. In the backseat, the dog snuffled questioningly.

"Sorry," I told it. "I was going to take you home and introduce you to my mother, but there's something we have to do first."

Although, come to think of it, bringing a dog to an exhumation might not be the best idea. I tried to dislodge the mental image of the dog grabbing some leftover piece of Beulah in its jaws and taking off with it. As a result, I was grimacing when Catherine came on the line.

"Savannah? What's going on?"

"They're digging her up," I said, as I steered the car with one hand and held the phone with the other. "They got a court order to exhume Beulah, and they're digging her up at four."

"Four o'clock?" I imagined Catherine checking her watch. "Where are you?"

I told her I was on my way back to Sweetwater from Columbia. "I can be at the cemetery in twenty minutes." Just in time for the exhumation to start. "I know we can't stop them, but I want them to know that we're watching."

"Them?" Catherine said.

"The Odoms. This is their idea. They're trying to prove that it was murder, and they're trying to pin it on Yvonne. We have to let them know that we're on to them."

Catherine didn't even hesitate. "I'll call Yvonne and meet you there."

She was gone before I could say anything else. I dropped the phone on the seat next to me and floored the gas pedal.

For some reason—perhaps because she owned property in town—Beulah had chosen to be buried at the Oak Street Cemetery in Sweetwater, instead of somewhere in Columbia, where she lived.

The cemetery on Oak is an old place, going back more than a hundred years. Several generations of Martins are buried there, while the generations before them—Caroline's contemporaries and earlier—are in the private cemetery behind the mansion. Most recently, Dix's late wife Sheila was interred at Oak Street, and a few years before that, our father was laid to rest here. It was also where Rafe's mother LaDonna was buried last summer.

I parked the car on the street and glanced into the backseat. The dog looked back at me, sort of hopefully.

"I'm sorry," I told it. "But I don't think this would be a good stop for you."

I mean, I didn't even have a leash for it. Or for that matter a collar. I'd have to find a store that sold those things. I suppose I could wrap a scarf around its neck and tie it, but Hermès would probably roll over in his grave if I did. So would my mother. And she wasn't likely to be excited about the concept of the dog to begin with, Rafe had been right about that. If news reached her that my new dog had slipped out of its Hermès scarf and crashed an exhumation at the Oak Street Cemetery, I'd never live it down.

No, much better to leave the dog in the car. Even though it could probably use a pitstop soon...

Pitstop or no pitstop, I decided I couldn't risk it. The dog would just have to hold it until we were done here. I couldn't imagine it would take all that long. "I'll try to be as quick as I can."

The dog whined, but didn't try to clamber out of the car. I left the window cracked for it, and headed up the hill toward the newer part of the cemetery, the one farther away from the street.

The Martin plot was quite near the street. There have been Martins in Sweetwater for more than hundred years, so we got first dibs when it was decided that everyone had to be buried in the public cemetery in town, instead of in the private one. I gave a nod to the family plot on my way past.

The more recent burials were in the back, up and over the hill. I could hear the sound of heavy equipment as I climbed to the top, and once I got there, I could see a small backhoe digging into the ground.

Catherine was standing halfway between me and the action. Yvonne must not have gotten here yet. She'd had farther to come than I had, so that wasn't surprising.

Closer to the backhoe stood a man in a trench coat. He had dark hair, but that was all I could see. I didn't recognize him. I did recognize the two women standing next to him. Mrs. Odom, in fur, and her daughter in cashmere. The latter's high suede heels were sinking into the soft ground.

"Detective Jarvis?" I asked Catherine when I reached her, indicating the man in the trench.

She nodded. "Yvonne's on her way. They didn't waste any time."

No, they hadn't. It was only a couple of minutes past four, and they had already reached the coffin. The backhoe drove to the side, and the guy inside grabbed a shovel and jumped down into the hole. He landed with a sort of hollow thud, and I winced.

I've never been to an exhumation before. I'm probably not alone in that. And I'm not sure what I had expected—maybe something grisly, considering what was happening—but it was all very simple. The guy in the grave shoveled for a minute—clearing the rest of the dirt off the casket, I assume. They wouldn't want to go too deep with the backhoe, for fear it might rip anything open.

Then he handed the shovel up to a buddy, and the buddy reciprocated by handing down a couple of long straps. In a horror movie, they'd probably have been chains, but these didn't rattle nor reflect the sunlight.

The guy in the grave worked the straps under the coffin and then his buddy gave him a hand up. They arranged a metal frame around the grave, and attached the straps to it. And began winding the coffin up.

By now Yvonne had joined us, clutching a soggy tissue. Her

eyes were wet, and her lips trembled as she watched the casket come out of the ground. "This isn't right. They shouldn't be doing this."

No, they shouldn't. I had a hard time wrapping my brain around how they'd gotten a judge to sign off on it under the circumstances, when there'd been absolutely no question of foul play.

I didn't say so, though. That would only make things worse. Instead, I put my arm around Yvonne from one side, while Catherine did the same from the other, and we watched the casket come into the sunshine before being loaded into a black hearse.

The hearse drove away with Beulah inside, and the two guys got busy putting up a tent over the hole in the ground. There was no point in filling it in again, I guess, since they probably didn't plan to keep Beulah out that long. Hopefully she'd be back in the ground sometime tomorrow, and wouldn't be bothered anymore.

The Odoms waited for the hearse to roll off down the hill, before they turned away from the grave. As soon as they did, they saw us, of course. Mrs. Odom's face darkened, and she quickened her steps, stomping through the graves. She might even have stepped on a few. Next to me, Yvonne gulped.

"What are you doing here?" She got all the way up to us, and leaned in, threateningly. It was kind of funny, considering that both Yvonne and I were taller than she was, and Catherine was at least as tall, and half her age.

Yvonne opened her mouth to answer, and Catherine pinched her.

"I would appreciate it if you wouldn't address my client directly," Catherine said coldly. While she's usually pretty easy-going, she's our mother's daughter, and can put on the lady of the manor act as well as the rest of us. "If you have anything to say, you can say it to me."

Mrs. Odom shot her a look that ought to have dropped her like a stone, but Catherine didn't even flinch. Mrs. Odom changed from a full frontal attack on Yvonne to addressing all three of us. "You have no right to be here!"

"It's public property," I pointed out. "My family is buried down there." I gestured with my thumb over my shoulder. "And my mother-in-law is right over there." I pointed in the other direction. LaDonna's grave was visible from where we were standing.

"It was a private occasion!"

By now Detective Jarvis and Ms. Odom had reached us, as well. Ms. Odom took her mother's arm. "Come on. Let's go."

Her mother twitched out of the grasp. "They shouldn't be here! Can't you arrest them?"

This was addressed to Detective Jarvis, who turned out to be a stocky guy with slicked-back, black hair and a brown suit under the tan trench coat. He shook his head. "I'm afraid not, Mrs. Odom. She's right. It's a public place."

"And we didn't intrude," Catherine added.

"But we're family! And they don't have the right to be here. She—" Her eyes, small and brown like raisins, drilled into Yvonne, "killed my sister-in-law!"

I could feel Yvonne flinch, as if from a blow.

"Nobody killed Beulah," I said calmly. "The M.E. already determined natural causes. Officers from the Columbia PD and the Maury County sheriff both saw the scene, and said there were no signs of foul play."

She didn't respond to that, not that I had expected her to.

"We all know what's going on here," Catherine added. "You lost the hearing yesterday, and with it your chance to get your hands on the restaurant. This is one more shot at that. And I have to say it's a disgusting tactic. Not only to have your sister-in-law dug up, but to accuse an innocent person of having killed her."

Mrs. Odom bristled. "I don't have to stand here and listen to this!"

I'm sure we all looked relieved at that statement. Her daughter and the detective certainly did, and Ms. Odom went back to pulling on her mother's arm.

Mrs. Odom wasn't willing to walk off without having had the last word, however. A couple of feet away, she turned and pointed her finger at Yvonne. It was tipped with a long, blood-red nail, and it shook, probably with anger. "They'll discover that she was poisoned, mark my words. And then they'll come for you. Don't think you're going to get away with this!"

She whipped around and stalked off, fur flapping, only slightly hindered by the gravestones and the uneven, grassy ground. Her daughter hurried after her, and the detective held up the rear. He turned and gave us a long look before disappearing over the hill and out of sight.

We stood in silence for a moment. I don't know about the other two, but I needed a second to breathe. The vitriol that had pumped out of Mrs. Odom's pores felt like it had poisoned the air around us. And anyway, as a conversation ender it was hard to top.

"That's not fair," Yvonne said eventually, her voice uneven. "I was Beulah's friend. They may have been family, but she didn't like them, and they didn't like her. They don't have any more right to be here than I do."

"Of course not." Catherine patted her arm.

"She left me her restaurant. Not them!"

"That's right." Catherine kept patting. She glanced at me.

"They won't get it," I said. "Like Catherine said, this is just a desperate last ditch effort, since they lost at the hearing yesterday. And I think it's horrible that they're digging that poor woman up for no reason!"

Yvonne's eyes filled with tears.

"I think it's good that they are," Catherine said. "This way, there won't be any doubt. Let them check again. When the M.E.

determines natural causes a second time, they won't have a leg to stand on."

Maybe not. I suppose we might as well look at the bright side.

Yvonne sniffed. "When do you think we'll hear something?"

"I don't think we'll hear anything at all," Catherine said, and didn't add, 'unless they come to arrest you.' Much better to leave that off. "I'll have to find a source."

"Try Patrick Nolan." She looked at me, and I added, "The Columbia cop Darcy likes. He and his partner picked up Yvonne this morning. And his partner just got attached to the Skinner homicides. She and Rafe are out there, talking to drug dealers. Nolan might be at loose ends, and be willing to talk."

Catherine arched her brows. "Maybe I'll have Darcy give him a call."

"It couldn't hurt."

"Meanwhile," she turned to Yvonne, "just go on home and relax. I'm sure this will turn out to be absolutely nothing."

Yvonne nodded, but didn't look convinced.

"I have to take the dog home to meet Mother," I said, as we made our way over the hill and down toward Oak Street, "but let me know if there's anything I can do."

It would take my mind off Rafe and the possibility that he and Lupe Vasquez were running into holdouts from Hector Gonzales's SATG.

"Dog?"

"Robbie Skinner's dog. It ran away from Animal Control and came back to Robbie's trailer. I found it there. Now I'm keeping it."

"What kind of dog? Not a purse pooch, I suppose?"

Hardly. "I'm not sure exactly what it is. A pitbull, maybe? But no, it wouldn't fit in a purse. It barely fits in the backseat."

"This should be good," Catherine said.

"Feel free to come home with me to see Mother's reaction.

I'm sure it'll be worth the trip."

Catherine smiled, but shook her head. "I have a husband and three kids to get home to. Dinner to make and homework to help with. I'll see you tomorrow."

She gave me a pat on the shoulder, and did the same for Yvonne, before she headed for the minivan parked in front of the Volvo. In the backseat of my car, the dog was pressing its nose to the crack at the top of the window. The glass was already streaked with what was either drool or snot.

"Lovely," I said.

"What?" Yvonne answered.

"Nothing." The window could be cleaned. "I don't suppose you know what Robbie called the dog?"

Yvonne shook her head. "I don't think he called it anything. It wasn't a pet or anything. I'm not sure it had a name."

That figured. "I'll find one," I said. "Before I get to the mansion. I have to introduce it to my mother as something. And 'Robbie's dog' just won't cut it."

Yvonne smiled. At least I had accomplished that much. "Let me know if you hear anything. About the Skinners or about Beulah."

I said I would. And then Yvonne got into her little car and drove away, while I got into mine and greeted the dog. "I'm sorry. Not much longer now. I'll let you do your business before I take you into the house to meet my mother. We want you to be on your best behavior when I do. Peeing on one of her antique rugs wouldn't endear you to her."

The dog didn't answer, but it did wedge its head between the seats to snuffle.

"We'll have to stop somewhere and get you a collar and a leash and some food, too. I should have thought of that when we were at Robbie's place. Although the sheriff probably wouldn't have let me take anything out of there, even if it was just dog food. Can't mess with the crime scene."

And by now, there was nowhere to stop between here and the mansion. Nowhere that sold dog food and paraphernalia.

The dog licked my ear. It was wet and weird and made me jump. Not at all the same thing as when Rafe did it.

"OK. Don't do that again. That's strange."

The dog subsided. Instead, it sat down in the backseat and panted.

"I'm sorry you had to wait," I told it, as I turned the key in the ignition. "But this was important. These people are way too desperate to get their hands on that restaurant. There has to be something more going on. Maybe the land is worth money."

It probably was, come to think of it. The cities are expanding all the time. Nashville south toward Columbia, and Columbia south toward Sweetwater. In fifty years, all of Middle Tennessee might look like Los Angeles. And a plot of land right on the Columbia Highway might be worth plenty.

"I should check with city planning," I continued, as we pulled away from the curb, "and see if there's anything being built in that area. Maybe that would account for it."

The dog bobbed its head. It wasn't a nod, but I decided to take it that way.

"I'm glad you agree. Here's something else that bothers me. Digging up a dead relative is a pretty big deal. Even if it's a relative you don't like and have never been particularly close to."

I thought for a second and added, "Hell—heck—digging up anybody is a big deal, whether it's a relative or not!"

The dog bobbed its head.

"I keep thinking about that last thing she said. Mrs. Odom. That they'd prove Beulah was poisoned, and Yvonne wouldn't get away with it. How can they be so sure she was poisoned? I mean... if someone killed her, it probably was with poison. That makes sense. The sheriff said there were no signs of foul play, and the police would have noticed if she'd been strangled or hit over the head. But there are drugs you can give people that look like natural death. Especially if they're taking drugs anyway. And Beulah was taking insulin shots every day. What's another puncture mark?"

Nothing anybody would notice, most likely. Not if she was giving herself shots once or twice a day anyway.

"So if she was murdered, she was most likely poisoned. But how would they know that?"

I looked at the dog in the mirror. It wagged its stub of a tail encouragingly. I felt like a slow student finally catching on.

"Unless...."

The dog barked. I fished out my phone and dialed Rafe.

SEVENTEEN

"I dunno..." Rafe said. "That's a pretty big leap, darlin'."

"Not that big. You didn't hear her. She said they'd prove that Beulah was poisoned, and you could tell she absolutely believed it."

"That don't mean they killed her," Rafe said. "It could just be they think they know something they don't."

Of course it could. But... "You didn't hear her. And anyway, it makes sense."

"How's that?"

"They want her restaurant. Maybe her house, too, although they can't have that. I'm sure they don't want to take on the Diabetes Association. But taking on Yvonne, that's a different story."

He had no answer to that, so I continued. "They probably figured that if Beulah died, they'd get it all. They may not have known about the will. They weren't close, so she probably wouldn't have told them, and it wasn't at her house. The sheriff said he found it in the safe at the restaurant. So even if they looked for it in her house—sometime when she wasn't there, maybe—they wouldn't have found it."

"So now you've got'em breaking and entering, too?"

"What's a little B&E if you're planning murder?"

He didn't answer, so I went on. "They were the only family she had. It made sense for them to think, if she died, they'd inherit. And they might have needed money. Yvonne mentioned that it was Otis who made the money. When Otis died and the money stopped coming in, they may not have adjusted their lifestyle to account for it. So they were living high on the hog."

"Yvonne says."

"Yvonne knew Beulah," I reminded him. "Beulah probably said so. And they thought, if Beulah died, they'd get the restaurant and the house. They could sell the house and get some cash that way, and they could keep running the restaurant. Or maybe the land is valuable. I have a hard time imagining them getting their hands dirty actually slinging hash at a meat'n three."

Rafe grunted. It might have been agreement, or maybe just a noise to make me go on. I went on.

"Beulah was taking lots of medicines anyway. Pills and injections. Nobody would notice another injection mark. And there are lots of ways to kill someone." As he himself had said not too long ago.

"I gotta agree with you there," Rafe said dryly. "But if you can't imagine them getting their hands dirty serving food at a meat'n three, can you really imagine them committing murder?"

There wasn't much I'd put past Mrs. Odom, to be honest. But he had a point. "How about this? Remember when Yvonne said Darrell Skinner had hooked up with some woman in the Pour House up in Thompson Station?"

"Sure."

"What if that woman was Ms. Odom? The daughter. Thompson Station is on the way to Franklin, and the Odoms live in Franklin. What if Ms. Odom was slumming and hooked up with Darrell? And talked Darrell into killing Beulah?"

"It'd take more than sex to get Darrell to commit murder," Rafe said.

"Are you sure? They were growing pot and running dog fights. How principled could he be?"

Rafe sounded amused. "It ain't about his principles, darlin'.

He didn't have none. It wasn't the murder he'd object to. But he'd wanna get paid."

Ah. "Well, then, maybe she paid him. Maybe that's why she was there in the first place. To find someone willing to kill her aunt."

There was a momentary pause. "I could see it," Rafe admitted. "So what are you saying? That the Odom women killed all the Skinners to make sure nobody talked?"

"You tell me," I retorted, as I pulled the Volvo into the driveway up to the mansion. The dog panted in the backseat. "If Darrell got paid for killing Beulah, would he have told his brothers?"

"Prob'ly. Not like they were gonna turn him in. Money's money. And they weren't too particular about how they got it."

No, they hadn't been. Between the dog fighting and the marijuana, it seemed like murder might not have been outside the realm of possibility.

"So whoever paid Darrell to kill Beulah, might have been worried enough to kill all the Skinners." Or all the Skinners old enough to talk. The baby had been spared, since it knew nothing.

"Might could," Rafe admitted. "If they weren't willing to take care of Beulah their own selves, I can't see'em executing seven people in cold blood, though. Can you?"

I couldn't. "Maybe they have an accomplice. Someone else who killed the Skinners." I pulled the car to a stop at the bottom of the stairs.

"Why didn't that someone kill Beulah, then?"

No idea. But he was right. If the Odoms had an accomplice who'd be willing to kill all the Skinners, they wouldn't have needed Darrell's help in the first place.

"Can you at least think about it?"

Rafe told me he would.

"So how are you two doing?"

"Fine. We're trying to find somebody to talk to. But nobody

wants to talk to us. Can't imagine why nobody'd wanna talk to a cop in uniform and a special agent. Can you?"

"Maybe you should ditch the squad car and uniform, and come borrow the Volvo."

"I love you, darlin'," my husband told me, "but your car's no better than this one. If I had your mama's Cadillac, that might make a difference."

"You can ask her if you can use it. She'll probably let you."

"I appreciate the thought. But I'm not taking your mama's car into places where it might get shot at."

"You're going to places you might get shot at?" I hadn't realized places like that existed in Columbia.

"The car," Rafe said. "Nobody's gonna shoot at us."

Sure. "You're being careful, right?"

"Always."

I rolled my eyes. "I'm home now. I'm going to let the dog out of the car to pee, and then take it inside to meet my mother. I want to make sure it doesn't pee on her rugs."

I could hear the smile tugging at his mouth. "Sounds like a good plan."

"Any idea when you'll be home? Or back here?"

"Can't tell you right now. But I don't think it'll be as late as last night. Don't hold dinner, though, We'll grab something while we're out here."

"Good luck," I told him. He wished me the same, and I hung up. And went around the car to open the door for the dog. It bounded out and over to the grass, where it squatted. I was pretty sure that meant it was a girl dog, but I bent over as best I could to peer at its underside anyway. Just as mother opened the door.

"What are you doing?" Her voice changed. "What is that dog doing on my lawn?"

The word 'dog' carried the same inflection as if it had been 'snake' or maybe 'weasel.'

"Peeing," I said, straightening up and putting a hand to my lower back. Moving was getting harder and harder. "It's my new dog. Its name is... um..."

Mother's brows rose.

"Fine," I said. "It's so new it doesn't have a name. Its previous owner didn't name it. I guess he didn't see it as worthy of having a name. It's coming back to Nashville with me and Rafe. In the meantime, it's going to have to stay here. It probably won't be for more than a day or two. Rafe has some very good leads on the Skinner investigation."

If I did say so myself.

Mother contemplated the dog, which was now nosing around the bushes in the flower bed. "Pearl."

"Pearl?" Of all the names I might have thought she'd come up with, that hadn't been on the list.

"I had a dog named Pearl when I was little," Mother said. "She was a white Chihuahua."

"Does that look like a Chihuahua to you?"

"It's white," Mother said.

"More gray."

"Light gray. Dappled." She shook her head. "You can call it anything you want."

"Pearl is fine." Not what I would have picked—I was leaning toward Killer or Xena, Warrior Princess—but if Mother was getting into the game and not telling me I couldn't keep the dog, I was willing to give her the name she wanted. And give the dog my mother's choice of name. "Is it OK if she comes inside? I can put her in the carriage house if you'd rather."

"Of course she can come inside," Mother said. Without a single demur. I wanted to ask who she was and what she'd done with my mother, but I decided it was better not to look the proverbial gift horse in the mouth. Hopefully the dog—Pearl now—would behave inside, and so wouldn't be banished to the carriage house later.

I got her attention and waved. "Come on, Pearl. Let's go inside."

I doubt the name made any difference, and she probably didn't understand what I was saying, but she trotted up the stairs behind me. Her nails clicked on the hardwood floors in the foyer. Mother winced, and then straightened her face. "You might consider taking her to see a veterinarian. If she's been living outside, she might need special care."

She might, at that. "The clawfoot tub upstairs is pretty deep. Would it be OK if I gave her a bath?" If her nails needed trimming, the vet could do that tomorrow. But at least she'd be clean.

"Of course," Mother said. "I'll find some old towels for you."

She clicked off down the hallway on her heels. The dog contemplated her, but didn't follow. Instead it—she—looked up at me. "We're going upstairs," I said. "To take a bath."

Her stub of a tail wagged.

"Do you know what a bath is? I hope so. If not, you're in for a rude awakening."

She didn't say anything to that, but after I'd hung up my coat and taken my booties off, she trotted beside me up the stairs and down the hall to the bathroom.

I filled the tub with warm water and suds from the shampoo bottle. We didn't have any dog shampoo, so human products would have to do. Hair is hair, I figured, so it would probably be all right, at least this once. Tomorrow, when we went to the vet, I'd find out. But it probably wouldn't hurt the dog to be bathed with my mother's *Acqua de Parma* shampoo for once.

The dog contemplated the tub and the water. I contemplated the dog. "I didn't really think this thing through very well, did I?"

The dog probably weighed about as much as my mother. There was no way I could pick her up and put her in the tub. The dog or my mother. And there was definitely no way I should try, in my condition. A pity Robbie's dog hadn't been a Chihuahua like my mother's.

"I don't suppose you'd like to get in?" I asked Pearl. "The water's nice and warm. And you've been living outside a long time. I'm sure you'd like to get clean."

Pearl looked at me.

"I'm afraid I can't get you in there. If you want to get in, you're going to have to do it yourself. I can try to help." Although she didn't even have a collar I could hold on to. And it wasn't like I could grab her by the ears or tail and guide her into the tub. "I should have thought of this. Maybe we should take a shower instead. Maybe that would be easier."

I could get under the spray with the dog and wash her. The biggest danger would be her knocking me into the wall. Or biting, I suppose. But I wouldn't be hurting the baby by trying to lift her.

The bathroom door opened, and Mother came in, bearing a stack of last year's towels. She took in the standoff and tsked. She put the towels on the vanity and moved past the dog to the tub. "Come on. In." She slapped the inside of the tub with her hand. Her wedding band clicked against the enameled cast iron of the old clawfoot.

The dog contemplated her with its head tilted.

"You can do it," Mother told it. "Come on."

The dog gathered itself. I could see the muscles in its hind quarters bunching. It jumped and landed in the tub with a splash that sent soapy water three feet in the air, splashing over the sides of the tub in a flood. Mother squealed as she got soaked. So did I.

Pearl stood in the middle of the carnage with water and bubbles up to her belly, wagging her tail. Every time she hit the bubbles, a few of them flew into the air.

"Good girl," Mother choked out. "That's a very good girl."

Her hair was plastered to her skull and her eye makeup was

smeared. I'm sure I didn't look much better. Mother gave me a look. "She's in the tub. Would you like to bathe her now?"

"I guess I'd better." My voice was uneven, but I managed to keep from laughing outright. "Thanks for the towels."

"Don't mention it," Mother said and stalked out. I could hear her heels clicking down the hallway in the direction of the master bedroom and bath, and her own, this-year, extra fluffy towels.

There was no point in me drying off since I was only going to get wetter, so I rolled up my sleeves and went about washing the dog. And while I won't claim to have done a particularly stellar job—it was my first time—she smelled better coming out than she did when she went in. I rubbed her ears with suds, and did the best I could with the snout, and rinsed her off with the handheld shower. She must have enjoyed it, or at least not minded too much, because she stood still for all of it, aside from wagging her tail and panting. It looked almost like she was smiling.

I pulled the plug from the tub, and as the water level sank, I was faced with the same problem as before, in reverse: in this case, how to get the eighty-pound dog back out of the tub so I could towel her dry.

Or maybe it would be better to towel her dry inside the tub, so she wouldn't track water everywhere...

No sooner had the thought crossed my mind, than Pearl leapt. She scrambled across the edge of the tub, skidded on the wet tile floor, and banged into the sink vanity. It took her a second to get her bearings after that, and then she shook. Water sprayed everywhere. It was like taking a shower.

I shrieked. Pearl took one look at me and headed for the door Mother had left cracked open.

"No! No!"

I threw myself at her—Pearl—with a towel. She evaded the first time, but eventually I got her tangled up in the towel, and proceeded to rub her dry while I crooned at her. "That's a good girl. Just a little bit longer. We'll take care of you. Once you're clean and dry, you can come downstairs and find something to sleep on. Like a nice rug or a pillow or something. But first you have to be dry. My mother will kill me if you shake all over Great-Aunt Ida's loveseat. She seems to like you—and I'll admit I'm a bit surprised by that—but she would not be happy if you ruined the heirlooms."

The dog stood still, tongue lolling, while I did my best to rub the water from her coat. As soon as I let go, she was out the door like a shot. I could hear her nails skidding on the floor, and then the sound of her paws bounding down the stairs. Then there was the same scramble on the floor of the foyer, and the bounding of paws toward the kitchen. I didn't hear my mother scream, so the dog must have stopped short of running into her.

I hung the towels to dry and took myself off into my own room to put on dry clothes. Everything I had on, all the way down to my bra and panties, was wet.

By the time I got downstairs, the dog was sitting on the kitchen floor, its short stub of a tail brushing back and forth. Its eyes were fixed on my mother, who was standing at the stove stirring something in a pan. It smelled good, whatever it was. I peered in. And recoiled.

"That isn't dinner, is it?"

"It's for the dog," Mother said, stirring placidly. "Ground beef, raw egg, rice. You should go buy a bag of dry dog food, but this dog needs good food right now. Poor thing, you can see its ribs."

You could. Partly, that was probably because it had very short hair, but she was right: the dog was too thin. When I'd had my hands all over it in the tub earlier, I'd felt several scars under the fur, too. It hadn't had an easy life.

"How about I run to the store now?" I said. "You look like you've got this under control. I'll buy a bag of food, a leash and collar, and some dog treats. And maybe a couple of dog bowls."

Mother's kitchen was full of fine china, and I wouldn't put it past her to serve the dog on Sèvres porcelain, but the bowls could go home with me (and the dog) when we left in a day or two. I had no suitable dog bowls—or Sèvres porcelain—in Nashville.

Mother nodded. "You go ahead. Pearl and I will be fine."

I had no doubt. The dog wasn't taking its eyes off the stove. But it was waiting patiently, and as long as it didn't attack Mother to get at the food, they'd probably be all right.

"I'll be right back," I said, as much to Mother as to the dog.

Mother nodded. "Drive carefully."

The dog didn't even look at me when I left.

The closest store to the mansion is the drugstore where Yvonne had been working since Beulah died and the restaurant closed. I knew she wouldn't be there—she was probably at home, trying to drown her sorrows in wine and a bubble bath, to take her mind off the Odoms and their attempt to railroad her into a murder charge. But drugstores usually carry dog supplies, I've noticed, so I made that my first stop. If I couldn't find what I needed there, there was a Walmart in Columbia I could go to, but I wasn't going to drive all that way if I didn't have to.

As it turned out, I didn't. The drugstore had a small bag of dog food—Pearl would probably make her way through it in a couple of days, but by then we'd be back in Nashville and I could buy something bigger, and have Rafe carry it for me—and a collar and leash that looked like it might fit her. The collar was pink, because I thought it might look nice with Pearl's coloring, and the leash was the kind that retracts into a big handle. I chose a pink handle, to coordinate. Then I chose a bag of minty chew-sticks—was I supposed to brush the dog's teeth? I couldn't imagine Pearl taking kindly to that, although I should probably ask the vet tomorrow—and a box of bone-shaped dog crackers. On my way up to the register, I grabbed a rubber bone that squeaked and a small, fuzzy, stuffed animal. Maybe she'd like the company.

I was standing at the register pulling out my wallet when the sliding doors opened, and in walked Ms. Odom, cashmere coat flapping around her knee-high boots.

I shrank back behind a display of chewing gum, hoping it would hide my increased girth. Although I needn't have bothered. She didn't look neither right nor left, just swept down the makeup aisle toward the back of the store.

I craned my neck, until the cashier popped an extra-loud bubble-gum bubble to get my attention. I paid her what I owed for the dog paraphernalia. But instead of leaving, I backtracked to see if I could figure out what Ms. Odom was up to.

My first impression was that she might be looking for Yvonne. Yvonne wasn't working today, though, and Ms. Odom had to know it, since it wasn't that long ago that she'd seen us at Oak Street Cemetery.

So maybe she was here to talk to Yvonne's boss? To try to get Yvonne fired? The Odoms had certainly tried to ruin Yvonne's life in other ways, so it might not be beyond them to try this.

I skulked through the aisles, keeping my eyes peeled for Ms. Odom's camel-colored cashmere. The plastic bag with Pearl's paraphernalia crinkled in my hand.

The manager's office was probably in the back. Behind the door that said 'Employees Only,' was a good guess.

I tried the door, but it was locked. It had a keypad on it, but of course I didn't know the combination.

Beyond the door, I could see restroom icons, and that gave me an idea. I was pregnant. I always had to pee anyway. Nobody would question it if I asked for the code so I could get back there and use the bathroom. And while I was back there, I could scope out the manager's office, and maybe hear what Ms. Odom was up to.

There were no drugstore employees in sight, but the

pharmacy was on the back wall in the opposite corner. I made my way in that direction, and stopped when I caught a flicker of camel cashmere.

Never mind the restroom code. Ms. Odom was standing at the window picking up a prescription.

I ducked behind the nearest display—walking sticks, some of them in psychedelic colors and patterns—and sharpened my hearing.

"Do you need to talk to a pharmacist?"

Ms. Odom's shiny bob swung as she shook her head. "My mother's been taking Epiclore for years. She knows what to do."

The pharmacist named her price, and Ms. Odom ran her credit card through the machine and received her medicine, or her mother's medicine, rather. I ducked out of sight before she could turn around and see me, absolutely no wiser than I'd been before I'd listened to the truncated conversation.

Epiclore? Epic lore?

It was a pity my sister-in-law was dead. Sheila had been trained as a nurse. She would have been able to tell me what it was.

A quick Google search on my phone netted me a Finnish heavy metal band, but nothing else.

Adding the word 'medicine' to the search didn't help. All it did, was take the heavy metal band out of contention and give me information on some sort of game playing instead.

I was probably spelling it wrong. Medicines are sometimes spelled weirdly. And I might have heard it wrong. And chances were I could stand here for hours trying different combinations of things without hitting on the right one. I considered asking the pharmacist, but she'd probably find it suspicious, right on the heels of someone walking off with just that medication. It would be obvious that I'd been eavesdropping.

So I headed out instead, and when I got there, I called Yvonne. "Sorry to bother you again today."

"It's OK." Her nose sounded stuffy, as if she'd been crying.

"When you work at the drugstore, do you ever work the register in the pharmacy? Enough to know about some of the medications?"

"Once or twice," Yvonne said. "They have certain people they schedule back there, because they're familiar with the process, but I've been back there a couple of times when someone's been out sick. Why?"

I told her about Ms. Odom. "She was picking up her mother's medication. And I've been looking for it online, but I can't find it. It sounded like she said epic lore. But that can't be it, because I can't find it."

"Epiklor," Yvonne said.

"Isn't that what I said?"

She spelled it.

"Oh. What is it?"

"Potassium chloride," Yvonne said. "Medication for low levels of potassium."

Oh. "Is there anything weird about it?"

"Not that I know of."

"I don't suppose Beulah was taking it?"

"No." She sounded very certain. "Beulah was taking pills for high blood pressure and insulin shots. Nothing for potassium."

"OK," I said. "Thanks."

"Have you heard anything about the autopsy?"

I hadn't. "I'm sure it's too early. The M.E. might not get to it until tomorrow. But I'll give Darcy a call and ask her to get in touch with Patrick Nolan. He should be able to tell us one way or the other." If he was willing. And hopefully, if Darcy asked, he would be.

Yvonne said thanks and hung up. I got in the car and called Darcy while I drove home to my mother and my dog.

EIGHTEEN

By the time I got home, Mother had fed the dog the rice and ground beef mixture from the stove. She was sitting in the parlor—Mother—with a glass of sherry, and Pearl was arranged at her feet, curled into an almost perfect circle. When I came in, she lifted her head and inspected me, but didn't bark.

"Good girl," I said, and got a wag of her stubby tail in response. "I bought something for you."

I pulled out the little stuffed animal. Her eyes fastened on it, greedily.

"I'll go put the bowls in the kitchen," I told Mother, as I tossed the stuffed animal to Pearl. "I thought maybe I'd put them over in the corner by—"

It was all I got out. There was a growl, a snap of jaws, a ripping sound, and then the stuffed animal was in two pieces on the floor, its head off and stuffing everywhere.

"Dear me," Mother said faintly.

I swallowed. I knew it was stuffed—had been stuffed—and it hadn't suffered, but somehow I got the feeling it wasn't the first time something like this had happened. This was what Robbie and the Skinners had trained Pearl to do. She was looking at me and wagging her tail, her tongue lolling. Looking for praise.

"Come here," I told her as I dropped to the floor and reached for her. I could tell my voice was uneven, and I think she could, too, because she whined. "It's OK. I don't blame you. You just did what you've been trained to do. I won't bring you any more stuffed animals." And I'd make very sure that whenever we were outside, I'd keep her away from puppies or kittens or squirrels or anything like that. "It's all right."

I scratched her ears and stroked her back, my hand bumping over ridges of scar tissue under the sleek fur. "I'm so sorry. They shouldn't have taught you to do that. You don't have to do it anymore."

Mother was still pale, and looked shocked as well as confused.

"The Skinners used dogs for dog fighting," I explained, while I continued to pet Pearl. "She has scars under her fur."

"The poor thing." I'm not sure whether she was talking about Pearl or the decapitated toy on the floor. Maybe both.

"We'll be kind to her from now on. Hopefully she'll learn not to do that anymore. But I won't give her any more stuffed toys for a while." I blinked the tears away and reached into the bag again. "Here, baby. I bought you a squeaky bone."

Pearl's eyes lit up as I squeezed the bone and made it squeak. When I gave it to her, she tossed it up in the air, chased it across the room, pounced on it, and laid down to chew contentedly on the rubber.

Both Mother and I let out a sigh of relief.

"Sorry about that." I got myself to my feet with the help of the coffee table. "I'll go put the bowls in the kitchen. I thought I'd put them over in the corner by the back door, where they'd be out of the way."

Mother nodded. "She ate some of what I made. The rest is in the fridge for tomorrow. You can mix it with the dry food. But she should probably just have dry food for the rest of the night. We don't want her to have an upset stomach."

No, we didn't. I wasn't in any kind of position to wake up and take the dog out multiple times a night. If I had to clean up dog poop from the floor, I'd probably vomit. And the thought of asking my elegant mother to do it was in equal measure inconceivable and hilariously funny.

Of course, Rafe would be home at some point. And would probably be up for taking the dog out as well as dealing with the poop. But it would be preferable if neither of us had to.

"Maybe it would be better to wait until tomorrow to give her any more food. She's had two chicken wraps and a bunch of ground beef already this afternoon. That might be enough for tonight."

Mother nodded. "She's in no danger of starving at the moment. Although you should make sure she has water to drink."

I should.

"And make sure to wash the bowl before you put it down," Mother added. "Germs, you know."

This was a dog that had spent its life outside, chained underneath a trailer. Somehow, I didn't think plastic germs were going to do it in. But there was no sense in arguing. I told my mother I'd be sure to wash the bowls well before I put them down, and headed out of the parlor and down the hall to the kitchen. Pearl lifted her head to watch me go, but then returned to chomping on the bone.

After washing the bowls and filling one with water, I put them by the back door on a dish towel. The dog food went in the cabinet along with the biscuits, and I poured myself a glass of juice and went back to join Mother in the parlor. "Did I tell you that they dug up Beulah Odom?" Or had that gotten lost in the excitement of the dog earlier?

Mother's eyes widened and she choked on a sip of sherry. Obviously I hadn't gotten around to mentioning it.

"The Columbia PD came and picked up Yvonne earlier," I added. "They're trying to pin Beulah's murder on her. But first they have to prove it was murder. Originally, the M.E. ruled natural causes."

Mother leaned forward and put the sherry glass on the table.

"They exhumed the body? Are you sure?"

"I watched them do it," I said. "Dug her right out of the ground down at Oak Street. With a backhoe."

Mother winced.

"A hearse took the coffin and drove off with it. I guess they plan to do the autopsy again. And come up with different results."

"Dear me," Mother said.

"I saw Ms. Odom when I was at the drugstore just now. She was picking up her mother's prescription. Mrs. Odom takes something called Epiklor. Yvonne said it's potassium chloride. I wonder whether it's possible to kill someone with it."

Mother's eyebrows rose. "I imagine it is. Your father took potassium chloride."

And had died of a heart attack, just like Beulah. Not that there was any question about my father's death not being natural.

"The doctors made sure we understood that it was only to be taken orally," Mother added. "To inject it can be fatal."

Really?

As I'd said earlier, who would notice another injection mark on a woman who injected herself with insulin several times a day?

"Wouldn't it show up in the tox screen, though? I'm sure they did one during the autopsy. The original autopsy."

"That I don't know," Mother said with an elegant little shrug. She picked up her glass again. "But now that you know what it is, you can probably find out."

I probably could. I put my juice down and pulled out my phone. This search was a whole lot easier than the previous, and also netted me more helpful information. Yes, you could poison someone with Epiklor and cause a heart attack. I won't bore you with the medical explanation, a lot of which went right over my head, but I did find out that it was possible. I also found out that potassium chloride occurs naturally in the body, and that elevated levels wouldn't necessarily set off any flags during autopsy. And apparently it breaks down after a few days, so at this point, the M.E. wouldn't find anything unusual in Beulah's corpse.

If it had ever been there, of course. Just because Mrs. Odom took potassium chloride, and just because potassium chloride could be used to poison someone, didn't mean that Mrs. Odom had poisoned Beulah. But it was something to keep in mind. If the M.E.'s verdict changed from natural causes to poison or undetermined, I could mention it then. And would.

And in the meantime, there was the dog fighting angle and the drug angle to investigate as far as the Skinner murders were concerned.

"Do you think the vet's still open?" I asked my mother. "I should probably call and ask about bringing Pearl in tomorrow morning. Just in case they're busy."

Mother allowed as to how that might be a good idea.

"I wonder which vet the Skinners used." If they'd used one.

"If they ran dog fights," Mother said, her lips tight, "I doubt they'd bother with a vet."

Probably not. But just in case, maybe I should drive Pearl to Columbia tomorrow morning, instead of the local Sweetwater vet. Just on the chance that the vet had her records already, and more to the point, so I could find out what, if anything, the vet knew.

I googled veterinary clinics in and around Columbia, and found three. I picked the one closest to Sweetwater, and dialed. When the phone was answered, I explained who I was and that I had just adopted a dog whose owner had died. "I was wondering whether Robbie Skinner took his dog to you?"

"We can't give out information on our patients," the receptionist told me, snippily.

"I'm not looking for information. I'm just trying to do my

best for the dog. If she already has veterinary records somewhere, it would be helpful to take her to the vet who is familiar with her."

"Hold, please." She disappeared before I could answer. When she came back a minute later, she told me, "Doctor Finster says to tell you we have no records for a dog owned by Robbie Skinner. Is there anything else I can do for you?"

I told her there wasn't, and dialed the next number on the list, and went through the same conversation there, with the same result. They didn't know Robbie Skinner and had no records for Pearl.

At the last clinic, the phone was answered by a man. "This is Doc Anderson."

"Doctor?"

"Of veterinary medicine. How can I help you?"

I went through my explanation again.

"I'm sorry," Doc Anderson said. He didn't even have to think about it. "We never worked on any dogs for the Skinners. But we'd be happy to take a look at yours. Is something the matter with her?"

"Not as far as I can tell. She's a little too thin, and has some scar tissue. And she just ripped the head off a stuffed toy. But other than that, she seems all right."

"No fleas? No demodectic mange?"

"Demo what?" I said.

"Scabies. Mites that burrow under the skin and cause itching and hair loss."

Oh. "No, she's not scratching a lot. And she has all her hair. We just gave her a bath." And wasn't it a little late in the year for fleas?

"Bring her in tomorrow," Doc Anderson said, "and I'll take a look. Nine o'clock?"

I could probably drag myself out of bed and to Columbia by nine. I told him I'd be there, and hung up, just as there was a noise at the front door. It sounded like the knob turning. Pearl's ears twitched, and the next second she was on her feet and barking, the hairs at the back of her neck standing up.

A second after that, she was on her way, nails scrabbling on the wood floors.

I found her in the foyer, barking at the door. I have no idea why, since she should be able to see Rafe on the other side, and recognize him. Nonetheless, she was standing there, teeth bared and barks reverberating under the two-story ceiling.

"It's OK," I told her, while I turned the doorknob to let him in. "You know him. You ate his sandwich earlier. You like him. He might even like you. Although if you jump on him and tear his throat out, I can guarantee you he won't. And I won't, either."

The dog didn't stop to listen. Rafe opened the door. "Quiet!"

His voice reverberated under the two-story ceiling, too. The dog dropped to her stomach and whined. If she'd been human, she would have been covering her head with her hands. As it was, she was clearly bracing for a blow.

Rafe saw it, too, and cursed. Softly.

"She's all right," I said. "She just doesn't know that that part of her life is over. It'll take more than a day for her to learn that we won't hurt her."

Rafe nodded. "Everything all right here?"

He was still looking at the dog, not me. I nodded anyway. "Fine. She took a bath. She ate. She didn't bother Mother or me."

And speaking of Mother, she was watching the proceedings from the door of the parlor.

"She has an appointment with a veterinarian tomorrow morning," I added. "I want him to make sure she's healthy before we take her home. But she's been good so far. It's possible she doesn't like men."

Rafe arched a brow, but didn't respond. Instead he crouched where he stood, just inside the door. "C'mere, darlin'."

For once, he wasn't calling me darlin'. This time, it was the dog. Who looked at him suspiciously for a second before creeping toward him, still on her stomach.

"It's OK. Nobody's gonna hurt you. There you go." When she got close enough, he reached out a hand and let her sniff his fingertips. I held my breath—what if she decided to bite?—but she didn't. She sniffed, and then allowed him to reach below her chin and give her a quick scratch.

He didn't push it. A few seconds, and then he got back to his feet. So did Pearl, but she looked a lot more comfortable. When Mother clapped her hands and called for her, Pearl bounded down the hallway to the parlor, and they both disappeared inside.

"Pearl?" Rafe said.

"Mother named her. She used to have a dog named Pearl."

He was silent a second. "I bet it didn't look like this dog."

I shook my head. "It was a white Chihuahua. But she's OK with Pearl staying in the house. She was OK with me using her hundred dollar shampoo on the dog, too. If she wants to call it Pearl, she can."

Rafe nodded. "Have you eaten?"

I told him I hadn't. "I've been too busy running around. Didn't you and Lupe Vasquez stop for anything to eat?"

He shook his head.

"So Pearl ate your lunch and you haven't had anything to eat since this morning?"

"That's about it, yeah."

"Go on and go out," Mother's voice said from the parlor. We couldn't see her, but she could obviously hear us. "The dog and I will be fine."

"Don't you want something to eat?"

"I had something when the dog ate," Mother's disembodied voice said. "We'll be fine here. Go on. I don't want to leave her by herself."

Fine. "Just let me grab my coat."

I did, and stuck my feet back into the booties, and we were out the door a minute later. "You go ahead and drive." I handed Rafe the keys. "I have to text my sister."

"Which one?" He held the door for me, and waited until I was situated before he closed the door and walked around to the driver's side.

"Darcy. We sicced her on Patrick Nolan."

"Lupe Vasquez's partner?" He turned the key in the ignition.

I nodded. "You got Vasquez for the Skinner investigation. We're surmising that Nolan might be assigned to Detective Jarvis for the Beulah Odom matter. And we want to know what he knows. And what Jarvis knows. So I called Darcy and asked her to find out."

"And?"

"She said they might be having dinner tonight. I want to know where they are, so we can go and surprise them."

"Let me know where to go once you figure it out," Rafe said, and put the car in gear while I dug for my phone.

By the time we made it to the Mexican Restaurant in Columbia where Darcy and Patrick Nolan had first met—I'd been there, too—I had managed to update Rafe on everything that had happened since I left him and Lupe Vasquez at Animal Control this afternoon. The exhumation, the scene with Mrs. and Ms. Odom in the cemetery, my trip to the drugstore, and Mother's information about the potassium chloride.

"If that's what it was, I doubt they'll find any trace of it now. According to the internet, it isn't detectable after several months. Or even several days. But if her potassium levels were high at the original autopsy—and nobody really thought anything of it, since potassium is one of those natural things that your body has anyway—that could mean that the Odoms killed her."

"Or that they didn't," Rafe said.

I gave him a sideways look. "I don't imagine you're suggesting that Yvonne did?"

"I don't know that anybody did. The place can't be worth much."

"Depends on how much of the land around it goes with it. If it's enough to build a nice, big subdivision, it would be worth plenty."

And with the Nashville area expected to grow by another million people in the next ten years, land within an hour of Nashville would all be at a premium.

"Anyway," I added, "as you've said yourself before, you can't ever really know what's a good motive for murder in someone else's mind. Maybe Beulah disliked her sister-in-law all these years, and her sister-in-law held off on killing her out of respect for Otis. But now that Otis Odom is dead, she has no reason to wait. It could be as simple as that."

Rafe shrugged. "If they can't prove Beulah was murdered, we'll prob'ly never know."

Probably. "Any news on the Skinner case?"

Rafe shook his head. "We drove around a couple hours, looking for people to talk to. Nobody wanted to talk to us. Officer Vasquez thought she might have better luck on her own."

And she might. She was known in Columbia, and probably known not to be a big threat. Rafe, on the other hand, had shut down Hector Gonzales. Whoever had taken over Hector's business in this corner of the world had to be worried that he was next.

"These are kind of crazy happenings for a little town like this. Aren't they?"

"What happened to the Skinners is crazy for anywhere," Rafe said. "I'm surprised we don't have national media here, sticking their nose in."

"I think maybe the sheriff has managed to keep a lid on it. And for all that it's seven dead, it's all the same family. It's not as sexy—if you'll excuse the term—as a serial killer targeting brunettes. Or hookers. Or gay guys. That makes for better copy."

Rafe nodded.

"Are you any closer to figuring out what happened?"

"You know about as much as I do," Rafe said. "Darrell was a dog. Robbie was a wife beater. I don't know much about Art, but he grew illegal drugs and ran dog fights. There are plenty of reasons for murder there. Money or revenge or just fighting against wrong. People against drugs. People against cruelty to animals."

"You haven't narrowed it down to one yet?"

He shook his head. "Could be any or all of'em. The M.E. finished all the autopsies. Cause of death was gunshot for everybody. Everyone but Robbie was killed with a single shot to the head. There were two different weapons. The same weapon was used on Art, Linda, A.J. and Darrell. A second weapon was used on Cilla, Matty, and Robbie."

"So two shooters?"

He shrugged. "Seems like it might be. Time of death was between two and three am for everyone. One person coulda done it all—the crime scenes are all close enough—but why use two different weapons? Not like there wasn't plenty of time to reload the one."

That made sense. Unless the shooter wanted to give the impression that there were two of him. Just to throw off the scent.

Rafe nodded. "There's just no way to know. Two guns, but it mighta been the same finger on the trigger. Or not. They started at Art and Linda's place. One of'em went into the mobile home and killed Art, Linda, and A.J. The other went into the trailer and killed Cilla and her boyfriend. Then they split up. One went to Darrell's place, one to Robbie's. Or they started with Darrell and Robbie, and met up at Art's after."

Or one person did it all. "Any thoughts on why Robbie was

shot in the stomach and not the head, like everyone else?"

"Plenty of thoughts," Rafe said. "Coulda been deliberate. Whoever did it hated Robbie more, and wanted him to have some time to think about what he'd done. Or it mighta been because Robbie woke up when the shooter came into his trailer, and tried to rush him. Or her. No time for a neat shot to the head, so the shooter did what he could and booked it outta there."

I nodded.

"Or it coulda been that Robbie killed everyone else and then shot himself, thinking he'd have enough time to make it to the car and outta there, and get help. And instead he died, too."

"Why would Robbie kill the rest of his family?"

"A million dollars in pot?" Rafe suggested.

"I thought you said the Skinners were close. One for all and all for one."

"They were. But I haven't seen'em in fifteen years. And a million dollars is a lot of money."

He had a point. We drove in silence a minute. Up ahead, I could see the bright lights of the Mexican place on State Street. *Fiestas de Mexico* lighting up the night in neon blue and orange.

I pointed. Rafe nodded.

"So I guess you're looking for two people who are willing to alibi each other for the night the Skinners were killed." A man and a woman? Or two homosexuals? Or a mother and daughter, like Sandy and Kayla Skinner?

Rafe shrugged as he pulled the Volvo into the parking lot next to the restaurant. "Most people don't have alibis for the middle of the night. Unless it's somebody that'd be together anyway, I'd be more suspicious of people who do have alibis, since it would be 'cause they expected to be asked."

Good point. "You're smart," I told him.

He chuckled. "Not so much that you'd notice. Stay there."

He exited the car. I waited for him to come around and open the door for me. The smell of grilling meat hung in the air. I could hear his stomach growl from several feet away, and it had been a long time since lunch. Longer for him, but he wasn't eating for two.

"I'm starving," I said.

Rafe nodded and put an arm around my shoulders. "Let's go feed that baby."

NINETEEN

Darcy and Patrick Nolan were finishing up dinner when we came in. And Nolan did not look happy to see us. Whether it was the prospect of us raining on his date with Darcy, or the prospect of us asking him questions about the Odom case, I'm not sure, but it was beyond obvious that he wished we hadn't shown up.

Since Darcy seemed delighted, he did his best to hide it, though, and forced a smile. "Mr. and Mrs. Collier."

After about five months of marriage, it still gave me a thrill to hear that. However— "Since you're dating my sister, you should probably call me Savannah."

"And under the circumstances," Rafe added, straight face, "I'll be Agent Collier."

Nolan grimaced. "That's clear."

Rafe grinned and pulled out the chair next to him. "Sorry I took your partner away from you." He gestured me into it.

Nolan gave in to the inevitable. "It's all right. Gives Chief Carter a chance to keep his finger in both pies."

"I guess you don't usually have so much excitement in Columbia," I said, watching as Rafe pulled out the chair next to Darcy and seated himself on it.

"We rarely even get one murder, let alone seven. But the Skinners lived outside the city, so until you wanted information about the drug scene, the chief had no reason to get involved." Nolan shrugged. "Any news?"

I wondered whether Rafe was going to tell him anything.

Then again, with Lupe Vasquez right in the mix, there was no real point in being reticent. Anything that happened, she'd have to relay. And would probably choose to share with her partner.

Rafe gave him the information about the two different weapons, and Nolan came to the same conclusion I had: that there had likely been two shooters, or someone wanted us to think so. He also brought up the same point Rafe and I had discussed on the way over here, but took it a step further.

"If Robbie shot himself, there would have been a gun in the trailer, wouldn't there?"

Rafe nodded.

"Was there?"

Rafe shook his head.

"So Robbie couldn't have shot himself."

"He coulda. If someone else was there to take the gun away."

Nolan chewed on that for a second. "So there were two shooters, and one of them was Robbie. Robbie wanted the rest of his family dead so he could keep all the pot for himself."

"It's a theory," Rafe said.

"And Robbie shot himself so it would look like he was attacked, too, but he accidentally ended up killing himself. And he had a partner in the marijuana trade, who took the gun away."

"Or his partner might have killed him," I suggested. "Accidentally—to make it look like Robbie was also attacked—or even on purpose."

Nolan tilted his head. "Why'd he do that?"

"Same reason that Robbie killed everyone else. To keep all the money for himself. This way, he wouldn't even have to share with Robbie."

"I dunno." Nolan shook his head. "That's a big risk to take. He's getting nothing now, that the sheriff found the pot."

"But the sheriff didn't find the pot on his own. It took someone calling and telling Rafe where to look." And that someone couldn't have been Robbie's hypothetical partner, since the partner would have had every reason to want to keep the police from finding the pot. Especially if he'd been a party to seven murders. Not like anyone would want to draw attention to that.

"Tell me about Detective Jarvis," I said, since there wasn't much more to say about the Skinner case at the moment. We could speculate until the cows came home, but that's all it would be: speculation. "I saw him at the cemetery earlier, when they were exhuming Beulah. He was with the Odoms. How did they convince him that she was murdered, when the medical examiner said it was a heart attack?"

"I wouldn't venture to guess," Nolan said, and closed his mouth primly.

"Is everybody in your department trying to get on the news, Nolan?"

This was Rafe's question, and Nolan bristled. "No. Jarvis doesn't care about that. He likes to close cases, but so does everyone else."

Not much anyone could say to that.

Nolan added, a little reluctantly, "The chief probably told him to look into it. The Odoms leaned on Chief Carter, and Carter told Jarvis to check it out."

"Do you have any idea whether he actually believes it's murder," I asked, "or is he just trying to humor the Odoms? And his boss?"

Nolan shrugged. He's a tall and pretty skinny guy, with a long neck, but the shoulders were broad inside a faded denim shirt. "Could be either. I don't think he would have gone to the trouble of getting an exhumation if he hadn't thought there might be something to it, though. We don't dig people up as a general rule."

I would hope not.

"I don't suppose the M.E. has had time to do the second

autopsy yet?"

"If he has," Nolan said, "nobody's told me." He glanced at Rafe and added, "Not like they haven't had plenty of other bodies to keep them busy at the morgue."

Rafe nodded.

Throughout this whole conversation, Darcy had sat quietly and watched one after the other of us speak. Now she opened her mouth. "We were just about to leave."

I think she followed up with a nudge under the table, because Nolan nodded and pushed his chair back.

"You're welcome to stay and have dessert," I said, since I didn't want to feel like we were chasing them off, and that's what it felt like right now.

But Darcy shook her head. "We're just going to head out. No offense."

"None taken." She'd had dinner with me—and Mother and Catherine—yesterday, and she hadn't seemed eager to get away then, so she must just want to spend some alone-time with Patrick Nolan.

I looked at him, as he held the coat for my sister. "Will you let us know if anything happens with the Odom investigation?"

Nolan didn't answer, and I added, persuasively, "I really think this is the Odoms doing everything they can to get their hands on Beulah's restaurant. They failed to get the will overturned yesterday. And today they're accusing Yvonne of murder. If they believed all along that Yvonne murdered Beulah, I can't imagine that they would have wasted time with a competency hearing. Can you?"

Nolan had to admit that he couldn't. "I'll give you a head's up if they get an arrest order."

That was probably the best I could hope for, so I thanked him, and watched them walk out. "Did you get the impression they couldn't wait to get away from us?"

Rafe grinned. "Young love."

They were both older than us, but OK. "They look good together, don't they?"

"Your sister's a pretty woman," Rafe said.

She was. Or maybe striking was a better description. And Nolan wasn't a bad-looking guy, in spite of the beaky nose and the slightly oversized ears.

"I feel like we didn't learn a whole lot."

"I didn't think we would," Rafe said. "He's a cop. Not like he's gonna be inclined to tell you much about an ongoing investigation. Specially when he knows you think they're investigating the wrong person."

Maybe so. "I'm used to talking to Tamara Grimaldi. She tells me things."

"She don't tell you everything, either. Not when it's none of your business."

Maybe not. "He had a point about the gun. If Robbie shot himself, there'd be a gun somewhere."

Rafe nodded.

"And there wasn't."

He shook his head.

"So maybe Robbie didn't shoot himself."

"Maybe not." He looked up as the waiter—short and Hispanic—approached the table. "*Buenas tardes, amigo.*"

He prattled on in Spanish, ordering me a glass of sweet tea and himself a bottle of Corona. And a bowl of cheese dip to go with the bowl of chips and salsa the waiter had put on the table. I was able to follow the conversation up to that point, mostly because I know the basic food names. I couldn't follow what came after that, so I didn't try. When the waiter took himself off to fill the drink order and bring the *chile con queso,* I arched my brows at Rafe.

"Just making conversation." He filled a chip with salsa and lifted it to his mouth.

"I keep forgetting how well you speak Spanish."

He shrugged and swallowed. "You don't spend ten years trying to work your way into a South American theft gang without having to learn some Spanish."

It had sounded like more than some, but what did I know? He had managed to pull off a few months undercover as Jorge Pena, professional hitman, though, so I figured his Spanish was probably pretty damn—darn—good.

We got what we ordered, anyway—or so I assume, since Rafe didn't send it back—and spent an enjoyable meal discussing murder, mayhem, and other related subjects. He detailed his march through the woods, searching for a way off the Skinners' property, including the time he'd been out of cell phone range and his worry that something would happen to him while he had no way to call for help. I made him laugh by telling him about Pearl's bath. Her brief dispatch of the small stuffed animal I'd bought her made him frown, though. "Not sure I like that."

I hadn't liked it, either. However— "It's not her fault. It's what she was trained to do."

"I'm not blaming her, darlin'. But there's a reason dogs that have been used for fighting don't make good pets. They've been trained to be vicious."

"Pearl's not vicious," I objected. "When it comes to us, she's just very protective." And so far she had listened to me when I'd told her not to attack, so I wasn't too worried about her going at the wrong person.

"I'm glad she's protective," Rafe said. "And I know you want her. But what happens when we have a baby crawling on the floor?"

I hadn't thought about that. I probably should have.

No, scratch that. I definitely should have.

"You don't think she would do anything to the baby, do you? I mean, there's a big difference between a baby and a puppy or a kitten. Or another dog."

"Maybe not to Pearl," Rafe said.

Maybe not.

"I have an appointment with the vet in the morning. I'll ask him what he thinks."

Rafe nodded. "You want dessert?"

I didn't. I had gorged myself on fajitas and cheese dip and chips and a lot of other things—some of which included sour cream and avocado—so I was full. "You go ahead."

"I had a different kind of dessert in mind." He winked.

"By the time we get back to the mansion, I'm sure I'll be up for that." I smiled back. Just give the food time to settle, and I'd be hungry for 'dessert,' too.

"Then let's get outta here." He signaled the waiter for the check, which arrived promptly. Rafe paid the bill and added an exorbitant tip. I'd even go as far as to call it obscene.

I arched my brows at him, but he just smiled. And then, when we were on our way out the door, after the waiter had picked up the receipt and seen the amount of money he'd been given, Rafe stopped to ask a question. I waited for a minute while the two of them went back and forth, and then Rafe nodded and came toward me. "Let's go." He put his hand on my lower back and nudged me out the door, into the chilly dark of the fall night.

"What?" I said.

He glanced down at me. "Since Vasquez struck out on the marijuana angle, I figured I'd tap another source."

"The waiter? How do you know that he knows anything about it?" He hadn't smelled like marijuana, and after this morning, I knew that smell well.

"I don't." He unlocked the car and opened my door. "But she said most of the trade is South American. I thought there was a chance he mighta picked something up."

I guess maybe the South Americans liked Mexican food, too. I guess it made sense that they would. And maybe they liked Mexican beer, or Tequila. And maybe, if they had a little too much Tequila or Mexican beer, they talked.

"Good idea," I said. "I guess that explains the tip."

"I figured it couldn't hurt." He shut my door and walked around the car to the driver's side. "Let's go home."

"Back to the mansion?"

He nodded. "Might as well wait somewhere comfortable."

I thought about saying something about the fact that he was comfortable enough there now to call it home, but then I thought that that might just make it awkward. So I didn't. But I noticed.

"Fine with me," I said instead. "You still owe me dessert."

He grinned. "Starting to get in the mood?"

"I'm always in the mood. I just thought it might be best to give the food a chance to settle. There isn't a lot of room left in my stomach these days."

He reached over. "Everything OK in there?"

"As far as I can tell." My stomach moved, and I smiled. "Did you feel that? He turned over. Or she."

We still weren't sure what we were having. The latest ultrasound had been undecided. The technician had ventured what she thought was an educated guess, but until I knew for sure, I wasn't going to make up my mind one way or the other. The nursery at home was yellow. Once we knew what we were having, I'd throw in some blue or pink to match, but I still had a month and a half or so to go. And maybe more, since first babies are often a little late.

The baby did another somersault, and Rafe chuckled. "Looks like we've got a gymnast."

"Or kick-boxer." I grimaced as a tiny foot got me in the ribs.

He rubbed soothing circles, I guess in an effort to make the little athlete inside settle down. Unfortunately, it seemed to have the opposite effect. Junior knew that Daddy was paying attention, and was getting excited.

"Let's just go home," I said, with both hands on my stomach now. It was literally shifting back and forth as the baby moved.

"Lean your seat back a little. You'll be more comfortable." He put the car in gear and we rolled out of the parking lot and down the street as I fumbled for the lever between the door and seat.

Leaning back felt better. The heartburn subsided, and the baby felt less squeezed. "I've had a pretty good pregnancy," I said, as I watched the streetlights flicker past outside the window. One. Two. Three. "After I stopped throwing up, anyway. And apart from all the extra visits to the hospital because something happened and we needed to check that the baby was all right. I haven't been feeling too bad the last couple of months. And I didn't get the gestational diabetes or anything like that. It's been good."

He glanced at me. "But?"

"I'm getting ready for it to be over. I feel like an elephant."

"It could be worse," Rafe said. "It could be ninety degrees."

True. And don't think I hadn't thought about that. "I'm starting to feel sort of unwieldy. It's hard to get out of bed in the morning."

"Hasn't it been hard to get out of bed all along? You've been sleeping a lot."

"It takes a lot of effort to make a baby. But that wasn't what I meant. It's literally hard to get out of bed. I can't sit up anymore. I have to roll, like a beached whale, over to the edge of the bed, and tip myself off onto the floor."

He chuckled. "You don't look like an elephant or a whale. You're gorgeous. But I get that it's tough."

"You can't possibly get it," I said grumpily. "You've still got your body. There's nothing stopping you from jumping out of bed in the morning."

"Sure there is." He grinned.

"Not like that." But I smiled back. It was impossible not to.

He reached over and took my hand. "It'll be over soon. By Christmas, we'll have a baby."

We would. His and mine. And life would never be the same

again. I folded my fingers around his and held on as the car left the lights of Columbia behind and traveled the dark road toward Sweetwater.

We were about halfway there—in fact, we were just coming up on the shuttered Beulah's Meat'n Three, although I'm sure that was a total coincidence—when Rafe swore.

I was almost asleep by then, or at least so relaxed and full of food that I hadn't been paying attention to our surroundings. Not until Rafe said a bad word and yanked the wheel hard to the left. I straightened my seat as we bumped off the paved road and into the graveled lot outside Beulah's. "What happened? Did we get pulled over?"

"You could say that." He fought the car for a few seconds until he managed to slow it down and turn it toward the road again. I looked out. There were no blue lights in sight. But as I watched, a big truck with round headlights and a row of lights on the roof of the cab followed us into the lot. And parked at the entrance to the road, so we couldn't leave. The interior of the Volvo was lit up almost as bright as day.

I squinted. "Who's that? Police?"

"No." Rafe's voice was grim. My heart skittered in my chest as he reached for his gun and the door handle. "Stay here."

He opened his door.

"Where are you going?" Panic laced through my voice. "Who's out there?"

He leaned down to peer into the car. "Just stay here. If something happens to me, scoot over to the driver's seat and get the hell away."

Have you lost your mind?

I bit back the words. "Should I call the sheriff?"

"Not yet." He straightened. "Just stay inside the car where it's safe."

That I could do. I wouldn't do anything to risk harming the

baby, at least not until I had no other choice. But if something happened to him, I was damned if I'd drive off and leave him there. And if he thought so, he didn't know me at all.

I didn't say that, either, just nodded and stayed inside the car. Rafe shut the driver's side door and walked toward the truck. His hands were up, with the gun clearly visible, although there was absolutely nothing about him that looked like he was surrendering. More that he was signaling he wasn't going to shoot first.

After a second, the lights on the truck turned off. A voice called out in Spanish, and Rafe turned toward me. "Kill the lights."

I reached over and flipped off the headlights on the Volvo. The clearing plunged into darkness.

TWENTY

It took my eyes a few seconds to adjust. Since nothing happened in those few seconds, it turned out to be no big deal.

I got my sight back in time to see the doors on the truck open. Two men got out, one from each side. And when I say that they got out, I mean that they climbed down. The truck was big, with huge tires, and the men were both short. Short and dark, with broad cheekbones and black hair.

This wasn't exactly how I'd hoped the waiter would come through with his information about the drug dealers. We could die here in this parking lot, and nobody would ever know what happened to us.

Neither of the men glanced at the Volvo, but I scooted down a little in the seat anyway. I knew it was stupid—if the waiter had tipped them off, they knew I was here—but it made me feel better. At least the baby was safely tucked below the dashboard. That wouldn't help if they shot me in the head, but it was the best I could do. I couldn't keep from peering out across the dashboard to see what was happening.

Rafe did nothing. Just stood there, a few feet from the corner of the Volvo. He'd lowered his hands, but kept the gun out and clearly visible. It was in his hand, but he wasn't pointing it at anyone. The South Americans did the same. Each had a pistol in his hand, but they weren't pointed at Rafe (or me). My impression was that they were more there for show than anything else. It was as if all three of them wanted the others to know that they were armed and dangerous, but that they wouldn't shoot unless the other team shot first.

I wondered whether they thought I was in here with a gun of my own.

If this kind of thing continued to happen, maybe it wouldn't be a bad idea to get one. And learn how to use it.

The two men stopped a few feet in front of Rafe. Close enough to talk, but far enough away that he couldn't reach out and grab either of them. With the windows closed, I had no idea what they were saying. And since they were presumably speaking Spanish, I doubt I would have understood much even if I had been able to hear.

I concentrated on watching, instead. Watching their hands, in case one of them suddenly decided to bring the gun up and shoot. And watching their faces, so I could pick them out of a lineup if I had to.

One was Rafe's age, a year or two past thirty. Short, with broad shoulders and skinny legs. The other was younger, early or mid-twenties. A brother, maybe, or just a friend. A little taller, with longer hair and a ratty, little goatee. They were both wearing jeans and dark jackets, and I memorized their faces as best I could, just in case I'd have occasion to identify them later.

Not that they were behaving in a threatening way. They weren't. Each was almost a head shorter than Rafe, and quite a bit smaller all around. If he knocked their heads together, he'd probably knock them both unconscious. And neither made any move to attack. The pistols stayed loose and low in their hands. In Rafe's, too.

The conversation continued for about ten minutes, during which I became aware of an increasing need to pee. It might have been nerves—the situation was scary, even if no one was shooting; I was quite aware that things could turn on a dime—although it was more likely to be the tea I'd had with dinner. Under normal circumstances, we'd be close to the mansion by now. Instead, I had to sit here in the dark, while my husband was having an armed discussion outside, and try to hold it.

A car appeared on the road, and conversation ceased as all three of them watched it drive by. It didn't pull into the parking lot, and when it was out of sight, they went back to talking. But the conversation was mostly over by now. About a minute later, the two strangers headed back to their truck. Rafe stayed where he was, outside ours, while they turned their lights back on and bathed the clearing in a glare. My heart started beating faster. Now would be the time to shoot him, if they were going to. As they were driving away.

But nothing happened. They backed off, into the street. Where they took off toward Columbia with a squeal of tires. Rafe waited until the truck was completely gone before he holstered his pistol and came back to the car.

He locked the door behind him and put his head back against the seat and closed his eyes. "I'm glad that's over."

"Scary?" I asked.

He rolled his head to look at me. "I've been in scarier."

I knew he had. "You'll excuse me for being a little worried. I thought they might shoot you."

"I thought they might, too. That's why I made sure they understood that I'm not working vice and I'm not interested in their business."

He leaned forward to put the car in gear again and headed for the road.

"Had you met them before?" I wanted to know, as we left the bumpy gravel of Beulah's parking lot for the smooth blacktop of the road.

He shook his head. "They knew who I was, though. Or Pablo did."

"The older one?"

He nodded. "He knew Hector. And couldn't be happier that Hector's out of the picture."

"That's good." At least we weren't looking at someone else who wanted to avenge their mighty leader's incarceration. One of those had been enough.

"I made sure he knew that the case against Hector is old news. I'm not interested in coming after him. All I wanted to know, was if they had anything to do with shooting the Skinners."

"And?"

He glanced at me. We were zooming toward Sweetwater at a good clip. "He said they didn't."

"Did you believe him?"

"Pablo pointed out that the last thing they'd wanna do is draw attention to themselves. It makes sense."

It did.

"He said, if they'd wanted to get rid of the marijuana crop, they'd have set fire to the greenhouses instead."

And all of the Devil's Backbone would get high from the smoke. I could just picture it. A haze of pot smoke all over Maury County.

"They alibied each other," Rafe added. "For the night the Skinners were murdered."

"Are they gay?"

He shook his head. "I didn't get that impression. They musta been together doing something, I guess. Either that, or they're lying."

"Wouldn't you be able to tell if they were lying?" He'd always been able to tell when I was lying, anyway. Then again, I'm possibly the world's worst liar. Not in the sense that I do it a lot; in the sense that I do it badly.

"Some people are good liars," Rafe said. "And it was dark. Not that easy to see. I didn't get the feeling that they were lying, but they mighta been."

So the suspect list now included Mrs. and Ms. Odom, Sandy and Kayla, and Pablo and his friend. In addition to Robbie and his hypothetical partner. I had no idea about the Odoms, or Kayla and Sandy, but at least we knew that Pablo and his friend had access to guns.

"The guns they were carrying..."

Rafe shook his head. "Ballistics came back as shotgun. Not pistol."

"But that doesn't mean they couldn't have two shotguns tucked away somewhere else."

He nodded. "Could easily be a couple of shotguns behind the seat in that truck, yeah."

So they weren't off the list. Even if Rafe seemed strangely inclined to believe that they'd had nothing to do with the Skinner murders.

"Did I tell you I'm taking Pearl to the vet tomorrow?" I asked. "I'm hoping to find out something more about the dog fighting thing. I tried to find whatever vet the Skinners took their animals to, but nobody would admit that the Skinners were patients."

"Dog fighting's illegal," Rafe said. "If a vet thinks a client's using dogs for dog fighting, he has an obligation to inform law enforcement."

"So if one of the veterinarians did know, and didn't inform, he wouldn't want me to know about it."

He nodded.

"Then I probably won't learn anything. But Mother said I should take Pearl in and make sure she's all right from living outside, so that's where we'll be in the morning."

Rafe nodded. "Not sure what the sheriff's got planned for tomorrow. The whole case feels like it's mired in molasses. Everywhere we turn is a dead end. We have a lot of info, and a lot of possible motives, but none of'em seem to go anywhere. They all end up in the parking lot at Beulah's with two people with alibis."

He turned the Volvo into the driveway at the mansion.

"I can't wait to get inside to the bathroom," I said.

He laughed.

Pearl had to put on a show before letting us into the house, of course. By the time that was over, I click-clacked my way down the hall to the guest bath without taking my booties or overcoat off first. By now, my need to pee had escalated to an absolute must, and immediately.

Rafe, meanwhile, went inside the parlor to visit with Mother. When I came in, she was talking animatedly, using her hands to make her point. But as soon as I showed up in the doorway, she stopped. "There you are." She smiled.

"I had to visit the ladies room," I said, taking a seat next to Rafe on the velvet loveseat. "The baby's squeezing my... um..."

Bladder. The word I was looking for was bladder. But I figured Mother probably wouldn't appreciate me using it. Too anatomical.

"Rafael was telling me about what happened on the way home."

Oh, was that what he'd been doing?

It hadn't sounded that way to me—it was Mother who had done all the talking, not Rafe—but his expression didn't give anything away.

"It was scary," I admitted. "At least at first. When we first stopped, and they had their lights on, and Rafe got out of the car, I was sure they were going to shoot him." And I'd be a widow after less than six months of marriage.

He reached out and took my hand. It was hard and warm. "They didn't."

Not this time. But telling him that I worried would be pointless. He knew. I turned back to Mother. "They ended up just talking for a while, and then the truck drove away. And we came home. Nothing happened. Everyone's fine."

She nodded. "I spoke to Bob while you were gone. He's

going to stop by."

Fine by me. I had suggested it myself, this afternoon. "We're probably going to head up to bed. I'm wiped out. And it isn't every night Rafe has a chance to get to bed at a decent hour."

Like last night, when he came in sometime in the wee hours of the morning. Before tramping through the woods half the day. He must be exhausted.

From the look he gave me, clearly not too exhausted for dessert, though.

"Go ahead," Mother said. "I'll let Pearl out when Bob leaves."

Bob was leaving? I had assumed he'd be staying the night once he got here.

Not that it was any of my business. They were consenting adults. They could do whatever they wanted. And there was no need to lie about it, if that was, indeed, what Mother was doing to spare my feelings.

Whatever.

"Thanks," I said. "I appreciate it. Once I get up there, I probably won't wake up again for anything but a minor earthquake. This making a baby business takes a lot out of you."

Mother nodded. "Just wait until the baby's born," she told me. "You won't get a full night's sleep for the first year."

Something to look forward to.

"I'll see you in the morning," I said. "I'm taking Pearl to the vet. If I'm not up by eight, will you wake me?"

Mother promised she would, and I caught Rafe's eye. He got to his feet, too. "Good night, Margaret Anne."

"Good night, Rafael," Mother said. And I couldn't help but remember a night last year—Christmas Eve—when he had shown up here to tell me that he had finished the investigation into Hector Gonzales's SATG and was ready to rejoin the human race, if I wanted him. I'd taken him upstairs to my room while Mother had glowered, tight-lipped.

A lot had happened in a year. Not all of it good, but as far as

I was concerned, we were all in a better place than a year ago.

Like last year, I held Rafe's hand up the stairs. Unlike last year, I didn't have to drag him behind me. "You can stay downstairs and wait for the sheriff if you want," I told him as we reached the second floor. "And update him on our meeting with the drug dealers."

"It can wait till tomorrow. If I let you go to bed by yourself, you're prob'ly gonna be asleep by the time I get there."

There was a good chance of that.

"And anyway—" He grinned, "the sheriff ain't coming here to see me. He wants to see your mama. I don't wanna get in his way."

"Good point," I said. "Let's get this show on the road, then."

We turned into my room. "What's the matter? Just wanna get it over with?"

"Tired. But I never just want to get it over with." It had been more than a year of us sleeping together at this point. And I still couldn't get enough.

"Good." He pushed my back up against the wall next to the door and bent his head to nuzzle my neck. I dropped my head back. "I'm not tired at all," he added, his breath warm against my skin. "I can do this all night long."

My toes curled into the rug. Rafe chuckled. And that's when the phone rang.

It wasn't inside my room. I could hear twin dial tones from downstairs, and from Mother's bedroom at the end of the hall. After a few seconds the ringing stopped, so she must have picked up the phone downstairs. I turned my attention back to my husband, who was doing wonderful things with his lips and my throat. Until—

"Rafe! Savannah!" It was Mother's voice, from the bottom of the stairs, and she sounded frantic.

Rafe didn't even hesitate. One second he was there, a hundred percent intent on getting me naked and into bed, the next he was out the door and on his way down the stairs, two steps at a time.

Good thing we hadn't gotten around to taking any clothes off.

I followed, a little more slowly. She'd called for him first, so chances were he was really who she wanted. I was just an afterthought.

They were standing in the foyer, and Rafe already had his boots on.

"What happened?" I asked.

He looked up at me, while keeping his hand under Mother's elbow while she slipped her feet into shoes. I don't think either of them realized just how far they'd come in a year. "Somebody shot the sheriff."

Oh, my God. "Is he OK?"

He had to be, if that had been him on the phone. Didn't he?

"OK enough to get himself to the hospital." Rafe's voice was grim. "Get your shoes on if you're coming."

Was I coming? I glanced at Pearl, standing in the hallway outside the parlor, looking from one to the other of us. "Maybe I'll just stay here with the dog."

"Nice try," Rafe said. "Get your shoes on. Let's go."

"You asked." But I made my way toward the booties over by the door.

"I ain't leaving you alone here. Not even with the dog for protection."

Fine. "Can we take the dog with us? I don't want to leave her here alone. What if she starts to chew on Great-Aunt Ida's velvet loveseat?"

Mother looked nauseated.

"She'll have to stay in the car when we get to the hospital," Rafe warned me. "We can't take her inside."

"Are you sure I shouldn't just stay here with her?" I'd gotten my booties on, but I still wasn't sure about this.

"I don't want you staying here by yourself. Just in case someone thought this would get us out of the house."

"Why would someone want us out of the house?" But I grabbed for my coat.

"Dunno," Rafe said. "But just in case someone's coming, let's give'em what they want. I don't want you here alone. Does the dog have a leash?"

She did. It was in the kitchen, where I'd left it when I stowed the food and biscuits earlier. Rafe hurried down there and got it. When he approached Pearl, she hunched her back and dropped her head and the stub of a tail dejectedly.

My heart broke a little. "It's OK," I told her. "We're not chaining you up. You're coming in the car. But there are leash laws. You can't just run free. Unfortunately."

She didn't respond. But when Rafe had buckled the pink collar around her neck and attached the practically weightless leash, she lifted her head and looked surprised.

"Guess somebody was expecting another chain," Rafe said and tugged the leash. "C'mon. Time to go."

"I'll take her." Mother reached out and took the leash from him as we passed through the door and onto the porch. "You two sit up front. I'll stay in the back with Pearl."

I had my mouth open to protest—how could I relegate my mother to the backseat?—but Rafe nodded. "Strap in. I'm gonna go fast."

"Thank you," Mother said, and crawled into the back of the car. After a second's pause, Pearl jumped in after her. I walked around to the passenger seat and strapped myself in.

"Everyone ready?" Rafe didn't wait for an answer, just peeled off down the driveway and onto the road without stopping.

"Is he at the medical center in Columbia?" I asked when I'd caught my breath.

Mother nodded. She wasn't as used to Rafe's driving as I am, and she was clinging to the door handle so hard her knuckles were white.

"How bad is it?"

Mother took a breath. "He was able to drive himself to the hospital. I imagine that means it's not life threatening."

I would imagine so. "Has anyone called Todd?"

Rafe glanced at me. "I'm sure the hospital did," Mother said. "He's Bob's next of kin."

He was. And she was right, the hospital had probably taken care of it. Nothing I had to do, then.

"Did he tell you what happened?"

"He was on his way to the mansion," Mother said. "I told you he'd called, and was coming over."

I nodded. "Where was he coming from?" Or from whence was he coming? "Home?"

Bob Satterfield, and Todd too, lived in an old four-square house in downtown Sweetwater. In case I haven't made it clear, the Martin Mansion is on the north side of town, on the Columbia Highway, near the city limits. It's probably not much more than a five minute drive.

"The sheriff's office," Mother said. "Someone shot at the car. And hit Bob in the shoulder. Instead of coming to the mansion, he drove straight to the hospital."

Smart man. "If he could get himself all the way there, I'm sure he's all right. I've been shot in the shoulder. Rafe has, too." And I wasn't sure I'd have been able to drive myself to the hospital afterwards.

However— "I don't think Rafe even went to the hospital." A couple of band aids and some Tylenol, and he'd been back on the job.

Rafe nodded. "It hurts like hell, but it's usually not a big deal. No organs or anything to damage up there. As long as the bullet didn't shatter a bone, they'll patch him up and pump him full of antibiotics, and he'll be back to normal in a week or two."

Mother nodded. She still looked a little pale, but that could have been the darkness and the occasional pair of headlights coming in the opposite direction, bleaching the color from her face. She kept her hand on the dog's back as we zoomed up the road to the medical center, either to give Pearl comfort or to take some of her own from the steady breaths of the relaxed animal.

TWENTY-ONE

The last time Rafe and Todd Satterfield had met in a hospital, Todd had said the wrong thing and Rafe had flattened him, right there in the corridor.

It was a year ago, give or take. I had just had a miscarriage. Rafe thought it was Todd's baby. Todd knew it was Rafe's. Neither of them was happy about it, and one thing led to another. Incidentally, it was just a week or so later that I got shot in the shoulder. Nothing to do with either Rafe or Todd.

When I peered into Bob Satterfield's hospital room and saw Todd sitting there next to his father's bed, it all came rushing back.

I turned to my husband. "Maybe we should just stay out here in the hallway."

Rafe gave me a look. "Your mama's gonna wanna see her boyfriend, darlin'. And I'm sure the sheriff has something he wants me to do."

"Todd's there," I pointed out. Couldn't he do whatever it was his father wanted? Between him and Mother, surely they'd have it covered?

"I see him, darlin'. Feel free to take him outta the room if you think he can't handle looking at me, but I gotta hear what the sheriff has to say, so I can go about trying to find who shot him."

"Would you like me to try?"

He looked at me. "I got it covered."

"I meant, do you want me to try to get him out of the room

before you go in?"

"No," Rafe said. "I want you as far away from him as you can get."

OK, then. I took a breath and pushed the door open, and pasted a smile on my face. "Evening, Sheriff. How are you doing?"

"I got shot," Sheriff Satterfield said. He was sitting up in bed, in a hideously ugly hospital gown. I could see the outline of bandages crossing his right shoulder under the fabric.

"I know. I'm so sorry." I smiled politely at Todd. "Hi again."

He nodded. To me and to Rafe. "Collier."

"Satterfield." Rafe nodded back.

A truce. Good. At least neither of them would end up on the floor.

"We won't be staying long," Rafe said, turning to the sheriff. "I just wanted to see what you wanted me to do about this."

The sheriff nodded, and then winced. Even that small movement must hurt. "They got the bullet out. I had them tag it for forensics. Just in case there's a connection to the Skinner case."

Rafe nodded.

"I think the shots mighta come from Oak Street Cemetery. I was on my way past there when it happened."

That was interesting. Or seemed so to me. Probably because I had just been at Oak Street Cemetery this afternoon.

That didn't mean there was any connection to Beulah or the Odoms. Unless it was a total accident—some kid taking potshots at cars on the road from his house—there aren't that many places on the road between Sweetwater proper and the mansion where someone could hide and wait. It's mostly private property along the road. And someone who was hoping to kill the sheriff would probably have enough sense not to go into someone else's yard to do it, just in case someone was home and got a good look at the shooter.

"Any chance it was an accident?" I asked, and the sheriff moved his eyes (only) to look at me.

"I wouldn't think so. The shot was too accurate for that."

"So do you think he was trying to kill you? Or make you crash? Or what?"

He shifted, and winced again. "I wasn't going fast. Even if I'd crashed, I don't think I woulda died."

"But you might have been laid up for a while."

He nodded. "I'm gonna be laid up for a few days now. But it's not like that matters. The investigation will go on. Even with me outta commission, there are other people who'll do the work."

He glanced at Rafe, who nodded. "Anything else you can tell me? Or something else you want me to do, other than checking the cemetery?"

"I can't think of anything." The sheriff shifted again, and winced again. It was as if he couldn't keep from moving, even though he knew it would hurt. "Forensics on the bullet'll come back tomorrow. We'll know more then. Anything new on your part?"

"I had a talk with a couple drug dealers on our way home from dinner." He outlined what had happened in Beulah's parking lot. Mother made unhappy noises, and while Todd didn't make noise, he didn't look happy, either. "They said they can alibi each other for the night the Skinners were shot. That ain't worth much, since they'd prob'ly lie about it. But for what it's worth."

The sheriff nodded.

"They took off back toward Columbia," I added, "after they were finished saying what they came to say. I don't know if they would have had time to get down to the Oak Street Cemetery to shoot at you."

Although if we had had time to go inside the mansion and spend a couple of minutes with Mother and upstairs before we got the call about the sheriff's mishap, maybe they would have. On the other hand, the shooting had taken place before we got the call, so maybe not. It might even have happened while we were in Beulah's parking lot, talking. And if so, Pablo and his friend were definitely off the suspect list.

"I'll go take a look," Rafe said, and turned to my mother. "You gonna be all right here?"

She nodded. She was a bit pale, too, and was holding onto the sheriff's hand. "Todd will give me a ride home later."

We all looked at Todd. He nodded.

"We'll take Pearl with us," I said. She was in the car in the parking lot with the windows cracked, since we couldn't bring her inside the hospital.

Mother nodded. "Don't wait up."

I had no intention of waiting up. And to be honest, I had a feeling she'd probably be home before us.

"I'll stop in tomorrow morning," Rafe told the sheriff. "Try to get some sleep."

We turned toward the door. And stopped when it opened.

A man a few years younger than the sheriff stuck his head through and looked around. When he saw Sheriff Satterfield, he pushed the door open and came in. "Sheriff." He extended a hand for shaking.

"Chief." The sheriff moved to take it, and then thought better of it, since it was his right shoulder that was hit. "Sorry." He inclined his head toward it.

The other man—Columbia chief of police Carter, I assumed—stuffed both hands in the pockets of his very nicely cut suit. If Sheriff Satterfield was tall and a bit raw-boned, a Gary Cooper type, the chief was Cary Grant. Dapper and almost a bit too good-looking, in an over-fifty sort of way. He gave my mother an appreciative look that lasted a second too long, and while I don't think she really noticed, both the sheriff and Todd did. Todd's eyes narrowed. So did mine.

Rafe took my arm. "We'll be back tomorrow," he told the sheriff again as he took a step—and I did, too, perforce—toward the door.

"Wait a second." Chief Carter turned away from the bed. "You must be Agent Collier. I'm Chief Carter."

"Nice to meet you." Rafe let go of my arm to shake. "We appreciate the loan of your officer to help us deal with this. Especially now."

With the sheriff out of commission. He didn't say it, but it was inferred.

"My pleasure." Chief Carter had a lot of teeth. They were impossibly white and straight, too. Almost blinding. He'd either had them straightened and bleached, or they were fake. "You know, I'm happy to pick up some of the slack until the sheriff is back on the horse. It's a big case, and one that's received a fair amount of notice in the media. We don't want it to languish because of this. I'm sure you could use another pair of hands while the sheriff's out of commission."

There was an almost imperceptible pause. I'm not sure anyone but me realized that Rafe was considering this suggestion very carefully. "We appreciate that," he said after the moment had passed, "but I'm sure you've got your own crimes to deal with inside the city limits, Chief. I've got Officer Vasquez's help, and the sheriff's deputies, and if I run short, I can always call in a couple other agents from the TBI. I've got three rookies up in Nashville just itching to get down here to do some investigating." He grinned, but there was an edge to it. I'm not sure anyone but me noticed that, either.

Chief Carter looked put out, but he didn't push the issue, just nodded. "Let me know if that changes. I'd be happy to lend a hand."

Rafe said he would, politely enough, and we left.

"What was that about?" I asked when we were outside the hospital and on our way across the dark parking lot toward the

Volvo. I had thought it better not to bring up the subject while we were still inside the hospital. You never know who's listening.

He glanced at me. "It's under control. We don't need any more help."

I nodded. That was most likely true. Just as everything else Rafe had said was true. He had Lupe Vasquez to help him, if he needed anything inside the Columbia city limits, and he had Sheriff Satterfield's deputies for anything in the rest of the county. And if he wanted more professional help—or someone to do grunt work—he could always call in the three rookies he was training up in Nashville. They were young men in their early twenties, and would probably be beyond psyched about a field trip to the Devil's Backbone. "You're not usually possessive. At least not about work. You've always been happy to work with Grimaldi and the MNPD."

He shrugged. "He's been trying to push his way into the investigation from the beginning. It's bothering me."

It would probably bother me too, to be honest. "Well," I said, "if you don't need him, you don't need him."

"I don't." He unlocked the car doors and opened mine. In the backseat, Pearl came to and scrambled to her feet.

"Hello, darling," I cooed as I slid across the seat.

Rafe closed the door behind me, and came around the car, and continued the conversation as if there hadn't been a pause. "It's not that difficult of a case. It's not like we're dealing with a serial killer. Just someone—or two someones—who wanted the Skinners gone. It's the same motive for all of'em. We're not dealing with somebody who's obsessed. I don't have to worry about when the next shoe's gonna drop. I don't think this guy— or these guys—are gonna do it again."

I nodded. He'd mentioned the possibility of a spree killer the first day, but since nothing had happened and no one else had been shot—except for the sheriff—I guess the investigation had moved away from that as a solution.

"How about what happened this evening?" I asked. "Any chance it was just random—some stupid kid with a gun—and not related at all?"

By now we were on our way down the road toward Sweetwater again.

"It don't have to be related," Rafe said. "You're right, coulda been a kid taking a potshot at the sheriff. Could be something to do with another case. Like the Beulah thing."

That thought had crossed my own mind, too. The coincidence of the cemetery being the scene of the shooting, after the exhumation this afternoon, was a bit hard to swallow. Even if I had rationalized it for myself earlier.

"I hope you're right. That would mean nobody's likely to take a potshot at you."

"Let's hope," Rafe said.

We drove in silence a few minutes, and I don't think I was the only one waiting for the gunshot.

When we passed the mansion, I said, "I guess we're headed to the cemetery? To look around?"

He nodded. "Dunno what we're gonna find in the dark. We'll have to get a forensic team out in the morning, to take a closer look in daylight. But I wanna see if I can at least pinpoint where the shooter was. That way they don't have to walk all over everything tomorrow."

"We'll come with you," I said. "Maybe Pearl can smell something."

I saw the corners of his mouth lift. "I don't think she's been trained for that, darlin'. But sure, you can come along. Unless you want me to take you home first. You and the dog."

"I want to be where you are," I said, firmly. There was just the chance—like this morning—that whoever had shot Sheriff Satterfield was still lying in wait behind a handy gravestone, and when he saw Rafe come up the hill, he'd plug him too. And since

Rafe would be straight on, and a lot closer than the sheriff had been in his car down on the road, chances were the shooter would get him in the chest or right between the eyes. And I wasn't about to let that happen, if there was anything at all I could do to stop it.

We parked in the same place I had parked earlier, for the exhumation, and made our way up the hill. I was holding Pearl's leash, and Rafe had a flashlight. A big one, that he could use to knock someone unconscious if he had to, but that he was using for its intended purpose at the moment. The circle of light seemed very small in the vast darkness. And let's be honest, graveyards can be a bit creepy at night. Not to mention the fact that they provide excellent cover—and lots of it—for anyone with a gun waiting to take out a special agent.

My heart beat overtime as we made our way between the gravestones, with Pearl sniffing eagerly at the ground. Once we got to the top of the hill—and it wasn't much of a hill, just a gentle rise, since you can't really bury people on a sharp vertical—Rafe started looking around.

"This is the most likely angle," he told me as he flashed his beam of light around.

I peered down the hill at the road, where the sheriff would have gone by. "No chance he could have made a head shot, then." We were high enough above the road that the sheriff's head wouldn't have been visible.

Rafe nodded. "I don't think our guy tried to take him out. Just outta commission."

"Do you know who?"

He glanced at me in the dark. "I have an idea. It's sorta crazy. I'm not gonna tell you about it."

Fine. "Be that way," I said, watching him prowl between the gravestones. Pearl sniffed a cross stuck in the ground at an angle.

"Looks like some depressions over here. The ground's still a little wet from yesterday."

"When you say depressions, I guess you mean footprints?"

"Something like that," Rafe said, looking at the road. "This looks good. If I were gonna take a shot at somebody in a car, this is where I'd be."

"I didn't know you had sniper training."

He grinned at me over his shoulder. "I don't. You don't need to be a sniper to take someone out at this distance."

"But it would take more than a pistol, wouldn't it?"

He nodded.

"So we're back to the shotguns used against the Skinners. How much do you want to bet one of the bullets is going to match?"

"Nothing," Rafe said. "I don't bet against the house." He gestured me—gestured us, me and Pearl—back toward the road and the car with the flashlight.

Driving from the cemetery to the house was like deja vu all over again. It was just a few hours since I'd done it, after the exhumation, with the dog panting in the backseat.

We pulled into the driveway, and Rafe looked up at the bulk of the house. "Don't look like your mama's back yet."

I shook my head. There was a light on in the parlor, but I was pretty sure we'd forgotten to turn that off when we left in such a hurry earlier. And no one had thought to turn on the outside porch lights before we took off, so they were dark. If Mother had come back, and had realized we weren't here, she would have turned them on to make it easier for us when we arrived.

Rafe pulled to a stop at the bottom of the stairs. "OK if I just keep the car here till tomorrow?"

I nodded. "Sure. That way Mother can tell right away that we're back." Which she couldn't if we put the car in the garage.

"Stay there." He opened his car door. I stayed where I was. I'm not sure exactly why, other than that he asked. I mean, it's not like I'm not capable of opening my own door. And while it's nice that he wants to do it for me, he doesn't have to do it every time we go somewhere. Especially not when it's dark, and late, and I can't wait to get inside. But I sat and waited. In the backseat, Pearl panted eagerly. She was probably ready to get out of the car and inside, too. Rafe shut the driver's side door and headed around the hood to get me. He'd gotten about halfway there, when there was a loud bang. Rafe dropped to the ground at the same time as the windshield shattered. I shrieked. In the backseat, Pearl started barking. Deep, reverberating barks I barely heard through the cotton in my ears.

"Rafe!"

I pushed my door open, as Pearl's barking reached a hysterical pitch.

"Stay down!"

I could barely hear Rafe, either. But the fact that he was talking penetrated. He was alive. For a second or two, I hadn't been sure.

Because he'd asked, or ordered, I crouched down low in my seat instead of bursting outside to see whether he was OK. Time stood still as I waited for the next shot.

It didn't come. Instead, it was Rafe who came, around the car at a crouch until he was tucked behind my open door. "You OK?"

"Fine," I said shakily. "Someone shot at us."

He nodded grimly.

"Did he hit you?"

He shook his head. "Can you walk? Let's get you outta here and into the house."

"What about you?" My teeth were shattering. Delayed reaction, I guess. In the backseat, Pearl kept barking frantically. I tried to shush her, but she wouldn't listen.

Rafe leaned back on his heels and reached to open her door. Pearl launched herself through the opening, skidded on the gravel, and then pointed herself in the direction from whence the shot had come. She took off for the woods still barking.

"C'mon." Rafe took my arm and practically hauled me out of the car like a cork from a bottle. "Let's get you inside while he's distracted."

The barking was fading into the distance.

"You don't think he'll shoot her, do you?" I clung to his arm as he propelled me up the stairs to the porch, covering me with his own body. Putting himself between me and whoever was out there.

"Better her than you." He fumbled the key into the lock. "He was prob'ly already running by the time she got out of the car, and once he saw her, he'd run faster. I'll have to see whether she could catch up."

The lock clicked. He pushed the door open and me inside. "Stay there until I come back. Lock the door but don't turn on any lights."

He didn't wait for me to obey, just took off down the stairs after the dog, already yanking his gun out of the holster.

I stumbled across the threshold, locked the door, and sat down, right there on the floor, in the foyer.

TWENTY-TWO

It was an eternity before he came back. Or at least five minutes. I kept my ears peeled for the sound of shots, but I couldn't hear any. Pearl's barking faded into the distance, or maybe it stopped. I sat there, on the floor, with my arms curled protectively around my stomach and tears running down my cheeks. Partly it was just reaction, but partly it was fear, too. Fear of what was going on outside. Fear that, after everything we'd been through, Rafe was going to get shot and killed by some nutcase with a gun right back here in Sweetwater, in my own backyard. I'd come so close to losing him so many times before. And that bullet had come awfully close. If he'd been moving just a little bit slower, he wouldn't be alive now.

A sound on the porch outside brought my head up. A scuff of a boot on the floor, and the outline of a man against the glass in the door. He'd told me to keep the lights off, so I had, but there was no mistaking that physique.

I scrambled to my feet and yanked the door open. And threw myself in his arms, sobbing.

"Sorry, darlin'. Sorry." He gave the dog time to strut through the opening before he kicked the door shut. "I didn't wanna leave you. But I had to see if I could catch him. Or at least see who he was."

I nodded, my wet cheek against the soft cotton of that gray hoodie he'd been wearing for the past several days. Somehow he still managed to smell good, like clean laundry and spice.

"You all right?" His hands were running up and down my arms, checking for damage.

I nodded and sniffed. "I wasn't hit. And car windows don't shatter the way other windows do. There was no glass."

He stopped touching to check for damage, and just held me for a moment, his breath warm in my hair. "That was a helluva thing."

It had been. "The same guy who shot the sheriff?"

"I'd guess so. I didn't see him. I followed the dog through the woods, but by the time I got out on the other side, all I could see were taillights."

"That's too bad." I burrowed a little deeper into his arms. "But at least you're all right."

"Mostly," Rafe said.

I straightened. "What do you mean, mostly?"

"The bullet grazed me before it hit the windshield."

Holy shit. Pardon my French.

"You mean you've been running around the woods bleeding? Let me see. Is it safe to turn on the light?"

"The guy's gone," Rafe said, "so yeah. But maybe it'd be better to go into the kitchen." And away from the big, open, double doors.

I pulled him after me down the hallway. "Sit." I pushed him toward the island while I fumbled for the light switch inside the door. When light flooded the room, I turned to him. "How bad is it?"

"I've had worse." But he was still gritting his teeth as he pulled the gray hoodie down his arm and off.

"Oh, my God." I took one look at the bloody furrow crossing his arm, and felt my head go light.

"It's not that bad," Rafe said, poking at the edges of the wound as I braced myself on the counter so I wouldn't crumple to the floor. "I've had worse."

I knew he had. But the sight still turned my stomach. "We

have to go back to the hospital. You need stitches."

He squinted at me. "I've got this, darlin'. It's not deep. Just see if you can find me some bandages."

I wasn't in any condition to argue. And as he'd said, he'd had worse. He probably knew what he could get away with and what he couldn't. I got down on the floor to dig out the first aid kit from under the counter, and I can't even begin to describe how nice it was to have the hard surface of the floor under me. I don't think I'd been in danger of fainting, but I was certainly not as steady on my feet as I wanted to be.

I lifted the box with the first aid supplies up onto the island, but stayed on the floor myself. "I'm sorry. I want to help, but every time I look at your arm I want to throw up. If you need me, I'll do my best. But if you don't, I'm just going to stay down here for another minute."

"It's fine, darlin'." His voice was steady, and I couldn't hear a lot of pain in it. "I've done this before."

Of course he had. I leaned back against the island and closed my eyes as he opened the box. The lock snicked, and then I heard his fingers rummage through the contents. Pearl nosed me, seemingly worried, and I roused enough to ruffle her ears so she knew I was OK.

Out in the front of the house, there was the sound of the door opening. Pearl took off down the hallway like a shot, barking frantically.

I lifted my head. "Did we remember to lock that when we came in?"

Rafe nodded, at the same time as Mother raised her voice. Pearl, naturally, had stopped barking once she recognized Mother. "Hello?"

"Kitchen," I managed, and listened to Mother's heels clicking down the hallway toward us, accompanied by the lighter clicking of Pearl's nails.

Mother came in saying something mundane, I'm not even

sure what it was, and then she stopped. "Oh, dear. Savannah, darling..."

"I'm all right," I said. "I just feel like I'm going to faint."

Mother nodded. "Rafael—"

And then she saw what he was doing, and turned pale. "Urk!"

He glanced at her. "It's OK. I've had worse."

Mother swallowed. I could see the effort it took. She was probably sick to her stomach, too, but she pushed through it. "Let me help you with that."

She disappeared out of sight around the island, and they got busy with band aids and gauze. Pearl abandoned me to stand there and watch, her tail twitching back and forth.

"This isn't a gunshot," Mother asked, "is it?"

"If it was a gunshot, there'd be a round hole." Rafe's voice was steady. "This is just a graze."

"From a bullet."

Rafe nodded. "He was waiting in the woods when we drove up."

Mother's hands stilled for a second. "I hope he's gone now."

"Pearl chased him off," I said, from down on the floor. "Rafe saw his taillights drive away."

"Good." Mother wound gauze around Rafe's arm, pure white against his dusky skin. "Do you need anything for the pain?"

"A couple Tylenol oughta do it. I don't wanna drop out, just in case we have more trouble."

Mother nodded and went to get him the Tylenol. "I appreciate that."

"Don't mention it." He was smiling. I could hear it in his voice.

It was probably time for me to get myself together, too. I wasn't the one who'd been shot, after all. Or grazed.

I dragged myself to my feet to take a look. Yes, neatly

bandaged. Nothing to see here. "Sorry I wasn't any help."

He shook his head. "Baby all right?"

"Seems to be asleep." At least there were no cartwheels anymore. I put a hand on my stomach. "We should try to get some of that, too. I don't think I'm up for dessert after all tonight. I have to be up early to take the dog to the vet. And you need to rest."

He nodded. Mother dropped the Tylenol into his hand, and he knocked them back, with a water chaser.

"What happens now?" She stood holding the glass and looking worried.

"We go to sleep," Rafe said. "Chances are the excitement is over for tonight. There's nobody else left to take a shot at."

"How about Lupe Vasquez?" If someone had shot at the sheriff and at Rafe because of the Skinner investigation, maybe they'd shoot at her, too.

Rafe glanced at me. "I'll send her a text and tell her to be careful. But if I'm right, I don't think she's in any danger." He suited action to words before he turned to Mother. "Set the alarm. The dog'll let us know if anyone stops by."

Pearl wagged her stub of a tail from where she was lying in front of her food and water.

"Does she need to go out again?" I asked.

He shook his head. "If she didn't take care of business in the woods, she can wait."

He had to push himself upright with his good hand. I moved to support him. "Hang onto me until we get upstairs."

"Don't mind if I do." He grinned down at me. It wasn't his best effort, but it made me feel better. If he could smile like that, he was all right.

We dragged ourselves up to the top of the stairs, and staggered down the hallway to my room. I dumped Rafe on the edge of the bed, and got to my knees in front of him to help him take off his boots. He grinned down at me. "If I wasn't about to

262 | BAD DEBT

drop dead..."

"Hold that thought," I told him, as I yanked, "for twelve hours or so." The boot came off and I started on the other one. "Unless it would make you sleep?"

He shook his head. "I don't think I'm gonna have a problem with that. And I'd rather be feeling good enough to participate."

I'd rather he felt good enough to participate, too. That's not to say I wouldn't do whatever I could right now to make him feel better. "Let's take your pants off. Can you stand for a second?"

He could. I unzipped him, and pulled the jeans down his legs. "OK. You can sit back down. It's probably best if you just sleep in the T-shirt. Wait until your arm feels a little better to try to take it off."

He nodded. "Night, darlin'."

"Good night," I said, and tucked him under the blankets before I got ready for bed myself, too.

I'd been worried about what else might happen, but we spent a quiet night. Nobody knocked on the door, nobody phoned, and there were no more shots outside. Obviously the unknown gunman had gotten what he came for. Rafe had dropped to the ground when the shot grazed him, so maybe the shooter thought he'd actually hit him, instead of just plowing a bloody furrow in Rafe's upper arm.

Somebody wanted him out of commission, obviously. He and the sheriff both.

Someone who wanted the Skinner investigation stalled? Someone hoping to get away?

But if someone had shot all the Skinners and wanted to get away with it, why had that someone even stuck around Maury County this long? He could have jumped in his car two nights ago, after plugging the last Skinner, and been long gone before anyone knew the Skinners were dead.

So whoever it was had a reason for staying. A reason that

was more compelling that the need to go. A family in Maury County? A job? A life?

And maybe no obvious connection to the Skinners, making it easier to believe he wouldn't come under suspicion?

Whatever Rafe was thinking, I couldn't imagine what it was. So I turned to look at him instead.

It was early-ish, just after seven. I'm not sure what woke me, since I don't usually wake up this early. Maybe it was the knowledge that I had to be at the veterinarian's office in Columbia by nine. Or maybe Rafe had moved or made a noise. Maybe I was just worried about him.

He was asleep now, anyway, his skin dusky against the white sheets. The wounded arm was on the outside of the blanket, the bandage still pristine. He hadn't bled overnight, then. That was something to be grateful for. And he was sleeping peacefully.

He's a good-looking guy, whether he's awake or asleep. Good bone structure, gorgeous physique. Pretty eyes, with long, sooty lashes that were lying against his cheeks right now. His lips were soft and slightly parted, and he was breathing quietly.

Mostly, he looks very capable of taking care of himself—and everyone else who happens to come along. Mostly, he is. But there's something about him when he's vulnerable like this that just tugs at my heart. I love him so much it hurts, but at times like this, I just melt.

He opened his eyes. From one second to the next, from sleep to alertness. "Morning, Goldilocks." His voice was raspy, sending shivers down my spine.

"Good morning," I managed. "How are you?"

"Fine." His lips curved.

I thought about telling him that yes, he was, but settled for a simple, "Me, too."

"So I see." He reached for me. "C'mere."

"I'm not sure this is a good idea," I said, even as I let him pull me closer. "Your arm..."

"Ain't gonna be bothered if you climb on."

Ah. Well, no. That shouldn't affect his arm. "Are you sure you're up for... I mean..."

He chuckled. "Yes, darlin'. I'm definitely up for that."

He was. "I don't want to hurt you," I tried.

"You ain't gonna. Walking around like this all day is gonna hurt more than taking care of it now. There you go..."

I positioned myself and sank down, and his eyes rolled back in his head.

I stopped moving. "Oh, my God! Are you all right?"

He smiled, his eyes hot under sleepy lids now. "Just keep doing that."

I kept doing it. And I'll spare you the details. They're private. Suffice it to say that when I staggered to the bathroom a bit later to clean up, we were both in a very good mood. And the bandage around Rafe's arm was still pristine.

"Are you going to the hospital this morning?" I asked when I came back out of the bathroom after showering and brushing my teeth.

He nodded. "I gotta give the sheriff an update on everything that happened yesterday."

"Any chance you can get them to take a look at your arm while you're there? Just to make sure you don't need stitches?"

"I don't need stitches." He was sitting on the edge of the bed preparing to get up. "But I'll ask someone to take a look." *Since you insist.* He didn't say it, but it was implied.

"Thank you," I said. "Do you need a hand up? Is it OK for you to take a shower?"

"It's fine." He accepted my hand to help him get upright. "I'm gonna unwind the bandage before I go in. Will you help me get it on again later?"

I said I would. By now, hopefully that bloody furrow in his arm had healed enough that I wouldn't pass out when I saw it.

Worst case scenario, I'd ask Mother to help again.

So he rinsed off while I got dressed and dried my hair, and ten minutes later we were on our way down the stairs together.

Mother was in the kitchen sipping coffee. Between the sheriff and a shooter right outside her house, she might have spent a restless night. I had no idea. I'd dropped off pretty much as soon as my head hit the pillow. But she did look closer to her own age today, a bit more drawn and tired than usual. "I want to go to the hospital and see Bob," she announced, with no preliminaries. "Would you like a ride?"

Rafe nodded. "I'll text Officer Vasquez and tell her to meet me there."

"The dog's been out." Mother turned to me. "She's ready to go to the vet when you are."

"I need something to eat first." The baby did uncomfortable things to my stomach lining when I was hungry. And I was hungry almost all the time.

"There's yogurt in the fridge," Mother said, "and oatmeal in the cabinet." She concentrated on pouring coffee into a travel mug, which she handed to Rafe. "Banana?"

"Don't mind if I do." He snagged one from the bowl and winked at me. "Looks like we're going."

It did look that way. "Stay in touch," I told him, while I poured instant oatmeal into a bowl and added water. Steelcut oatmeal made properly on the stove is better, but I didn't have that much time, either. This would have to do. "Please get someone to take a look at that wound. It's great that it's stopped bleeding, and it's probably OK, but humor me."

He nodded. "Take care."

"I'm going to the vet," I said. "It isn't like I'm the one chasing down dangerous criminals."

"Humor me." He dropped a quick kiss on my mouth, and then followed Mother out the back door. Pearl moved aside, politely. I closed and locked the kitchen door behind them, and watched them walk across the dead grass to the old carriage house, now the garage, where Mother's car was parked.

By then, my oatmeal signaled its completion from the microwave, so I didn't stick around to watch them drive away. I did hear the car pull past the house and go off down the driveway, though.

Pearl and I only stayed long enough for me to finish my oatmeal and a glass of milk. Not only did we have an appointment to keep, but I felt a little uncomfortable in the house by myself, to be honest. What if someone was watching? What if someone had seen Rafe and Mother drive away, and knew I was here by myself?

I bundled Pearl into the car, and didn't draw a deep breath until we were both locked in and on our way down the driveway.

The drive to Columbia was uneventful. Nobody shot at me. Nobody stopped me. Nothing untoward or interesting happened. The phone didn't even ring. I pulled into the Animal Hospital's small lot with almost fifteen minutes to spare, and sat in the car for a minute to look around.

A handful of vehicles were parked on the other side of the lot. Employees, most likely, staying out of the way and leaving the parking spots right up front to paying customers. (Yes, I had parked right up front.) There were a couple of seen-better-days small compacts—I guess maybe you don't get rich from working in a veterinarian's office—and a beat-up pickup truck. A nice BMW probably belonged to the doctor of veterinary medicine—Anderson, wasn't it?—and then there was the big white truck with the multiple doors on the sides.

Animal Control.

I arched my brows and opened my door. "C'mon, Pearl. I know we're early, but let's go check it out." And see if maybe the young woman I had met at Robbie's crime scene two days ago was here.

Was that significant, if she was? If she knew Doctor Anderson?

Or was she here to take Pearl back? Yesterday, they'd told me I could keep her. But maybe it wasn't that easy. Then again, possession is nine-tenths of the law. She was mine now. And in my possession. Wearing the leash and collar I had bought her.

Bottom line, if anyone thought they could take her away from me, they had another think coming.

I squared my shoulders and marched toward the entrance, ready to do battle. Only to be yanked back when Pearl dug her claws in and refused to walk through the door.

I bounced back, and turned to her. "What's the matter, sweetheart?"

She was cowering, her head and stub of a tail drooping.

"It's all right," I told her, stroking a hand down her back, where the bones of her spine stood out too prominently. "I won't let them hurt you. If they have to give you a shot, it's so you'll feel better. But nothing bad's going to happen to you. I promise. You're coming home with me."

She shivered, and kept shivering. My hand came back covered with tiny hairs.

Maybe this wasn't a good idea. If there was a puppy or a kitten in the lobby, would Pearl feel compelled to attack it? And could I hold her back if she did?

Maybe it would be better if I checked and made sure the lobby was empty before I took her inside. For everyone's safety. And then had them take her directly into an exam room.

I looped her leash over a handy hook that seemed to be there just for that purpose. "I'll be right back."

I took the couple of steps toward the door and pushed it open, into the lobby. Now that I wasn't holding on to Pearl's leash anymore, and wasn't trying to make her move, Pearl seemed more inclined to go with me. Or maybe she was just concerned that I'd run up against something I couldn't handle, if she wasn't there to protect me.

The lobby was empty, and by now Pearl was standing next to me, ready to bark at any sign of trouble. I stepped back to unhook her leash, and we walked in. She started shivering pitiably as soon as we were inside, but by then we had made it through the door, and there was no turning back.

"Savannah Martin," I told the young woman—pink-haired—behind the counter. "Collier."

"That the name of the dog?"

I shook my head. "That's my husband's name. I'm just getting used to it. The dog's name is Pearl. I spoke to Doctor Anderson yesterday."

She nodded. "We have you on the schedule. Fill this out, please." It was a sheaf of papers a half inch thick, attached to a clipboard.

I looked at the top sheet. "I don't know any of this information. I've had the dog since yesterday. We think she was used for dog fighting. If she wasn't, she's spent her life chained outside, underneath a trailer, without much to eat or drink. I just need someone to take a look at her to tell me if she's healthy. But I have no idea about her history."

"Do the best you can," Pink Hair told me.

That would be easy enough, anyway, since the only thing I could do, pretty much, was sign the bottom of each page.

"Do you have somewhere we can go, maybe? As I said, I think she was used for dog fighting. She decapitated a stuffed toy yesterday. I don't want to be responsible for the consequences if someone brings a puppy or a kitten in here." Or, God forbid, something even smaller, like a pet hedgehog or guinea pig. There wouldn't be anything left.

She looked at me in silence for a moment before she nodded. "Just a sec."

It was no more than that before the door between the waiting room and clinic opened and she waved us through. "You can wait in Exam 1. Doctor Anderson will be right in."

"Thank you." I pulled Pearl, shivering like in a strong wind, into the empty exam room. "Sorry."

"She can smell the other dogs," Pink Hair said. The voice of experience.

I reached down to pet her. Pearl, not Pink Hair. "I saw the car from Animal Control outside. Is... um..." What was the name Rafe had given me two days ago? " —June here?"

Pink Hair lowered her voice conspiratorily. "She and Doc Anderson are dating."

No kidding? "How long has that been going on?"

"A year or so," Pink Hair said, with a flip of those pink tresses. "How do you know June?"

"Oh, I don't really." I reached to give Pearl another stroke. "I just met her at a crime scene a couple of days ago. When she picked up the dog."

"I heard about that." She nodded. "A family up in the hills was shot."

"The Skinners. Did you know them?"

But she hadn't. Or said she hadn't. Doctor Anderson had said the same thing, so it was probably true that the Skinners didn't bring their dogs here for treatment. They probably hadn't brought their dogs anywhere, the bastards. Just put a bullet in their brains if they got sick or hurt.

Just as someone had done to the Skinners.

I forced a smile. "I'll just wait for the doctor here. You can let June know I'm here, if she wants to talk to me. I didn't see her when I went to Animal Control to talk about the dog yesterday."

Pink Hair nodded and withdrew. The door closed with a little click behind her. I sat down on the only chair in the small room, and got busy scratching Pearl's ears and assuring her she'd be all right between signing my life away on the admittance forms.

TWENTY-THREE

Doctor Anderson walked in just a few minutes later. He was on the tall side, and handsome, in a distinguished sort of way. Prematurely gray, at a guess, since his face didn't quite match the pallor of his hair. I'd put him in his late thirties; ten years or so older than me. He was dressed in jeans and a blue shirt under the white coat, and sported a friendly smile. At least until Pearl started growling at him, her neck hair standing up.

"Sorry," I said, while I tried to calm her down. "She's protective."

"That's OK. It's nice that she has bonded with you so quickly." He held out a treat. Pearl's nose twitched, but she didn't accept it.

"Go ahead," I told her. "He's not going to hurt you. He's just making sure you're all right."

It looked like she contemplated that. I don't think she actually understood a single word, but she could tell I wasn't afraid, so she backed down.

Doctor Anderson wisely refrained from touching her while she was chomping on the treat. She might have taken his hand off if he'd tried. Instead he talked to me. "Tell me about her."

"I told you all I know on the phone yesterday. She's a rescue. I found her two days ago chained outside a trailer up near the Devil's Backbone. Her owner had been shot. Your girlfriend came and picked her up, and she must have run away, because yesterday afternoon she was back up there, probably looking for

Robbie."

The vet was back at the previous thing I'd said. "My girlfriend?"

"Your receptionist told me that you and June are involved. I saw her truck in the parking lot."

"Oh." He flushed.

"Just out of curiosity, where were you the night the Skinners were shot?"

His brows arched. "Are you accusing me of something?"

"Just asking a question," I said. "See, it occurred to me that someone might have killed the Skinners to rescue the dogs. Most people wouldn't consider a human life a fair trade for a dog—let alone seven—but someone who sees neglected and abused animals all the time, like you and your girlfriend..."

I trailed off, suggestively.

"If someone killed the Skinners to rescue the animals," Doctor Anderson said stiffly, "wouldn't they have taken the dogs with them?"

"I'm not sure. That would make it kind of obvious that the dogs were the target, wouldn't it? And anyway, you and your girlfriend would have known that Animal Control would be called in, and she'd get her hands on those dogs anyway, a few hours later. Anybody else who killed seven people to rescue dogs might have taken the dogs. You two didn't have to."

"That's crazy," Doctor Anderson said, but without a whole lot of conviction.

"I'm not accusing you of anything. Just curious. I don't suppose you'd tell me where you were last night? Between seven and ten, say?"

"What happened yesterday?"

He sounded sincerely concerned, which was a point in his favor. I also didn't get the sense that he already knew the answer to his question, although I'm not as adept at winkling out lies as Rafe, so I could have been wrong about that.

"Someone shot Sheriff Satterfield. And the TBI agent who's in town helping him." The TBI agent who happened to be the love of my life and the light of my existence. Although I didn't mention that.

"That's terrible," Doctor Anderson said. I thought he looked a bit pale, honestly. "June and I were together last night. We had dinner. That was probably around six-thirty or seven. We spent the night at home. My home."

"Alone? Together?"

"We're consenting adults," Doctor Anderson said dryly. "Yes. Alone, together."

"So neither of you has an alibi."

He shook his head. "We didn't realize we'd need one. Is the sheriff serious about suspecting us?"

"The sheriff is in the hospital after having a bullet dug out of his shoulder. He's mostly concerned about finding who shot him. We think there's a connection to the Skinner homicides."

Doctor Anderson looked at me for a second. Then he leaned back and opened the door to the hallway. "June!"

A moment later, rapid footsteps sounded outside. "Eric? Are you OK?"

She stuck her head through the opening, and took in me and Pearl. Her voice changed. "Oh."

"They think we shot the Skinners. And the sheriff and his deputy."

"Agent," I said.

"The sheriff?" June's confusion looked real, as well.

I told her what had happened. "We think there's a connection between the shootings yesterday and the Skinners. I think, when we get the bullets back, they'll be from one—or both—of the guns that were used in the Skinner homicides."

She looked at me for a second. "Your husband is the TBI agent who came down from Nashville, right?"

I nodded. The love of my life and the light of my existence.

"Is he all right?"

"The bullet mostly missed," I said. "He bled some. The sheriff took one in the shoulder, and had to spend the night in the hospital."

She shook her head. "That's terrible."

I couldn't agree more.

"She asked about our alibis," Doctor Anderson told June. "For the night the Skinners died, and last night."

June turned back to me. "We were together last night. At Eric's place. The night the Skinners were shot, I think we were together, as well."

"At the Skinners'?"

She rolled her eyes. "No, not at the Skinners'. Are you serious? I love animals, but I wouldn't kill people over them. Not when I could have just called the cops. That's what we've been working on. Getting enough evidence of the dog fighting to call in the sheriff."

She sounded sincere. And it did make sense. Nonetheless, there were two of them, just like there were—had been—two shooters at the Skinners'. And I didn't believe for a second that they wouldn't lie for each other, so their alibis were worth squat.

Of course I didn't let her know that's what I thought. "I appreciate it," I said instead, and changed the subject. "I guess your colleague down at Animal Control told you I want to keep Pearl? She made her way back to Robbie Skinner's place yesterday afternoon, and she seems to like me."

"She damn near went for my throat when I came in," Doctor Anderson added, as corroborative evidence. A bit of an exaggeration, but appreciated, nonetheless.

June hesitated. "I can't keep you from keeping the dog. You've got her. She's in your possession. You didn't have to let us know that you planned to keep her."

"But?"

"You realize she's been mistreated and neglected and

probably abused? She's going to have issues."

"I've already learned that I have to keep smaller animals away from her," I said, giving her a scratch behind the ears. "Other than that, she's been great. I'm not worried."

Doctor Anderson moved forward. "Let's get her up on the table. Give me a hand, June?"

June gave him a hand. Pearl didn't look thrilled, but she allowed herself to be hoisted onto the slick metal table, where her nails scrabbled for purchase. She started shedding like crazy, and shivering like a leaf. I stroked her and cooed at her. "It's OK. It'll be over soon. He's just looking at you. After this is over, we'll go home where you'll be safe."

The examination didn't take long. Pearl had no broken bones and no lacerations. I already knew that, since her fur was short and if she'd had open wounds, I would have noticed. She also didn't have fleas or mange. She got a pill for heartworm, a couple of shots for other things, had her toenails cut, and then I was allowed to walk out with her, a lot poorer, but with a few interesting tidbits of information. Pearl looked beyond happy to be done, her tongue wagging and her stubby tail sticking up jauntily as she made her way toward the Volvo.

I opened the back door for her, and she jumped in. I pulled out my phone and called Rafe.

It took him a few seconds to answer. "Collier."

I assumed from the greeting he wasn't alone. Or maybe he just hadn't taken—or had—the time to look at the display.

"It's me," I said. "Everything all right?"

"Fine."

OK, then. "I wanted to update you on my visit to the vet. Turns out he and June, the Animal Services person, the one who came to pick up the dogs from the Skinner properties the other morning, are involved. They're each other's alibis for last night and the night the Skinners were shot."

He made some sort of noise.

"I don't know whether they have access to shotguns, but it wouldn't surprise me. This is the country down here."

He made another noise.

"Pearl got a pill and some shots, and we're on our way home. Or somewhere else. I'm not sure yet." The implication being that I'd be happy to drop everything and meet him somewhere if he suggested it.

He didn't.

"Where are you?" I asked. "Still at the hospital?"

"We left a few minutes ago." 'We' being him and Lupe Vasquez, I assumed, since he had said earlier he intended to have her meet him there.

"How's the sheriff this morning?"

"Grumpy," Rafe said. "The pain's worse the second day. After the adrenaline and anger wears off."

Did that mean he was in more pain today, too? "Did you have anyone take a look at you?"

He said he had. "The doc offered to put in a couple stitches, but it's already healing on its own, so he said it wasn't necessary. It was just if I wanted to."

"Let me guess. You didn't want to."

"Why'd I want stitches I don't need?" He didn't wait for me to answer. "I forgot to dig that bullet out of your backseat last night and get it to forensics."

I glanced into the backseat, beyond Pearl, who had settled into a pretzel-shape, with her nose on her back legs. "I see the hole." Round and neat in the middle of the leather. We'd have to patch the upholstery, I guess. Or get used to driving around with a bullet hole in the car. Maybe, when the baby came, I could position the car seat in front of it. "I could use a new windshield, too," I added.

The cracking wasn't too bad. A sunburst going out from a small hole in roughly the middle of the window. I'd been able to see all right while I was driving, but it would be easier without the cracks.

Rafe swore. "I didn't remember that. I can't believe I left you with a broken windshield."

"Mother didn't give you much time to think this morning," I pointed out. "And it isn't that bad. I can drive with it. Although we'll have to have it replaced at some point."

I heard his voice talking, but not to me. After a second, he came back on the line. "There's a repair shop a couple blocks north of where you are. Drive up there, and we'll pick you up."

"Are you sure? I don't want to interrupt your work. I can make it back to the mansion. I made it here."

"I want it fixed," Rafe said, "before we have to drive back to Nashville. There, you'll be stuck at home. Here, at least your mama's around, and you have sisters and a brother who can pick you up if you need to go somewhere."

He had a point. And it was nice of him to think of it. "I'll see you there, then."

"Tell'em to leave the bullet in the backseat alone."

He hung up before I could tell him that I had no intention of letting anyone into the backseat as long as Pearl was there. And Pearl would be there until Rafe showed up with another car to put her in.

The repair shop was easy to find. As he'd said—as Lupe Vasquez had no doubt told him—it was just a few blocks up the street from the Animal Hospital. I pulled into the lot in front of a garage bay, and parked. "We'll wait here a minute," I told Pearl, even as a man in mechanic's overalls came out of the little office next to the bays, and toward me. "Excuse me a second. It'll probably be best if I take this outside."

Definitely best, since Pearl had already seen the guy, and was rumbling low in her throat.

"Just wait a minute," I told her. "Rafe will be here soon, and then we'll get you out of there."

She didn't look happy, but she settled back down. I stepped out of the car and closed the door. "I'm waiting for my husband to get here to pick me up. Me and the dog."

The guy—his nametag said his name was Greg—glanced into the car and turned pale. "I need a new windshield," I told him.

He looked at it. "That looks like a bullet hole." The accompanying look was accusatory.

"We'll dig the bullet out of the upholstery before we leave the car with you."

He had no answer to that. "I should be able to get the windshield done today. Dunno that I can do anything about the seat."

"Don't worry about it," I said, as a Columbia PD squad car pulled into the lot. "I'll take care of the seat. You just worry about the window. This is them now."

The squad car pulled up next to the Volvo, and Rafe opened the passenger side door. It looked like he'd lost the argument over who was driving again today. The mechanic—Greg—took one look at him and swallowed.

"My husband," I said.

He gave me a look—something like mingled respect and horror—and nodded. "We... um..." His voice cracked, and he tried again, "I just told your wife I think we can get this windshield fixed today."

Rafe nodded. "Scuse me." He pulled a knife out of his pocket. Greg turned a shade paler. I couldn't help but smile, although I tried to hide it. He practically collapsed against the side of the car when Rafe stepped past him and opened the back door. "C'mon, sugar."

He lifted the dog out of the car. "Get the door." He nodded to the squad car.

I hustled to open the back door, and he loaded Pearl inside before turning back to the Volvo and crawling into the backseat.

Greg looked like he was thinking about running away, but

thought better of it. "I'll... um..." He gestured to the office.

I nodded. "Someone will be in to talk to you in a minute."

Greg looked less than thrilled as he slithered along the side of the Volvo before making a break for it across the parking lot.

Rafe backed out of the car and straightened. It hadn't taken long to dig out the bullet.

"Did you get it?"

He nodded and showed it to me, flat on his palm. "Forensics'll match it to the one they dug out of the sheriff, and the ones they recovered from the Skinners."

"Bet?"

He shook his head. "It's gonna be one or the other of the same guns. Not sure it matters which. The one they took outta the sheriff yesterday matches the gun used on Art and Linda."

"So this might be from the gun they used on Cilla and her boyfriend."

"Might could." He walked around the squad car to Lupe Vasquez's window. "Take care of this for me." He dropped the bullet, or slug, or whatever it's called, into her hand. "I'm gonna go inside and deal with the mechanic."

Lupe Vasquez nodded. "I'm sorry," she told me as Rafe headed for the office, "but you're going to have to sit in the back with the dog. Behind the partition."

"No worries. I've been in police cars before." I crawled into the back with Pearl. She waited for me to get comfortable—as comfortable is it's possible to get in the back of a police car—before she settled down with her head in what was left of my lap. Between the size of Pearl's head and the size of my stomach, she was hanging off my knee, pretty much.

"So what's new?" I asked when we were situated. "Rafe didn't tell me a whole lot earlier."

"Sheriff Satterfield is fine," Lupe Vasquez said. "He'll be released this afternoon."

"That's good." And would make my mother happy. He

probably wouldn't be able to take care of himself very well, with what I assumed would be an arm in a sling. Mine had been in a sling when my shoulder was hit last year. Would Mother move into the sheriff's house with him for the duration? Or would she invite him to stay with her? That had the potential to be awkward, for all of us, if Rafe and I were still there.

Or maybe she'd do neither. Todd lived with his father. Between the two of them, they'd probably manage.

"Forensics came back on the bullet that hit the sheriff. It matches the bullets from some of the Skinners. We'll test this one," she held it up, inside a ziploc baggie now, "but I'm sure it'll turn out to be the same story."

I nodded. I was sure, too.

"When we're done here," Lupe Vasquez continued, "we'll take you and the dog home, and walk through the woods where the shooter was hiding when he shot at you, to see if we can find anything he left behind. Footprints or a gum wrapper or a cigarette butt or something like that."

"Any news about the Beulah Odom investigation?"

"Nolan contacted me," Lupe Vasquez said, "to say that Jarvis heard back from the M.E. It'll be a while until the new toxicology results come back, but on the face of it, nothing's changed from the last time he did the autopsy on Ms. Odom."

I had a hard time believing that. After two months in the ground, I'm sure quite a lot had changed. Not that I was about to say so. "Did Jarvis say anything about potassium chloride?"

"Nolan told Jarvis about the potassium chloride," Lupe Vasquez said, "and Jarvis said he'd check with the M.E. Then he called Nolan back a few minutes later and said that the potassium levels had been a little high at the first autopsy, but not so high that they'd raised any flags."

"Mrs. Odom—Beulah's sister-in-law—takes a medication called Epiklor. It's potassium chloride. And it can be deadly when injected."

Lupe Vasquez nodded. "Nolan said you'd shared that with him. He said he'd share it with Jarvis and see what Jarvis wanted to do."

Hopefully Jarvis would do something. While I was positive Yvonne hadn't poisoned Beulah, I was less certain that the Odoms hadn't. If nothing else, someone would look into it.

"So things are moving forward," Lupe Vasquez said, as Rafe came back out of the repair shop. He had his phone to his ear.

The call ended before he made it to the car, and he dropped the phone into his pocket. "Change of plan," he said, when he'd opened the door and fitted himself into the front seat. "Sorry, darlin'."

This was directed at me, not Lupe Vasquez. At least I hoped so. He glanced into the back of the car at me, and his lips twitched.

"What's the change?" Lupe Vasquez wanted to know, as she turned the car and headed out of the lot.

"We gotta go back up to the Devil's Backbone before we can go to Sweetwater. Our old friend who called to tell us about the marijuana grows, called again. He wants us to meet him there."

"How do you know it was the same guy?" I asked. He hadn't talked to him yesterday. Mother had.

He glanced back at me. "Guy with a handkerchief over the phone to disguise his voice? I don't figure there's more than one of them around. And he knew about the greenhouses. He wants us to drive up there and meet him."

By now, I assumed rather a lot of people knew about the greenhouses. But OK. "So he has some more information for you?"

"Said he knew who killed the Skinners," Rafe said. "Sorry, darlin'. But I don't wanna put him off while we drive all the way down to Sweetwater and back."

Of course not. "I don't mind," I said. "Pearl and I will just go along for the ride. It's not like we have anything else to do."

Without transportation, our only option was hanging around the mansion all day, and to be honest, I'd rather tag along with him and Lupe Vasquez. At least I wouldn't be going out of my mind with boredom. "I don't suppose you got any kind of indication who this guy is?"

"Sorry. Coulda been anybody. Coulda been the sheriff, for all I know. That handkerchief, or whatever it was, did a good job."

Too bad. I had wondered whether, if Rafe had picked up the phone yesterday instead of Mother, he would have recognized the voice. Now I guess we knew that he wouldn't.

"It was a guy, though? Not a woman?"

He shook his head. "Definitely not a woman. Not unless she was a baritone, and that's unlikely."

It was. If nothing else, I guess we could eliminate Kayla and Sandy.

"He said to come in the back way," Rafe added. "The route I walked yesterday. I'll talk you in."

Lupe Vasquez nodded. I settled back in the seat and put my hand on Pearl's head. At least now, I'd get to see how Rafe had spent such a large part of yesterday.

It was a bit of a drive. We passed the entrance to Robbie's place, and then another driveway a mile or two further on, to Art's and Linda's place. Then after that, another. "Darrell's place," Rafe said. "In another mile or so, there'll be what looks like another driveway, but there's no mailbox next to it. That's what we're looking for."

We kept driving. In another mile or so, there was the driveway with no mailbox, and Lupe Vasquez turned in.

"There's a gate just up ahead," Rafe told her, "so don't get going too fast."

"On this surface?" She shot him a look. "No chance of that."

The road here was no better than Robbie's drive, and might have been worse. The car bumped over ruts and the wheels sank into holes and puddles. I kept my fingers crossed, praying that the shocks would hold out.

A few yards in, we did indeed come to a cow gate. It was open, and leaning drunkenly to the side.

We kept going. Lupe Vasquez's hands were white-knuckled on the steering wheel as she fought to keep the car moving forward.

"What a horrible road," I said.

Rafe glanced into the backseat. "The better to keep you out, my dear."

I guess so. The Skinners wouldn't have wanted anyone accidentally wandering down here. And to make sure no one did, the sides of the road were festooned with the same kinds of signs that had lined Robbie's driveway: *No Trespassing* with pictures of automatic weapons.

While it isn't nice to rejoice in someone's death, I had to admit—to myself, at least—that I was happy that the Skinners were gone and nobody would be shooting at us.

After some harrowing minutes, we came to another narrow road that led up to the right. Rafe told Lupe Vasquez to turn. "This is the track that leads back to the greenhouses."

It looked familiar. The same two ruts in the ground that we'd walked along yesterday, from Robbie's pot operation to Art's. Except there was more vegetation down here. Up on top of the hill, the track was sort of open. Here, branches brushed the sides of the car and swatted at the mirrors.

Lupe Vasquez gunned the engine to get up the hill. I held onto Pearl. I'm not sure exactly why, because gunning the engine on such a narrow and badly surfaced track didn't result in a whole lot of speed. We might have been going thirty-five or forty by the time we reached the summit, and burst out of the trees into the more open area.

And that's when the shot came. Loud and close. I screamed. So did Lupe Vasquez, as she fought to keep control of the car. It rocked this way and that, and life slowed down as the wheels left the furrows in the ground and plowed across the grass. I saw the treeline come closer and closer, in slow motion.

"Shit," Rafe said, and that was the last thing I heard before we hit a tree trunk with a grinding crunch of metal and tinkling of glass.

TWENTY-FOUR

For a second we just sat there with our ears ringing. Rafe gathered himself first, and I guess that shouldn't have come as a surprise. "Savannah? You OK?"

"I think so," I said, my voice shaky. "I'm not noticing any pain."

I'd strapped in when I got into the car, so while I'd probably have some bruises from the seatbelt, everything else seemed fine. I'd been strapped over and under the baby, so I didn't think the baby had been hurt when I'd been yanked forward and then back.

I'd let go of Pearl in the impact, and she had flown off the seat and slammed against the wall separating the backseat from the front. I think she must have had the wind knocked out of her, because she wasn't barking. She also wasn't moving, but was just lying on the floor, and on my feet. But she was breathing, and her eyes were open. Hopefully she hadn't broken any ribs or anything like that.

"How are you?" I added.

"I'll live." Rafe's voice was grim. He had not been strapped in, nor had Lupe Vasquez. Cops often have to exit and enter their squad cars quickly, and can't always take the time to buckle up properly. And out here, I guess they'd both figured there'd be no danger of getting in an accident. We'd been going so slowly.

"How about Vasquez?"

It was hard for me to see through the grid separating me

from the front seat. Rafe leaned over with a wince. "She's out. I think she slammed her head against the steering wheel."

She was so short she probably would have. Rafe's head looked like it might have connected with the windshield. He'd probably bruised his torso on all the instruments and gadgets on the dashboard when he was flung forward, too.

"She didn't get shot," I asked, "did she?"

He shook his head. "I think what happened was that the shooter took out the front tire, and she couldn't maintain control of the car, so we crashed. She just knocked herself out, I think."

He reached over and wrapped his fingers around her wrist. "Her pulse is strong. I don't think she's hurt."

"We should check and make sure." I fumbled for a door handle, but couldn't find one. "What the hell—I mean, heck?"

"Squad car," Rafe said. "They transport prisoners. You can't give them a chance to open the door and just walk away."

I guess not. "Can you let me out, then? So we can make sure she's all right?"

"Not on your life," Rafe said. "There's somebody out there with a gun. What do you think's gonna happen when one of us opens the door?"

"He'll shoot at us?"

Rafe nodded. "I need you to stay right where you are."

Since I didn't have any choice, I nodded. At my feet, Pearl began to stir. She whimpered and then panted.

"She OK?"

"I'm not sure," I admitted. "She's down here on the floor, and I can't lift her. She hit the wall, so she might have broken something. Or just banged herself up."

"Hang on." He opened his door.

My voice rose. "Have you lost your mind? Stay inside the car!"

"He hit the tire on the other side," Rafe said. "He's over there." He nodded to the woods on the other side of the car.

"How do you know there aren't two of them? There were two guns!"

"I think there's only one shooter," Rafe said.

"With respect, I'd rather not take your word for that. And I don't want you risking your life for Pearl. I love her, but I love you more."

He didn't say anything to that, but he didn't get out of the car, either. In front of me, Pearl was getting to her feet. I put a hand on her head. "You OK, sweetheart?"

She looked up at me for a second.

"Would you like to come up?" I patted the seat next to me. Pearl contemplated it before she gathered her haunches and jumped. Up on the seat, she walked in a circle twice and lay down.

"I think she's all right," I told Rafe. "We can have her checked out again later, but for now, I think she's the least of our concerns."

He nodded. "Check your phone. I don't imagine it works, though. Mine didn't yesterday, when I was walking through this area. I had to get out close to the main road before I could call the sheriff."

I dug my phone out of my bag while he was talking, and... nope. No service bars.

"We're as far as we can get from the trailers while we're still on Skinner property," Rafe said. "Back that way," he gestured beyond where we'd been driving, "is all wilderness. That's the Devil's Backbone up there. Not much coverage. We're either gonna have to make our way closer to the trailers, or back down to the man road, if we wanna call for help."

"What about the police radio? Doesn't this car have one?"

"I imagine the crash prob'ly took it out." But he searched the dashboard for it and flipped the switch. "Dispatch? Anybody there?"

Nobody answered.

"That's not good," I said.

Rafe shook his head. "Somebody's gonna have to walk back to where we can get a signal on one of the phones."

Sure. "I expect you'd want that somebody to be you?" As if he hadn't gotten enough exercise walking this road yesterday.

"I don't want it to be you," Rafe said. "Somebody's out there with a gun."

"If you walk away, he could shoot you, and then come back for us. And you won't be here to protect us."

"Vasquez can protect you. When she wakes up."

"I think we should stay together," I said, while inside I marveled at the fact that we were here, within about twenty minutes of Columbia by car, and within an hour or so of civilization on foot—if you could call the Skinners' trailers civilization. And we were cut off from everyone.

It wouldn't have been a problem but for the man with the gun, of course. If we'd just been dealing with a broken down car, all we'd have to do is walk to where we could get cell service. But the fact that someone was out there taking potshots at us with a rifle complicated things.

"Whoever was out there mighta left by now."

Maybe, maybe not. "Maybe we should open the door and see. If he wants us to stay inside the car, and the door opens, he'll shoot at it, right?"

"Or maybe he'll just wait until one of us is outside the car and then pop us in the head."

I didn't like that idea very much, and said so. In the front seat, Lupe Vasquez was beginning to stir. We watched in silence as she twitched, and moaned, and finally opened her eyes and sat up. "Shit." Her voice was weak, and edged with pain. "What happened?"

"We think someone shot out the tire," I said. "But we haven't been outside to check."

She turned her head a half turn, and must have thought

better of it, because she focused on Rafe before she got close to looking at me. "Why?"

"We figure he's still out there."

Lupe Vasquez nodded, and immediately regretted it. "Oww." She lifted a hand to her forehead. "I have a bump."

"You slammed into the steering wheel," Rafe told her.

"How long was I out?"

"Just a couple minutes. Two, maybe three. If it's a concussion, it ain't a bad one." He gave her a second or two to digest that before he added, "We're still trying to figure out what to do."

No sooner had he said it, than another bullet sang through the air and smacked into the side of the car. I squealed and ducked. Lupe Vasquez did the same. Pearl jumped up and started barking, and Rafe swore.

"I guess he realized I woke up," Lupe Vasquez said, her voice shaky.

Rafe nodded. "We gotta get outta here." Another shot zinged the car, emphasizing his point.

"Isn't that what he wants?" Lupe Vasquez asked. "To get us out and running so he can take us out, one at a time?"

And leave us here, up in the woods on private property, where nobody was likely to find us.

"If he hits the gas tank," Rafe said grimly, "the whole car goes up."

And if we were inside it, we'd go, too.

"I vote for taking our chances outside." Not that anyone had asked my opinion, but I didn't like this feeling of being a sitting duck. I hadn't liked it before the question of blowing up the car had come up, and I liked it less now.

"At least a nice explosion would bring some help out here," Rafe said.

"That won't matter if we're dead." I waited a second and added, "I don't want to be dead."

He shook his head. "It's something to think about, though. But I'd rather control it than sit here and wait for someone else to blow us up. Let's go."

He opened his door, on the side of the car away from the shooter. I opened my mouth, but closed it again. If there was another shooter on this side of the car, we'd find out. But he might be right, and there was just one guy with two rifles.

What that did to my suspect list, was something I didn't have time to think about right now.

He slithered out and onto the ground, staying low. I held my breath, but nothing happened. "C'mon." He gestured for Lupe Vasquez.

She began to make her way across the car to the passenger side, climbing over the big console between the two front seats. Meanwhile, Rafe crept the few feet to the back door and pulled it open. "C'mon, darlin'. Let's go."

I started inching my toward him, expecting, at any second, to have a bullet slam into him from the other direction.

But nothing happened. I swung my legs out of the car and crouched on the dry grass. "Come on, Pearl. Time to go."

"Take her leash off," Rafe said softly, as Lupe Vasquez scrambled out of the front seat and onto the ground. She had a bump and a cut on her forehead, the blood smeared from where she'd touched it earlier. I opened my mouth to argue, and Rafe added, "We don't have time to stop and untangle her if she gets stuck. Better to let her make her own way next to you."

Since that made sense, I unclipped Pearl's leash from her collar and slipped it into my pocket. "Come on, sweetheart. Let's go."

With us all outside the squad car now, and crouching on the ground behind it, we took stock of the situation. Or the other two did. I felt a bit out of my element, to be honest. So I contented myself with scratching Pearl's ears while they were discussing options and peering through the car for a muzzle flash on the other side.

"There," Rafe said, a second before another bullet hit the car with a loud ping. "I've got him."

I looked over at him. "You're not going over there, are you?"

He looked back at me. "Somebody has to. Or he'll just keep us pinned here. His weapon has more range than ours, and he's prob'ly got more ammunition, too."

While that might be true, I still didn't like the idea of him going over there.

"Here's what we're gonna do." He glanced at Lupe Vasquez and then at me. "Savannah and the dog'll go straight back from here. Hopefully the car'll provide enough. Besides, he prob'ly doesn't even realize they're here. He was expecting the two of us. So you," he looked at me, "get lost in the trees up there, and once you're clear and outta sight, you head up the track toward Darrell's place. Keep checking your phone. Once you get close to the nearest greenhouse, you should be able to call out."

I nodded. "What are you going to do?"

"We're gonna split up," Rafe said. He looked at Lupe Vasquez. "You're hurt. It's better if you stick around here. And—" He hesitated a second. "If that's who I think it is, it's better if it's me taking him on anyway."

Lupe Vasquez looked like she wanted to demand an explanation. I certainly wanted to. But Rafe gave neither of us the opportunity to ask. "You head down that way." He pointed away from the car, down the way we'd come. The brush was thicker down there, and would provide more cover. "Take a couple of potshots at him. Your weapon doesn't have the range to actually get there, but it'll keep him occupied and in place. Meanwhile, I'll cut through the woods with Savannah until we're outta sight, and double back around."

Lupe Vasquez nodded. "Keep me covered until I get to the trees?"

"Course." He glanced at me, probably close to giving me the

nod to go.

"I have a better idea," I said. "If he sees Vasquez headed down that way, and then there's no more activity around the car, he'll realize that you have moved on, too. He'll either be looking for you, or he'll come down here and try to take Vasquez out. Either way, he won't stay where he is now. Wouldn't it be better if you gave me your clutch piece—" the one he kept strapped to his ankle, "and I'll stay here and take potshots at him with that while you go through the woods and double back around? That way, he might not realize that you're coming."

For a second nobody spoke. Then— "You don't know how to shoot, darlin'."

"I can point and pull the trigger," I said crossly. "You said yourself he's too far away, so it doesn't matter if I wouldn't actually be able to hit him. I'm just providing a distraction to let you get away. If he doesn't realize I'm here, maybe he'll think that you sent Vasquez off for help and you're the one still hiding behind the car. He'll think he has you pinned, so he can just wait you out."

There was another moment of silence.

"It's not a bad plan," Lupe Vasquez murmured.

Rafe glanced at her, and then back at me. "I want you safe."

"I won't come out from behind the car. I promise."

"What if he blows it up?"

"He probably won't," I said, with a lot more confidence than I felt. "Once she gets into position, Vasquez will keep him too busy to worry about me."

Lupe Vasquez nodded.

Rafe looked from me to her and back. I could tell he didn't particularly like the idea, but he knew it was more likely to work than otherwise. When he reached down and pulled the small gun he keeps strapped to his ankle, and handed it to me, I knew he'd capitulated.

"Hold it like this. Point that. Pull the trigger."

I nodded.

"Be prepared for some kickback. It's a small gun, but it'll still have some."

I nodded, even though I wasn't entirely sure what he meant.

"Ready?" He glanced at Lupe Vasquez, who was crouched at the rear end of the car, ready to take off. Her gun was in her hand.

She nodded.

"Keep her covered," Rafe told me.

I nodded.

"On three." He counted down. Lupe Vasquez took off like a shot, the gun in her hand spitting fire in the direction of the woods across the track. Rafe took off at the same time, into the trees and brush behind us. And I leaned a hand on the hood of the car, and let fly a bullet in the direction of the gunman.

The gun jumped in my hand. *Kickback.* OK, then.

I aimed and squeezed the trigger again. And by then Lupe Vasquez had thrown herself headfirst into the trees and brush farther down the track, and I could stop shooting. Behind me, everything was quiet. Rafe was gone, without so much as a snapping twig to mark his passage.

The rifle across the way spit out another bullet. Not aimed at the car this time, but aimed at Lupe Vasquez. I held my breath, but didn't hear her scream. He must have missed.

That didn't keep him from trying again. For the next several minutes, he practically peppered the area where Lupe Vasquez had disappeared with bullets. I hoped to God she'd managed to get away. Or that she was flattened on the ground holding her breath, or something. She didn't return fire, I do know that much. But that might simply be because she couldn't. Not because she was dead, but because the number of bullets coming her way kept her pinned down.

I sent a desultory shot in the direction of the gunman myself, and got an answering shot back, before he went back to taking potshots at the area where Vasquez had disappeared. It must be more important for him to stop her from getting away, than to take out Rafe, whom I assumed he thought was back here. The only good thing about it all, was that he didn't seem to have realized that Rafe was gone. The few bullets thrown in my direction, and the many, many directed at Lupe Vasquez, left no room for shooting at Rafe. He must think that Rafe still was pinned back here behind the car, when, in fact, he was on his way through the trees, preparing to land on the gunman like the wrath of God.

I won't lie about it. It was the longest fifteen or twenty minutes of my life. That's how long it took before I heard activity across the way. When bullets weren't flying, it was quiet out here in the woods, and I had no problem hearing the scuffle on the other hillside. Voices, thumps, and then a single gunshot.

I was on my feet before I realized I'd stood up. "Rafe!"

"Get down!"

It came from the left, where Lupe Vasquez was up on her feet now, too. In one piece, thank God.

I dropped back down behind the car while I waited, breathlessly, for a flurry of bullets. When none came—not my way, not hers—I thought it might be acceptable to hope, just a little, that that single shot we'd heard had either been Rafe putting a bullet into the gunman to slow him down, or said bullet had gone wild and hit a tree trunk or the ground.

A minute passed. Then another. And a third. A small eternity in seconds ticked by, heartbeat by heartbeat. Pearl whimpered, and I reached down to ruffle her ears while I kept my own peeled. Next to me, a few yards down the road, Lupe Vasquez did the same. She hadn't dropped to the ground again after telling me to get down. Instead she was standing, half hidden behind a tree trunk, her gun in her hand, but not pointed. Until the sound came that we'd been waiting for. The sound of movement on the other side of the road.

Lupe Vasquez lifted her gun and sighted. I rose on my knees, high enough to be able to peer through the car window and out on the other side.

Something moved between the trees. I held my breath. Was it Rafe, coming to make sure we were all right? Or was it the gunman, who—having disposed of Rafe—knew that it was just the two of us women down here?

Not that I wanted to disrespect Lupe Vasquez by implying that she couldn't take care of herself. I'm sure she could. She could probably take care of me, too. And I did have a gun of my own, with—hopefully—a few more bullets in it. I wasn't entirely sure how many I'd used—maybe three or four?—but since I also didn't know how many had been there to begin with, it didn't really matter. I looked at the gun, turning it around, but there was no cylinder with bullets *a la* Dix's old Old West cap gun I could look at. And Lupe Vasquez hissed at me—probably because I was waving a loaded gun around and pointing the muzzle at myself—so I turned it back around. It was tempting to shake it, to see if I could hear rattling inside, but I wasn't familiar enough with guns to know whether that would be a good idea. It didn't particularly seem like one.

Pearl growled. The sound of someone moving through the trees on the other side of the track was louder now, and the fur on the back of her neck stood up. I should have kept hold of her, I know, but by the time that thought occurred to me, she had already moved. Around the car and into the middle of the track, where she stood with her feet planted and her shoulders hunched, fur bristling, barking in deep, threatening woofs.

I saw a flash of movement between the trees. Something pale blue, like the sky. A pair of jeans?

And then someone stepped out of the trees, and all the breath left my body on a big, relieved sigh.

"Shut it," Rafe told the dog. "It's me."

It was. Alive and whole and—as far as I could tell—with no

blood on him. Pearl hesitated, and her stub of a tail gave a tentative wag.

"Good girl." He gave her a pat on the head on his way past. By this point, Lupe Vasquez had left the tree where she'd taken cover and was on her way toward us. I got there first, of course, and threw myself at him.

He caught me, and without any kind of telltale grunt of pain. Another indicator that he hadn't been hurt.

There was no need to tell him I'd been worried. He knew. "I'm all right."

"Me, too," I said, into his chest. "So is Pearl. And as far as I know Lupe Vasquez."

He nodded, and let go when the latter reached us.

"Everything all right?"

"Fine," Rafe said, keeping his arm around my waist. Down on the ground, Pearl had realized that this was a happy occasion. She was jumping around us with her tongue hanging out, looking like she was smiling.

"Did you get him?"

Rafe nodded.

"Who was it?" I asked. "Anyone we know?"

He hesitated. "I think I'd better just show you. Not sure you'll believe me otherwise."

Interesting.

He led the way back into the trees on the other side of the track. I did my best to keep up, while Pearl danced around me. Lupe Vasquez pulled up the rear, trying not to stumble over the dog. She had holstered her gun, but still had her hand on it. "Is he dead?"

Rafe shook his head. "I cuffed him. He ain't going nowhere. And since his hands are behind his back, he won't be shooting at us."

Good to know.

Even so, when we got to a point between the trees where we

could see him lying there, we all stopped.

I didn't recognize him. Not from this angle. He was flat on the ground, and blended, to a degree, with the faded grass and dead leaves. He was dressed in camouflage; not military, but hunter. A pair of coveralls and a hat that covered everything but the hands that were cuffed behind his back. Pale skin, so we weren't looking at one of the South Americans. He was facing away from us, so we couldn't see his face, and what I did see wasn't familiar. He might be someone I'd met, but he wasn't someone I knew well. Or at all.

Lupe Vasquez, on the other hand, caught her breath quickly. I glanced at her, and saw that her eyes were wide and her mouth open. Obviously, she knew who it was. Or thought she did. "Oh, my God," she said. "Is that...?"

Rafe nodded.

I looked from one to the other of them. "Who?"

TWENTY-FIVE

"Chief Carter?" Sheriff Satterfield repeated, with a heavy dose of 'I have a hard time believing that' in his voice.

It was later that evening. And we were all gathered in the parlor at the mansion. The sheriff had been released from the hospital, and Todd had driven him to see Mother. They were both there. So were Rafe and I. So were Lupe Vasquez and Patrick Nolan. We were all sitting around, on chairs and Great-Aunt Ida's loveseat, looking almost like we were having a friendly gathering instead of a debriefing.

Rafe nodded. "I caught him shooting at Savannah and Officer Vasquez, so it's not like I could be wrong."

"Dayum," the sheriff said, and then shot an apologetic look at my mother. "Sorry, Margaret."

Mother shook her head. "Are you sure you're all right?" She divided a look between Rafe and me.

We both nodded. "I was hunkered down behind the car the whole time," I said. "Rafe was the one who risked his life going after the guy."

He gave me a look. "You were risking your life the whole time you were behind the car, darlin'. I spent most of my time walking. The only risk I took was those couple of seconds it took to make him put down his gun."

"Those couple of seconds during which he could have shot you."

"Those couple of seconds when he wasn't shooting at you,"

Rafe said.

It wasn't worth arguing over. And anyway, he was right. We'd both been in danger. So had Lupe Vasquez, who was watching the conversational ball bounce back and forth like a spectator at a particularly exciting tennis match. She had a band aid covering the bump on her head, but looked otherwise all right.

I turned back to Sheriff Satterfield. "Yes. Chief of police Carter. Decked out in hunting gear and taking potshots at us with a rifle. Probably the same one he used to shoot you last night."

"Why?" the sheriff asked, and that was, indeed, the question of the hour. Or evening. The whole day.

"He wasn't real cooperative in interview," Rafe admitted. "We brought him down to the sheriff's office, since we couldn't very well take him to his own station."

The sheriff nodded.

"I did the interview. Cletus Johnson sat in, since you weren't available."

"How'd that go?"

"Fine," Rafe said. "It was professional. He don't like me much, but he likes his job. So he did what I told him to do."

The sheriff nodded.

"Officer Vasquez," Rafe glanced at her, "gave a statement about what happened out on the Skinners' property, and then she stayed in observation. I didn't think it'd help to have her in the room with us. I figured her boss'd try to dominate her if he could."

The sheriff nodded. So did Lupe Vasquez. So did I, not that I'd been there. After Rafe had shown us the handcuffed chief back there in the woods, he had tracked down the chief's car, which was parked some yards farther up the road from where ours had hit the tree. He had loaded us all into it, including the chief, and driven far enough that we could get a cell signal. Lupe

Vasquez had called her partner for help. Once Nolan showed up, she and Rafe had driven Chief Carter to Sweetwater in the chief's car, while Nolan had taken me and Pearl back to the mansion. He'd gone to the Sweetwater sheriff's office to watch the interrogation with Lupe Vasquez after that, and Pearl and I had stayed home until Rafe came back. Vasquez and Nolan had driven the chief's car back to Columbia. Rafe and I had taken Nolan's squad car to the repair shop to pick up the Volvo, had dropped the squad car back outside the Columbia police station, and had ended up back home. And now here we were, going over all of the details.

"He admitted to shooting at us," Rafe said. "Not much else he could do, when we caught him holding the gun."

The sheriff nodded.

"He admitted to shooting you last night, and trying to shoot me. We matched the second bullet since it would tie things up nicely, but we have his confession."

"Did he confess to killing the Skinners?" Todd wanted to know. Preparing his case, I guess.

"He didn't have to," Rafe told him. "He was carrying the same two rifles that were used in the shootings."

"That doesn't mean he pulled the trigger."

I refrained from rolling my eyes. But really, could Todd be any more of a lawyer if he tried?

Rafe nodded, acknowledging the point. "He said he did it. He used two different guns to make it look like two different people were involved. And then he used one of those guns to shoot at the sheriff, and the other one to shoot at me. And Savannah."

Everyone turned to look at me.

"He called here yesterday morning," Rafe added, "to tell us about the greenhouses, since we hadn't found'em on our own. He wanted to make sure we did, since it made a good motive for the murders. He told me he didn't think anyone would ever actually solve the case, and he was trying to blow as much smoke as he could."

"So what was his motive?" Todd wanted to know.

"He wanted a big case," Rafe said. "Nothing much has happened in this part of the state since Savannah's high school reunion in May."

I nodded. The others did, too, since they obviously all remembered the serial murders that had taken place then.

"Rumor has it Chattanooga's gonna be needing a new chief of police in the next few months. He didn't think his record was flashy enough to apply and get in."

Todd's eyes widened. "He killed seven people for career advancement?"

Rafe lifted a shoulder. "Pretty much, yeah. He figured a big case like this would put him on the map. He didn't foresee the sheriff calling me instead of asking him for help. He thought he'd be playing a big part in 'solving' the case. The pot would tie to the drug scene in Columbia, and he could get rid of the Skinners and clean up the drug problem at the same time. And go off in a burst of glory."

"So he killed seven people to make himself look good?"

Both Lupe Vasquez and Patrick Nolan looked faintly sick, probably because they'd been working for him.

"That was the biggest part of it," Rafe said, "yeah. He knew the Skinners were growing pot. And he knew about the dog fighting. It was a way to stop all that. And advance his own career and reputation at the same time."

"That's obscene," Mother said angrily. "What's wrong with him?"

Pearl lifted her snout from the carpet and gave a soft sort of woof. Mother glanced down, and then reached down and petted her head.

"Some kind of narcissistic disorder?" I suggested, since the chief certainly sounded like someone who saw himself as the center of the universe.

Rafe shrugged. "Or he's just a selfish bastard who doesn't care about anyone but himself."

There was a beat while we all digested this.

"Did you record the interview?" Todd asked.

Rafe nodded. "Course."

"I'm going to need a copy of that recording."

"You'll have to take that up with the sheriff." Rafe glanced at Bob Satterfield, who was sitting on Great-Aunt Ida's peach velvet holding my mother's hand. "I'm just helping out."

Sheriff Satterfield nodded. "We'll talk," he told his son.

I turned to Rafe. "Now, you suspected someone earlier than this morning. Last night, you told me you had a suspect, but you wouldn't tell me who it was."

He nodded.

"Was it Chief Carter?" the sheriff wanted to know.

Rafe made a face. "Yeah. I figured, if I accused him of anything without proof, you weren't gonna listen to me, though."

The sheriff didn't respond to that, but I thought there was a good chance Rafe was right. When you accuse the chief of police of seven counts of murder, especially when your own past is more than a little checkered, you'd better have your ducks in a row. He's more than proven himself since those early days— Rafe, I mean—but I had a feeling the sheriff would have been more likely to side with the chief of police anyway.

"What tipped you off?" Todd wanted to know. He sounded genuinely interested, and not at all judgmental. It was a nice change.

Rafe glanced at him. "It wasn't really one thing. Gut feeling, I guess. That, and he kept trying to insert himself into the case. He showed up at Robbie's that first day knowing about the murders. None of us called him. It was easy to explain away—lots of people there, any one of'em could have given him a call—but it wasn't us."

The sheriff nodded. "It made sense that he'd come and offer help, though. I didn't think anything of it."

"Sure. But then he kept showing up. He showed up at the hospital last night, and did everything he could to get himself officially attached to the case. That's why he tried to take you out, you know. He wasn't trying to kill you. Just put you outta commission for a few days, so he could offer to step in. And when that didn't work, he tried to shoot me."

And in that instance, I wasn't entirely sure he'd been shooting to wound. Rafe had been hit in the upper arm. A foot to the right, and it would have been the middle of the chest. And a bullet there was likely to have taken him out permanently.

"I guess he was hoping to blame those shootings on the South Americans," I said. "He knew you were looking into the drug scene. He assigned Lupe Vasquez to take you around."

I glanced at her. She nodded.

"But he didn't realize that you'd been speaking with the South Americans when Sheriff Satterfield was shot. Nor that you made sure they knew you weren't interested in their business. They had no reason to want to get rid of you."

Rafe shook his head. "I started suspecting him after he showed up at the hospital. When someone shot at us last night, I was pretty sure he was involved."

"So when he called this morning, why did you take us up into the hills?" Lupe Vasquez wanted to know. "Didn't you suspect that something would happen?"

Rafe made a face. "I thought it was one of Pablo's guys. Pablo said he'd ask some questions, and I thought it was a call from somebody who wanted to pass on some information. I shoulda known better."

"I didn't consider it, either," I said, slipping my hand into his. "I was worried the first time we went up there. When we got the call telling us to look behind Robbie's trailer. I was worried that someone planned to get you out there by yourself, to kill you. But since that didn't happen, I didn't think anything of it this time. I just assumed it was the same guy, and he was harmless."

"It's not your job to think about stuff like that, darlin'." He squeezed my hand.

"You can't think of everything, Rafael," Mother said. "And you saved Savannah. And Officer Vasquez."

Rafe glanced at Lupe Vasquez, and at me, and grinned. "They held their own."

"I packed our bags while you were out this afternoon," I told him. "We're ready to go home, unless anyone needs Rafe to stay longer?"

I glanced at the sheriff, who shook his head. "I'm sure we can handle it from here. Unless... You don't wanna be interim police chief of Columbia, I suppose?"

"No," Rafe said, "thank you."

"I could put in a good word. Maybe make the position permanent."

"No. Thank you."

The sheriff nodded. "I thought not. But I figured I should ask."

"I already have a job. One I oughta get back to."

"We appreciate you taking the time to come down here and help out. I know you don't like coming back."

Rafe grinned. "I like it better'n I used to. Maybe in another dozen years, I'll take you up on that job offer."

"By then you can have my job," the sheriff said, and stood to shake hands. "Thanks for the help."

"Anytime." They shook, carefully, and Rafe turned to me. "I'll go get the bags."

I nodded. "Upstairs in our room."

He headed out, and I turned to Mother. "Thanks for having us. And the dog."

Mother assured me it was no problem. I addressed Pearl.

"Time to go, sweetheart."

She flapped her stubby tail once, but didn't get up.

"Go outside?" I tried. "Car ride?"

She grinned, but didn't move.

"Come on, Pearl." I took two steps closer and bent.

Pearl flopped over on her back with all four legs in the air, exposing a pink tummy. I don't think it was to make it easier for me to pick her up.

"I don't think she wants to go," my mother said.

I looked at her. "She has to go. That was the whole point. I was going to take her home with me. She can't stay here."

"She can stay here," Mother said. While I stared at her, she added, "I've gotten used to her. It's nice to have a dog again, after all these years."

Had she lost her mind? "She's not exactly a Chihuahua." Or some other elegant designer breed Mother could carry around in her purse.

"I like her," Mother said. "She makes me feel safe."

There was no arguing with that. She made me feel safe, too.

"I'm happy to leave her," I said, "if you're sure you want me to." Mother nodded. "But if things don't work out, I want you to let me know. Don't just take her to the pound or anything like that."

"As if I would." Mother sniffed. "We'll be just fine." She glanced down at Pearl. "Isn't that right?"

Pearl slapped her tail against the floor in response.

OK, then. I guess it was settled. I was out the price of a pink collar and leash, and minus one dog. "Before I go," I said to Todd. "Does the DA's office have any plans of charging Yvonne McCoy with the murder of Beulah Odom?"

He shook his head. "Not that I've heard. In fact, as far as we're concerned, it's still death by natural causes. We don't charge people in those circumstances."

"Detective Jarvis is trying to prove that it was murder. After the Odoms lost the competency hearing, they started saying that Beulah had been murdered and that Yvonne did it. They even got an exhumation order and dug her up."

Todd nodded. "I heard."

"The second autopsy didn't reveal anything the first autopsy didn't," Patrick Nolan volunteered. "And Jarvis claims Chief Carter pushed him to reopen the case."

Another attempt to make himself look good, perhaps. "I think the Odoms did it," I told Todd, and followed up with all the reasons why. "I understand that they may get away with it. If you can't prove that it was murder, you can't charge them with anything. But if you're going to charge somebody, I'd much rather have it be the Odoms than Yvonne."

"I'll keep that in mind," Todd told me, his lips twitching.

By now Rafe had come back from putting the bags in the car, and was standing in the doorway waiting. "Ready?"

I nodded. "Pearl's staying here."

He glanced from me to the dog to Mother and back. "I figured."

He'd been quicker on the uptake than I had, then. Although I have to admit that part of me was relieved about it. I didn't think Pearl would do anything to harm the baby, but as they say, better safe than sorry.

"You'll have to come down and testify," Todd told Rafe.

He nodded. "We'll be back before then. Thanksgiving's in a few weeks."

It was. And while I hadn't received a formal invitation, it seemed Rafe had.

"We'll see you soon," I said. And turned my husband around and pushed him out the door. "Quickly. Before they try to stop us."

He grinned down at me. "Problem?"

"I think the sheriff's staying the night. I know he and my mother have sex, but I don't want to be in the house when they do." We passed through the front door and into the night.

The bags were already in the car, and now Rafe tucked me into the passenger seat.

"So," I said when he'd walked around the front of the car—with no one shooting at him this time—and gotten behind the wheel. "Interim chief of police?"

He grimaced as he turned the key in the ignition. "Not a lot of jobs I'd want less than that one."

I could imagine. "Except maybe Maury County sheriff?"

He gave me a look as the car began to roll down the driveway toward the road. "You want me to be Maury County sheriff?"

"You can be anything you want to be," I told him. "It doesn't matter to me. If you decide you'd like to live in Sweetwater and keep the peace in Columbia or Maury County, I'll be behind you all the way. And if you don't, that's OK, too."

Just as long as we were together.

He nodded. "We've got some time to figure it out."

We did. One day at a time. I leaned back against the seat and watched the mansion disappear in the distance as we made our way up the Columbia Highway toward Nashville and, for the time being, home.

# # #

About the Author

New York Times and *USA Today* bestselling author Jenna Bennett (Jennie Bentley) writes the Do It Yourself home renovation mysteries for Berkley Prime Crime and the Savannah Martin real estate mysteries for her own gratification. She also writes a variety of romance for a change of pace. Originally from Norway, she has spent more than twenty five years in the US, and still hasn't been able to kick her native accent.

For more information, please visit Jenna's website: **www.JennaBennett.com**

Made in the USA
Middletown, DE
10 March 2017